HINTERLAND

DAVID E CATTERMOLE

ISBN 978-1-5272-2519-0

The Solstice Press

7 Seager Court, Crockatt Road, Hadleigh, Suffolk. IP7 6RL.

www.davidecattermole.com

For Mel and Sam and Gabe

I must go down to the seas again, to the lonely sea and the sky . . .

JOHN MASEFIELD

PART ONE

JERUSALEM TIDE

1

I hear it. I can't see it yet, but I hear the roar of the waves. I feel the salt air on my skin and I can taste it too. Only just, but it's enough.

Must stay calm.

I can't see Joyce either, or hear her. But I feel her.

I've got to go down there, back down there to the shingle and the gulls and the wind.

Soon.

I'm on the edge of the woods, by the path that leads across the marshes. The wind is in the winter trees, sighing, knocking. But I still hear the sea.

Must stay calm.

I sit on the old steps cut into the bank, the boards move to cushion me, they feel softer than I remember. I sit and wait for Joyce. She's definitely coming. It's like waiting for a bus. Except Joyce is the entire route and the bus all at once. It's how it is here. She's a promise, a potential, stretched across all the places she visits. Along the way, the promise is always kept.

She's coming.

Joyce told me that I was the same as her. But I don't believe it. I'm present all the time here, I know I am.

Although perhaps that's the way it feels when you're on the bus?

But I know the difference. I used to be distracted. I know exactly how that feels. You see, for me life was fluid. My seasons and years rolled along, merging like a song without verses. Punctuation coming only as fleeting moments, pivotal events standing out like pins in the map, marking where I'd been and what I was doing on those rare occasions. Oh, I know the difference.

She's coming.

*

The last time I went back to see Vince in Brighton, one of those pins in my map came up. Not the day the two Brightons collided or the night that fate mugged me, nothing like that, but nonetheless, a moment that truly left its mark. We were up at Devil's Dyke and, as always, got to talking about old times while we watched cloud shadows over the Downs.

Tom wasn't with us, I don't know why, I can't remember.

It was spring and in the sun it was warm. I was sitting on the grass. A breeze was coming cool against my back and smelling of pine from the cops beside the big pub there. Vince was lying down, squinting at the sun. He was wearing a black suit, of course he was, that's all he ever wears, right from the days of the Heroes. The jacket was buttoned because he was shirtless underneath. He'd kicked off his old Birkenstock sandals, his bare feet golden against the grass. He looked like a fallen priest in some Sergio Leone western. His hair wasn't in dreadlocks, hadn't been for a few years by then, in fact it was close cropped but managed to unkempt nonetheless. To complete the whole spaghetti western thing, stubble covered his square jaw like a sandy down. His hands were tapping a rhythm on the grass, his mouth silently moving to form the words to whatever tune it was. I thought that it might have been 'Somewhere Over the Rainbow', but that was because it had been in my head since hearing snatches of it while clicking up and down through the radio stations on the drive from Suffolk. I'd been saying that we'd had our prime.

'What? No!' Vince laughed, interrupting his drumming and raising a hand to shield his eyes.

'It's true! Well it's definitely true for me, anyway,' I replied.

'*Definitely?*'

'Yeah— well, I know when I peaked, I know exactly when I peaked.' I would have said more, but the shadow of a cloud swept down the slope and poured into the farmland toward Ditchling.

'What?'

'Yeah,' I nodded. And I did.

'All right, when? *When* did you peak, Maggie-May?'

'Third of July, 2007 . . . about seven p.m.,' I replied with confidence. Confidence because it really was one of the larger of my map pins, sticking out proudly from the dizzy blur of the rest of that year. I explained that it was when I was in the French Alps, when I climbed Mont Blanc. I had the summit to myself for a few brief moments before Christophe, my guide, caught me up. No one else had made it, but I'd jogged, as much as you can in crampons, the last few metres until the snow-cap stopped going up. 'I looked down at Chamonix and then across the mountains in the evening light to Italy, Austria and Switzerland,' I recounted. 'Seriously, Vince, it was just this moment of beauty . . . beauty and privilege . . . and I knew I'd never have it again.'

Vince lifted himself up on to one elbow and turned to face me, his sinless cornflower-blue eyes analysing me. 'Beauty *and* privilege?'

'Yeah.' I knew what was coming. I shrugged. Then it came:

'Fuck off!' he laughed, lying back down and arching his back to get his cigarettes out of his pocket. I watched another cloud shadow   sail away from me. Vince lit up, inhaled deeply, then lay still, looking up at the sky with his cigarette sticking out of his mouth like a tiny mast. 'Fuck off,' he said again, philosophically this time, cigarette ticking back and forth with the words. His smoke-filled breath chasing away the pine scented air.

I lay down flat, the grass damp against my back, and joined him in his vigil.

'Did I tell you that Danny gave me a shitload of hazel?' Vince asked. I frowned. 'Nicely dried out and everything,' he added before I could respond.

'Who the fuck's Danny?'

'Oh, just this geezer who had a shitload of wood.'

'Well, yeah . . . I got that—'

'I'm gonna build a yurt with it . . . rent it out for festivals and that.'

'Fuck off!' I laughed.

*

Vince. I wish he were here now. Well I wouldn't wish that on him but, well. The wind's really picking up, starting to howl through the trees. Not enough to cover the sound of the sea though. And there aren't any cloud shadows.

Must stay calm.

Joyce still isn't completely here. I finger my wedding ring, turning it slowly with thumb and forefinger. Time's ticking.

Perhaps I should go on alone?

I breathe deeply. I close my eyes. I squeeze the edge of the step I'm sitting on.

No… not a good idea. I'll wait.

Oh, this is stupid. I used to love it here.

I used to come here with Mum and Dad when I was little. And then with Vince and Tom when we were boys: lazy days, skimming stones and smoking cigarettes.

I brought Isla here on our first visit to Suffolk, when we were thinking of leaving Brighton. It was late autumn. We drove up in the Triumph, just after we'd bought it. We got a room in a hotel on the seafront at Southwold. On the first day, we decided to walk to Dunwich for lunch. It was bitterly cold and stormy. We never made it. In fact, we barely got halfway. The waves were booming on to the shingle and the wind was driving spray everywhere. We played around for a while, me swinging wildly to hurl stones high over the huge breakers and Isla leaning into the wind at impossible angles, giggling like a child with her arms out like an aeroplane. Then we huddled together, Isla feeling so small in my arms, even through her winter coat. We had matching red woollen hats, a his-and-hers set from Camden Market, which Isla insisted we wore as preparation for old age together. She wore hers pulled down against the wind, her dark hair coming from beneath it to frame her oval face, those warm brown eyes shining up at me when I reached down to kiss her. I made sure mine was loose. The wind took it and that was that.

On the way back, Isla took some pictures of the water crashing over the sea defences at Walberswick. They were great pictures and one of them ended up hanging in the flat in Brunswick Square and in the hallways of all our homes since.

We spent the afternoon by the fire in a pub, the Bell Inn, thawing out and drinking pints. Isla eating salt and vinegar crisps with a wince and daring me to buy one of the giant pickled onions in the jar at the end of the bar, only to put her head in her hands laughing when I crunched into it with my eyes watering. We got chips on the way back to the hotel, ate them in the lee of the lifeboat station, and then stayed in our room for the rest of the weekend. I loved every minute of it; we both did.

2

The first time I saw Isla was in the summer of 1993, on the evening the Heroes played our first gig in London. The summer of 1993 was a fine time for me. Back when I truly was a bluesman, baby.

Kelly - friend and musical cohort - and I walked out of Camden tube station into a busy world of light and heat and noise. It was August and it was hot. You could taste the exhaust fumes and smell hot tarmac as London seared. We stopped and stood looking across the traffic to the World's End pub. It was a big building. It felt like a proper venue. It felt like a big, proper London venue!

I don't remember exactly what time it was; I wouldn't have known then anyway because I didn't do watches and had no idea that all the clocks in my life had been ticking toward that day and would always keep time from it. To and then from the greatest of all my pins in my map. The pub disappeared behind two red buses passing in front of us as if to confirm we were definitely in London. They were full of tired-looking people in suits so I guess it must've been the end of the afternoon. The World's End came back into view. Kelly looked at me, I looked at her and we grinned. We grinned because we knew we were ready. That was really all we knew then, all we needed to know.

I was wearing my boots, black jeans, a t-shirt and sunglasses, because that's all I ever wore, except when I was on stage, of course, when it had to be a black suit. Kelly had khaki trousers, a white vest top and her John Lennon glasses, because in the Camden of the summer of 1993 that was exactly the right look and she was one who just had that knack. Kelly was tall with a straight, boyish figure, almost as tall as me. She made up the last couple of inches with spiked hair that changed colour so often I have no idea what was natural for her. That day it was a shocking red. Chosen to match the buses, I guess. She looked stunning. She was always lustrously tanned, although she denied using sunbeds in the winter, and her green eyes told you in no uncertain terms that she was one of the smartest people you were ever going to meet. She was carrying her guitar case; protecting the 1961 Fender Jazzmaster that never left her side and that Vince claimed sounded like God. As always in those days, I carried nothing except my door key and some cash stuffed in my pockets. Our black suits were on their way with Vince and Tom.

The sound of an angry horn had us turning and looking across the junction to the High Street. It seemed our timing that day was perfect just as it always was on stage. The Heroes' van, Vince at the wheel and Tom in the passenger seat with his face in his hands, had arrived. Few had air conditioning then, not even Mercedes drivers by the look of the red-faced man cursing them as Vince made an illegal U-turn right across his path and disappeared behind the pub. I grinned at Kelly again, then ran across the road after them.

I grew up with Vince and Tom. Tom and I were at primary school together and Vince's family moved into the big house at the end of our lane when I was nine. Vince grew into a handsome man of classic good looks, right down to the chiselled line of his jaw. But when he first came to our school Tom and I couldn't stop taking the piss out of him: it was as if his man's chin had arrived early and the rest of his head was still growing to catch up. He was therefore, immediately, Jimmy Hill. We worked around the whole chin thing though and quickly became friends. Good friends. It was during adolescence that we realised we all had a shared laziness, a shared fear of work and a shared love of music. A shared love of the blues to be more precise, which, while everyone else started to worship Indie music, left the three of us in Vince's massive bedroom with its amazing Georgian acoustics, listening to our own pantheon of gods – Floyd Dixon, the Soul Survivors, Sam and Dave, Stevie Ray Vaughan, Bettye LaVette and, of course, John Lee Hooker. We finally formed our own blues band during A-levels. We were actually quite good, but too lazy to really get anywhere. A-levels came and went and in order to avoid work we all drifted through clearing and ended up at the University of Brighton together.

Our band continued along the same lacklustre road as our academic careers, until our final year at college when we met Kelly. Kelly was a couple of years older and living with her partner, Lizzie, in Hove. As a guitarist and songwriter, she could have been just like so many of the people we knew; except she wasn't – she was different. Where Vince and Tom and I and every would-be musician we knew *dreamed* of making a living out of music, Kelly *planned* and *worked hard* to make it happen. And she was good. Her lyrics were great, but her true gift was guitar. She heard us play at a mutual friend's birthday and liked most of what we were about. Afterwards she bought us a Scotch each and, without any introduction, sat us down and spoke while she eyed us over like someone buying horses. She said she was putting a band together.

'Putting the band together!' Vince cut in with his best James Belushi impression. Kelly ignored the interruption. It was to be a band that she would manage and that would make us real money. With our student life drawing to a close and the wolves of proper jobs almost at the door, we finished our whiskies and said we were in.

Although Kelly was lesbian she'd nonetheless – in her own way – harboured a lifelong crush on Clint Eastwood and that's where the band's name came from. We all thought Clint was a star and so we didn't argue. Looking back now, I think – again in her own way – she was in love with Tom too, because he was the best of us.

We practised regularly for the first time. Kelly and I found that together we were far better songwriters than either of us could've hoped to be individually and things started to really come together. She insisted that I was too pretty just to hide behind a guitar and had me singing out front. 'As a skinny streak of eye candy with a come-to-bed voice', as she put it. How could I not have gone along with that? By the time we'd finished our degrees, *Kelly's Heroes*, the new blues sensation, were filling pubs across Brighton.

We'd had three years of pubs and venues across the South East before we got our first proper London gig that August in Camden. I think by then we all realised that we were never going to hit the big time, but I was loving it. I was making enough money to have my own place in Brighton, a beautiful one-bed flat on the seafront in Bedford

Square, and life was quite literally wine, women and song. And that was everything I wanted. Or so I thought until Camden.

The driver's door flew open and Vince jumped out. 'Maggie May!' he shouted. Vince was wearing his black suit; there was never any time wasted in changing before and after gigs with Vince. He had a black t-shirt on under it for once and wore a pair of faded yellow espadrilles that matched his mane of blonde dreadlocks.

'All right, Vince!'

Vince ran over, ducked left, ducked right and delivered two fake punches to my stomach. I grabbed him in a lock and knuckled his hair.

'And Kelleee . . .' He grinned, holding out his arms to hug her.

'Can't believe you let him drive, Tom,' I laughed.

'Don't, Mags; it's not funny. I *honestly* thought we were going to die on the M23.' Tom was the total opposite of Vince: where Vince was skinny, Tom was broad, and where Vince looked like that preacher from Clint westerns, Tom was sharp, with his black fringe swept just above his grey eyes, a tailored jacket, stiff shirt with needlepointed collars and leather shoes that were only a breath away from pimp.

'Fucking, London,' Vince announced, hugging Kelly. 'Fucking, London!' he shouted, letting her go. He drummed excitedly on the van's bonnet.

'Yes, Vince . . . fucking, London,' Kelly smiled.

'Picture!' Vince shouted suddenly. 'Picture, picture!' he repeated, reaching into his inside pocket. He produced his tattered Olympus compact camera.

'Oh, for fuck's sake, Vince,' we chorused. Christ knows how much he must have spent on film and processing over the years. It was an obsession that would not abate until he bought a camcorder for Christmas '99 to capture the end of the century.

'Yeah,' Vince laughed, assuming, as always and wrongly, that we were joking. 'Come on, with me,' he continued, reaching round behind Tom to pull us all together in a tight bundle. 'Van in the background!' he announced to himself. 'Say cheese!'

'Cheese!' A red light on the camera blinked manically, then the flash blinded us.

'That's gonna be a keeper,' Vince said, again to himself. 'Nice one, Kelleee, you've done us proud this time . . . you've done us proud,' he continued, biting his bottom lip and nodding while he surveyed the litter-strewn alleyway with its graffiti, flaking black ironwork and carpet of crushed cigarette butts that smelled of piss and fast food from the burger place next to it. 'Done us proud,' he said again, putting his camera back in his pocket.

'Thanks,' Kelly replied quietly. 'That's really—'

'Jesus, I forgot, I really need a piss,' Vince interrupted, walking away from the van and fumbling with his zip.

'Vince! They'll be a loo in the . . .' Kelly began, but it was too late. 'Oh, never mind.'

I smiled at Tom. Kelly shook her head as she walked into the pub to sort out business.

'Fucking, London!' Vince grinned over his shoulder.

That was it. I started laughing and when I laughed Vince laughed, and when Vince laughed I laughed. We started messing around. Vince kept running back down to the street and trying to make friends with people. Tom tried not to, but caved in the end. We went for cigarettes, found a Seven-Eleven around the corner and ended up buying a bottle of Jim Beam. Tom even pulled his signature drunk move of picking a passer-by's pocket just to call them back and return their wallet with a theatrical bow and an 'I believe you dropped this, sir'. Now, that really is a long and separate story. But, in summary, Tom was an amazing pianist and guitarist not solely because he had his mother's gift for music. Tom also had his Uncle Frank's grace of hand. Uncle Frank, however, had used his gift for crime. By all accounts Uncle Frank was a truly talented thief whose career finally ended with an extended stay in Norwich Prison, from which he returned a retired, mostly reformed and lovable old rogue. Retired Uncle Frank and Tom, aged six when Frank came home from Norwich, had doted on each other and Tom grew up on a diet of

Frank's old tales of misadventure. Tom was no thief, but channelling the talent he'd got from Uncle Frank into piano and guitar was never quite enough. So, he kept the old family tradition alive through what he viewed essentially as street theatre and sleight-of-hand conjuring. And, like old Uncle Frank, Tom was good.

Somehow, we managed to get the van unloaded and set up our gear. I think Tom and Kelly did most of that, though. By the time we were up for our first set we were as arseholed. But that was fine: when we were drunk we were relaxed, and when we were relaxed we were good. Vince always said that a hit of whisky before he played his drums made him reach *It*. I think Jack Kerouac was the only thing he'd ever read. And it worked. That night we were good. By then we'd stopped experimenting and settled into the honest twelve-bar blues with an F, C and B-flat chord progression that Kelly and I always seemed to end up at when we wrote together. Yeah, we really were a great little blues band.

I remember about twenty minutes in, looking out through the smoke to the moving bodies and the faces staring back. I was giving them my moves, I was gyrating – well kind of – I was pointing, I was winking and they were loving it. Vince was on drums behind me, Tom on bass in my left flank, Kelly to my right, and everyone in front of me moving to my voice, our music, our words and our rhythm. I knew we had them; we had that proper London space and all the people in it. If there was or is an *It*, I think we probably had it right there and then. I sang and flirted with the eager eyes looking back at me, all wanting to stand out, all wanting to get my attention.

My attention!

I was happy. I was doing my thing and I was happy! And when I was happy I sang happy, happy from my soul, happy that made me think of my dad's singing. And when I sang happy I was good and people loved it. It lit me up.

If I had done watches then, if I had done time then, I would perhaps have been aware of the final seconds ticking by. But I had no premonition, no feeling or sense of life's second hand sweeping purposefully on toward one of those life-changing moments. Toward that pin of pins. It just happened. Out of the blue, or rather out of the disco-lit smog and sea of faces.

NIKON.

I saw that first. Don't ask me why, but that's what I noticed and I can still see it as clear as the word SCANIA. Then behind the word I saw the camera, and behind the camera the photographer.

Isla.

She stepped forward from the crowd, crouched and took her shot. Everyone moved and flowed seamlessly around her as if held back by some invisible shield. The two security guys looked but didn't approach, and I bet they didn't know why. She had this amazing presence. She was beautiful. A real-life Audrey Hepburn, right there in Camden, right there in front of me. I just wanted to hold out my hands and smile at her. Years later I read that Richard Burton said when Elizabeth Taylor walked into the room and he saw her for the first time she was so beautiful that he laughed. When I read that I thought of that moment in Camden. I stared at her and she looked up from behind the camera, looked right into my eyes. That was it. The room reversed. My world flipped. If I'd had *It*, then she'd just taken it. Now I was the one wanting to be noticed. Now it was my eyes eagerly seeking attention. Isla's attention.

3

Joyce is here now and we've come down on to the beach, right where Isla and I were. Right where I lost my Camden hat. The wind's still howling and there's sand coming with it against my face. The sky's grey like old metal and the sea's angry.

I'm glad you're here Joyce.

Joyce is slender like Isla, but taller. There's something noble about her, about the way she stands. Something elegant and something disciplined. Her hair is a white blonde, always so neat and set in waves. It seems immune to the wind. She's wearing a fitted sage-green tweed jacket and pencil skirt that match her eyes. She could be straight from a 1950s movie: Grace Kelly to Isla's Audrey Hepburn.

Joyce doesn't speak in the way you would imagine. I think actually it's because she's so old. Oh, she looks younger than me, but I think she's been here a long time, a very long time. I think she's as old as the sand in this wind. That's why she's further off than me. I think she'd find it hard to connect at all.

Gulls soar overhead! The wind's like a catapult when they come over the shingle, sending them wheeling out across the sea. Little flashes of brilliant white.

I look up the beach, I look down the beach.

We are alone.

So, what now, Joyce? We wait?

Joyce says yes. She touches my arm. Her eyes are kind. I nod. I breathe deeply.

Joyce says it will be okay.

I finger my wedding ring and look along the beach again.

*

Still nothing. As far as I can see toward Dunwich and back to Southwold, the beach is empty. The Tide's going out and it'll be dark soon. And still nothing. I don't want to be here, down here, when it gets dark.

Must stay calm.

Must see this through.

You see, we're not here by chance, Joyce and me. Those pivotal events, those pins in my map, continued. They continued here on this beach. Since that day I haven't dared return, not to the waves and the gulls and the shingle, even though I know this is where I must be, where I'll find my answers. So many of the songs I knew thought we'd all find ourselves at a crossroads, possibly playing our fiddle. But for me I've always known it would be here, here on the shingle where the sky meets the sea. I don't know how I know it, but I do. I'm sure of it. Joyce still had to work hard to persuaded me to come back though. She's sure I was wrong about that day, wrong about it being something dark, about there being evil in place.

It was a day when the sea was as I've always loved it best: not rough, not still, but just so. Churning, rolling, swelling, tireless. The sky was endless blue and the waters were all greens and browns with pure white crests. Foam fanned out across the hard-packed sand in front of me, rolling right over to the shingle bank and barring my way. I looked up. There was the lighthouse rising from Southwold in the distance. I turned and looked the other way along the gentle curve of Sole Bay to Dunwich, hazy and equally far off.

Oddly, no memories of the many days I'd spent on that beach came to me. In fact, my mind was empty. I was alone and I felt calm and peaceful. I watched another sequence of waves fan out in front of me. It was a perfect day. I looked inland, across the marshes to the woods beyond. The trees were bare, leafless, architectural forms. With the sky so blue I'd thought it was summer, but I guessed it must be winter, or early spring perhaps. I looked at my watch, but it was gone. I realised I had no memory of coming to the coast. It was as if I'd just woken to find myself looking at the sea. I had no recollection of any thoughts I'd stirred from.

How could I have lost my watch?

How could I have thought it was summer in the wintertime?

Where had I been?

I looked back and there were no footprints.

I stood watching the sea. That's when another pin fell on to my map. Not the one that changed things, not the voice that was to come that day, a quiet, simple, but nonetheless important, moment of truth: I remembered I was dead and for the first time it was okay, I didn't mind.

4

The Tide's almost out. I look along the beach, up and down, up and down, and then back toward the woods. Always back to the woods. I finger my wedding ring. Joyce takes my hand. I jump. She smiles warmly. I look toward the woods. She squeezes my hand.

I don't think we should have come, Joyce.

I think of the voice I heard that day.

Joyce says I was wrong about it.

I'm not so sure, Joyce. Now that we're here I'm not so sure. I look at the sea. The waters are the darkest grey. The light has almost gone. I look back to the woods again.

We should go.

Joyce gives my hand another squeeze. I look at her, her face still so warm and kind. I love Joyce. She takes my other hand. I nod slowly.

I need to see this through, I need to know the truth. I need to know.

We stand facing each other and wait together.

I'm glad you're here, Joyce.

*

Right from my first days in this place I spent my every waking moment searching. Trying to reach out to Isla and Jack and May. I would go to places we went in life, special places, family places looking for them, everywhere and anywhere I could think of — everywhere except home that is, I've tried to reach home, reach our house, again and again but I don't think it's meant to be, at least that's how it feels.

Day after day I would search for them among the living. You see I had to know. I had to know where they were. I had to know for sure, one way or the other. But even in those first days the living were distant. Sometimes shadows, sometimes more, but always a way off. Always out of reach. Nonetheless I would try to find my family day after day.

I had to know.

I wanted to find them there.

I wanted them to know that I was sorry, but more than anything I just wanted to find them, find them there among the living.

But of course, I could never close the gap, never cover the final distance. Sometimes, though, I felt I got close. It was as if the Tide took me to them, to places where I was sure I could feel them. Sometimes I even imagined that I caught a glimpse of them far off among the distant living. But I could never be sure. I could never be certain. And that's what I needed, I needed to be certain. I had to know for sure. But it seemed I would never have my answer.

The day I heard that voice was one of those days. It started when I finally stopped staring out to sea and noticed people up the beach in the distance: a couple with a dog that was racing in and out of the waves. They were a blur, but they were there. I began to notice more and more: people walking down from the woods, people further along the beach toward Southwold and people back nearer Dunwich. Families, I thought: mothers, fathers and little ones. And then, there among them, shimmering in the distance, I was drawn to three figures. It was as if they were in a heat haze, no more than bending, shifting shadows, but I was sure it was a woman and two young children. Isla, I thought. Jack, I hoped.

'May,' I whispered.

I started running up the beach to get closer. Wash from the breaking waves bubbled around my feet, but I couldn't feel the water. I ran and ran but they remained distant. Closer perhaps, but still distant. I had to reach them. I had to know. I ran with my head down. On and on.

I had to get to them! I had to know for sure!

But when I finally raised my head the gap remained and still there were just three flowing shadows way off ahead. My run slowed to a jog, then a walk and finally a last step. Then I shouted. I shouted their names. Christ, I screamed them. I wanted sound and light to work the way it always had, but the waves broke, the breeze stirred the sand and nothing of me reached them. Whoever they were. Finally, I sat on the shingle bank with my head in my hands.

I don't know how long I'd sat there on the shingle. A good while, I think, because when it spoke it took me a moment to realise what was happening. It was a voice and it was talking to me. After so long in solitude a voice from right beside me, in my space, and definitely talking to *me*.

'Enough,' it said.

I was running before I thought about it. Instinct screamed at me to run and I did. I ran and I ran, my feet gouging into the shingle. I didn't look back, not once. I just kept going and going until the light started to fade and the Tide with it.

The next thing I knew, I was in a dream. At first, I thought I was awake, I thought the Tide had taken me somewhere, because I was lucid. I'd always had dreams since I arrived, but I was always an observer, I was never in control. They were fixed replays of life. Sometimes a comfort, bringing days with the children and Isla back to me. The children always busy, little May toddling, with her chestnut bob and her mother's big warm eyes, and Jack, older but still a little boy, skinny and baby-faced. Both of them making the most of me, showing what they were making or drawing or playing with or imagining; Isla peaceful and amused by their running and racing and excited chatter and my enthusiastic but ever so slightly confused encouragement. But mostly, I relived the moments before my crash, vivid and haunting replays: speeding through the country lanes, roof down and the early-morning July sun blinking through the trees. The car leaning and pitching with the road, working the gears round each familiar twist and turn. Radio on, me clicking through the stations. Tyres humming on the new surface down the hill toward the bend, hedges and banks rising around the sunken road. The bend, the final bend. The lorry, the huge wall of a lorry with the giant letters across the grill:

SCANIA.

Fear. Every muscle locked, rigid against the seat and the brake. Wheel turning. Tyres screaming. Car sliding. Eyes closed. Isla, the children, Mum, Dad. Being carried as a small child. Holding Jack and

May. Isla. A final sense of nakedness, of privacy and self lost, all gone. Eyes closed. Isla, Jack, May . . . What had I done?

But the dream I woke to was different. I was in control. I was in my family's old beach hut that had been lost to a storm years ago. I was laying on the bench. It was daytime. The yellow curtains that once hung in my parents' living room were drawn across the front sliding doors; thin and threadbare with pinpricks of bright sun coming through the weave here and there. I didn't want to look at them directly. I had a beach towel over me. There was the sound of the sea and children playing outside. And the all-pervasive smell of damp. There was the scratched and scored Formica table with the faded plastic clock above it, camping stove with a blue gas bottle beside it and the triangular cupboard in the corner by the back door. Everything just as it had been when I was a child. I was even small. I knew it was afternoon and that I, little more than an infant, was having my afternoon sleep. Mum and Dad and my sister Julie would be outside, enjoying the sun. And I knew that it was for me to choose when to end the dream and wake. I knew that all I had to do was open the back door.

It's a dream that since that first time has come to me over and over, and every time I step down from the bench and reach up to the oversized handle to wake from the comforting sound on waves breaking on the beach of childhood summers.

*

The sun's gone and I can barely hear the waves now. Sounds always fade when the Tide goes out.

I was hoping it would make sense if I came back here, Joyce.

Joyce says that it still might.

I hope so.

I want to understand about the voice.

Joyce says that I already do. She says that there *is* help here.

You can say that, Joyce. You have faith.

But what I don't know, still don't understand, is why I had that dream and why it keeps coming back. That's why I'm here, where it started. Maybe my mind just found a place of safety buried in my childhood memories, a little blue shed that always felt like home. But maybe it means something.

Oh Joyce, I hope we're still here when the Tide comes back in.

5

After the Heroes' gig in Camden there was no sign of Isla. No sign of the photographer, the girl, the woman, who'd stepped out from the crowd and beguiled me. Actually, I don't know about beguiled. *The Beguiled* is another Clint Eastwood film that we thought briefly about naming the band after, but Kelly had said beguiled sounded too predatory, so Kelly's Heroes it was. And perhaps she was right, and perhaps beguiled isn't the right word. Enchanted maybe? No. The girl who turned my head?

Yes.

The girl who turned my head and left me looking in a new direction, a direction where the defining feature of other women was that they weren't her.

I looked everywhere. I pretended not to, of course, making excuses while we packed up. I didn't actually need to piss every five minutes, but I figured everyone needed to visit the loos sooner or later, so loiter like some pervert in basement corridor with the sickly stench of old Victorian sewers I did. I didn't really need to step out for air a hundred times either, but wander through the groups of people spilling out on to the street to escape the jostling heat and sweat of the World's End I did. So many faces, but never the one I wanted. She'd gone. Vanished. And I had no idea how to find her again.

In the end, between my wanderings and everyone's drinking, we managed to get our stuff back into the van. Kelly got the train back to Brighton, to home, to Lizzie and their cat. Vince had, as always, sniffed out a party. So, reluctant to give up my search, after a final wander around the remnants of the crowd, I said I'd come along. Tom locked up the van and we set off to find the address in Kentish Town that a tall gothic girl, who'd helped us pack up, had written on Vince's hand. The felt-tip lettering was fuzzy because she'd slowly licked from his fingertips to his wrist before writing on him, but we managed to find the house anyway.

Vince sang as we walked and I laughed. We all had our black suits on still, but he was barefoot now, with the espadrilles officially MIA. It was one of his made-up songs about breasts and bums and girls that made him do dirty things. I must have heard a hundred variations, all basically the same, all obscene and yet profoundly childish. He danced around as he sang, waving a bottle of Becks, like some modern-day prancing jester with dreadlocks for a hat. He would suddenly lean in right up to our faces to repeat the chorus, eyes wide and shining. Vince loved parties – we all did – and with the high of the evening's performance he was buzzing. By the time we got there, Tom and even I, despite my preoccupation with the photographer, had joined in the singing.

'It's the band!' somebody shouted, in that half-chuffed, half-sarcastic drunk way of needing to make your observations a public announcement. We walked through the overgrown front garden, filled with people, patches of bare earth, tangled plants and the smell of ivy coming thick in the humid night air. We were three young men, with three black suits, two shirts and two pairs of shoes: an arrangement that we carried off damned well. There was an old fridge on its side next to a heap of bicycles piled against the house: a once grand, but by then run-down Victorian mid-terrace student let with peeling paintwork, posters on the walls and, at time of arrival, Happy Mondays blaring from open windows.

'Ladieees!' Vince called out, stepping into the hallway, with its grubby black and white tiles and people nodding to the music. It was smoky as hell and even closer than the air outside. Two or three voices cheered, again in a half-drunk, half-chuffed sort of way, and the tall gothic girl appeared from one of the inner doors.

'Hey, hey!' Vince beamed, opening his arms, bottle in one hand, cigarette in the other. 'I was just singing about you, baby!'

The gothic girl – I don't think I ever did know her name – strode over and kissed him. In that space, she seemed taller and with all her get-up was, I have to say, a truly striking sight. She gripped his face and sucked at his mouth, black lipstick smearing and tongue flashing. Vince's arms remained as they were, only his head moving to accommodate her, his eyes wide open and still lit with mischief. At the time, it was one of those things that you don't exactly dislike seeing, but in the back of your mind somewhere you know you're glad you're not sober. I looked at Tom and we both laughed. That was the last I saw of Vince for the night; no doubt he was busy enacting the thrust of his song.

The kitchen was a little less crowded and the table was covered in bottled beers so we helped ourselves. A couple of the girls in there recognised us as Heroes and bubbled with compliments about my singing. Another made a beeline for Tom. She was a tall, pretty brunette and had Tom written all over her. She asked Tom to hand her a bottle opener from the table. Tom picked it up in his right hand, flipped it over his knuckles and it was gone. The girl's eyes widened. Tom then produced it from behind her ear with his left hand. Seamless. I was watching carefully and I knew what I was looking for, but still it was seamless. That was it: they settled right in, talking comfortably. Then another girl, a little older, came in from the back garden. As soon as she saw me she started chatting. She was cool and I liked her. She was smoking and I asked for a cigarette. She looked me in the eye, drew on the one she was smoking and then slowly held it up, lipstick-marked filter and all, to my mouth. I took it. She asked if I wanted another beer; I said no. She shrugged, stepped to the table behind me, grabbed a Budweiser and pinched my arse. I looked around and said, 'Oi'; she bit her lip and held my stare.

She was fine and confident, I liked her a lot and usually that would have been enough. But my heart wasn't really in it. In the brave new world in which I found myself, she simply was not the photographer, she simply was not Isla.

6

I wake. It's morning. I'm alone. I'm far from the beach now, the Tide has put me in the woods close to where I lived. I come here sometimes.

Joyce has gone. She doesn't come here.

I love Joyce. I love her absolutely.

I've been dreaming, dreaming about Tom. Something important about Tom, but already its fading. In my waking moment it was so clear, but as I focus now it's already fragmented. Only the feeling of importance lingers. I finger my wedding ring. I run over the dream. I try to recover that waking understanding.

I was in Wales, the Brecon Beacons. I love the Beacons. I used to walk there with my dad when I was a boy and later with Tom. Vince would come along but stay in Brecon, in a pub somewhere, and wait. He never did understand why Tom and I wanted to walk so far.

I was on the summit of Pen y Fan, looking over to Cribyn. I'd been watching cloud shadows scudding down into the valley and then away toward the English distance. But a mist had come up all around, rolling in and covering everything except the summits of the Beacons themselves. The tops of Corn Du and Cribyn were suddenly ghostly islands rising from a white sea.

Then I heard Tom's voice. He was calling out for me.

'Mags!' He sounded distressed.

'Tom?' I called back, looking all around but seeing only mist.

'Mags?'

'Yes!' I answered. 'Where are you?'

'I'm not here anymore. Remember?' Came his reply.

Snap. I'm awake. Crouching in the woods.

Crouching usually means I'm hiding. But it's okay, I don't feel as if I need to be hiding. It's just because this is where I came to hide after hearing the voice, when my time here shifted from lost wandering and searching to an existence of hiding and fear. Hiding because the voice confirmed fears that had been growing in me. Fears that I was being watched. Stalked.

Joyce always tells me there is nothing out there, nothing watching me, nothing to fear. So does Henry for that matter.

I love Henry too, absolutely.

Like Joyce, Henry doesn't come here.

They both say that they're sure the voice is from somewhere good. But going back to the beach yesterday bought it all back and I'm not sure that anything *good* could make me feel like that. I think maybe it's all part of something much darker than they know. Perhaps they were better people than me. Perhaps I was a bad person and it's here for me, just me. And that's why they wouldn't know about it.

It started in my early days here. The wind would suddenly bring a sense of someone or something and the living would seem to move further off. Much further off. I'd get gooseflesh. I'd look all around, see nothing but I'd be sure there was something watching. Something hidden. I don't know what I expected to see: some dark shape in the distance, something prowling, something looking for me. Or worse still, some dark shape in the distance that I'd know was looking directly at me. Just like one of the Black Shucks – hell hounds – in so many of my dad's stories. Dear old Dad, he loved his stories.

I kept telling myself it was just my imagination – fuelled by a whole childhood of those stories – but after the voice I was sure I'd been right all along. That someone, something, had been watching me. So, I came here, to the woods. It was always somewhere I escaped to in life when things were hectic. In death, it felt familiar and safe. So safe in fact, it took me a long time to muster the courage to step out into the open again. Not just courage to be honest, but resolve too. You see, it was a sanctuary that I was happy to be in and for the first time in all my days I didn't get bored just standing quietly. It felt like a timeless time. It was so peaceful. I found myself always looking up through the trees to the sky. It came all shades of blue and grey, cloudy by day with the sun passing over as the Tide flooded through the trees, with calm herringbone sunsets and bright stars at night. The constellations Dad had shown me wheeling overhead. And the weather! Rain and wind, sun and showers, great storms filled with angry snow, summer calm. I could have watched that forever. It was as if it was passing through me and I was part of it, part of the energy and the motion and the sweep of day and night, night and day.

In the end, it was guilt that finally broke the spell. I felt guilty about the living. Sometimes I'd think I'd caught a glimpse of them walking among the trees, just on the edge of sight. I knew they couldn't see me, but I wondered if they could feel me. Sense me somehow. I was sure one or two of them got twitchy. Especially one little girl who always wore a yellow raincoat. Dearest little thing, reminded me of May: big inquisitive eyes, a beautiful little rounded face and shy glances. She often used to look my way and seemed to get nervous. They say that children can see spirits don't they, or is it dogs that can see them? It dawned on me that by remaining there I was haunting the place. Such a lovely place, it didn't seem right. So I had to leave.

*

I've moved to the edge of the wood, looking out over fields. There's a frost on them. The low sun's starting to reach through gaps in the trees and hedges, clearing the frost in patches. There's birdsong and a rook is rasping. The Tide will come any moment. I feel it. Then I'll get going. I'm going to head west. There's a monument, a little war memorial, on the edge of a village in that direction. I'm going to walk to it. It's something I've wanted to do for some time and I think finding myself back here is a sign. A sign that this is the right time.

I drove by it in the early days when I still had a car here. There was a man beside it. He looked so sad. I mean truly, desperately sad. I thought he was one of the living, he was far off you see. But there was something different about him. I think now that he was a spirit, and if he is I can't bear to think of him being so sad and alone. Being lost. I told Joyce about him and she said if he was part of my story I'd come across him again, that the Tide would take me to him. And here I am, in the woods close to him. Joyce says that's what it's all about here. We all have a story that needs to be told, a story that we must tell to ourselves, and that we must hear. And I think she's right. I always find myself going over my story.

Until I met Joyce I was so alone. I thought there would be people waiting for me. I thought people who went before me would be here. But that's not how it works. They're not here. So that's why I want to go to him, because it's down to us, those of us who *are* here, to help each other.

I assumed people would be waiting for me because of Dad. He always believed people waited for their loved ones, that they would be reunited here. Some of his old stories were about that sort of thing. He would often talk about a place called the Folk Meadow. It was a Norse story. He loved those old legends – they're where the Black Shucks came from. He said it was a beautiful valley between the sea and the mountains and the forests, where people waited and travelled on their way to their final rest. A halfway step, a hinterland between heaven and earth. I've often thought that this must be it, that he got it right. Well, almost right.

He first told me that story when I was little and very ill in hospital. He sat by my bed all night. I woke up wanting a drink. He handed me a plastic beaker with orange squash in it. It was warm and weak and tasted of the cup. I asked him if I was going to die.

He said no.

I asked him what he'd do if I did.

That's when he told me about the Folk Meadow and he said he would come and find me, that he couldn't bear the world if I was gone, so he'd come and find me. He said we could climb up to the high country and explore the mountains and forests together. That's the first and only time I saw my dad cry. He didn't realise I saw because I pretended to be asleep. I think that's why I ended up walking hills and climbing mountains; the idea of exploring them stuck with me for the rest of my life.

But if this *is* the Folk Meadow, surely he'd be here waiting for me?

*

I wish Joyce were here. It would be good to have someone to walk with. When I was here watching the skies come and go I went over my story many, many times. And I see it so clearly now. At first, I thought it ended with my death. But that's not it at all. Joyce describes her story as being an hourglass, with her death the central pinch point between the life she lived and her time after it in equal measure. I see mine as an hourglass too now, with all my days bound around a single focal point which everything was either leading to or flowing from. But for me that moment wasn't my death; it was when I met Isla.

Joyce says that I lie about my story and that's why I've been here so long.

But that's just not true, I haven't been here long and I don't lie.

7

All of the world is asleep apart from him. She sleeps next to him, duvet discarded. He lies naked and far away. Sleep is a blessing he knows he will not receive. He fingers his wedding ring, watching the featureless dark where the window is hidden. The only breaks in the blackness are the red numbers on the clock, coming to him double-slow, crawling through minute after minute of each endless hour. He listens into the dark, wondering if he will hear their children stirring. But they, like her, like all of the world except for him, are sleeping.

Silence.

For a while he turns on his side to face her, breathing her in. His hand reaches out for her but stops short, fingers folding in. Jaw muscles flex, a sternness resolves itself across his face. He rolls back to look at where he knows the window is. From far off in the unseen distance, a dog barks and in doing so confirms the world is still there.

No breeze touches him. His flesh is clammy with becalmed humidity. His thoughts read messages glimpsed:

MESSAGES.>

He cannot stop them. He swallows. His tongue passes over dry lips. His eyes flick toward her again, but this time he does not turn.

Finally, the window is revealed, the dawn coming blue and lazy. A cool blue that tells of early-morning cold but brings none. In his sleeplessness, the change in light is like waking. His mind escaping from what had been read and what could never be said, to work:

First to arrive, turning into an empty car park.

White painted initials in the space close to the door.

Leaving car with roof down.

Hot coffee from the machine, paracetamol and chocolate from his desk drawer, his favoured substitute for sleep.

The rest of the sales team drifting in. The light banter of the start of the day.

Relaxed by the controlled tick-tock of the daily routine ahead, his guard drops and his face is kind again. In that honest moment, red numbers on the clock quickening and the countryside beyond the window stirring, he quite unexpectedly slips into sleep.

8

The Tide flows over the land and engulfs me. I step out of the wood. Out into the open.

It's beautiful!

I just can't help but hold my hands out and smile into it. Like cool rain on a hot day. I start across the field. The air is filled with the scent of new green things, of growing things.

I'm still trying to remember what it is about Tom? Henry and Joyce both say not to think too much about the dreams. But I think they mean something. The more I have, the more certain I am. I can't get the dream about Tom, about the Brecon Beacons, out of my mind. I keep trying to connect it with that last trip to see Vince in Brighton. I'm sure they go together but I can't make them fit. I think that's why I had the dream, because I'd been thinking about that last trip to Brighton. Perhaps that's also why the Tide bought me back here, perhaps the soul at the monument is part of it too? I just need to work out the connection, I'm sure it's there. I wonder if it was the cloud shadows? I said to Vince that if he liked watching them he should climb the hills if we went to Brecon again. He said cloud shadows were cloud shadows and you could drive to see them at the Dyke, so why walk?

No, I'm sure that's not it. There's something else.

*

Vince and I left the Dyke when the clouds thickened and it started to rain. We drove back into Brighton, back to Vince's new flat. It was close to the works yard he rented in Hove. We were in my car and Vince was smoking, the stink of his cigarette filling the cabin, despite the fact I'd put all the windows down and the air was streaming cold against my face and the rain was in it. Whenever I've asked him not to smoke in my car he always assumed I was joking. I asked Vince if he'd settled in yet or whether his stuff was still in boxes.

'Boxes! I've been in for just over a year now. Burnt all the boxes in the yard to keep warm in January,' Vince laughed. 'Take a left up here, where that fat bastard's crossing,' he added, pointing across the dashboard and grinning, his mouth curling around his cigarette.

'A year? No…'

'Moved in last March.'

'You're telling me I haven't been down since last March?'

'Before then, Maggie. The last time you came down was the Christmas before. But you couldn't stay and come out on the lash for a laugh with your old besties 'cause you had too much fucking work on.' He pulled a face like he was looking at someone throwing up when he mentioned working over Christmas, then smiled around his cigarette again and winked. I didn't rise to the bait.

'Yeah, I remember that, but surely—'

'Follow the road round and then take a right.'

'Right.'

We turned into a broad road of tall white terraced houses, with black painted railings and a double strip of parked cars down the middle. We'd managed to get ahead of the rain for the time being so, parked in the middle strip, I left the windows cracked open by a couple of inches to clear the cigarette smoke. As soon as I stepped out of the car, it was as if I'd never been away. Brighton was an old, old friend. The soundscape of traffic and people, a siren in the distance somewhere, the smell, that smell of fumes and concrete and fast food all mixed with the sea, the light off the white buildings, the bicycles by doorways, everything. Always familiar, no matter how many months or years.

*

I'm following a track through a huge field that covers a broad basin of land. There's barley all around me. The sun's behind me in the east, warm and steady. There isn't a breath of wind. The barley is completely still.

Shame. I love it when the wind stirs through it as if it's water.

Wait—

I remember thinking that before. Did I come here in life? I don't think so, not this way. But it *feels* so familiar.

I stop and look around. I'm right in the middle, out in the open. Nowhere near the hedges along the crest. I finger my wedding ring. I scan the path behind me and the hedges circling the bowl.

I must get moving. The Tide won't wait forever.

I jog forward.

This is so familiar. Have I been here before? No, when could I have been?

*

Vince's flat was a mess, but I have to say I liked it. It was like every other flat Vince had rented, like so many flats I'd been in before in Brighton. Like my own before I met Isla. In fact, I was sure I'd been in it before, years ago for a party or something. Relaxation seemed to ooze out of every piece of furniture, every odd thing discarded on the floor, every pile of books, every loose CD and empty bottle, even out of the motes of dust serenely idling in the sunlight angling in through the living room's sash windows. And it was quiet, city-quiet if you know what I mean: lots of background noise, nothing distinct, nothing requiring attention and all muffled by the old walls. We walked through to the kitchen. Well, I say kitchen; it was actually a festering shithole that just happened to have a sink and a cooker in it. We were greeted by a debris field of dropped and decaying food, a many-times-overflowed mound of bin bags that looked more like a *Star Trek* monster, and a great mass of unwashed and long-abandoned crockery on or near the draining board. Fortunately, an all-prevailing smell of curry masked that of the bins and the decay. The window was open and looked out on to the back of shops in the next street: flat-roofed extensions, fire escapes and cooling units adding to the background hum.

'Make us a cup of tea, Maggie-May,' my host requested, dropping into one of the two chairs at a tiny table all but covered by an over-filled ashtray.

I felt compelled to summarise the room. 'Your kitchen's a bastard,' I said, walking over to the kettle. Some long-forgotten pasta cracked under my feet. Vince leaned back in his chair and smiled thoughtfully, obviously assuming I was joking again. I filled the kettle. The cold-water tap had one of those little rubber hoses on it that I hadn't seen since my nan's house in the seventies. The rubber was cracked and pitted and rasped against my skin when I ran my thumb against it. The clicker wasn't working on the cooker, so I lit it with Vince's lighter and joined him at the table while we waited.

'Seriously though, Vince. Don't you ever want to get yourself sorted? It's like student days in here.'

Vince shrugged. Every so often the rogue left his face and a wise soul showed itself. 'I like it like this,' he said simply. I just smiled. I always just smiled when he was like that; what else could you do? He reminded me of his dad at such times, of what his dad would bring to people. It was a shame they no longer talked. I guess that's the problem with people so much alike.

Vince lit another cigarette and inhaled deeply, cupping his hand across his mouth. He stretched his legs out under the table and leaned back over the chair to look upward. He exhaled lazily. The plume of smoke passed in front of a great fern, fronds cascading down from the shelf behind him. It was a beautiful plant, a deep healthy green, just like springtime. I hadn't noticed it when I walked in. I looked through to the hallway and saw two yucca plant sentries by the door, also healthy and bright. There were other plants in pots all over, spider plants, some devil's ivy on top of the fridge and loads I didn't recognise. All well-tended and in perfect condition. I'd forgotten how much Vince loved plants. And photographs: the walls were covered in them, truly plastered, almost no space left uncovered. A collage of his history; often my history too. They were hypnotic. I could have spent hours finding moments I remembered, connecting them, expanding them, reliving them and rediscovering what had gone.

I made us tea, after scrubbing the mugs almost to destruction. Vince stayed at the table; I stood, leaning against the sink and looking out of the window. City views, warts and all, were a treat. Vince screwed his cigarette into the overflowing ashtray.

'Perfect cuppa. Cheers.' He raised his mug.

I tipped mine in exchange. 'You smoke too much.'

'Hmm,' Vince nodded slowly.

'No, seriously, you should give up.'

Vince sighed sharply. He looked down at the table and prodded the ashtray. It didn't move, but the table wobbled a little. 'What for?' he asked quietly. 'What's the point?' he added, looking up, face uncharacteristically glum, those sinless blue eyes searching mine.

*

Tom!

That's why Vince was like that. Something wasn't right, just like my dream. That's why I keep thinking about that day in Brighton. Tom wasn't there. I need to remember. Dreams *do* come for a reason, I'm sure of it.

I'm still in the huge field of barley. I look at the sun, now moving round me to the west, and then at my wrist where my watch used to be. My eyes scan the track behind me. My focus lingers on patches of shadow. I jog on, faster now.

I wish I could remember about Tom, but I honestly can't.

9

He lies on his side, facing away from where she sleeps. The pillow is drawn up under his arm. The room is bright now. The sun, already climbing, already hot, burns away the mists that rose around the house at dawn. The steaming breath of plant and soil, hemmed into ordered shapes by hedgerows, now liberated by the sun, now destroyed by the sun.

He breathes steadily. His face still and peaceful. The red numbers on the clock beside him appear faded in the bright new light. Unobserved, they change and update steadily with the world now. A breeze reaches in through the window. The muslin curtain, its whiteness touched by the golden sunlight, lifts and billows inward. The breeze continues and the curtain rises and falls, wave-like, regular and silent. He sleeps on.

Birdsong reaches in with the breeze, passing the flowing curtain and gently filling the room. The distant movement of traffic is heard: people hurrying to early starts, demands made on engines emerging from bends on winding rural roads. Footsteps sound from away in the house. The bed moves, pitching gently while springs complain. Still he sleeps on.

A shadow falls across him, something passing across the window. The door latch clacks against its stopper; the door creaks. Sounds from the house – footsteps and children's voices – grow louder. The door creaks again; the latch clicks. Children's voices fade.

Under his lids his eyes begin to move, darting rapidly. He dreams now. He is far away from the house and the countryside, from his garden, the fields and the woods and the heathlands reaching to the shingle and the sea. He is on a busy city street. He is in London. He is bobbing and weaving through a crowd, trying to pick his way against a tide of people. He looks at his watch; it does not show the time, but he knows he is late for his train.

He must catch his train.

His face moves to a determined frown. He continues to work his way up the street toward Liverpool Street station. He reaches into his jacket pocket to check for tickets. Fingers find them.

'Excuse me, do you have the time?' a stranger asks from the crowd. Too polite to ignore him, he stops for a moment despite his rush.

'Yes.' He looks at his watch; still it does not show the time. He frowns and holds it up to the stranger. The stranger looks and his eyebrows knit together.

'Oh,' the stranger says. 'You'd better hurry, then; we'd all better hurry.'

With a nod, he is off again. He works his way through the crowds. He is pushed and jostled. Polite apologies and excuse me's. Again, a stranger stops him, an elderly woman this time. He wants to ignore her but she looks worried and his nature won't let him.

'Do you know where I am?' she asks, holding up an *A to Z*. He smiles and carefully takes the book. The page isn't one he recognises, but Liverpool Street station is marked in the middle, a big red icon with all the streets radiating from it.

'You're near here,' he explains, pointing to the station. 'That's at the end of this road,' he adds, gesturing down the street.

'Thank you. That's a long way. I'd better hurry,' she replies, taking back the book. 'We'd all better hurry.'

'Yes,' he nods.

He is running now. Jumping through the people. He reaches the tube station on the corner and pushes on across the road. He races by a statue of children and a McDonalds. He pauses at the top of the stairs to look at the giant departure board. Only one train is listed – his; the rest of the board is a huge clock giving a countdown. Seconds only. Below him the concourse is empty. The crowd has gone. He jumps down the steps and makes for the platform. The countdown running over his head: tall, red, ticking numbers.

Too late: the train is pulling out.

10

When I first got here I still had my watch. In fact, the first coherent thing I remember doing after I was killed was to look at it. To begin with I was in chaos; everything in those first few desperate hours is a blur to me now. All I could think about was my family.

Isla, Jack, May.

Isla, Jack, May.

Isla, Jack, May.

Their faces, their future, their love, their pain. Their terrible pain. You see, from the first moments here I was irrelevant and they were everything. They were all that mattered. It was an epiphany of being that tore away everything except my love for them. It left a truth that was naked and desperate and haunting. I could think of nothing but them and I could do nothing for them. Nothing.

What had I done?

What had I done to them?

The question that, although I have searched and searched, I cannot answer.

I just drove, I drove until night fell and I found myself at the end of a rough track on a hillside. It was as dark as it ever gets in early July. My mind wouldn't stop, wouldn't let go of what I'd done, of Isla and Jack and May. I just sat there, staring out across the shadowed farmland below. I was lost.

I remember nothing of that night, absolutely nothing. It's as if I ceased to be until I felt the dawn cold. Not a deep cold, a gentle early-morning summer cold. The car was filled with pale blue light and smelled new and fresh. There was birdsong. From nowhere a sense of peace filled me in that first new moment of awareness.

The windows were fogged with condensation. That's when I looked at my watch; it was fogged too and I had to run my thumb over it to see the dial. I didn't want to lose track of how long I'd been there. How long I'd been dead. It was a diving watch I'd been given for Christmas.

Last Christmas, *my* last Christmas. A watch that from the day I got it seemed to draw time away from me, right from when I first wore it on Christmas morning.

Like every Christmas morning we were running late and I ended up waiting in the car. Not the Jaguar that I was to journey here in; we had a Land Rover Discovery for family trips. It was really cold that morning. Proper cold. I'd gone out to get the heaters going before the children got in. It took ages before two patches of clear glass finally started to grow across the windscreen, the blowers roaring behind the dashboard. I looked out to the house. The door was open but there was still no sign of anyone. I sighed. I looked at my brand-new watch:

10.41 a.m.

I'd said we'd be at my sister Julie's by 11.30 a.m. It was an hour's drive to my sister's house. The maths wasn't difficult. I sighed again and looked up at the sunroof. It was covered with an intricate frost pattern, swirling fronds laced together.

I got out of the car and walked up to the house, feet crunching on the gravel, trying not to march. Actually, I say gravel, but we'd had the old gravel replaced with a lighter pea-shingle after we'd had the house repointed. That was the trouble with improving things: it always seemed to leave other things unmatched and in need of change. Things that used to seem important. I stopped at the door.

'Come on, guys!'

'Now coming,' Isla replied, walking out of the dining room. We looked at each other. She smiled.

'We'll be late.' She looked beautiful. She'd curled her hair and dressed for the occasion: distinctly sophisticated in the easy way that was hers alone. 'You look . . . lovely,' I said quietly. 'Really,' I added. She smiled again. A smile that meant *thank you*; that meant *I love you*.

Isla touched my arm. 'It's okay, Julie won't be expecting us on the dot . . . ' she said quietly. 'We're—

'Daddy! I'm going as this. I was going as Obi-Wan because I got him too from Father Christmas, but you and Mummy got me knight stuff,' sang Jack, a miniature Knight Templar, complete with tabard, woollen chain-mail jerkin and a slightly mismatched lightsabre. It was Jack's seventh Christmas and I guess it doesn't get much better than that. Skinny as ever, his blonde hair was an unruly tangle of random tufts; his green eyes flicked left and right to follow the blade of the sabre.

'Cool . . .'

Isla roughed-up his hair even more and then stepped back into the dining room, her hands going to adjust her earring.

'Daddy, Daddy, Daddy!' May screamed with excitement, running down the stairs. May was all pretty smiles, beautifully brushed dark hair and big bright eyes filled with the magic of her fourth Christmas. 'Sally's coming too!' she shouted.

'Wow!' I said, trying to fall in with her eagerness. 'Who's Sally?'

'Sally!' May tutted, holding up a new life-sized baby doll wrapped in winter blankets.

'Oh, I didn't know she was called Sally.'

May frowned at me. 'Silly Daddy,' she said.

I got them both into the car, me fumbling with the straps on their seats, they giggling and chattering about Christmas. I kissed each of them.

I got back in the car. I looked out through the now clear windscreen to the house: no sign of Isla. I took my work phone out of my jacket and had a quick scan through emails. Nothing from James. James and I were collaborating on a sales bid. We were sure it was going to rocket both of us to the highest reaches of the company. James didn't have a family and I knew he'd be working over the holiday. I started to write an email, a few suggestions I'd thought of earlier, eyes flicking between the screen and over to the house. The list grew into more of a draft section, the high-voiced Christmas discussion from the backseat fading as my thoughts focused and my eyes settled on the blue-white display.

'Shall we go, then?' Isla asked straight out of nowhere, her tone more accusation than enquiry.

'What?' I almost dropped the phone. Jack and May exploded into more giggles behind me. 'Oh . . . yeah.'

The car was cold again, from Isla opening the door I guessed. I glanced at Jack and May in the mirror. May was covering her mouth with her hands but her eyes were laughing. I looked at my watch: 10.53 a.m.!

I turned to Isla and her eyes met mine. I looked away, returning the phone to my pocket. I looked back, Isla's eyes were still waiting. She raised her eyebrows and opened the glove compartment. A squeak of escaping giggle came from Jack. I retrieved the work's phone, reached across and stowed it in the glovebox. Turning to face forward, Isla clicked her seatbelt into place. I started the car.

'Come on we'll be late, let's get a move on . . . ' she smiled.

*

I'm almost there now, I'll be there soon. I'm at the end of the track on top of the rise. I can't see the monument, but the little river that leads to it is below me. Not far now. The sun's low and bright. I hold my hand up to shield my eyes and stare into the distance. I see the church tower and trees that mark my journey's end. I slow my pace to a walk. I look back. A breeze picks up and stirs across the barley. It moves in waves. I stop for a moment. I watch the swaying patterns and see the path I've followed stretching away back into the distance.

I remember this, this view. Being glad I'm not still down there, out in the open. I'm sure I do.

Wait!

I think I saw something large moves across the track down in the field. I scan along the path. There's nothing there now. But I'm sure I saw something. I walk slowly backwards. I don't blink. I don't take my eyes off the sea of barley. What did I see back there? What *is* following me, watching me?

Must stay calm.

*

'Whooa! Watch Out!' my sister shouted. We – or rather everyone except me – were playing Jenga. It was my brother-in-law Clive's turn. Yeah, that's right: *Clive*. Julie, Clive and their two dogs lived in a small semi-detached house on a 1980s development near Ipswich. It smelled of the dogs and Clive's experimental cooking and always needed work doing on it. The Jenga tower was shot and no one was giving much for Clive's chances as he tried to steady his hand.

I looked at my watch:

4.05 p.m.

'Daddy, can you open this for me?' Jack asked, handing me a walnut and the crackers. He still had his party hat on. So did Isla and Julie. May had lost hers so I'd given her mine. She'd lost that too. Jack's voice startled me; my mind had drifted off from my watch to the sales bid. As I remember there was this idea, well concept really, I'd had and I was trying to think it through, get it straight.

'What? Oh, yeah . . .' I replied. 'Sure!'

The shout went up: the tower of blocks had fallen. Everyone was laughing, even Clive, although, man-to-man, I could tell that he was pissed off. Clive was always such a fucking cock; everyone thought so – even Mum – and none of us ever knew what Julie saw in him. Isla caught my eye and winked. She looked happy and her eyes told of wine and desire. I smiled back. She winked.

'My go, my go!' Jack announced, jumping over to the Jenga rubble.

'Oi, your nut,' I called after him.

'Hmm, don't worry. I don't like nuts. I just wondered what those weird ones looked like inside.'

Everyone started rebuilding the tower. I got up to put the walnut shell in the bin. I walked through to the kitchen but I didn't stop. I just carried on out of the back door without really even deciding to. I closed it behind me, silencing the laughter filtering out from the living room. It was cold and pitch-black. I had to feel my way around the side of the house to the street, my hands on the rough brick and folds of mortar.

The air was freezing and thick with the smell and smoke from the neighbour's wood-burner. Before I knew it, I was sitting in the passenger seat of the car with my work phone, eating the walnut while I read through a draft of the bid that James had emailed over.

*

The fleeting moment of distracted peace that I awoke to alone in my car on that first dawn after the crash disappeared when I looked away from my watch. Absolute despair took me. Isla, Jack, May, my beautiful family. What had I done? The undeniable naked truth of my situation filled me with a blackness from which I couldn't imagine escaping. A blackness that was complete.

But then the Tide came in for the first time. You see, it's not a sea tide, not a normal tide, not something I could even see back then, but it came with the sun, flooding over everything and I felt it. The moment it touched me I knew it was there and I felt less alone. I felt loved.

Many years before, I'd read – and until that waking moment forgotten – a tale of a Cistercian monk, Brother Alberic, who had collapsed whilst labouring in the fields he tended. He was feared dead, but after being carried back to the abbey – on a gate I believe – he regained consciousness. When he woke he spoke of a tide, a divine flow that had touched him and brought him hope. It was so profound that he was to leave the abbey and spend the rest of his life as a wandering white friar, spreading word of what he had experienced to all he met. I knew for me there could be no awakening, no recovery, but I knew instantly in that first dawn that what he'd glimpsed in his brush with death was now flooding the land around me. I knew I had found Brother Alberic's Jerusalem Tide.

11

It was Joyce who showed me how to actually see the Tide, but I found I could sense the ebb and flow of it, knew when it was coming and when it was going, right from that first morning. It's so much part of nature here. Part of nature full stop, I think for the living too. It's a beautiful thing. When it comes it's like arriving home or meeting an old friend; it makes me think of when I was little and being comforted by Mum when I was hurt or upset. It reminds me of lifting May or Jack from their beds when they had woken in tears from bad dreams, gathering them up, their warm little bodies against my chest. And most of all it feels like lying next to Isla when we were younger, when I would wake to find her arms around me and lie still, listening to her breathing and knowing I had everything I wanted in the world. It's all of those things, all at once.

*

I wandered out of the house in Kentish town that first evening I'd seen Isla and found myself in the back garden. I paused, struck by the view. It was teaming with tiny lights, strings of fairy lights and candles, some naked, some in old jars, all burning with tall, still flames in the breezeless, humid air. It was like some beautiful, hidden, holy place. In no particular hurry, I made my way from the house, still smoking my scrounged cigarette. There were people scattered around, but the one I wanted, the photographer, was not among them.

There was a shed with a small veranda – well, more of a covered area of decking. I remember the whole thing smelled of varnish and the wood was smooth and new; it seemed out of place alongside that rundown old house. There were a couple of steps leading up to the deck so I sat down on the top one, leaning against the side rail and cradled my beer while I looked back at the lights. And that's where I stayed , just sipping my beer and listening to the music and the people sounds coming from the house. I couldn't relax, though; couldn't stop thinking about the photographer. I was tempted to run back to Camden just in case she was still near the pub or maybe turned up to get the tube. But then it seems fate decided to smile on me, decided to adjust the universe in my favour. Isla walked out of the darkness between all the tiny lights.

She was wearing a white fitted blouse that looked like a man's shirt complete with epaulettes and a sort of khaki skirt that was short and not fitted. Very *National Geographic*, I thought to myself. She had a huge shapeless bag slung round her like a hammock, which made her look all the more petite. Her dark hair was straight then, shoulder length and framing that beautiful, pale, Audrey Hepburn face that I'd been searching for her all evening. She walked straight to me. Turned out her interest was professional at that stage; she'd been looking for me in the hope I'd give an interview.

'Hello,' she said, voice happy and, I thought at the time, quite posh. I played it cool, of course: I didn't get up, just moved my head to look at her directly and selected the sharpest reply from my list.

'Hi,' I said – it was a short list.

'Hi, I'm Isla,' Isla smiled. Oh my god, I even loved the name! I'd never met an Isla before – well, there had been Isla St Clair on *The Generation Game* with Larry Grayson, but I'd never met her. 'Mind if I sit?' Confident, sexy, beautiful and called Isla, with those Audrey Hepburn 'give me your soul now' eyes and definitely a little posh: did I fucking mind?

'Help yourself.' I gestured to the step, using my bottle as a pointer. She walked round and sat next to me, laying her bag down on the bottom step by her feet. I took in every graceful movement. She sat with her knees pressed tight together and angled away from me.

'Ahh,' She exhaled, putting her hands on her knees and smiling wide-eyed in a *right let's get to work* kind of a way.

'No camera this time?' I asked.

'Hmm? Oh! No . . . you recognise me from earlier,' she realised aloud, 'In the bag,' she added.

'Ah,' I nodded. 'Of course I recognised you from earlier,' I said sincerely. 'Seeing you isn't something I'd forget,' I added – post-gig bravado I think.

Her eyes, reflecting the myriad candle flames from the garden, smiled in reply. 'I'm here doing some work for the *Sussex Review*, an article on Kelly's Heroes . . . followed you up from Brighton.'

'*Sussex Review* . . .' I repeated out loud by accident, a bad drinking habit of mine.

'Yes. Have you heard of it?'

'Yeah, course I have,' I lied. She studied me, for a surprisingly comfortable moment, those keen, deep brown eyes reading me.

'You so never have!' She laughed, eyes staying on mine. She was beautiful.

'No . . . sorry, I was just being a bloke. You can't expect me to admit to not knowing things.'

She laughed and adjusted her position, leaning a little closer, her knees turning toward me. 'Oh, fuck it,' she sighed, abandoning professional interest. 'It's a shit magazine anyway.' It was my turn to laugh. We laughed together. And that was it. We were talking. No interview, no further bravado, just Isla and me. It was immediately comfortable, immediately intimate and immediately closed to all others at that shabby old house in Kentish Town on that muggy August night of 1993. We talked and we talked right there on the wooden steps. At dawn, we walked back to Camden, still talking. We talked over coffee and Danish pastries from a place by the lock. We talked on the first tube back to Victoria and we talked all the way back on the train to Brighton, right up to when it was time to go our separate ways.

The morning was cooler than the previous days had been. The station was quiet with a scattering of Friday-night refugees slumped on benches and a few people in shop uniforms hurrying to work. The clatter of shop shutters being rolled up for the day's business and the occasional clash of stock cages were the only interruptions to the sound of gulls. A breeze blew up Surrey Street and moved litter around our feet as Isla and I walked out to the taxi rank and bus shelters. I noticed the breeze didn't smell of London. Of course, I was wondering and hoping what would come next. So many assumptions. Isla stopped, touched my arm and brought me round to face her. I smiled at her. I always smiled at her. She smiled, but her eyes didn't. All of the clocks of my life that had ticked toward our meeting, the pinch in my hourglass, and were by then marking time from it, slowed for the placing of a completely unforeseen pin in my map.

'Well,' Isla said. Her hand moved flat against her chest, thumb finding a tiny gold cross on a fine chain that I hadn't noticed before.

'Well.' I suddenly felt foolish smiling.

She let go of the cross and took my hands in hers. 'This . . .' She paused and finally her eyes smiled, but this time her face was neutral, controlled even. She squeezed my hands gently. 'This has been . . . beautiful.' It was a strange thing to say. I smiled like a fool again, but my knitted brows questioned her. 'Completely unexpected,' Isla added before letting go of my hands. There was a silence that I felt I had to fill.

'Well, come and have a coffee with me.' I gestured to a place down the hill a little way. 'You can tell me all about how unexpected I've been—'

'No, I should go,' she replied, pointing to the cab at the front of the rank. It was a shitty brown Volvo with the white bonnet livery of an official Brighton and Hove carriage.

'No!' I replied, feigning shock. 'You can't go yet, you just can't . . . I'll be sad, I'll get depressed . . . I'll end up neglecting my pot plants and they'll *all* die. Do you *really* want that on your conscience?'

Isla smiled, her eyes and her face this time, just for a moment. 'No, I really must go.'

'Tonight, then. Come and have a drink with me . . . We may still be able to save the plants.'

'I have to get home . . . to my husband.'

What the fuck? It was absurd. She was twenty-six and already married. I didn't know anyone who was married – well, only older, grown-up people. Marriage was nowhere in my life, in the lives of people like me – people like Isla, forchristsake. But I didn't laugh, I knew she wasn't joking. In fact, I immediately did nothing. I just looked at her. She looked down, she looked sad. Then she got into the back of the shitty brown Volvo and it drove her away from me. I shouted my address as it drew away. I played it really cool and dignified by running alongside it and desperately shouting my address until it left me standing in the middle of Queen Street. Isla didn't look at me. Her eyes were fixed on the road ahead as she worked the tiny cross between thumb and forefinger.

I'd never known anything like it. Emotional Jenga – not that I'd heard of the game then; parties were still about sex and booze at that point in my life. I have a memory of it raining as I walked home along grey streets, but it didn't; the sun shone on the white buildings. I just didn't notice. I was looking with different eyes. I didn't see the truth.

12

He wakes. He sits upright. He turns to the clock but ignores it. Pushing it aside, he grabs his watch. He blinks sleep from his eyes and stares at the dial. His eyes screw shut; anger flushes over his face. He turns to look where she slept. The sheet is pushed back and she is gone.

His thoughts jump to what was read, before he can stop them.

MESSAGES.>

Memories from a distant night so many years before come for him. Buried memories of a day when two worlds came together, of a friend's door, of rage, of despair.

The muslin curtain billows up to the ceiling. His eyes flick to it. The grip of his memories is broken. He jumps from the bed. Fumbles through drawers for shorts and socks. He pushes into them, falling back to sit on the bed, his focus on the suit and shirt hanging on the wardrobe door. He clips his watch round his wrist, frowning at the dial. Pulling at the hanger, he lays the suit and shirt on the unmade bed and dresses quickly.

The kitchen is busy. His children eat cornflakes from white bowls with a blue floral pattern. His daughter is drinking orange from a small glass. The carton stands in the middle of the table. His son spoons down cornflakes greedily. He hurries in, pulling his tie into position. The smell of coffee meets him. His son looks up and grins.

'Hello, Daddy!'

He casts around the worktops. 'Keys! Have you seen my car keys?'

His son stops smiling. He lays his spoon in his bowl and stops eating. His daughter looks from her brother to him.

'Help me look!' He scours the worktops, running his hands over the odds and bobs, opened letters, books, toys and kitchen things. Without speaking, his son responds with determination. He gets down from the table and runs through to the living room. His daughter, younger, seems amused and asks her brother where he's going.

'Looking for Daddy's keys!' replies her brother, urgently.

He spins around looking toward the hallway. The clock on the wall, with the same floral pattern as the bowls, ticks at him.

'Where the hell are they!' he demands.

She walks in from the hall. They stop in front of each other. Their eyes meet. She bites her lip, her eyes sadly searching his. She lifts her hand to him. He delays for a moment. His jaw muscles flex. He brushes by her into the hall. She looks down and does not move. His daughter looks intrigued now. She climbs down from her chair and follows after him. He looks around, feeling through the pockets of a jacket hanging on the hooks beside a framed photograph of waves crashing over the sea defences at Walberswick.

His son bursts in from the living room. 'Daddy!' he cries simply, holding up a bunch of keys, standing straight like a soldier making good on the oaths he has sworn.

He pauses for moment, staring at his son. Frustration leaves his face. Relief follows.

'Good boy.'

His son beams proudly.

He grabs the keys and opens the front door. He dashes out, pulling the door behind him.

'Daddy, there's a lady coming to our school today,' his daughter begins with excitement. 'She's going to show us all about pianos and—'

The door slams. His daughter's voice is lost. He stops and turns back. His hand moves toward the door. He frowns. His hand stops short, fingers folding in. He turns away again and runs across the gravel drive to his car.

13

I've made it to the river. It's a lazy river. It will be green by the summer. But at the moment it's like a mirror, reflecting the sky until the breeze messes it up.

I hurry along the path.

I'm sure I'm doing the right thing. I've felt sure I need to go to that man at the monument. No one should be alone, not here.

Wait.

I remember . . . I remember thinking this before.

I hurry toward the church, nearly there. I look over my shoulder.

Must stay calm.

I'll be at the monument soon, really soon. I'm certain now that whoever he is, he'll be there, I can feel him. It will be like having Joyce or Henry with me. I'll have to be careful, though; if I'm the first person to meet him here he'll be nervous, just as I was when I first saw Joyce.

Joyce and I met a while after the beach and the voice, after I finally stopped hiding. After I decided I had to stop haunting the woods for the sake of that little girl in the yellow raincoat who reminded me of May. I'd returned to spending time as near to the living as I could, although it felt as if they were getting further and further away all the time. By then my hopes were fading. In my heart, I felt increasingly sure I would never find Isla or Jack or May there and that that was my answer. That I'd—

I can't say it.

But I've never been able to let them go, not until I know for sure.

There's always hope.

I returned to visiting places where perhaps they might be. The Tide still seemed to bring me to those places in fact. I would sit and think of them and send my love, and hope that it would reach them, and sometimes I believe I got a sense of them, a sense of them in the Tide.

On this particular day, I found myself in Woodbridge. It's a lovely market town where we used to go shopping. It's close to the coast, but not that close; at the time if it had been any closer I wouldn't have been able to go there. Not after the voice. The town *felt* busy, the distant living somewhere down the streets that led away from me: the bustling sounds of a crowd and even the occasional glimpse of movement. And this was one of those days that I thought I could feel them: Isla, Jack and May. Call it hope, blind hope, or imagination, the desperate imaginings of a lonely man perhaps, but sitting there I could feel them and the sense of it warmed me.

I knew Woodbridge well in life, and I sat alone, as always, on a favourite spot – the steps of the old hall in the middle of the market square. I focused on my feelings, trying to hold on to that sense of Isla and Jack and May, trying to focus on it. I so wanted it to be carried up from the living.

Then a woman walked along the edge of the square. Although she was a way off, it surprised me how close she was. And I could see her clearly. I watched her. She glanced at me without pausing. I continued to watch her. She was quite tall, elegant, and she had the blondest hair, set with a wave through it. She wore a shift dress, perfectly cut, perfectly fitted around a slender, gently curving figure. She was striking, not just because she was so close; even in life, in a crowd, I would have noticed her. I watched her every move, her every step. Not because she was an attractive woman – that really isn't relevant here; I simply felt drawn to her. I stood up on the steps and watched her walk out of sight. I thought about following her but I knew it would be a waste of time, that I wouldn't be able to close the gap. So just I stood there, staring at where she'd gone. Wondering how she had come to be so close. Closer even than the little girl in the woods.

Then after a minute or so she reappeared. She stood at the corner for a moment, staring right at me. I looked back. She turned quickly and was gone again. I didn't know what to think. Had she seen me? I mean, really *seen* me? Or had she felt me, like that little girl had?

Or was she?

Could she be?

I wasn't afraid. Not at all. Not like when I heard the voice. She felt very different. She felt *good*. Quite simply my heart told me that I'd just seen a friendly face, possibly even a fellow traveller in Dad's Meadow. I fingered my wedding ring, my eyes fixed on the now empty corner. I walked down the steps, slowly. I scanned the square and then looked back to the corner. Willing her to reappear, I took another few steps forward. Nothing. The corner stayed empty. The sounds of the distant living floated on the air.

I started running. I ran to the corner and continued round. The road went down a hill and there, a hundred yards or so away, I saw her. She was looking up at me. I stopped. She turned and started to walk away.

I wanted to call out, but I didn't.

I wanted to run after her, but I didn't.

I didn't know what to do.

Then she stopped. Dead still.

I took a few steps forward. She turned. She looked directly at me again. I stopped. We stood, staring. I didn't dare move, I didn't dare breathe. Slowly she raised her hand: Friend.

I raised mine. She smiled.

I ran down the hill like an excited child. As I got close to her it was the sound of living faded, withdrew. That's the first time I experienced it, her being further off somehow. But it didn't matter. She was right there to me. I stopped in front of her, closer than I usually would have. Her eyes were kind, rich-blue and filled with love. We put our arms around each other and I held her to me. She was real.

In that moment, I loved her. I loved her absolutely. I was always faithful to Isla, but if I'd have met Joyce in life there would have been an attraction and that would have defined how we interacted. In life, we would first and foremost have been man and woman. But there was nothing of that. I love her like I love my children and like I loved my parents when I was a child, like my sister, like my dearest friends and more, all at once. It was as if the Tide was flowing through us both. I was shaking.

That's how it is here. It's not about sex, whereas in life it is, to the tiniest detail. It was exactly the same when I met Henry, the same sense of the Tide washing over us. Although I can't remember exactly how we met. How can I have forgotten that?

*

I run. I run now, toward the church and the monument.
I remember this, I'm sure I do—

Henry!

I think of Henry as I run. I remember I was running from something when I met him. I'm sure of it. And Tom – when did I run with Tom? Both fill my thoughts. Questions without answers.

I *know* Henry. I remember conversations we've had and how he loves to throw stones. Always, whenever we sit, if there are stones on the ground he'll pick a target, a post or a bigger stone up ahead, and spend hours trying to hit it. He'll have me drawn in too, stone after stone! But I remember nothing of meeting him. I remember how I felt. I remember love, just like with Joyce. But different too, I remember the living being close when he stood with me, really close, not far away like with Joyce. And I'd been running. I was afraid.

I look back. I see movement! It's hidden in the evening shadows and too far away for me to make out what it is. But I definitely see it. I stumble. I manage to keep my feet. I run hard. I race the Tide.

I pass the church and see the monument up on the hillock. The sun is setting behind it. I hear the living in the village.

Safer now. I slow my pace.

The monument's a tall stone cross, ringed by white painted railings. There's a tatty, decaying poppy wreath at its base. I jog the final yards.

I see him! The man I saw from the car. He's faint in the sunlight. He's old and tall and standing, bent forward, beside the cross.

I take the final steps to him. He is far away. The sound of the living is silenced. His face is sad. He looks at the names carved on the stone.

Hello.

I don't know if he can hear me.

He looks up now but past me to the west. He looks so sad.

Hello!

He moves, stepping close. I feel rain in the air around him, cold rain. But it's not raining. I feel his sadness. It's everywhere. He looks as if he is going to weep. He is familiar. He walks around the monument. Right by me. He doesn't react to me. His eyes don't settle on me. I step back. He walks down the path, straight toward the sun. I raise my hand to shield my eyes.

Hello! Don't go!

He's coming back!

Wait, wait. Jesus.

I knew he was going to come back. Not because he heard me. He doesn't know I'm here. But I knew. The sun is coming through him. He's like a ghost. Even here he's like a spirit.

He walks back to where he began, old and tall and standing bent beside the cross.

No. Oh, no.

I've watched this before. I know I have. I remember.

I back away. I finger my wedding ring. It's all he does. It's all that's left of him. He's almost gone, faded. Faded to nothing. Always he reads the names and looks west. Surrounded by a great sadness, and in the sadness there's winter cold and rain. He's locked in his pattern, locked into nothing, and he can't see it.

How could I have forgotten?

How many times? Is this all I am, a shade locked into a pattern? Repeating over and over just like him? Is this my route? Am I like Joyce now?

Oh God. Oh God, I've got to get out of here. I've got to—

Someone calls my name.

Henry!

It's Henry! Henry's walking up the path from the church.

Oh Henry. Thank God.

He smiles. Everything about him is kind, right from his deep green eyes to his shining round face and great portly body. Apart from his thick white hair, he's like a Buddha.

How did you know I'd be here? This is where I met you, wasn't it? He nods apologetically. And it's true, he always meets me here.

He says it's okay. He says . . . he says it's okay, that Tom sent him.

TRANSITION

Tom. Tom's ill, that's right. How could I have forgotten that? That was why he wasn't there that last time in Brighton. . . But how could he have sent you? He's ill, not dead. Tom's not dead, he can't be. He—

Henry holds my shoulders. His big hands are heavy on me. The Tide rises up and flows around us. I love Henry. I'm shaking.

He's say's it's okay.

He's, he's—

I can't breathe.

He's—

I look at the man who's always here. He's walking again, back to the monument.

I push Henry away. He steps back. He raises his hands for calm.

He tells me it's okay.

He is, isn't he? Dead. After me. I remember you telling me before . . . Oh God, Henry, I remember.

But why isn't he here?

Henry says he had no need to stay. He was at peace.

I push past Henry. I run over to the man. I shout at him. I shout for him to see me. I stand in front of him and shout again. I feel the cold rain around him where there is no rain.

Henry calls my name.

He doesn't know I'm here. It's just like when I shouted across the beach at the figures I hoped were Isla and the children. I can't make myself heard. He doesn't see me.

Henry! What's happening?

Henry says the man is almost gone.

Is this it? Is this what's happening to me? Am I . . . am I a pattern like him?

Henry doesn't reply. There is love in his eyes, those calming, deep green eyes. He's holding up his hands again. Silently appealing for me to be calm.

How can I be calm, Henry? I don't want to end like this. I gesture to the old man who is looking to the west again. Not like that!

Henry shakes his head urgently.

He says I don't have to. I can find peace before that, just as Tom did.

But how? I am at peace!

Henry says I must stop lying. Truth is the only good.

I don't lie!

The Tide is flowing away. I can feel it.

Henry says it's okay again. He looks into the Tide, his face warm and kind. He says we should leave this place. He says he'll take me to Joyce.

But how?

I still can't breathe. I want to shake the man. Make him hear me. Drag him from his pattern, his tiny, pointless loop.

Henry touches my shoulder. I feel the Tide, the last of it ebbing through him. It brings my breath back with it. I breathe easily.

He says to take his hand.

I take it. Henry smiles and for a moment his eyes are like a child's. Like Jack's and May's last Christmas when they ran into our bedroom shouting that Father Christmas had been! I feel the excitement cutting through my thoughts.

The land drops away from us, the monument, the church, the dear, old, sad man, diminishing. I see it all in a perfect hemisphere below me, impossibly wide-angled and perfectly sharp. We're in the Tide!

Oh my God!

PART TWO

THE VEIL

14

I wake into joy. I blink into the sun. Its golden light bursts at me like jewels. The Tide flows with it, pouring over me, filling everywhere. For a moment I am with it, in every place I can see and every place I know. I am a dream in the woods, the beach, the hills, the sky, and I am loved.

I am sitting. My face rests against something hard and coarse. I hear the sea. I'm not afraid now. But I'm not brave either, nor do I feel the comfort it used to bring. I sit up and open my eyes fully, looking down away from the sun.

I flinch!

I am sitting on an oak branch above a clearing at the edge of a wood, my face against the trunk. I grab the branch. I do not fall. I think of Henry. He's not here. I have no sense of him. The monument and the man in his tiny pattern rise in my thoughts. The panic has gone. Only love for him remains. My feet hang ten feet above the woodland floor. It's thick with plants and the tree is in full leaf. It's a beautiful summer morning and ahead of me blue sky stretches away over marshes. I am near Dunwich again.

Someone calls my name. The voice is familiar. I look into the Tide and feel the warmth of the sun. The voice has called my name before. It woke me. It's a woman's voice.

Magnus, it calls.

It's Joyce, but it reminds me of Isla, when she would wake me at dawn, long before we needed to rise.

*

Isla leaving in that brown bastard of a taxi heralded a completely new and strange time for me. Brighton seemed to change somehow. It was as if I'd had fallen out of step with it. The people, the sights and the sounds and the background summer hum of hope and fun continued just the same, but for the first time I wasn't part of it. I was an observer only. Whether watching life down below in Bedford Square from my tiny balcony or walking through the crowds on my way to buy milk and cigarettes, I was remote. Brushing shoulders, weaving through the good people but never holding eye contact, never engaging, never being part of it all. Even Big Najat at the Spar on Western Road seemed to sense it and respectfully stopped telling me jokes. To begin with I carried on doing everything I always did. We rehearsed, we went to the pub afterwards, we played our gigs. I even continued to write songs with Kelly. But it was lacklustre, empty. So, slowly over the weeks, I began to fall back, my life contracting. First, I stopped writing songs. Then I started leaving the pub early. Then I stopped going altogether.

One evening in early September during this time, a breeze came in from the Downs ahead of a storm. I'd just got home from practice in the Salvation Army hall on Carlton Hill that we hired some weekday evenings. The light in my flat was low and all was still. I loved it when it was like that, when I came back to the quiet calm and shut the door on the busy world. On evenings like that I would walk barefoot, enjoying the feel the cool wooden floor and soft rugs, tiptoeing around with the lights off so as not to break the spell. I don't know why, but it always reminded me of when I was little and I'd come home from school to find that Mum had tidied up my bedroom – although my bedroom never smelled of incense failing to cover stale cigarette smoke.

I was by the breakfast bar that separated kitchen from living room in my one-bed sanctuary when the breeze came. I'd just finished making a cup of tea – peppermint tea, just to show how far I'd slid from the rock 'n' roll path. The breeze blew in from the balcony, through the French doors that had been open since June. It lifted the net curtains and went leafing through the sheet music and open notebooks filled with half-finished lyrics, poems to become lyrics and much annotation in Kelly's handwriting that lay over the sofa, the rug and the old upright piano that had clenched me renting the flat in the first place. It was like some unseen animal was scurrying through them, turning them over and leaving them to settle in its wake. It was cool and welcome on that muggy night. I knew it was from the Downs because it didn't smell of the sea. Coming across Hove, it brought the strange mix of smells from the McDonalds up the hill and jasmine from the big Thai restaurant on Church Road. Cradling my tea, I walked across the room and out on to the balcony. The world outside was polarised. Above, huge black clouds were reaching over the town, whilst below them the whites of the buildings blazed brilliantly. Just ten minutes before, I'd walked home through crowds of people in their vests and summer shorts, lazily wandering between cafés and bars. Then nothing could have hurried them; torpor and the contentment at the end of a long hot day by the sea had set in. But I looked out to find just a scattering of people, all suddenly in a hurry, scurrying to doorways and cars, glancing up to the Old-Testament-like thunderhead as it reached over the Gomorrah of East Sussex.

I leaned against the door frame and sipped my tea. It was hot and clean and the peppermint filled my nose. Suddenly lightning lit the great cloud from within. I stood straight. Then the thunder came, exploding and shaking the doors. A chorus of shock answered it from the seafront: excited cries, startled shouts, children's screams, merging into a single rolling 'Wow!' The yellow electric lights filling the windows across the square dimmed for a moment. The breeze blew into a wind. I moved back into the corner and sipped my tea again. The strings of fairy lights wound around the balconies opposite me were dancing. The wind always made me think about Dad and, even though he'd only been gone just over a year then, I smiled. The French doors started to bang. I went to shut them but the wood had swollen since they were last closed and they rasped and jammed an inch short of latching.

Lightning came again, followed by another explosion of thunder. This time all the lights I could see went out for a few seconds. Another cry rose up from the beach. A heavy raindrop hit my plastic table with a knock that sounded like a stone on a car windscreen. More raindrops came, dinting against the railings and rapping on the table. The ashtray in the centre jumped, throwing out ash. A raindrop hit my hand, cold and heavy. The ashtray jumped again and again. Then the clouds truly broke. The individual impacts became first a cacophony and finally a roar above the cries from the beach. I shrank right back into the corner, protected from the worst of it. The brickwork was rough and surprisingly warm against my back. I watched the world through a curtain of water. Below, people raced for shelter, holding bags, magazines – anything they had – above their heads. Rain splashed back from the table, the ashtray now overflowing with filthy black water. I laughed aloud with the electric excitement. The smell of wet concrete rose up from the square. Then a great crack of thunder and a flash of light came together. I flinched. Gooseflesh rose on my arms. The lights across town blinked out and didn't come back. And there I remained, watching the downpour, the splash-back all around gradually and inevitably soaking me, until I thought I heard my name called out. I leaned forward and listened for it again.

'Mags!' It was Tom, shouting up from the street.

'Maggie-May! Let us in, ya cunt!' Vince was with him.

Instinctively I sloshed the remainder of my tea out before jerking open the reluctant French doors and stepping inside. The door-release button on the intercom had never worked, regardless of whether the power was off or not. Instead, to save me running down three flights of stairs to let friends in, I had a door key tied to an oversized plastic tennis ball I'd won on the Palace Pier's giant grabber-claw game. I found it on the sofa under a stapled photocopy of Jelly Roll Morton's 'Hesitation Blues' for the piano. I went back out into the wall of water that was the balcony and dropped it over the railing.

'Key!' I shouted.

'Cheers!'

15

I slide from the branch, hanging for a moment before dropping to the ground. My landing is soft. I expect pain to jar my knees, but it doesn't come. Joyce stands in the middle of the little clearing that's more of a bite in the edge of the wood, smiling directly at me. Her hair is golden in the sun, perfectly set as always. She is alight with the Tide as it ebbs back around her. I can't take my eyes off her. It's as if she's part of the summer morning and the beauty of the new day. I feel her love in the Tide. Her eyes are as green as the verdant woodland world around us. My thoughts are distant. No words come to me.

Joyce says she knew it was me up there. She nods to the branch above me. She says she knew I'd be here.

How?

My thoughts race back. Pity for the man at the monument fills me. I breathe quickly.

How did you know?

Joyce steps toward me, her arms out. She says it's okay.

How did you know I'd be here, Joyce? I thought when Henry came and I remembered, I thought that I'd broken free. I— But is coming here, you finding me here, just the next, the next—

She puts her arms around me. The Tide pours over us as it follows the sun, flowing away through the wood. I sigh and breathe easier. It feels like the day we met. I slide my arms around her. We hold each other.

She kisses my forehead. She says it's okay.

I step back and nod slowly. I smile. But I mean no. I mean, no, it's not okay.

Joyce lowers her arms, her eyes searching mine.

A breeze comes up, waking the trees and stirring the dappled sunlight. I smell the brackish green of the marshes. I look up and think of Dad for a moment.

Joyce doesn't say a word. She's waiting. I don't know what to say to her, I don't know where to start.

I saw Henry yesterday. He helped me.

Joyce says she knows.

How? How do you know?

Joyce says he always helps me when I go to that place alone. She says I shouldn't keep upsetting myself.

But I . . .

She takes my hands and stares at me. She says I don't *have* to be upset, that it doesn't *have* to be hard. She squeezes my hands. She frowns at me. The sort of frown I used to give May when I couldn't convince her that there were no monsters under the bed. The sort of frown Mum used to give me when I was little and she couldn't convince me that there were no monsters under the bed. I feel the breeze on my face, it's from the sea.

But, Joyce. It's easy for you, you didn't leave anyone, you don't know what it's like. You... You don't understand what it's like for—

Joyce lets go of my hands and looks away.

Joyce?

She won't look at me.

I look at her. I look at the ground. I hear waves breaking on the beach way off. I listen to them. I look up. Joyce has walked away. She glances back at me. Her eyes are no longer glad. She looks away again, up at the trees.

And after Henry helps me?

I wait for an answer.

Joyce says that he brings me here just ahead of the Tide.

I nod slowly. It's true.

How many times?

Joyce says many. She turns and frowns in that same there-aren't-any-monsters-under-the-bed way. She says too many. She looks sad.

But it can't be, I haven't been here long enough to— I can't have. I look away.

Tom.

Joyce asks if I mean my friend Tom.

He's dead, isn't he?

Joyce nods.

But he was ill. He wasn't dead!

The breeze stops. The million-chequered lacework of light settles again.

Joyce says that I saw him. Says that I saw him on the hills that I go to.

She whispers: remember.

*

I opened my front door to Tom, his hand raised to knock. I could hear Vince still tramping up the stairs. Tom was literally dripping wet, water pooling round his Italian shoes, and his usually sharp-cut black hair lay flat over his forehead. His white shirt was transparent with the wet but, clinging to his sun-shy white skin, it made little odds. Two seemingly miraculous dry patches reached down to the knees of his blue trousers that looked as if they should have been on a highwayman. All very Adam Ant, I thought.

'Jesus, Mags, we were buzzing for ages. We're soaked!' He waved his wrist and, as if by magic, suddenly there was my door key and giant plastic tennis ball fob. He pressed it, spongy and wet and cold, into my hand.

'Sorry, I didn't hear. The power's off and I was on the balcony—'

'Fuck's sake, Maggie-May.' Vince's head came into sight above the landing rug. The sound of his heavy feet on the steps echoed round the stairwell.

'Sorry, I couldn't hear the—'

'It's all right. We all get caught wanking every now and then,' Vince reasoned graciously.

'Yeah, in fact we feel bad intruding on your *special* time,' Tom agreed, brushing flecks of god knows what off his shirt.

16

Joyce is sitting now. She's on a fallen tree at the edge of the clearing. I don't think it was there before. I'm sure it wasn't. I look at her. She doesn't look at me. She spins a little flower – that she must have just picked – between her thumb and finger, studying it in silence. It's a violet, I think.

Joyce.

She doesn't respond.

The Tide has settled now and the day is warm. Above the clearing the summer sky is happy. The trees are still. There's birdsong, but I still hear the lullaby of waves on the beach. They tell of a calm, lazy sea. Insects move among the leaves around us. One – nothing more than a bright speck in the slanting light – spirals near Joyce. It doesn't touch her, though.

Joyce.

I love Joyce. I love the stillness of high summer. I love the cool of the woods. I love the sea and the beach. Warm sand and white crested waves under cirrus skies and, later, herringbone sunsets. Tired, contented evenings, bare feet on the carpets and salt-stiff hair. My thoughts stray to long summer days of childhood. I see the sea. Joyce is further off. I feel those happy days with Mum and Dad and Julie.

No.

The clearing is cool. Insects continue to busy themselves. A cuckoo calls from far off in the trees. Joyce continues to study the bright little flower. They're both so delicate and slight. I take a step toward her. Still she doesn't look. If I love all of these things – the woods, the sea, Joyce – why am I not happy?

Help me, Joyce.

Joyce looks up. She lays the violet beside her on the fallen trunk. She stands. The breeze comes again. I smell brine. I think of the voice, down there on that day. The trees stir.

Joyce says I've never asked that before.

I smile. I'm not a pattern. I do new things!

Joyce walks over to me. She takes my hand. She asks how she can help.

I want to enjoy this, I say. I look around at the oaks with leaves flickering in the breeze, at the chestnuts, hazel and alder, the bright greens of the clearing giving way to richer, cooler tones in the deeper wood. I think of the moss and ferns running along the sloping ground to the willows and ash nearer the streams that feed the marshes. The little mossy burns so busy each spring, which Vince and Tom and I would try to dam when we were boys.

Joyce nods.

The warmth of the sun and the cool of the deeper wood come to me both at once. I see far.

I see it all! I see it, Joyce!

I see the marshes and the sea. The summer skies of dawn and noon and dusk are over the wood and over the beach and over the sea and over me. Joyce takes my hand. She is with me!

Joyce!

We feel warm. We feel sand under our bare feet. We taste ice cream and cola. We are children! We run. We sprint over the sand. We laugh. Our arms are in the air. We hear my parents, Mum and Dad, and my sister's voice when we were little. We are in the waves, blue and green and white, jumping through them, their weight thudding against us. We are children *and* we are parents. I hold Jack and May as we jump over gentle bubbling waves. Joyce holds a little blonde-haired girl almost as pretty as May in her arms. I am a child holding Dad's hand, my sister holding the other as we jump the waves. On the beach, I hold curious shells and stones in my hands with pride. There is contented tiredness and my sister's sleeping head resting in the warm evening. Joyce is still with me and the little girl is with her. We are Joyce now and we are the little girl.

Joyce . . .

We are in a church. The sun streams through high-vaulted windows. Dust swirls in the warm, slanting ribs of sun. White ribbons are tied along the pews. It is a wedding. There is a crowd around us. Voices are raised in song. Joy fills us. We squeeze our mother's hand and look up into her happy face. The little girl squeezes our hand and we look down and smile at her. We look at the altar and the priest with love and wonder. Such joy, such wonder. We are special.

The clearing is around us again. The brief sense of joy slips away from me. My heart is racing.

All of this, Joyce. All of it.

The breeze leaves us. The clearing is still again.

All of it. I want to remember how to enjoy all of it again.

Joyce smiles. The Tide is all around her. She says we should go down to the beach. I swallow. The sound of waves comes again. Joyce squeezes my hand.

She says it's okay. She says this will just be a lovely day.

I nod.

She says Henry will meet us there.

Really?

She says yes, she knows he's there.

She tugs my hand.

I linger, the little girl whom Joyce held in the waves is in my thoughts for a moment.

Joyce says it's time to find Henry.

17

After lighting, some of the many half-burned candle stubs dotted around, Vince began systematically searching my flat, methodically checking every cupboard, corner and bookshelf. He was looking for biscuits. You wouldn't have thought it to look at the tall lanky man that he had become, but as a child he was so greedy his mum had to hide biscuits, even lock them away. He always searched for biscuits. Tom hung back, hovering by the door and looking at his feet every time I glanced over. Vince ended up leaning against the breakfast bar, idly opening the cupboards below.

'I'm out of biscuits.'

'You sure?' he replied, his eyes a silent inquisition, searching my face for truth. I nodded. He let the door swing shut. Little droplets of water were trapped in the fuzzy blonde edges of his dreadlocks, catching what little light there was like morning dew on spider webs. I was sure I could see wisps of steam rising from his soaking black suit. He smelled just like my family dog – Wellington – when I was little. He grinned at me, eyes sparkling now. I knew he'd come for a reason. I looked over at Tom. He glanced down at his feet again so I looked back at Vince. Still smiling, he started fingering the stud through the corner of his bottom lip: the original Elvis-head earring that Mary Delaney had pierced him with against an ice-cube from her gin and tonic while the old romantic fools were enjoying coitus in the back of the Heroes' van.

'I'd make some tea . . . but there's no power,' I said finally.

'Oh, there's clearly been quite enough of that already,' Vince observed, turning to Tom and nodding at the box of peppermint teabags. Tom exhaled slowly, looking directly at me. I swallowed.

'They're not for me, they're—'

'Just the mugs, Mags,' Vince interrupted, pulling a flat half-bottle of Scotch out of his jacket. Tom walked over and stood at the end of the breakfast bar between us both. I slid three mugs in front of him.

Vince poured a couple of inches in each without looking away from me, without so much as a single downward glance. He didn't spill a drop. There was a pause. Finally, Vince raised his cup in salutation and took a hit.

'Right then,' he said, with a wince. I took a sip. It was cheap supermarket blended Scotch that burned foully and made Bells taste smooth. I took a longer draw immediately, half draining my mug. I looked at the bottle and wanted it all. I sucked on my bottom lip. The dull burn reached down to my stomach.

'Right then, what?' I asked.

'Right then, what the fuck's up with you, Maggie? We've come round to sort it out, whatever it is.'

'We've been worried,' Tom added.

I looked from Tom to Vince. Vince took another sip. No wince this time.

'There's nothing wrong.' I drained my mug, the burning less intense. Scotch always made me a special kind of manic, crazy drunk. A place I suddenly wanted to be.

'Oh, fuck off, Maggie! Fucking tell us!' Vince laughed.

Tom glanced at Vince. 'Tell us, Mags,' he said simply.

I held out my mug. Vince poured most of the remaining whisky into it. 'Okay . . .' I took another sip. The windows suddenly lit up and everything was bathed in brilliant white light for a moment. Jagged shadows etched every edge. Then dim half-light again. Thunder rolled in the distance. 'It's this girl—'

'Girl! You've been moping around, not coming to the pub and drinking fucking mint tea, mint fucking tea!' Vince paused to tap the box of teabags, 'Over a bird! For fuck's sake!'

'Was it that girl you met after the gig in Camden?' Tom asked, ignoring Vince's outcry.

'Yeah.' As I acknowledged it, a sense of hopelessness filled me. 'Yeah,' I said again. Tom nodded thoughtfully.

'Camden, Camden . . .' Vince frowned, his eyes moving from side to side as if scanning an invisible diary. Then realisation came to them and he looked at me again, even more incensed this time. 'But you said you didn't even knob that one?'

'Yeah, I didn't.'

'For fuck's sake.'

'Her name was Isla, wasn't it?' Tom asked.

'Yes!' I was so pleased he remembered her name. I liked hearing it used. I liked my friends thinking about her in connection with me.

'All right,' Vince announced, raising his hands, his voice calmer. 'All right.' He lit a cigarette. 'Well, that's good, isn't it, then?' he asked Tom. I took another hit of whisky. I didn't notice any burning at all. 'I mean, it could have been worse . . . We thought you were ill – you know, fucked or something.'

Tom nodded.

'Easily fixed, easily fixed,' Vince carried on, speaking mostly to himself, I think. He drew on his cigarette. 'Right, this is what we do, Maggie-May! You finish your Scotch and then get your coat.' He paused to take another draw on his cigarette and turned to Tom. 'We're taking him out to get him pissed-up and laid.' Tom nodded in thoughtful agreement. 'Best way to get over a bird is to climb on the next one, Maggie.'

The whisky was already beginning to hit its mark. Vince's logic seemed faultless. I nodded just as the fridge's compressor started humming and the landing light came back on and reached in around my front door.

Fifteen minutes later I walked out of my bathroom a new man, pulling my t-shirt on, Scotch buzzing in my head. I was ready for a night on the town. Tom was thumbing through the LPs in my vinyl shrine. Vince had found my biscuits. Chocolate Hobnobs. Okay, I lie sometimes.

18

He drops into the driver's seat. The leather creaks and complains. He heaves the door closed. It thuds into place.

He looks back at the house reflected in the mirror. The front door stays shut. His focus moves to the angry stranger staring back at him. He looks down at his lap. He runs his hand over his face and blinks sleep away. His head aches, persistent and dull.

He looks up at the oval clock set into the dashboard.

He ignores the clock and looks at his watch.

He frowns.

He puts the key in the ignition and looks down at the steering wheel with the cat on the boss and starts the engine. He holds down a switch and looks up. Servo motors whine behind him and the windows drop a half-inch. The roof above him lifts and begins to retract. He continues to look up as the canvas folds and draws clear, the cream lining replaced with bright early-morning summer sky. A single feathered contrail spreads out across an otherwise faultless blue dome. The air has a chill to it and is heavy with the smell of the conifers along the driveway. The servos stop and the car chimes. He releases the switch and pulls away. Fat wheels crunch at the gravel.

The lanes are empty. Hedges stream by. Rolling patterns of fields, glimpsed and snapshotted through gaps and gateways, drift at a slower pace. Dappled light from overhanging trees slides up the bonnet and over him. Wave after wave. The low sun winks and starbursts through the blurring foliage. Again, he looks at his watch. He accelerates, the big engine answering with its deep voice. The car begins to ride the uneven road like a speedboat. He feels the rises and falls in his stomach.

Despite the speed, his thoughts drift away from the familiar route, from each known and anticipated bend and curve. He thinks of work. The nervous faces looking at the clock.

'Should we call him?'

'They'll be here soon . . .'

'Who can cover him? We can't send them away—'

'Call him.'

Without fully returning to the car and the empty lane and hedges flashing by, he glances at his watch again and then the speedometer. The maths resolves itself in his half-present mind. He smiles now. Powering the car through bends, down and back up through the gears, his demands obeyed by the machine, his thoughts still in the office.

'Okay, I'll call him now…'

'Wait! That's him, turning into the car park – look.'

Confidence replaces tiredness across his face. He shakes his sunglasses open and pushes them on, the dappled sunlight reflected in the dark lenses. The car powers on and the dashboard clock marks time.

19

Vince looked up through a cloud of cigarette smoke. Somehow the smoke had resurrected and amplified rather than masked the smell of peppermint tea, but I didn't really care by then. Actually, I wondered if he was smoking menthols. Elmore James's 'Dust My Broom' was playing low from the turntable I'd had since my fourteenth birthday, that timeless voice of his filling the room like a lazy afternoon. After the steam of the bathroom, the air coming through from the balcony was cool, gossamer hairs on my arms standing to greet it. It was still raining outside, with a steady pap-tap of raindrops coming from the balcony door. Vince hadn't moved from the breakfast bar where he was flicking through some lyrics and notes that Kelly had scribbled on an A4 pad. His mouth was moving silently, forming Kelly's words while he nodded and tapped out a rhythm on the counter that didn't match Elmore's.

'The little hand says it's time to rock 'n' roll!' Vince grinned. 'I'll bring these, shall I?' He waved the packet of Hobnobs. I nodded before picking up the bottle of Scotch from the breakfast bar and taking another long tug. A welcome tingling along the sides of my tongue came and quickly faded.

'Pint at the Cricketers first?' Tom asked rhetorically, returning Wilson Pickett's *The Midnight Mover* seventy-eight edition to its sleeve with reverence. Tom was kneeling before the shrine, basically four deep shelves running from the chimney breast across to the balcony wall that I'd made myself and painted gloss white. They were home to my compulsively hunted, cherished and loved eclectic horde of the rare, the classic, the comedic and the beautiful music of my world. Below them were my three turntables and collected memorabilia on the grand old sideboard that came with the flat. Kelly had decorated the entire thing with fairy lights the previous Christmas and they had stayed ever since to mark it all out as a holy place.

'Careful with that,' Vince cautioned.

'Cricketers,' I agreed.

Tom, ignoring Vince's call for care, stood up, spun the cardboard sleeve as a diamond between his two hands before slotting Wilson back into place on the top shelf. He walked over to the door. I followed.

'Wait! Wait, wait,' Vince demanded. Tom and I groaned. We knew what was coming. He took out his battered Olympus.

'Vince . . .' Tom objected.

'Fuck that, Vince. I want some more booze.'

'No, no, no. This is important,' Vince insisted, setting the self-timer and positioning the camera on the breakfast bar. He backed away and joined Tom and me. 'One day you'll want copies of these. You'll see.'

The cheap whisky continued to hum through my brain. I jumped and put my arms around both their necks, weighing them to a stoop and bringing their heads close to mine. 'Glad you came round, boys!' Vince's hair was still damp and still smelled like dear old Wellington.

The tiny red light blinked manically.

'Now say "arseholes"!' Vince shouted, doing his best to look up at the camera.

'Balls!' we shouted together.

The flash fired, the camera clicked and the motor wound the film forward.

'That's going to be a classic,' Vince said. He put the camera back in its case. He beat out a drum solo along the breakfast bar on his way to the door. 'Fucking A!' he announced. I grinned.

Then it came: a single short buzz from the door intercom. I let go of Tom. Then two more came, close and sharp: *Buzz, buzz.*

I pressed talk. The customary whine faded into the sound of the street below, rain still pattering in the background.

'Heh-low.'

'Magnus?' A female voice crackled over the tinny speaker.

'Yeah,' I replied.

'It's Isla.'

20

Isla had always had something – call it empathy, call it a sixth-sense, call it luck, I never really knew which – that would bring her to me when I least expected, but most needed. A few years ago, when May wasn't much more than a toddler, in the November of Jack's first term at school, I'd been in London all day. It had been an awful day from the moment my alarm woke me into the cold blackness of five thirty on a rainy early-winter morning. Just reaching over to slap the button and turn it off sent cold air streaming down my back and made Isla pull the duvet round herself. Jack had brought a cold home from school and I'd caught it straight away. It always worked that way: if Jack got a cold, I'd get it and Isla would be fine; if May caught something, it would usually skip me and Jack and go straight to Isla. That's inheritance, I guess. So, I dosed myself up with Lemsips before Carl, a sales colleague, picked me up and drove us through the blackness to the station where we waited in silence, stepping side to side like a couple of penguins to keep warm, while I sipped a latte from the little stand by the ticket barriers.

Then came the first meeting. It was a disaster. The project was floundering so I'd expected it to be difficult, but from the moment we walked in and I tried to look well and positive it was obvious we'd already lost the battle and the account with it. Carl went back to Liverpool Street after that. The second, a lunchtime informal over a pint in the Sherlock Holmes off Northumberland Avenue just down from Trafalgar Square, turned out to be a depressing waste of time. Time that I watched leak away painfully on my watch in a series of a hundred surreptitious glances while my morning Lemsips wore off. This left all my hopes with the third and final meeting of the day, over in the Soho end of Dean Street at the offices of the PR agency on a new project. It turned out to be a great oozing turd of a meeting. A disappointed client politely, yet cruelly – and, I have to say, deservedly – deflated the egos of the PR team and drew what should have been another six months of revenue for us all to a premature close. Even the pyramid of Diet Cokes in the middle of the oh so very chic – oh so very wank – 'graffiti meeting table' seemed to lose their shine. I was beat. I was cold, I was tired, I felt like shit and I was far from home.

I managed to say a few constructive and conciliatory words to the client in the lobby that I hoped would have them back to us, if not the Dean Street agency, then wrapped my heavy coat around myself and walked out into the fading light. It was still raining and even the smell of doughnuts from the coffee shop across the street didn't excite me. I remember wanting a cigarette, even though my throat was on fire and I'd quit six years earlier when we discovered Isla was pregnant. People were hurrying by and a YO! Sushi scooter wove through the chicane of cars, parked vans and brave cyclists. My coat felt warm and I wanted it to grow to envelop me completely and create a little private space in all that hubbub. I walked up past the Soho Theatre to Oxford Street to get the tube from Tottenham Court Road. The rain started getting heavier, falling cold against my face and soaking my hair. I gave in and waved down a cab. I was thankful that the driver didn't speak much or try to make friends on the way to Liverpool Street, leaving me to blow my nose and watch the streets slip by as we jerked through traffic.

On the train, I got a cup of tea, swallowed a couple more tablets, then slept with my head against the cold window. A text coming in from Vince, telling me he was drinking coffee at a café in Ho Chi Minh City on one of his extended travels woke me just in time for my stop. I felt sweaty. I read the text twice over. I wondered how it was that our days could be so different. I thought about phoning to book a taxi home from the station but decided there'd be plenty at the rank.

The train juddered to halt at the platform so violently I thought it was broken. An announcement was echoing around the station. For some reason, a lot more people than usual got off the train. Friday rush for the weekend maybe. We all started walking as quickly as possible in order to get to the taxi rank, in that polite and tactical way you do when you don't want to look as if you're racing. But it was no good. I just felt too ill to race. So, accepting the inevitability of a day fated to be bad having to end with a queue for a taxi in the freezing cold, I slowed down and let the crowd get through the barriers.

It was dark when I walked out. I paused to button up my coat as a car pulled into the set-down bay in front of me, its lights picking out the fine drizzle and blacking out everything behind it. A bus, its yellow windows filled with tired-looking faces, pulled away, leaving the smell of diesel that I've loved since I was a boy, and a car horn sounded angrily from away down the hill toward the town centre. The bus and the angry horn reminded me of Camden suddenly, except this time I had nothing but empathy with those tired folks in suits on the bus. The last button fastened, I shrugged my shoulders and stepped out into the drizzle toward the taxi queue.

'Magnus!' Isla called from the car beside me.

I turned quickly. The driver's door was open with Isla standing beside it and the interior light was on. Jack was learning forward from the back seat, waving madly with a piece of paper in one hand. May was strapped in her seat but just visible beside Jack, her little face bobbing with excitement.

'Huh . . . hello,' I said. 'How did you . . . What are you doing here?'

'Oh, just hanging around, looking for someone handsome to take back to my place.'

'Oh, well, I'll move along, then.'

I got in next to Isla, my coat bulky and getting in the way, my case in the footwell. Isla leaned over and kissed me while she clipped her seatbelt in place.

'Daddy!' Jack shouted.

'Hello, mate! How are you feeling? And how's my beautiful girl?' May didn't reply. She still wasn't speaking much then; she just wriggled in her seat and flashed the most beautiful smile at me.

'I've drawn you a picture!' Jack continued to shout, stuffing the piece of paper he'd been waving against my face.

'Wow, thank you . . . What is it?' I asked, wrestling with my coat and seatbelt to get a hold of it.

'It's you with a massive red nose 'cause you've got my cold!'

'Wow, yeah, it's very good! Thank you.'

'It was all your own idea as well, wasn't it, Jacko?' Isla encouraged, smiling in the mirror at Jack. 'And May helped colour,' she added. 'Now sit back. Are you still strapped in?'

'Yes!'

Isla winked at me. We pulled away. I turned back and settled in my seat.

'Thank you so much,' I said. 'I can't believe you're here. Where have you been to?'

'Nowhere. We were worried about you,' Isla explained, her eyes flicking to me as we pulled up at the traffic lights by the station exit. 'It was so cold and awful this morning, I didn't want you to go. 'And we've hardly seen you all week, so since it's Friday we thought we'd come and collect you and have a lovely dinner.' The lights changed and Isla pulled out on to the road.

'Is it Friday? I didn't—'

'We helped Mummy make a trifle!' Jack cut in. 'As a surprise.'

Isla and I laughed.

'Thought we'd grab you before you had a chance to sneak off and work this evening.' She squeezed my knee before changing gear. I watched her glance in the mirror then caught her eyes as she looked at my reflection. She was happy. She was happy and beautiful.

We had homemade pizza, Jack making a face with tomato eyes and pepperoni smile, then a surprise pudding of, yes, trifle, followed by a DVD and popcorn. It was a perfect evening.

21

I stared at the grill on the intercom box. The sound of the street and rain continued to whine from it. I turned and looked at Tom and Vince. Tom was smiling. The whisky hum faded like clouds when the sun breaks through after a storm. I was suddenly sober. I looked back at the grill. My finger was shaking on the talk button.

'Hello?' came Isla's voice again.

'I'll be right down . . . the door release is – I'll be right down.'

'If it's a bad time, I can—'

'No, no, don't go anywhere!'

'Okay, I'll wait right here then . . . in the rain.'

I turned to Tom and Vince again. 'Hide!' I said.

'What?'

'Look, I've got to . . . Look, Vince. . . No! Don't hide, go . . . use the fire escape.'

'What? What the fuck are you talking about?' Vince laughed.

'Now's not the time for her to meet you, Vince . . . I need to—'

'Be a shame to cramp the boy's style,' Tom stepped in.

'Take the biscuits, take 'em, they're yours—'

'You can introduce us. We'll tell her you've been moping around after her like some kind of cock . . . set things up for you,' Vince explained, giving me the thumbs up.

'Fire escape! Please, Tom.'

'If we do . . . are you gonna cheer up?' Vince asked.

'Yes. Yes! Now go . . . It's out of the bathroom window – you know the way,' I urged, turning the two catches on the door to the landing.

'You owe us one, Maggie-May!'

'Absolutely. Cheers, guys.' I opened the door and made for the stairs.

'Maggie!' Vince called me back.

I grabbed the banister to stop myself and leaned back. 'What?'

'Give her one for me!'

I ran down the stairs, vaulting them in threes and fours.

The hallway – with its broad chequered black-and-white tiled floor, final grand sweep of stair, high-vaulted ceiling and wide wooden door, gloss black on the outside, white with tired, chipped edges on the inside, and a stained-glass side panel – would once have been the proud threshold of the Georgian home that filled the building. In my time, it was a shabby communal space shared by the six flats of which mine was one. The chandelier was long gone and the ornate ceiling boss boasted only a single bare bulb hanging from a kinked flex. Junk mail and fliers for sex and pizza littered the floor around the four mountain bikes and a green pushchair that hadn't moved since my residency began. I hit the floor with a thump from three steps up. I stopped dead. A slender silhouette filled the length of the stained glass, a shadow hanging over the South Downs mosaic. Isla's silhouette.

22

I looked over Tom's head to Isla. She closed the fridge door and frowned sympathetically. Tom was sitting across our kitchen table, old oak cut long before any of us were born. His head was bowed, his eyes fixed on the tumbler with an inch of the peaty eighteen-year-old Laphroaig that I'd just poured him. Isla walked over and put a plate of cheese and crackers and pickles between us. Tom looked up gratefully and went to stand. Isla pulled her dressing gown against the cold and smiled warmly. Tom relaxed and stayed in his seat.

'Thanks. I'm sorry I got you out of bed . . . I didn't realise the time. I—'

'Don't be silly, Thomas.' Isla put her arm around him and kissed the top of his head as if she was saying night-night to Jack. 'You come to us any time you need to. Now, I'm off to bed . . . and don't forget that the little people are asleep, so when the Scotch runs out keep the Wilson Pickett down, okay?'

Tom laughed through his nose and looked back down at his glass. Isla kissed me, touched my hand and smiled. A smile that said *poor Tom*, a smile that said to be brave, that said take care of him and a smile that promised to take care of me in return.

That night was definitely a pin in the map of my thirty-eighth year, a true waymarker in my life. So strange that I forgot it here for a time. I'd been lying in bed trying to sleep and trying not to watch the red digits on the bedside clock tick by impossibly slowly: I'd been lying in bed not sleeping and watching the red digits on the bedside clock tick by impossibly slowly. Isla had been sleeping peacefully beside me, her even breathing as rhythmic as the numbers on the clock. The winter eiderdown was heavy over us. Then, at 1.15 a.m. precisely, I heard a car on the lane. I listened to the engine note change down and back up through the bends by the old police house. Finally, gravel crunching, it pulled on to our drive. I sat up. Isla woke up.

Tom walked across the drive and I opened the door before he rang the bell. The night was bitter and still. The tink-ting of cooling metal from his Volkswagen was the only sound. He was in a state. His eyes red from tears, I thought. I don't think he was really aware of what he was doing. When I said hello he actually looked surprised to see me.

'Mags,' was all he said.

Isla came down and we got him in out of the cold.

'I . . .' was all he added.

Isla sat him at the kitchen table while I poured us a drink. A cup of tea clearly wasn't going to cut it. Isla asked if he was hungry. Tom nodded without really hearing the question. All Isla and I could do was look at each other and guess. I thought perhaps he'd split from Catherine. Isla said afterwards she knew it was more than that, and I believe she did.

23

I didn't wait. I couldn't wait. I didn't compose myself or think of something cool to say. I didn't straighten my clothes or even run a hand through my hair. I just stepped up to the door and opened it.

Isla's eyes met mine. Those sensuous brown eyes from Camden. She was standing in the shallow porch to keep out of the rain, barely two feet away. There was the face I'd been wanting to see ever since that brown bastard of a taxi took her away from me. I could have reached out and touched her easily. I could have pulled her to me and kissed her. There was the woman I had met once and didn't know at all, but whose absence I had felt everywhere. The umbrella she held at her side had clearly done its job; her raven hair was dry and in the same perfect bob as before. She wore a simple sleeveless summer dress, white with a floral pattern, that stopped just above her knees, marking her figure with a few simple lines. The lightness of the dress highlighted her smooth tanned legs and slender arms. All so elegant and easy, a feminine to my unkempt masculine – all, that is, apart from her watch. On her left arm, she wore an old heavy-looking man's watch with a brown leather strap that looked as if a dog had been at it. It was a great tired club of a thing that just didn't fit. Accessorising to carry off the whole *National Geographic* theme she'd had going on that night in Camden, I concluded with a spectacular error.

No words came to me. I wished I had composed myself and thought of something cool to say. I wished I had straightened my clothes, my hair. Then she smiled and the steady patter of rain, the light from the naked bulb high over my head, the sound of cars along the seafront, the smell of rain on concrete and brick, the lingering taste of cheap Scotch, all the houses and all the people and all the interwoven lives of Brighton, all of the world, fell away: there was just me and Isla and it was suddenly easy. That was her gift.

'Hello,' I said.

'Hey.'

My hand was still on the door and I was standing across the entrance. I stepped aside. A cloud of tiny insects brushed over me on their way up to the bulb. 'Come in.'

Isla's eyes searched mine for a moment. She drew her lips together like she was tasting her lipstick. 'No.' The world, the people, Brighton, the rain, the moving patterns of light cast down by the insects around the bulb all came rushing back. 'No,' she said again after a pause. 'I don't want to disturb your evening. I just wanted to check that . . . well, that you're okay.'

'Thanks, but I'm not scared of thunder.'

'No,' she laughed quickly. 'I mean . . . You know what I mean.'

'I'm not sure that I do,' I lied.

Isla looked down and then back at me. We were alone in our own private universe again. 'Yes, you do,' she said flatly. 'In Camden . . . We both know what would have happened if I hadn't been married.'

I was reminded of a Dutch girl – Sabine, her name was – who, with what I thought at the time was exclusively Continental directness, had asked me whether I thought that we would have become lovers if she hadn't had a boyfriend. Twenty minutes after she posed her question we became lovers in the back of the Heroes' van, but I had a hunch that things weren't going to play out like that with Isla.

'Oh, I was going to play hard to get anyway.'

She smiled. Our universe held. 'I'm sorry,' she said simply. Then she turned to walk away. Our universe popped and I fell back to Brighton.

'Sorry for letting me chat you up or sorry that you're married?' It was my turn to be direct.

She stopped, her umbrella half raised. She turned back. Her eyes spoke of thoughts far away for just a moment. 'Sorry – just sorry,' she paused. I didn't say anything. 'I shouldn't have come.'

'Yes, you should have. I'm glad you did.'

'No, I shouldn't be here. I—'

'But here you are. So come in.'

'No, no, I can't.'

'Why not? You're here. You must have wanted to see me?'

'Yes, but—'

'Then come in.'

'It's not that simple—'

'Yes, it is,' I dismissed, stepping closer. 'Yes, it is,' I said again, looking into those eyes.

'No.' Her eyes searched mine. 'No, it's not,' she whispered. We stood very close just looking at each other, neither of us speaking.

It was Isla's strange old watch that finally broke our silent stare. It chimed the hour, with one simple single note. A perfect E, in fact. It was clear and surprisingly delicate. I liked it. It looked too old to have electronics; it looked too old to work. Turned out it was mechanical, winding itself automatically with the motion of the wrist, and complete with the unusual feature of a mechanical alarm, a tiny precise bell no bigger than a match head at its heart.

We both looked at her arm and then back at each other. Isla breathed in. 'I'm going now,' she said and I knew she meant it. I couldn't think of what to say. She turned and walked down the steps to the black railings and the street, raising her umbrella. The rain started to patter on the taut fabric. A car passed a few feet beyond her, throwing up a wash of water from the overflowing gutter. None of it touched her; I don't think it would have dared.

'Wait!' I called, looking around suspiciously for brown taxis. She started to walk away toward the sea front. I pulled the door to and jumped down the steps. 'Wait,' I said again. 'Just wait!' I insisted. Isla stopped and turned around. Perfection under an umbrella halo.

'You're getting wet,' she said.

'Look, I totally get that you don't want to come up to my flat . . .' I paused, regretting the choice of words. 'But let's just have a drink—'

'I—'

'Just a drink,' I cut in before she could say no. 'A sit down, a chat . . . then we can say goodbye and it will all be cool.'

'I—'

'Come on. What harm can that do?'

'I'd like that!' she finally managed to say. 'Yes, I'd like that; it would be nice.'

We both laughed. It was a good laugh.

'How about the Cricketers? It's always all right there,' Isla suggested, holding up her umbrella to make room for both of us.

'Yeah, cool . . . No! No, I'm not that into the Cricketers . . . How about the Temple, it'll be quieter?'

24

Tom and I sat in silence. Isla's footsteps on the stairs faded to nothing and the house was still. I ran a finger along the rim of my glass, hoping he would look up and speak. I studied him for the first time in years. He'd lost weight and not necessarily in a good way. He seemed slighter, smaller somehow. His hair was short and gelled to stand in a peak. Whose wasn't? The glass whined under my finger, the tiny sound making me flinch. Tom didn't seem to notice. I started to finger my wedding ring, spinning it round between thumb and forefinger. My feet were bare and the tiled floor was numbingly cold.

'Tom,' I said finally. 'Tom, what's up, mate? What's happened?' Tom breathed deeply and looked up, running his hands over his scalp to the back of his neck where they stayed for a moment. He looked at me, his grey eyes finally sharp and present. His hands returned to the tumbler.

'I'm fucked, Mags.'

'What? How d'you mean?'

'I've not been well . . . not been for a long time.' The fridge burred into life, the compressor vibrating. We both glanced over to it.

'What d'you mean? You look fine . . .'

'I've been getting pain, a lot of pain.' Tom's hand moved to his throat. He swallowed. 'And bleeding . . .'

'Tom, I—'

'And bleeding, so I . . . well, I ignored it and you know . . .' He was suddenly speaking quickly, his eyes moving like he was reading it all from a script. 'But then I went to the doctor and he said it was probably nothing but referred me to make sure and . . .' He stopped, his hand moving from his throat to his temples, massaging them. I stood up. I don't know why.

'Tom—'

'So I went to the hospital and had tests and . . .' He looked up at me. 'It's cancer, Mags. Fucking cancer!' He ended in a shout. I just stopped. I didn't move. The fridge gave a final rattle and then the room was silent again. Tears welled in Tom's eyes and he looked just like Jack after one of his nightmares, when I'd go to him and find him sitting in the corner of his bed, eyes wide with fear. Tom looked down.

'Sorry . . . sorry, Mags,' he said into his glass.

I reached out to touch him, to put a hand on his shoulder, but my hand stopped short. My legs felt wrong. I used the table as a rail and slid back to my seat.

'They're good, you know,' I found myself saying. 'They can cure all sorts—'

'Like they did with your dad?' Tom spat. I bit my tongue. I looked away. I breathed and thought about cigarettes. 'Oh Christ . . . I'm sorry, Mags,' Tom – the normal Tom, the old Tom – said.

'It's okay . . . I think you're allowed to, Mate.' Tom nodded slowly. 'Are you saying they can't do anything?'

Tom swallowed and his hand went back to his throat. 'No. No, they say there are some treatments – surgery and then drugs . . .'

'Good. Well, there you go, then. For fucking's sake.' I took a sip of my Scotch. Smooth peaty heat rolled down my throat.

Tom smiled briefly. 'But it's not good, though. I asked him to be straight with me and he sure as hell was.'

'Did he give you a—'

'It's early days yet. Depends on what they find when they go in, how far things have really gone . . .'

There it was: the first of us to be ill, seriously ill. Sitting there in my kitchen on that winter night, I realised that cancer wasn't something that older generations or other people got. My thoughts were instantly selfish: how would this affect me and Isla, how would our world be changed? Then I noticed the silence.

'How's Catherine?' I asked.

'She doesn't know,' Tom said matter-of-factly.

'Doesn't know?' I was surprised. My thoughts were back on Tom. 'What do you mean, she doesn't know?'

'I didn't want to worry her,' Tom explained.

'But . . . but you've got to . . . You've got to tell her. Don't you think she'll be worried anyway? She'll have worried about the results as much as you—'

'She doesn't know I went to the hospital—'

'You didn't tell her you were having tests?'

'She doesn't know I'm ill . . .' Tom paused, his hand massaging his neck now. He swallowed slowly, carefully. 'I didn't want to worry her about it. I—'

'You haven't told her anything?' My voice was louder than I meant it to be. I glanced up at the ceiling. I leaned forward. 'She doesn't know anything about it – the doc, the hospital, anything?' I checked, my voice a whisper.

Tom looked guilty. He looked down and shook his head. 'No.'

'Oh, Tom . . . mate.' I found that I was shaking my head too. 'How long? How long has this been going on for?'

'I got the results two weeks ago.'

'The results! You mean, you've known this for two weeks and said nothing to her?' I failed to keep my voice down.

'Yeah . . .' Tom nodded. He looked ashamed.

'Have you told anyone?'

'No . . . No, nobody.'

'Tom—'

'I couldn't sleep, you see, so I got up . . . got in the car,' Tom shrugged. 'I just drove and ended up here—'

The sound of the loo flushing upstairs interrupted him. I guessed my voice had woken Jack; he'd always been a light sleeper. I glanced at the ceiling again. 'Oh, Mags . . . I feel like such an arse,' Tom finished.

'You are an arse!' I laughed. I didn't mean to; it just came with the realisation that this was typical Tom. I thought of all the times I'd gone to him for help, for advice, for healing. All the times we'd all leaned on him. Never once, though, had the need been his. A cold shiver reached up from my numb feet as I thought of that blackest of nights in Brighton when he saved me, when I was lost but found my way to his door, when the two Brightons collided.

25

It was warm in the car. Tom and I sat in silence as I drove through the night, following the A146 out of Suffolk and into Norfolk. The moon rose to the east of us just before three, its brightness masking the stars and revealing a landscape white and bare. Frosted fields and hedgerows rolled by and the headlights found wisps of cold hanging over the road. Despite taking the family Discovery, the steering felt light, especially when we dipped through the gentle valleys where the ice looked like shining pools across the tarmac. The heated seats, thrum of tyres and warm whisper from the air vents that smelled of cheap perfume from the freshener combined into a lullaby. I blinked often. For the most part Tom sat slouched with his face turned to the window. I would wonder if he was sleeping, but then he would turn slightly and run his hand over his neck, his fingers green in the light from the dashboard. It wasn't until later, on the way home, that I dwelled on his news; as the moon rose, my thoughts were mostly on work. It was an escape I suppose.

Tom and Catherine lived in Norwich close to the city centre in a small terraced house that they shared with their two cats. It was clear to all that they were very much in love. They doted on each other – they had since they met – and Isla and I had always thought it a shame they didn't have children. Tom would make such a good dad, Isla would say.

Tom had agreed that he had to tell Catherine. Of course he did. I knew how much she would be worried if she woke to find him gone and I'd wanted him to phone her, to tell her that he was with us and that he was okay. Sleep at ours that night and drive home to her in the morning. But Tom insisted that that just wouldn't work: she'd want to know why and then he'd have to explain over the phone. So, we agreed I would drive him home and we'd sort out getting his car back later. There was no way I would have let him drive himself.

Once we got to the city's ring road, the yellow sodium lamps changed the night and Tom sat up, the leather of his seat creaking. The roads were black again, but the frost lingered on the neatly landscaped embankments.

'D'you remember the way?' Tom asked. They'd been in Norwich for five years by then but I'd only managed to get over a couple of times.

'I think so. We follow the road left and then take a right at the next roundabout on to the big road into town centre, don't we?' I checked.

'Yeah, Newmarket Road.'

'You'll have to remind me which one it is after that,' I admitted, glancing over to him. A car passed the other way, moving slowly, wipers still cutting through ice on its windscreen.

Tom nodded thoughtfully. 'Thanks, Mags,' he said quietly, moving in his seat.

'It's no problem, none at all.'

'I really do feel like a twat,' Tom continued, massaging his neck again.

'Don't,' I said without looking at him. 'It's a shit deal, Tom. And I'll do anything I can to help.' I indicated to turn left and slowed at a broad junction. 'I mean it –anything, anything I can,' I added.

Tom studied me. I looked away, over my shoulder, to check the road was clear. We accelerated again. I glanced back. Tom was still studying me. 'Thanks, Mags,' he said finally.

Ten minutes later we'd made our way through narrow streets lined on both sides with cars parked bumper to bumper. I was glad I'd be heading back to the countryside. The streetlamps were on but the rows of terraced houses were dark. The city was definitely asleep. All except for one house ahead.

'It's this one, just here,' Tom announced finally. He was pointing to an end terrace, with steps up from the street to a tiny front garden of pebbles and tall plants in wooden tubs. Their broad leaves seemed untouched by the frost. The lights were on, all of them; the bay window downstairs and the bedroom window above it were blocks of matt yellow contrasted against the night and the rest of the street as if cut through a movie set to reveal the lit studio beyond. Clearly Catherine was not sleeping. The windows made me think of Edward Hopper paintings. I stopped the car. There was nowhere to park. I kept the engine running. I looked at Tom. Behind him the downstairs curtain moved. He sat forward, the leather of his seat creaking again, his hand going to the door handle.

'Thanks,' he said. 'I would ask you in but – well . . .'

I waved the notion away. 'Call me tomorrow evening and we'll sort out your car.'

'Oh, I'll get Catherine to give me a lift,' Tom stopped. He thought for a moment. 'I'd better go . . .'

I nodded. He opened the door. The lights in the car came on and a shock of cold reached in. I watched him step out. 'Tom,' I said. He ducked his head back into the car. 'Good luck, mate . . . and you know where we are, both of you. Isla and I have been . . . well, you know, with my dad and everything . . .' I screwed my eyes shut for a moment and let go of the steering wheel. 'But everything will be fine. You'll be fine. They'll sort you out . . . They're really good. They're . . . They're—
'

'I know,' Tom acknowledged quietly. He ducked back out and closed the door, pushing it into place with – I presumed for the greater good of the street and his neighbours – hardly a sound. I watched him walk up the steps. He didn't look back. The door opened and Catherine stepped out to him. I pulled away.

26

Joyce tugs my hand, we run along the beach now. There's shingle under my feet. But I don't sink or crunch. The waves are big but lazy. Long sweeps of foam like slowly spreading butter. I remember the voice on the day when the waves were just so. But it's okay, Joyce is so full of light and joy.

She looks over her shoulder and calls that it's Henry. She nods toward Southwold. I follow her stare. A man stands alone in the distance. He shimmers and wavers in the hazy heat. Joyce waves her arm in long sweeps.

Dad?

No, but he's like Dad. I recall the silhouette of Dad waiting up ahead on the beach, like a vertical collection of fluxing inks flowing in the summer holiday heat. I remember him walking faster than my sister and me. I remember the three shapes shimmering in the distance that I thought might be Isla and Jack and May. The impossible shimmering distance that I couldn't close or call across.

I stop.

Joyce's hand separates from mine.

Dad.

I look out across the water. I search for a sailing boat. A fast little sailing boat with a red sail.

Joyce stops. She's running back to me and gesturing up the beach to the flowing distant figure. The heat haze yields and the shimmering, sliding shapes coalesce. It's definitely Henry. Too round for Dad.

She takes my hand. The Tide brings her joy flooding back.

We run again. We hurry over patches of hard-packed sand like giant fingernails cut out along the shore. I turn to look out to sea again. There's a bank of cloud gathering out there, low on the horizon. They look almost like hills? I just can't help searching for a sailing boat, for a flash of red in front of those clouds. It feels as if it's close as if he's close.

Dad.

*

The last thing I remember about Norwich that night was the dashboard clock saying 3.52 a.m. as I drove away from Tom's house. The next thing I knew the clock was saying 4.49 a.m. and I was close to home. The winter night was still cold and frost-silver under the moon. I had to blink away tears to bring the numbers into focus. I was thirsty and my head ached dull and heavy. Tom's news had opened a floodgate in my mind, a gate that I hadn't expected to ever budge again. It wasn't about Tom; I felt sure he'd be okay. I'd been thinking about Dad. I'd been thinking, finally after so many years, really thinking about his last year with us. I'd thought about it all. From my phone ringing one afternoon when I was writing an experimental ballad with Kelly. Dad asking me to come home for the weekend. The quiet announcement to Julie and me that evening, Mum and Dad's hands clasped tightly together. Right to the final weeks and days as the last of him left us. Awful days that only Dad handled well. Visits home each week and the shock at the speed of decline. Dad standing tall with Mum, waving me off as I pulled away in the Heroes' van, only to find him sitting in a wheelchair, nodding with sleep in the shade of the trees along the edge of the garden, once the treatments had started two weeks later, his face replaced by that of a gaunt stranger who had stolen my dad's loving eyes. The cloud over everything I did. The guilt when I laughed and forgot for a short while. Walking out of the hospice without a word to Mum or Julie into a new day that Dad wouldn't see. The semi-conscious drive back to Brighton. The Little Chef meal that I ate greedily and then threw back up in the car park. Letting myself into my flat when I knew I should be with Mum and Julie and didn't know why I'd left them or why I was in Brighton. Getting into bed, screwing myself into a ball under my duvet with the bright sun streaming through the open window. The first day he missed was such a beautiful day. Waking in the late afternoon. Tom arriving after Julie had phoned him, patiently listening to my stream of consciousness as he drove me back to Suffolk in the Heroes' van.

Dad was basically a countryman. A big, softly spoken, honest man who worked with his hands, looked after his friends and didn't put up with shit from anyone. He was truly the best dad a boy could have wished for. There was always time for playing and joking and making and teaching and singing – and, of course, storytelling. He loved to tell stories. I remember him as a contented and peaceful man, but apparently he wasn't always so. In his younger days, he had a taste for adventure and as soon as he was old enough he joined the army in a bid to see the world. Get a change of sky, as he put it. Despite being a Suffolk boy, he followed in my great-grandfather's footsteps and joined the Royal Norfolk regiment. At age nineteen he saw action in Korea where by all accounts he proved to be a fine soldier. So much so in fact that he was seconded out of the regiment into 'special duties' for the remaining five years of his service.

He never really spoke about those years, so I don't know much about them. I'd always planned to find out more one day but left it too late. What I do know is that when he returned home it was with the conclusion he never wanted to leave Suffolk again and he rarely ever did. I also know that after he got back he lived a colourful few years, being no stranger to drinking and fighting or the odd night in the cells. At the time, there was quite a well-organised underground bare-knuckle scene around the pubs in rural Suffolk and Dad had the flattened nose and swollen ears to prove his internship in the circuit. When I was a kid there was a picture of him from those days on the sideboard, bare above the waist with fists ready to box, which always reminded me of the Pogues' *Peace and Love* album I bought when I was in my teens. It wasn't until he met Mum, eleven years his junior, in 1965 that he gave up fighting and found the peace I knew him for. The only thing I know for sure about those years of service was that they gave him his love of the sea and boats. My earliest memories are of the family beach hut, the one I dream about here, and watching Dad repair, rebuild, improve, love and sail his fourteen-foot Lark dinghy, with its dark blue woodwork and bright red sail.

In the summer, we'd spend endless days there, driving over in Dad's bright yellow Ford in time for breakfast *at the hut*. We all thought that that car was the coolest thing in the district and we were right. Julie and I would build sandcastles with Mum, go swimming, chase each other around the beach, play Swingball, the post always tipping because the beach material was too loose, and eat ice cream while Dad worked. And sometimes we'd help him in his world that smelled of turpentine and marine glues that gave me a headache in the summer sun. My favourite was watching him scrape old paint away with a portable blowtorch that used black gas cylinders the size of bean tins with an owl stencilled on them and a triangle-headed scrapper that looked as if it should have belonged to Doctor Who. It was always such an alien and delicately shiny thing in his big hands. In fact, I often used to borrow it from him to play Doctor Who, our blue beach hut being the TARDIS, of course, and the scraper my trusty sonic screwdriver. With tireless fascination, I would watch the paint blister and bubble before he scraped it clear, the flakes blowing away on the sea breeze to reveal age-old grey wood. He would look up, see me hopping with excitement and give me a smile. When he smiled, his big kind face was always etched with lines and crags. It's not that he was an old man then; it's just that he'd spent a life working outdoors and the fierce East Anglian sun and the tug-of-war wind between land and sea that shapes everything had left their mark. And Dad's face was a map of each season that he had laboured through. But, paint stripping aside, mostly we played while he worked and then, when the sea was calm, he'd heave the boat into the water, Mum would jam lifejackets on us and we'd be off, tacking back and forth. Julie would snuggle against Dad at the tiller; I'd be at the bow with the wind in my face and my hand in the water, cutting like a blade until it felt numb. Mum would sit 'amidships', ducking under the boom and telling me to be careful. When the sea was rough, we'd sit at the hut and watch him sail alone, cutting along with white foam surging at the bow and spray in his face. By the time we went back to school in the autumn Julie and I were always as brown as berries.

Best of all were the evenings when Dad pulled the boat back up and lit a fire on the sand. We'd build it on the same spot each year in the lee of the old wooden groin that cut the beach by the hut. Always it would be set among our eight blackened stones that had been found before I was born and which we scratched for and pulled out of the sand each spring. I can still picture them: the five rounded ones, the jagged fist and the two large flat slabs that mum always stood the coffee pot and pans on. We'd fry our tea of eggs, fish fingers, sausages and scalloped potatoes. The flavours would combine in a way that cannot be recreated indoors, strong and salty mouthfuls that tasted more of potato than meat, forked down with ketchup and finally leaving a taste of the sausage and fish in the grease on my lips. Then there'd be marshmallows for dessert. We'd try to toast them on long forks and our fingers would be sticky and taste of sugar until we got home.

When we were settled, Dad would tell us stories, with Mum adding atmospheric *ooh's* and *aah's*. He knew so many stories: legends of ancient Greece, sagas that had come to Suffolk with the Vikings a thousand years ago, tales of knights and heroes, wizards and dastardly villains. We loved them all, but our favourites were the scary ones: local tales of Black Shucks and other things that prowled the beaches and countryside of Suffolk and Norfolk. These he would save until the August light was fading and the fire was embers and gentle blue flames with occasional bright cinders riding the thermal up and away on the night breeze. Dad's eyes would sparkle in the firelight as he told of demon hounds and wildmen-of-the-sea. He'd pause just at the right moment to hold our suspense, taking a sip of the brown-bottled Tolly Cobbold beer that he let me have sips of sometimes – it tasting like tar and me pretending to like it. I'd sit by Mum, to keep her safe, and Julie would be on Dad's lap, her eyes screwed shut, her hands fists as she shook with excitement and fear.

*

I finally got home at 5.05 a.m. My head was full of Dad and Tom and everything that had happened. I knew I wouldn't be able to sleep. I don't know why but I made myself a hot chocolate, the first I'd had in years, and sat at the kitchen table sipping it. I remember it being delicious, sweeter than I'd expected, and making me feel warm. Isla had heard the car and came down. She had a hot chocolate too. She kissed me on my brow but said nothing until she brought her seat around and sat next to me at the end of our ten-seat table. Things were already breaking by then, but that night we were close, beautifully, wonderfully close. She put her hands on mine, lifting them clear of my hot chocolate, and held them tightly. She leaned forward, her face directly in front of mine, our noses almost touching, her eyes searching mine. Finally, she asked what had happened. I told her about Tom and about Catherine and taking him home. We laughed about Tom not telling Catherine. Laughed because we loved him and because we didn't want to cry. It didn't work. Isla asked all the same questions that I had: how bad, what are they going to do, what's next? Then we both wept, Isla sobbing, me silently with her head buried in my arms. We didn't cry for Tom; we cried for our fathers.

27

We walked and we talked, Isla and me. It was just as it had been in Camden: comfortable, relaxed and consuming. Her company drew me in, made me welcome and left me not wanting to leave. The cheap whisky crept back and left me with the gentlest buzz. We were close under her umbrella; her breath smelled of mint and her hair touched my face when the wind blew up from the seafront. The wet pavements were slippery and we fell against each other as we navigated our way round the puddles stretching across them. When I spoke, she smiled and her eyes held mine and it was easy. It was so very easy. We talked about everything and nothing and I don't remember a word of it. The subject was not important on that humid early September evening in 1993.

Finally, we stopped walking. Well, Isla stopped and I followed. She moved her umbrella and looked up at the sky. The storm had cleared, the rain had stopped and there were even a few determined stars showing through the tangerine haze of the streetlights.

'Oh!' Isla laughed. She shook her umbrella and pushed it closed. There was her wristwatch again, its big scratched face catching and flashing in the light from the shop window we'd stopped beside. A tall, slender girl – about twenty years old, I guessed – crossed the road beside us. She wore tight jeans and a top that was soaking and clinging to her. Her hips swayed and she moved with confidence. Her hair was blonde and dead straight to the base of her neck. Her narrow, sharp-featured face was attractive but not in a pretty way. She noticed me and smiled, holding my gaze as she walked. I was having my dog days back then and guessed she'd seen the Heroes play. She glanced dismissively at Isla before walking on.

Isla retuned her stare with a flat indifference. 'Where's . . . The Temple Bar?' she asked, turning away to look back along Western Road in the direction we'd come from.

'It's . . . Shit!' I laughed. 'It's back that way, isn't it?' We'd gone completely the wrong way and not noticed, walking instead toward the town centre, along the street with all its people and bars and shops that we hadn't noticed either. So, I turned to walk back and for the first time in my life hooked my arm and offered it to a woman. To Isla. I thought of Mum and Dad as I did it. It didn't matter where they were, didn't matter if they were just walking across Sainsbury's car park, Dad would always offer Mum his arm and they'd stroll as if they were on the promenade at Southwold. Isla paused and looked at me. I couldn't read her eyes – not sure I ever could. Had I crossed a line I shouldn't have? Then she turned away and looked down Preston Street down the hill and the rows of little restaurants to the seafront.

A car turned off from the esplanade below and raced up toward us, its engine complaining between gears and its lights reflecting off the wet road; a random oily rainbow pattern swimming across the tarmac. My eyes were still on Isla. She raised her hand and pointed down the hill. The car's lights appeared in miniature on her watch for a moment. I guessed she was about to say that actually she would head home. I thought I'd go and catch Vince and Tom at the Cricketers.

'Are you hungry?' she asked, in a voice that sounded as if she'd surprised herself.

'Yeah . . . always.'

'Me too!' With that she put her arm through mine and spun me round ready to walk down the hill. 'Chinese or Italian?'

'Either . . . both . . .'

So, we walked, arm in arm. For me it was a promenade. Isla stopped and read menus by doors and asked my opinion. All very alien and forward-thinking to me back then. If I was hungry I jumped into the first place I found unless the one next door smelled really good. About halfway down the hill we read the menu outside a little Italian place. It was simply called *Papa's*. I didn't need to read: the door was open and the smells were already making my mouth water.

'Here?' Isla checked, her eyes steady on mine. She looked beautiful.

'Absolutely.' I stepped inside without further discussion. Isla, arm still hooked through mine, had to come too. We bumped the doorframe. I realised this promenading took some skill. She smiled the loveliest what-are-you-like smile at me. A moment that the proprietor interrupted with a pleasant 'hello'. He was a squat, kind-faced, balding Italian in a white shirt and black trousers and he realised instinctively he'd intruded somehow. His name was Luca, but I wasn't to learn that for a few months.

'Excusi.' Well, what else was he going to say?

'Sorry,' I said by default as an Englishman. 'We'd like a table.'

'For . . .' The little man paused and looked at Isla and me. His face beamed. His eyes actually twinkled, somehow looking sad yet joyful at the same time. He sighed, a low, thoughtful breath that I think took him somewhere else for a moment. 'For two.' He held up his hands as if to praise us. 'A table for two, a table for a beautiful couple.' Isla politely looked down. I grinned at him. I liked him a lot.

28

The sea's still lazy. The breeze has gone. I look ahead to Henry. The heat haze yields and the shimmering, sliding shapes of him coalesce. It's definitely Henry. Too round for Dad.

Joyce calls his name. Her voice is happy. She waves her arm in big lazy sweeps again, just like the sea.

It's so beautiful today.

Henry raises his arms in reply. It makes him look less squat. I look out across the fanning waves. Beyond the surf the sun is reflected as a million tiny floating lights. Sparkles. The clouds are still on the horizon, stretching far and rising in domes and bluffs. They really do look like hills, like land. I look for a boat again, a sail against those clouds. A bright red sail. Of course there's nothing. I look up to the sky. Why am I looking for a plane now? The familiar feathering contrail of a passenger liner. Not here, no chance. But my car was here. I had it here for a while.

Joyce hugs him. A gentle hint of the Tide moves over them. I wait for him to look at me. Joyce steps back. We three stand together on the sand and patchy shingle. We none of us cast a shadow. And it's okay.

I love Henry.

I love Joyce.

Henry raises his arms. He holds them out. I've never noticed before that Henry's the same height as me. I thought he was wearing black, but he's not. He has blue trousers and a white linen shirt. Must have been a trick of the light, the heat haze, that made him seem so dark. His feet are bare. His white hair is tousled, telling of the breeze that's gone now. His face is so kind. Proud but kind.

Trustful!

That's it. A face that I trust. Noble features, but his skin is tanned leather like a working man and his white whiskers make him look wise. And those eyes, bright and just like the sea. I see the Tide in them! He smiles at me, at us. Crow's feet fan out beside his eyes. I think of Dad again. I glance to the sea for a moment. There is no sail, only the clouds on the horizon. They *really* do look like land. And birds! A 'V' of geese, I think, flying high, heading for those clouds!

I look back. There is peace here. All around us.

I thank Henry. I thank him for coming to the monument.

Henry says that it is his pleasure. But he says that I should be better to myself. I frown. I don't understand. Henry smiles again.

Joyce says that I asked for help. She says it that simply. I look down. Henry puts his hand on my shoulder. Joyce takes my hand. The Tide flows through and around us.

Henry says that that's good.

I look up at him. He's pleased.

Joyce says that I should show Henry what I want. She says just as I showed her. I'm not sure I can. I look along the beach, back toward Dunwich. I think of running on the beach as a child.

I remember running again!

I run with Julie chasing me, my heart racing with excitement! Mum and Dad wave at me. I watch Jack and May chasing each other. Isla takes my hand as we wave at them. They are giggling. Their little voices come to us over the sea, babbling springs of joy. Isla leans against me. The sun is warm on our faces. My toes are planted in the cooler sand. I look to Isla. She smiles. Lines tell of a million smiles before. This is not long ago. I am happy. Another child is running behind May, a little girl with blonde hair. She is from Joyce. I know she is.

Joyce steps back. The Tide stops flowing between us. I catch my breath. Henry is smiling at me. He understands. He nods. He takes his hand away from my shoulder and sits down, crossing his legs like a schoolboy, like Jack on the chair in my study. He moves like he is young and not old.

He says to sit. He gestures to the sand.

I sit, crossing my legs too, the sea and the lazy waves to my side. Joyce sits beside us, bringing her knees together.

29

Tom's aging Volkswagen sat on our driveway for nine days. We very quickly stopped noticing it, even though it was there all the time. It was early Sunday evening, already black but surprisingly mild after the cold snap we'd had. I'd just got home – I'd been at the office – and the house smelled of the roast dinner Isla had made for herself and Jack and May. Isla and May were in the living room, watching a *Black Beauty* DVD, cuddled together on the sofa, tears flowing. I was in my study, sorting out some papers for a big meeting in London the next morning, and Jack was with me. I was kneeling by the antique teachers' cupboard that we'd found at an auction in Woodbridge and used as a stationary locker and printer stand. Jack was slowly spinning around on my desk chair, also an antique. He was grilling me about *Jurassic Park*.

'So if the flying 'dactas flew away because they can fly . . .' he was saying, voice fading as the chair swivelled his face away from me.

'They're called pterodactyls,' I corrected, looking up in time to see him come back round. He was in his flannel striped pyjamas that looked as if they were from the 1940s, only shrunk. He was sitting cross-legged on the chair, sitting over his Jedi slippers that somehow also seemed to be from the 1940s. He'd had his bath and his fine blonde hair had dried sticking out in all directions as if he'd been struck by lightning. His blue eyes opened wide and darted left and right with thoughts about what I'd said.

'Yeah,' he said finally, 'the 'dactas . . . the flying ones. What if they flew to England where we and all the people live?' His face showed the question was born of hope and excitement rather than fear. He yawned with his whole body, bending and rising up to reveal Obi Wan Kenobi and Anakin Skywalker on the front of his slippers.

'Well, I guess we'd have to call the army or the RAF to come and sort them out,' I replied, turning back to my leather satchel that Isla had got me for the Christmas after May turned two. The leather was stiff and cold to the touch after being in the boot of the car.

'What, to bomb them up and machine-gun them?' His voice faded again.

'Yeah . . .' I managed, while I leafed through printouts.

'But couldn't we mind-link our minds to them so they would let us ride them?' His voice got loud again. 'Then we'd be powerful!'

'Hey?' I got to the end of the papers again and realised I'd left the latest copy on the printer at the office. I was going to have to drive back or get in even earlier to make sure I had it for the meeting.

'Meld our minds and in-charge them!' Jack clarified. 'We could make a 'dacta air force and—'

'Shit!' I sighed. 'Shit!' I stared at the satchel, hanging open like a lazy mouth stuffed with A4.

I heard Jack drop off the chair. I turned back to look but he'd already darted out of the door.

'Jack . . .' I called after him, reaching out to the door that was still gliding open at a snail's crawl. There was no reply. I heard his feet running across the hallway and the sound of *Black Beauty* got louder as he opened the living-room door. 'Shit...' I sighed. I sat in my chair that was warm from Jack. I held my hands to my face, massaging round in slow circles. I could hear Isla's voice, the tone soothing, the words lost to the television.

It was then that headlights swept across the study window and I heard a car on the drive. I looked at my watch and frowned. I looked out just as the security light came on. A small Renault had pulled up. It was old. The headlights went out and the interior light came on. It was Catherine. Tom appeared at the far side, looking at the house.

I put my head around the lounge door. Isla was now in the middle of the sofa with May on one side and Jack on the other. She had her phone in her hand. Isla and May looked up; Jack didn't. Isla put her phone down on the seat beside her leg. She smiled at me.

'It's Tom and Catherine . . . just pulled up on the drive—'

'Our drive? Now?'

'Yes . . .'

'Christ. Come on you two, pick your toys up!' Isla announced, standing up and straightening her sweater down over the top of her trousers. She looked around the room. 'Take these mugs out to the kitchen—'

A light rap on the front door interrupted her. I ducked back out into the hallway. I stopped beside the framed photograph of waves crashing over the harbour wall at Walberswick, to nudge the mat we'd bought on holiday in Morocco back into place, but it was stuck to the tiled floor and wouldn't budge.

I opened the door. Tom and Catherine were standing together, their arms interlocked. The night air reached in.

'Hello, guys!' I said enthusiastically. 'Come in!'

'Hi, Mags,' Tom answered quietly. Catherine just gave the briefest smile and then looked at Tom.

'Hi,' was all I could think to say, in a much quieter voice.

'We don't want to disturb you. Sorry it's late. Just came to get my car.'

'You're not disturbing us. Come in—'

'No, it's late. We'll just get the car. I just wanted to say hello . . . and thanks . . .' Catherine looked at me again and this time I got a small nod as well as a small smile. Catherine was a beautiful woman, but she looked awful – they both did. She was petite and always very smartly dressed. But that night she had jeans and trainers on and a big coat wrapped around her.

'Cathy, Thomas,' Isla said from behind me, her voice soothing. Catherine gave another small smile and then pressed against Tom. 'Come in. It's cold.' They stepped inside. Catherine and Tom had visited us many times; they knew the house and they had known Jack and May from birth. Usually there would have been hugs and kisses. But on this occasion these customs went unobserved. Instead Tom and Catherine walked together, avoiding eye contact with us. I closed the door and watched them follow Isla into the living room. I was reminded of the Tylers. I hated that, but there it was.

The Tylers were twins, Peter and Chrissy, who joined our school when we were ten and being two years below us they must have been eight. I don't know where they had come from before they moved to Framlingham, the small market town where we grew-up, but there family was poor, proper old-fashioned country poor. God knows what home life must have been like for them, they were always scruffy, unkempt and unwashed. And it was like the kids at the school could smell blood. They bullied them, they taunted without mercy, until Vince, Tom and I stepped in. Vince was always on a bit of a mission because of his Dad's job and I can't stand bullies. Never could. Anyway, until we sorted things out they looked like they were hunted. They would always be together, trying to keep each other safe, helping each other past the groups of kids in what must have seemed like a land of evil mobs.

I love Tom. I loved him like a brother from childhood. And Catherine in turn like a sister. Seeing them like that was hard to bare. There were my two friends, my dearest friend Tom, peering out on to a cruel world that had just dealt them such a vicious body blow, staying close, frightened, keeping each other safe. Just like the Peter and Chrissy Tyler. It was as if some spark, something essential, some vital thing, had been ripped from them.

I took a breath and followed them into the living room. They sat huddled together in the corner of the sofa opposite Jack and May, with Catherine squeezing Tom's hand.

'Hello, Uncle Tom and Auntie Catherine,' May chimed. She was wrapped up in her pink dressing gown with a pony on the pocket, her rich chestnut hair tumbling in waves and curls around her tiny round face. Catherine gave her the largest smile of the evening. I thought she was going to cry.

'Hello, May' she whispered.

'Hello, May. Hello, Jack,' Tom added.

'Greetings!' Jack replied without looking away from the TV. Isla smiled and shook her head. Finally, Tom smiled. I had no idea what to say so I just sat down next to May.

30

Papa's restaurant was a classic little bistro. The walls were covered with swirling rough-combed, carmine-red plaster. There were beams across the ceiling. The tables were fitted-in haphazardly, but all had matching red-and-white chequered cloths and nightlight candles burning in little red-tinted glasses. The only other light came from candle-effect bulbs in wall fittings. The room was cosy, filled with conversation, soft music, the chink of cutlery on china, and it smelled of home when Mum had seen Delia Smith preparing pasta on television and took to cooking spaghetti bolognaise as a Saturday-night treat. Our host led us, beaming all the while, through the tables to the far corner.

'Here?' he checked, gesturing proudly.

'Perfect,' I said. And it was.

His grin broadened. He pulled back a chair for Isla. He could clearly sense the youthful romance, the earliness of our relationship, or rather my longing for a relationship, and he was going to enjoy it. Isla graciously sat. She didn't look at me. I noticed she absent-mindedly adjusted that old watch, sliding it around her wrist. I sat opposite. Isla still didn't look at me.

'I will give you a few moments,' our host said, placing two menus on the table. He melted away.

Isla looked up. 'I think he's got the wrong idea,' she whispered.

I didn't think so.

A young waitress – Luca's granddaughter, Sabina, as I was to later discover – set the table around us. She worked quickly and precisely. Heavy, much striated cutlery, glasses and folded white cotton napkins positioned silently while 'Come Back to Sorrento' played softly in the background. Isla sat motionless with her hands in her lap while Sabina wove around the table. Isla was serene. The candlelight from the red glass played across her bare arms, her skin warm and lustrous. Sabina kept looking at me. I could tell she was trying not to, but her eyes kept finding mine and then she would look away shyly. Isla noticed but didn't say anything; only her eyes smiled. I was about to suggest some wine – I had a feeling that whisky would be inappropriate – when the music stopped prematurely. I looked over to the little bar in the opposite corner, I don't know why. There was Luca smiling and looking right at me. Despite the low lighting and sea of tables between us, I was sure that he winked at me. It was a mischievous, boyish wink that made me think of Vince. Then it came: beautiful new music and a soprano haunting yet lifting. Around me twenty conversations lulled for a moment; faces rose, registered the change, smiled and then the conversational hum returned. I grinned and nodded. I didn't recognise the recording or the voice, but I wished that my own could be so voluminous, so powerful even when quiet.

'Do you know him?' Isla asked.

'No. But I think he chose the music for us . . . Isn't it beautiful.'

'Like I said, I think he's got the wrong idea,' Isla whispered, leaning conspiratorially forward over the table toward me. Her face was happy. This time I definitely didn't agree. Sabina withdrew with a final more daring, lingering look.

Isla watched her walk away and then turned back to me. I leaned forward too; we were very close.

'I wouldn't have had you down as an opera man.'

'It's an aria.'

'An aria?'

'Yes, Puccini's 'Ricondita Armonia', from *Tosca*.'

'You're teasing me?' Isla guessed, leaning back to stare at me. Her face still happy.

'No.' I said, and I wasn't. 'It means hidden harmony. It's sung by a painter in a church. He's painting Mary Magdalene, and he sings about the contrast between Mary and his lover, a beautiful singer – Tosca.'

Isla didn't say anything for a moment. Her eyes searched my face. I think she expected me to laugh – laugh and announce a set-up. I listened to the song. It floated on what was left of the whisky in me and all I could think about was kissing Isla. She sat back, slipping into the red light of the candle and the shadows of the corner. Her eyes were bright. 'How do you know that?' she said finally.

'I'm a musician,' I shrugged.

'Yeah, but you're a blues man. You're a—'

'Doesn't matter,' I said honestly. 'If you've got music in you, you only need hear Puccini's work once.'

'You're full of surprises, aren't you?'

I laughed. 'Not really. Besides, Puccini *is* the blues. He died before his time, left so much of his work unfinished.'

'Really?' Isla moved forward again, resting her arms on the table, her hands cupping close to the candle.

'Hmm . . . throat cancer in his sixties.'

Isla nodded slowly, her eyes fixing on the candle.

31

I looked at Tom and Catherine. Tom smiled bravely. Catherine squeezed his hand again. I still couldn't think of anything to say. Then Isla said exactly the right thing. She stepped forward and knelt down in front of them both. She put her arms around them as she would Jack and May.

'I'm so sorry about everything, Thomas,' she said simply. 'Cath . . .' she continued, moving her hand over her heart. 'You're being so brave . . . and I know it will be okay, I know it will . . . You'd better make sure it is, Thomas!' It broke the gloom, blew away the clouds for a moment. Catherine finally let go of Tom's hand and hugged Isla properly. She put her arms around her and sobbed. May jumped down from the sofa and ran over to hug both of them. They looked down and Isla burst into tears too. I looked at Jack and then Tom.

'We'll make a cup of tea, shall we?' I suggested.

'Yeah, I'll help,' Tom agreed, standing up and sidestepping Catherine and Isla and May. Jack shuffled closer to the television.

I set mugs out along the worktop. We'd chosen Welsh slate because of the Brecon Beacons. By then I never seemed to have the time to go walking so it was my way of having something of them around me. It was always cold to the touch. Tom leaned back against the units in the corner and watched.

'You had roast?' he asked. 'Smells beautiful.'

'Oh, yeah . . . I think Isla did one for her and the children. I had to work today.'

'But it's Sunday, Mags.'

'Yeah, I know . . . I've got this really important—'

'Nothing's all that important, mate,' Tom interrupted. I looked over to him. 'Seriously,' he added without blinking. I looked away. I adjusted the mugs, lining them up neatly.

'Tea or coffee?' I asked finally. 'I can put the machine on if you like,' I added, nodding to Krups close to his elbow.

'Tea for me,' Tom replied. He ran his hand over his throat.

'We've got Breakfast, Darjeeling, Earl Grey, Laps—'

'Just tea.'

I nodded and threw two bags of Twinning's English Breakfast into the teapot.

'Sorry about leaving the car here all week,' Tom said, walking over and taking a seat at the table. The same seat that we'd put him in nine days earlier.

'That's all right . . . plenty of room out there. I should have called you anyway. I could have come and picked you up or sorted something . . . Just really busy, you know,' I finished quietly.

'Vince offered to come and pick it up – on his bike!' he announced cheerfully.

'What, cycle here?' The kettle built up a head of steam and gave its first hint of a whistle.

'Yeah, he came up, you see . . . to Norwich. Drove up in his van, brought his bike with him.'

'Did he?'

'Yeah . . . Well, I gave him a call the day after . . . after you dropped me home, you know—'

'Yeah.'

'Well, after I talked it through with Cath—'

'Is that all okay? Catherine, I mean.'

'Oh, yes. Yeah . . . fine, fine. We're good, she's been fantastic . . . and we're . . .' Tom searched for something, for the right words. The kettle started to whistle properly. 'Looking after each other . . . we're going to look after each other!' he explained loudly over the kettle. I turned the stove off and I filled the teapot.

'Yeah, anyway, so I called Vince about teatime.'

I smiled. It had been a long time since I'd had tea. I'd been on breakfast, lunch and dinner for years.

'He was really shocked. He didn't really say much, just, you know . . . he was sorry to hear it and . . . you know.'

I nodded. 'I'm surprised he didn't tell you to stop being a wuss and get better.'

Tom laughed. 'Then about ten o'clock there's a knock at the door. Catherine and I had gone to bed early. I came downstairs and there was Vince.

'What, he just turned up?'

'Yeah. As soon as he'd got off the phone he just got in his van and drove up.'

'What, just like that?'

'Yeah. I couldn't believe it. He stood there with this sapling in a pot as tall as him—'

'What?'

'Yeah, an oak tree – three years old apparently. Said they brought *strength, health and endurance*.' Tom counted them off on his fingers. 'Wanted me to have it. Said he'd come round to see if there was anything he could do – help with the garden, the house, that sort of thing.'

'Bloody hell.' I poured the tea.

'He stayed for three days in the end. Said he'd booked in a B and B, wasn't there to impose, but just wanted to be around in case I needed anything.'

'Good old Vince . . .'

'Yeah. To be honest, I just wanted time with Cath. I'm not being mean, or—'

'No, no, I understand. I'd be the same.'

'But it was a real help. He got it just right. He seemed to be at the house and then off out at just the right times.'

'I guess he learned how to do that from his dad.'

'Yeah!' Tom nodded enthusiastically. 'That's exactly what Cath and I were saying to each other on the drive over.'

'Who would have thought that?' I laughed. 'Never had Vince down for following in his dad's footsteps.'

'No,' Tom agreed thoughtfully. 'Imagine if he did! I mean, actually as a career!' We both laughed. Tom smoothed his hand down his throat.

'Surely they'd turn him down . . . surely,' I decided aloud.

Tom thought about it. 'I wish he'd talk to his dad. I mean, his dad's cool and it's so sad they don't talk and—'

'Whole can of worms that I've tried to open with Vince but . . .'

'Yeah.' Tom nodded slowly before changing the subject. 'He brought some drums with him – not a full set, sort of folk jobs – and I got my guitar and Cath sang. We, you know, just jammed . . . I always play, but haven't really made music properly for ages. It was good.'

'You've kept up your playing?'

'Yeah . . . course. Actually, Vince was saying we should get together, come to Brighton and play a gig. Just for old times' sake. Once I'm . . .'

'Yeah, I guess so. I don't really sing now. I don't really have the . . .' I stopped short.

32

I had spaghetti bolognaise and Isla had cannelloni. The food was simple and delicious. I mopped up every last drop of the rich tomato sauce that tasted of pepper and basil and the big tomatoes from Dad's greenhouse when I was little. I was happily sated. I ate greedily as I always did in those days. Isla ate slowly and carefully. I finished long before Isla and she laughed. But it wasn't just me eating greedily that made me finish first; it was because Isla had talked and I had listened. It seemed that she already knew much about me, having done her homework before going to Camden to cover the Heroes' first London gig. So, I asked her to play fair and tell me about herself, about how she'd come to Brighton. You never met an actual born-and-bred Brightonian; everyone was from somewhere else and everyone had their own particular tale of how life had brought them to London-by-the-sea. And the sharing of these stories was always an integral part of getting know someone. Our bowls were empty and we rested our elbows on the table, our faces close. Isla had chosen the wine, a beautiful Barolo that I thought tasted of blackberries, which were still a fruit in those pre-email days, and I was happily, comfortably, gently, drunk. Isla was flushed and pretty. Her eyes sang about the wine and lingered on mine from over her clasped hands. She'd just concluded her *how-I-came-to-Brighton* story. She lived with her dad – didn't mention her mum – in Oxford. At eighteen, after a very conservative education as a non-border at the local catholic school, she'd come to study photography at Grand Parade. Not because she had in mind a career as a photographer but because she'd always enjoyed photography and didn't know what she wanted to do. I got the impression her dad hadn't really approved, but I didn't want to push her on that. It turned out she was good. Very good. Three years later she finished college with a first. Again, I got the impression that things weren't so good with her dad. She said that the little girl who'd stepped away from the nuns and her father's cotton wool had gone by then and that returning to Oxford wouldn't have worked for father or grown-up daughter. But she didn't just stay in Brighton; that wasn't her story at all.

She had wanted to get away and see the world, and she sure as hell did – big time. I don't know why I found it surprising – probably because I was profoundly uninterested in politics and world affairs at the time – but Isla was very political. She was a Fabian and social campaigner. A month after graduating she volunteered to work as a photographer for a charity working across Africa, especially in Somalia, Ethiopia, Sudan and through to Chad. Again, again, I got the impression this wasn't with the approval of Dad back in Oxford. Initially, it was to be a three-month placement but it quickly became permanent. Her great empathy gave her the perfect eye for capturing the human suffering that she found there. Her work found its way into magazines around the world, especially in the US, and boosted the charity enormously. Even as we'd sat there in Papa's, tears had come to her eyes as she talked about what she had seen. It was the tip of the iceberg really; later I was to hear of her being taken at gunpoint from an aid convoy, mugged and beaten for the sake of her camera and seventy US dollars on the streets of Bosaso in northern Somalia. About the murder, the loss, the suffering, the dignity and indignity, the hate and the kindness she had borne witness to; a great edifice of emotional damage on young shoulders that would come crashing down on her when she returned to England.

'In the end, I was there for twenty-six months,' she concluded. 'You sort of burn out in the end. I came back for a break and to see Dad. I was in Oxford initially, but in the end I found myself back in Brighton and just . . . stayed.'

It took me a moment or two to realise she had finished. Wasn't going to say anything else. The story didn't seem to be over. I wanted to hear more. I loved hearing her talk; I loved the sense of getting to know her. I knew what she was sharing with me was intimate, not just for anyone, and I loved it and I wanted the rest, the real end of the story. So I waited, but she just looked down at her hands and I knew she'd finished.

'Wow . . .' I said. She looked up and smiled modestly. 'Well! I'm not going to bore you or embarrass myself with my meagre tales of drunken bar fights after gigs and a two-two geography degree.'

Isla laughed and pressed her lips against her hands. 'I can't imagine that you'd ever bore me,' she said. Her eyes flicked to the candle.

'Oh, I bet I could!'

She looked back. 'No . . .' She looked sad. Her eyes returned to the candle.

Silence again.

I studied her hands. There was that watch and a truly giant ring with three diamonds set next to each other. It looked too big for her hand; I was surprised it stayed on.

'Now, that is a serious piece of jewellery,' I noted. Isla looked up and then looked at her hand.

'Oh, yes.' She seemed embarrassed. 'It's my engagement ring.'

'Wow . . . Your husband really went for it.' *Shit*, I thought, really not wanting to talk about her husband.

'Yeah . . .' Isla nodded. 'He's very old-fashioned—'

'Oh?'

'Yeah, he has this thing that you should spend three months' earnings on an engagement ring.'

I nodded. I had a distant memory of Mum saying something along those lines. It was suddenly a strange conversation to be having. 'Yeah . . . I think I've heard that before.'

'Hmm. Silly really; anything would have done.' Isla turned her hand round, studying the ring. There was a rubber band wrapped around it underneath.

'Elastic bands another old-fashioned thing?'

'Oh, no! I don't know if I've lost weight or something since we bought it, but I feel like I need to have it resized. I don't wear it much.' *We*. I didn't like that. I wanted to change the subject, but at the same time I didn't want to. I wanted to stick my nose right in the middle of it. I wanted to know why she was having dinner with me rather than Mr Big Fucking Ring.

'So what does he do?' I found myself asking.

'Duncan.'

'Sorry?'

'His name's Duncan.'

'Right . . . Sorry.'

'He's a solicitor.'

I wasn't ready for that. I was expecting a 'he's studying to be' or a 'he drives a van at the moment but he's really an actor or a writer' or something equally Brighton. 'Wow,' I said inanely for the second time in one conversation. I didn't like the sound of this Duncan.

Isla smiled as if she'd anticipated my surprise. 'He's older . . . older than me,' she explained simply.

'Oh. Right . . .' I hesitated, wanting to ask the question but not sure whether I should. Again, Isla smiled. She knew the question and seemed amused by my hesitation. I moved in my seat; the chair scraped against the tiled floor.

'He's fifty-one.'

'Fifty-one!' I closed my eyes. I think I winced; I'd virtually shouted it. Someone of fifty-one may as well have been eight hundred and fifty-one. It was ancient, it was old people, it was people's mums and dads – it was fucking geriatric. I definitely didn't like the sound of this Duncan cunt at all. 'Sorry,' I said simply, pulling a face as if she was going to slap me.

Isla laughed. 'It's okay. I get that a lot.'

'Yeah . . . but still, I'm sorry.'

'It's fine,' Isla insisted and she meant it. 'I'd have been the same before I met him, but I knew straight away. He's lovely and he makes me feel safe.'

I honestly didn't know what to say to that. It struck me as a strange thing to say. 'No wedding ring?' was the best I could manage.

'No, I lost it. That's why I so paranoid about this one...' She waggled her finger to make the point. 'We went for a walk on the Downs one day last winter, I guess in the cold my fingers shrunk, and when we got back it had gone.'

We, we, we! 'Oh, no . . .'

'Yeah, it was awful. I felt terrible. So, I wear this as both.'

'Or not at all.'

Isla frowned quizzically.

'Sometimes you don't wear it . . . and then those of us you come and talk to after our gigs don't get fair warning.' I explained, making a joke of it.

Isla twisted her big old watch around her wrist. She bit lightly on her lip. 'I'm sorry.'

'Don't be,' I said, laughing it off as nothing.

'No, I am. I am sorry.' Isla took my hands in hers as she said it. She looked sad again. She pulled me back into our own private universe. Silence. I thought she might kiss me.

We looked at each other. *Kiss me*, I thought in the dead silence.

'Finished?' came Sabina's voice from somewhere. Pop! Back in a shared universe: the dozen conversations, the chink of cutlery, laughter and 'The Carnival of Venice' playing in the background.

We both laughed. Sabina looked embarrassed and then stared at me. Isla sat back in her seat. Sabina cleared our bowls and we both ordered ice cream for pudding. Again, Sabina smiled at me for longer than she should have before blushing and walking away.

Isla watched her go and then smiled at me. I shrugged. 'Don't know what's with her,' I said.

'Or the girl out on the street earlier.'

I grinned like a child. 'Yeah, or her.'

'It's because you're beautiful,' Isla said calmly. I laughed and shook my head. I'd been called many things, including gorgeous, sexy – I even got a *fucktastic* at a big wedding reception gig the Heroes played in Hastings – but never *beautiful*.

'No, you are,' Isla said, and suddenly I knew she meant it. 'I'd like to keep you in a little box –' she outlined a square with her hands – 'so that I could open it up and look at you whenever I felt sad.' She looked away the moment she said it, into space somewhere beyond me. She started twisting her watch again.

'I don't think I'd fit into a box; we could try a Travelodge, though.'
I didn't really want to say it; it just sort of came out.

Isla laughed quickly and flicked an imaginary something at me. The
conversation had been rescued from discussing the elephant on the
table: the fact that Luca was right about us. Although a big part of me
wanted to talk about that elephant.

*

We sit on the warm beach together. Henry, Joyce and I. Summer light
is everywhere. The lazy waves sparkle with myriad tiny stars, just like
the candles in that garden in Kentish Town where Isla and I first sat
and talked. I see them reflected in Henry's eyes. Joyce's too. I can still
feel Isla's hand in mine from when I remembered watching Jack and
May.

Isla.

I look down. I look away from Henry. I see Isla, Jack and May.

Henry says that I need not feel guilty.

I look up with surprise.

I don't.

Joyce turns away.

Henry says that I can have joy. The joy I showed him. Henry says
that everyone can.

How?

Henry looks toward the sun. His face is turned right into the Tide!
Its fingers reach around him like steam from a kettle just before it
comes to boil. Light in the light! Moving over him.

Henry says I must choose to have it.

I shake my head.

It isn't that easy.

Henry says it isn't easy but it's simple.

How? Show me.

Henry says that first I must be truthful, I must not lie.

I don't lie.

Henry turns back from the Tide and looks at me. Joyce turns back too. They are both looking into my eyes.

I don't lie.

33

He slows at a junction. He does not stop. Hedges of hazel, thorn and elder rising from rich banks of grass curve away and yield a view, a glimpse only, of clear road to the left, clear road to the right. He accelerates hard, turning the padded wheel. He races away. A dead tree, stark and white amid the summer land, flashes by.

He glances at his watch.

His sunglasses reflect the world, blurred and racing collage of hedge, and sun and sky and the dead tree now diminishing.

He watches the needle sweep. Speed increases. Maths again. Ten minutes to spare, grows to eleven.

He smiles. The car jumps and skips on the flat, straight road first made by Roman hands. Faster still. His hand leaves the gearstick, finger extending. He reaches for the stereo, the big control at the centre. He moves to press it. He thinks of music. His finger pauses, hovering by the I/O button. His jaw muscles flex. His hand returns to the gears. He drives on in silence. Only the note of the engine, the thrum of low tyres and the hiss of the streaming air parting around the car with the sleek cat on the badge are heard.

Ahead a lone car joins the road. It catches the sun and shines white and bright in the distance. His eyes settle on it. The car skips and pitches. He feels the rise and fall, rise and fall, fall and rise. Both hands on the wheel now, knuckles paling. The road narrows in a rush. The gleaming oncoming car blooms in size. The car passes like a bullet fired from a gun somewhere up ahead. For a fragment of time, in a pocket of still air, he looks at a woman with straight blonde hair. She and her shining white car are reflected back in his glass. They have gone. Hedges race by again. His eyes flick to the rear-view mirror. He sees the white car with the blonde woman shrinking away.

The road descends now. Dropping down between growing banks and the great bend before the next junction and the B-road beyond. He feels the car try to fly from the gentle ridge and then sink and rise on its suspension. He holds his speed. His hand returns to the gearstick. His foot finds the clutch, his fingers flex around the stick. The known and familiar distance counts itself down.

His mind returns to work: pushing the glass door open, the new chap at reception smiling at him as he walks through the atrium. The MD looking down from the open corridor above, a knowing nod exchanged.

The distance halves, then quarters. His grip on the stick tightens. Dappled light rolls over and over. The sun is warm on his face.

A jog up the stairs. Walking through the open-plan office to his door, his door to his office in the corner. Passing by the co-workers who greet him.

34

Henry is still looking at me. Joyce turns away. Henry studies me. The lights from the sea have left his eyes. He looks sad. I don't like this. I love Henry. Why is he sad?

I turn away. I look at the sea and the sweeping lazy waves spreading across each other, layer after layer. The shingle clatters and slides under them as they withdraw. They come again. They come again. Long reaches of cloud cling to the horizon. They're dark and brooding at the base, lighter, whiter, happier above. I count the waves. They rise, spread, break, fan and withdraw in slow motion. It's a timeless pattern that I've always known.

The soul at the monument comes to my thoughts. The old man looking to the west with rain in the air, his own slow, timeless pattern.

Henry says that I should stop going there, that I can if I choose. His voice startles me. I was far away.

Is it all a pattern, Henry? Is that all I am?

Henry says no.

Do we always end up here afterwards?

Henry and Joyce say no together.

I turn away from the sea to look at them both.

Henry says no again.

Joyce says it again too.

This is new?

Henry nods.

Good.

I like that. I feel calm. I breathe deeply.

The lazy summer sun is way across the sky now. Its light is red and burnt orange. Its glow is in Henry's face. Joyce's too. I lie down.

I'm on my back looking up.

35

'I've stopped work,' Tom announced.

'Have you?' I was surprised.

'Yeah, the doctor signed me off.'

'Of course . . .' I paused. I fingered my wedding ring. I looked from Tom to the mugs and back again. 'How is all that . . . what's happening with . . .'

'Tuesday,' Tom replied simply. 'I go in for surgery on Tuesday.'

'Wow, that's quick.'

'Time's important.'

'Yeah, yeah, of course.'

'Mags . . .'

'Yeah?'

'It's okay to talk about it, or not . . . I don't want you feeling awkward—'

'Oh, no, I . . .'

'Or any fuss. It's fine . . . Cath and me, we're going to be fine; we'll get each other through it.'

'Course you will.' I sat down at the table. 'Fuck. I'm sorry, Tom. I don't know what to say.'

'There's nothing to say, Mags.' We sat quietly for a minute or two. It felt like a long time.

'I can't believe, Vince,' I said in the end. 'Just coming round, heading up . . .'

'Yeah, he's a star.'

'You know that I'm here too. If there's anything . . .'

Tom nodded thank you.

'So, are you going to be on sick pay – sick pay and Catherine's money?' I pried.

'Yeah, well, Cath has stopped work too.'

'Really?' Surprise again.

'Yeah.' Tom smiled understandingly. 'She – we wanted to be together through this.'

I fingered my wedding ring again and looked at my hands. 'I guess things will be tight, then?' I said, looking up.

'Oh, yeah, but we'll manage.'

'Well, look, if you need some help . . . I can—'

'No. No, that's really kind, but no. We'll be fine.'

'Yeah, of course . . .' I looked at my hands again.

'So, where's our tea, then?' Isla asked, walking in with Catherine.

I looked up. Tom and I had been sitting in silence again. The interruption was welcome.

I poured the tea and the four of us sat at the table together. Tom sipped his carefully and Catherine watched him. Isla's phone beeped and Catherine said they shouldn't keep us up. In the end, we sat there for an hour drinking tea. We talked about our lives in Brighton, laughed about how old we sounded talking about *the old times*, and then Catherine noticed the collage of photographs of Jack and May on the wall. It was a huge piece of work, a metre tall and two wide. Isla had put it together at the end of the summer. It started on the August bank holiday weekend. It was rainy so we stayed in and I worked in the study. She started printing photographs, tens and then hundreds. She had to take the Discovery and the children to Ipswich to buy more ink and paper while I worked. She brought back pizza so she wouldn't have to cook. By late evening, when Jack and May were asleep and I'd finished work, the conservatory floor was already covered. Over the next week the wicker furniture had to be stacked against the wall and pictures covered the floor and the windows. She worked tirelessly until it was done: sifting, shortlisting, selecting, grouping, rescaling, retouching and reprinting. It became all-consuming. It was as if she was pouring her soul into it. I remember when I was in the study working I heard Jack telling May not to disturb me.

'But Mummy's crying,' came her tiny voice.

'But Daddy's working,' Jack said very seriously.

I went through to the conservatory, Isla was sitting cross-legged in the middle of the floor with her MacBook, editing pictures. Tears were rolling down her face. I asked what was wrong. She seemed startled. I'm not sure she even realised she was crying.

After eight days, it was done. She had a frame specially made by this this guy she found in the parish magazine adds. She insisted that the frame should be simple. Finally, it was placed in the kitchen on the big wall between the two doors. She was very quiet for weeks afterwards. I didn't know why.

36

I thought about that big old elephant lying there on the table in front of Isla and me at Papa's. I considered talking about it all honestly. Being truthful. I thought about trying my luck and waking him up. But in the end, I decided to roll with things and ignore him. Ignore what I was increasingly sure was mutual chemistry, bubbling with the catalyst of candlelight and wine. I decided I liked it when Isla laughed; she looked even more beautiful and it made me smile – so why end the smiles?

'So anyway, what's with the big old Second World War watch, then? And what the hell's the time anyway?' I teased.

'Oh, I don't know . . .'

I frowned by way of making my lack of understanding clear.

'It doesn't work any more . . . doesn't' keep time properly,' Isla explained.

'What? You weigh yourself down with that thing and it doesn't even tell the time!' I continued to tease.

Isla looked sad again. 'I wear it when I need to be brave.' She held her hand to her chest, pressing her palm on her sternum.

'I like that,' I said, and I did. 'What did you have to be brave about today?'

'Coming to see you.'

'Yeah, right. What was it really?'

'Really.' A moment slipped by. 'It was my . . .' Isla began to whisper. Her eyes held mine as they filled with tears. She didn't blink. In that moment, I guessed at so much and got it all right. I reached across to take her hands. I almost made it.

'Oh . . . God, I'm sorry,' she said, snatching her hands from the table and looking away from me.

'Don't be silly, it's—'

'No, I really am,' she went on, looking around the floor by her chair. She picked up her bag. She still didn't look at me. It was like a landslide; she was collapsing in on herself right there as I watched. She lifted her bag on to her lap and then pulled her watch up her arm until it jammed.

'I can't believe I . . .' She broke off. Both hands were on her bag now. I didn't know what to do. I wanted to help. I wanted to jump over the table and hold her and tell her whatever it was it would be okay.

'Really, it's—'

'It's been lovely,' she said quickly, still not looking at me, looking around the table and then the room beside her – everywhere but me. The landslide, the disintegration of the cool and collected young woman I'd been admiring all evening continued unchecked.

'Isla? Isla, look . . .'

She stood up. Her chair scraped on the tiles. The guy to our left looked over for a moment and then made a show of reaching for his wine and looking away. I stood up too.

'Thank you. I'll have to owe you for dinner. I'm sorry,' she continued, still without looking at me.

'Isla, wait—'

She finally looked at me. Just a fleeting glance. Tears were flowing down her face. 'Goodnight,' she said. With that she hurried away, weaving through the tables toward the door like the place was on fire. The background music must have been running on a loop because 'Come Back to Sorrento' started again. I stood there watching her. I looked down at the table. The door jingled. I took a step from the table. I looked over to the little bar. Luca was watching me and making no attempt to hide this. I looked back at the door. Isla was gone. I thought I saw her pass by the window, heading down the hill toward the sea.

I thought about running after her. I thought about not running after her.

Luca was a man who understood his business, understood the business of eating and dining and the emotional interplay that had filled his restaurant since it was his father's and he had helped wait on tables as boy after school. He knew it was time for him to come to the table, come to me. I stood there, filled with indecision, turning from table to door, table to door.

'Twenty pounds will cover it,' Luca said calmly, his voice fatherly and sympathetic, not accusing, not worrying that I intended leave without paying my bill, his words as much suggestion, as much advice, as commerce. I looked down at him. He nodded *yes*. I fumbled in my pockets for cash. I pulled out some screwed-up notes. My door key spun out with them and rang on the tiled floor beside Luca. He picked it up. I stretched out a twenty-pound note, smoothing it against my leg, and we swapped.

'Down the hill, toward the sea,' Luca said simply. I really did like him a lot.

I ran out of the door. I looked up and down the street. I couldn't see Isla. This was starting to feel like a bad habit repeating itself.

I reached the bottom of the hill and stopped, breathing deep and sharp after running. I looked left and right along the seafront road. No Isla. Traffic bumped past with tyres sloshing through puddles that told of the earlier downpour. The pavements were busy with groups of people moving between pubs and clubs. A drunken whoop came from across the road. I could smell doughnuts from somewhere and cigarette smoke mixed with engine exhausts. A young guy in his teens pushed past me, moving against the flow, tall and skinny with a black t-shirt and jeans. He looked upset and angry. I jogged along toward Old Steine, jumping high, trying to catch sight of Isla. Nothing. I could feel my heart racing; I wasn't used to running in those days. After the Metropole Hotel, I scanned the twin snakes of jerking head and tail lights, up toward the Palace Pier and back to the wrecked West Pier. I saw a gap and jogged across to the promenade. Here I stood close to the road, rising up and down on my toes like a yoyo, scanning left and right along the front. My breathing steadied. I finally stood still. I became aware of a dull thudding in the air and through my feet from the Zap Club in the arches under the road.

'Shit,' I said, surrendering to no one in particular.

I turned my back on the traffic. An angry horn sounded back toward Hove and was answered with a distant shout. I sat down on the steps to the beach in front of the Grand, feeling the wet cold on my arse as soon as I did so. The lights at the end of the Palace Pier pulsed through the old friend of a pattern, tracing the struts and beams and hoops and curves of the funfair. I lit a cigarette, the last in my pack, inhaling deeply and holding the smoke hot in my chest, before looking up to the orange-haze sky and exhaling. I thought about trying to hook up with Vince and Tom. I wondered if they'd be in the usual haunts or if they'd go somewhere new.

37

I finished my cigarette in no particular hurry and flicked the glowing butt spinning out over the beach. I walked along the seafront for a bit, stepping out of the way of a kid no more than ten or eleven who shot by on roller blades. I remember thinking it was late for him to be out. I watched him weave off through the scattering of people, mostly couples at that point. A little further along, there was a homeless guy sitting on one of the benches, sorting through two bulging shopping bags full of old random crap. He looked like a broken old man to me, his hair and whiskers matted and filthy. Looking back, I doubt he was as old as fifty. Despite the warm evening, he was wearing two long coats. I hated walking past folk like him. I heard Vince's voice in my head: *Don't give them money. They'll just spend it on booze or drugs . . . You won't be helping them.* I knew where Vince was coming from, but he spent his money on booze so why shouldn't that poor old bastard? I hated seeing people broken like that. I wished the world wasn't that way.

My deliberations were cut short when he spoke to a guy of about my age walking the other way toward me. The guy was wearing a sharp suit and I guessed he'd gone for drinks after work and was on his way home.

'Got a li'l' change?' The old man's voice was an apology, his expression one of need and neutral expectation of kindness or cruelty. There was no hope in his face at all. He truly was broken.

'Fuck off!'

The old man looked away in absolute submission, lowering his head until it almost touched his shopping bags full of rubbish. I thought of the Tylers. It was horrible. To my surprise the man stopped. 'Why don't you get a fucking job rather than scrounging off me, cunt!' he shouted. The old man turned his head away in anticipation of being kicked or punched or spat at and mumbled something I couldn't make out.

'That's enough of that, mate,' I said.

'You what?' replied the prick in the suit, turning away from the old man to glare at me. At that age I hadn't finished filling out but I was already a big chap and I don't know whether I had my father's eyes or if the experience of many a scrap after the Heroes had played at tough clubs showed in me, but no one ever seemed to guess that the last thing in the world I ever wanted to do was fight or hurt anyone.

'You heard,' I replied, squaring up to him. He blinked. He snorted dismissively and walked away.

'Shouldn't waste your time with wankers like that,' were his parting words.

I turned to face the old man. He was looking at me but turned away immediately. I guessed there were two sorts of people who stopped to do anything more than drop a few coins in his hand: those who talked about Jesus and those like my smartly dressed new friend who said *fuck off*. I guessed the old man was more at home with the fuck-off-ers. I looked at the side of his head and then decided to go with Vince. So I crossed the road and called in at the West Pier News. Inside, the strip lights were so bright and harsh that they actually hurt my eyes. It smelled like a butcher's shop. The tiled floor was covered in black half-dried footprints dragged in from the wet pavements. I pulled a large bottle of orange juice from the refrigerated display unit and went over to the till. I squinted at the man behind the counter. He looked bored. I put the orange juice down and pointed out a soft pack of Lucky Strikes, gesturing for two packs, and a flat half-bottle of Bells. I also grabbed a giant bar of fruit-and-nut chocolate the size of an A4 sheet of paper from a special offer pile by the till. He put everything in a paper bag. I pulled a single note from my pocket and he gave me some coins back.

I came out and went back across the road. The old man was still on the bench, rummaging through his bags.

'Got a li'l' change?' came his apologetic litany. It was as if the last ten minutes hadn't happened.

'Sure,' I said dropping the coins I'd just been given into his hand.

'God bless you,' he nodded and turned back to his bags. I put the giant bar of chocolate, the orange juice and one of the packs of cigarettes on the bench beside him. He looked over at them and then up to me. His face showed nothing. He said nothing. There was nothing to say.

I dropped down and walked on the beach itself. I always liked the beach at night, or rather looking back at the lights of the buildings from down there. With the glare of the lamps the sea was black and hidden but I could hear the shingle clattering and the swish of small quick waves. I twisted the whisky cap, breaking the seal, and took a long chug. My tongue was numbed, my lips tingled and a brief hint of spice gave way to a sour grain that drew on my mouth and made we wince as I swallowed. I took another before the burning in my gullet had a chance to ebb away. I screwed the cap back on.

Then it happened. I smiled. I was happy. I didn't know when or if I'd see Isla again, but I realised there wasn't anything I could do about it. What I did know is that there was definitely something between us and that she knew where I lived. Beyond that I knew the Heroes' had a gig in Portsmouth the next night in one of my favourite venues. It was as if the storm earlier in the evening had cleared away the clouds that had been over me for the past weeks. I looked back at the lights of the buildings and cars and smiled again. In that moment, all those lights and cars and people seemed to be a teeming tapestry of endless possibilities. Anything could happen there and I lived right in the middle of it! It was time I found Vince and Tom. It was drinking time for Heroes.

*

I love that we haven't been here before. I feel freer suddenly. I turn my head and smile at Henry and Joyce. They smile back but Henry eyes speak of distant thoughts.

I love it!

Joyce nods. She says that she loves to see me like this.

Like what?

She says happy. I nod. It's true. It's as if I've been asleep. As if I've missed so much. I close my eyes and breathe, the sun warm on my face.

I feel free, Joyce. That's why I'm happy.

I think of Dad and the song he would sing when he sailed or laboured on his boat beside the beach hut. The same song I'd sing to Jack if it was just the two of us in the car, him sitting up front with me and the roof down. Dad's *happy song* about the wind and the sea a-blowin' him wherever he pleased. I don't know if he made it up, but it was a beautiful song. I sang it to Isla too, first by accident and then often when we were drunk and young.

I want to sing. Oh God, it's been so long since I sang

*

I guessed Vince and Tom would be at the Madeira Hotel bar, known to the world as the Catfish Club after ten o'clock Thursdays to Saturdays. I used to sing there all the time. It was a fantastic place: a big smoky basement filled with rhythm and blues, soul and Motown until two a.m. We knew the regulars and we knew the management. They always had the same DJ – 'Southampton Barry' from Hayling Island, who we also knew well – but the best thing was that they encouraged musicians to play live between Barry's sets. They kept a drum kit and this old piano on the low stage opposite the bar. It was a beautiful thing – an antique Steinway and Sons – and anyone was welcome to *get on up* and play. Right from the early days the Heroes used it as a place to test out our new material and also have some fun covering our some of the greats. We'd bring our guitars and cover Ray Charles, Solomon Burke, James Brown, Aretha Franklin, the Delfonics, the Commodores, all of them. Then we'd move on to our own stuff. It caught on and by 1993 had a name as the place to catch new bands trying to make it and catch those, like the Heroes, that normally played bigger venues. It attracted the fans and the music press. Hence the management loved us.

That was it – just what I needed! I decided to go back to my flat, pick up my guitar and then get a cab over to the Madeira. If Vince and Tom weren't there I'd play and sing solo or find some folks to jam with. So, I walked up the beach ready to step back into the tapestry, to take my place in the great and colourful world that was Brighton of 1993. And I started to sing. I started to sing Dad's song. I sang and I sang. I sang about the sea and the wind and travelling the wide world. And this was no humming to myself. I lived to sing and make music and I lifted my voice. I sang as if I was already in Portsmouth in front of that big crowd.

Back up by the road a group of three couples walking together on their way somewhere stopped as I passed by. They were smiling. One of the women gave a whistle. Her man smiled and shook his head. The rest turned and smiled too. I spun around, raised up my arms and sang louder. I sang the cheeky bits about the women a-waiting for me that used to make Dad's eyes twinkle. My voice filled the air. I held nothing back; I hit every note. They applauded, right there on the street. The whisky lifted my soul and my singing set it free!

*

I want to sing. I want to sing Dad's song. I want to sing it right now. It's in my heart. I'm singing in my thoughts, but I can't sing aloud. I can't.

God, I want to.

I think of Isla. I think of Isla when we were young and Isla when we weren't young any more. Holding her. Touching her. I want to sing of the girls a-waiting for me. My eyes are closed. The sun is warm on my face. I turn toward the warmth. The sun is red through my closed lids. In my thoughts, I sing on. I recall Dad's words of the winds and the sail and the shores they'll take me to. I want to fill the air with my voice! I want to sing the words in my head, sing of going where I choose and sing of luck and love.

I haven't sung since I got here! I want to sing!

Joyce sits down beside me, close to me. I feel it in the sand.

I turn and open my eyes. Dad's words continue in my thoughts. They are joyful.

She is smiling at me. Her eyes are happy. Henry is beside her and now he is happy too.

*

I turned the corner into Bedford Square, leaving my audience behind. I kept my arms outstretched, whisky bottle raised in one hand, and directed my singing to the flats and my neighbours around and above me. I sang of my little boat and the oceans and the tides and tomorrow. I walked and wove up the pavement, tapping the bottle against the black railings. I thought of Dad and his boat. I wasn't sad; it felt as if he was close. I thought of racing over the waves with my hand in the water like a blade as I sang of turning tiller and cutting home. Then I stopped singing. I stopped because there was Isla sitting on my steps. Slight and beautiful, her knees together, her hands in her lap, one just covering that bloody watch. Her head was down, her hair hanging in front of her face. She could have been sleeping.

*

I finish the song in my thoughts. I could not sing out loud. I shall never be able to sing again.

How could I? How could I after what I've done?

But Dad's words were a joy, were a comfort. There is a sudden stillness. The sun is lower now.

How long did I think of Dad's song?

The Tide is ebbing away. I raise my head. Henry has moved. He is sitting along the beach a little way off. He looks west into the fading Tide. He picks up stones and throws them forward lazily. Joyce kisses my forehead. I feel the Tide.

She says the song was beautiful. She lies down next to me and looks at the reddening sky.

How do you know, Joyce?

She says she could feel it.

She's right. I knew we could all feel it. I love to sing. I'd forgotten how much.

I lie flat again. I feel the sand against my back. I close my eyes. I push fingers into the sand. It's warm and damp.

I feel content, just as I know Henry does. All is quiet. Even the sea is whispering. The waves breaking and falling back, breaking and falling back, are like the breath of a sleeping giant.

38

My sleeping had been deteriorating for over a year by the time Tom and Catherine came to pick up his Volkswagen. My ubiquitous dull headache from tiredness had peeked into an oppressive heaviness by the time they left that night.

'Are you sure you won't stay? It's late to be driving to Norwich, especially in separate cars,' Isla was saying. We were all standing in the hallway while Tom and Catherine put on their coats. Our hall was a big space where the staircase came down in a curve to meet the twin front doors, some plants, a leather Chesterfield sofa bought from a restoration place in Woodbridge, an occasional table and a photograph of huge waves breaking over the seawall at Walberswick. A single lamp on the occasional table and the warm yellow light pouring out of the living-room doorway gave it a sleepy calm. Tom and Catherine stood close to each other, Catherine holding Tom's parka for him while he slipped his arms through. It made me think of Jack on school mornings.

'No. It's really kind, but we need to get back,' Catherine replied graciously.

'Yeah, and nothing beats your own bed,' Tom added lightly, reaching into his coat sleeves and turning to face Isla.

Isla was standing across from me. She nodded her understanding. 'Well,' she said. The word seemed to hang in the air. Catherine turned to her but didn't step away from Tom. Isla's steady brown eyes smiled at them both. No one spoke. Tom looked down. Isla step forward and hugged Catherine. 'Everything's going to be okay,' she said finally, leaning back to look directly at Catherine. Catherine nodded bravely, her mouth clamped shut, her face determined. Neither cried. Isla stepped to Tom and kissed him on the cheek. 'Go and get better, Thomas,' she ordered.

'Righto,' he said.

'Lovely to see you again, Catherine,' I said, stepping forward. We kissed each other, her hand on my shoulder.

'Bye, Mags, and thanks for bringing this one home safely the other night,' she said. I smiled.

'See you, mate,' Tom said simply.

'Yeah, see you, Tom. We'll hook up with Vince, go and get proper pissed as soon as you're sorted.'

Tom nodded. 'Yeah,' he said quietly, touching my arm. 'Thanks, Mags.'

And they left, holding hands and knitted together so that they touched at the shoulder and hip. Again, I was reminded of the Tylers as I watched them walk across the drive to their cars like two wounded soldiers, helping each other to safety before more harm befell them. The security light threw their shadows out across the gravel and hid the garden beyond in blackness. The night air was cold while Isla and I waited silently at the open door. We waved as they drove away, Tom leading in his Volkswagen and Catherine following in her Renault, their faces white and brave and scared in the clinical light. Their brake lights flared bright at the road and then they were gone.

The next time I would see Tom would be with Vince, but we weren't drinking and Tom wasn't sorted.

I closed the door. Isla and I stopped smiling. I looked at Isla. She looked sad.

'Poor, Tomas,' she said, glancing at the closed door.

'Yeah . . .'

'It's going to be a tough time for them.'

'Yeah,' I said again. I looked at my watch. It was already eleven thirty. 'Shit.'

Isla turned back from the door, her eyes warm and concerned. 'He'll be okay, though,' she reassured, laying her hand on the side of my face.

'Oh, yeah . . . yeah, definitely. Sorry. I just realised the time,' I explained. Isla looked confused for a moment and then lowered her hand. 'I've got a big pitch tomorrow and I've still got stuff to do.' I nodded toward the study door. 'And I brought the wrong bloody papers home with me so I'll have to get into the office early on my way.'

'Right . . .' Isla whispered.

'It's important!' I insisted instinctively. I looked up at the ceiling and then started again. 'It's really important. I really don't have any choice,' I went on.

'Magnus . . .' Isla started but broke off.

I went to put my hands on her shoulders but stopped short, ending up in more of a 'don't shoot' stance. 'What?'

'Never mind—'

'It really is important!' I hissed, glancing up at the ceiling again.

Isla looked down and nodded slowly. She took a breath. 'I know,' she conceded. 'I know,' she repeated, I think for her own benefit. 'It's just that . . . I thought you'd want to talk. I think perhaps we should . . .'

'Should talk?'

'Yeah, poor, Tomas.' She paused and sighed. 'But not just Tomas. These things are important . . .' Again, she paused, trying to find the words, frustration on her face. 'They make you think.'

'About life?' I guessed.

'Yes!' She nodded quickly. She took my hands in hers and studied my face, her brown eyes like chocolate in the warm yellow light. 'It's so precious. And we seem to—'

'I know.' I squeezed her hands. 'I know how busy I've been and I know you and the little people miss me—'

'I don't mean it like that. I don't . . .'

'I know,' I reassured. 'But it's true. It's just this is a really important time. I have to get this right and then we'll be sorted and we'll be able to have all the time we want – soon, really soon. We could go on holiday, we could—'

'I know, I know, but it's not . . .' Isla's eyes were wet now and still so sad. 'We never seem to stop and enjoy what we have.'

'What we have takes a lot . . . It—'

'Is Uncle Tom going to be dead?' came Jack's voice from up the stairs. Isla and I looked up into the semi-darkness. Jack was sitting a few steps down from the landing. I smiled at him.

'Have you been eavesdropping on grown-up conversations again?' Isla asked.

'No, I've just been listening to you . . . and Uncle Tom when he came round before as well,' Jack explained.

I went up and sat on the step next to him. I looked at my watch as I sat down: eleven forty. I looked down to Isla at the foot of the stairs. 'No,' I said softly, 'he's not.'

'He's not going to be dead?'

'No.'

'Are you sure?'

'Yes,' I lied.

'Honestly?'

'Yes, I don't lie,' I lied again.

'Daddy's right. Uncle Tom is going to fine and there's certainly nothing for you to worry about,' Isla added. Jack seemed immediately reassured. I squeezed his knee and stood up. He looked up at me and smiled.

'Now come on, you, back to bed,' Isla ordered, walking up the stairs and pointing to the landing. I ran my hand over Jack's hair and went down. I stopped at the foot of the stairs and looked back. Isla had her arm round Jack and was guiding him back to bed. She looked back at me. She smiled a strange brave sort of smile that I hadn't seen before and then turned away. I watched them disappear into the dimness of the landing.

'Sweet dreams,' I said to where they had been, before turning and walking into my study.

39

I wake.

No, wait, this is dream, I'm not awake.

I'm in the beach hut. A towel is lying over me like a blanket. I roll on to my side. The heavy old bench cushion complains under me. The cushion I'm using as a pillow smells damp but it's dry against my cheek. I look across at the old table and the gloss-painted boards of the wall – blue paint on the bottom half and white above. I reach out from under the blanket-towel and run a tiny hand over my whiskerless face. My skin feels so soft. I am a child. I lie still. I hear the sea outside and voices, laughter. I think of Mum and Dad and Julie. They are just outside. I listen. I stay dead still. I cannot make out what they are saying but they sound happy.

I sit up. Pinpricks of light wink between the boards of the walls and the varnished roof. I swing my bare legs over the edge of the bench. The towel falls to the vinyl floor. I sit, my feet swinging and not reaching the floor. The air is warm and smells of damp like the cushion. I touch the wall in the corner beside me. It's cool to the touch. It's dim in here but I can see okay. There's light coming in from the front doors, through the threadbare curtains that used to hang in Mum and Dad's house. I don't want to look at them, though. I look at the backdoor instead, it's edged with a pencil line of daylight. I hear laughter again and the pok-bok of Swingball. I don't want to look at the front doors, not yet, not this time, but I know I'm going to.

I look at the front doors. The old orange curtains covering the windows are glowing bright with sunlight. Sharp pricks of light burst through the worn material. I hold my tiny fingers. I have no wedding ring. I look at the brightness and listen to the voices, to Mum and Dad, and Julie's laughter. I count into the pok-bok rhythm of the Swingball. It's like a metronome.

I look at the backdoor. I look at the handle. I want to stay, to listen to Mum and Dad and Julie. But I know I should wake. I want to wake.

I want to turn the backdoor handle and wake. I don't want to wake and leave them. I don't want to turn the handle and wake.

I step down. Everything is big. I look up at the table. It's like a giant's cave. I look at the front doors, at the old curtains with the sun blinking through them. I hear the voices and the laughter and the pok-bok of racket against tennis ball: the sounds of summer fun. I wait. I stand in the middle of the floor.

I reach up to the backdoor handle. I turn it.

*

I wake. I wake into darkness. No, not darkness: night.

It's night time!

I haven't seen the night for . . . I never see the night now.

I'm on the beach. I'm right where I was lying. I haven't moved. I'm not somewhere else. I sit up.

I feel calm.

I'm on the beach at night and I feel calm!

Joyce and Henry aren't here. They're somewhere else. But I can feel them. They're promises.

The moon is bright and low on the horizon and those clouds are still there. The moonlight makes them look even more like land, like a distant shore way out across the sea. The night is bright and the sky isn't black. It's all shades of deep purples and blues.

It's so alive!

The sea is silver and white. The beach is silver-grey. I look up. The stars are sharp. I look inland across the marshes.

The stars are even brighter there!

The teeming stripe of the Milky Way reaches over me south to north into Lyra, like a brushstroke of lights across the bruising heavens. Mum always said it was like spilled sugar. Dad always marvelled at the billion suns and their worlds. Both worked for me.

It's beautiful! I've missed the stars!

I see the woods beyond the marshes. The trees are black against the sky. I watch them swaying. I can't hear waves. The sea is silent. I look around. The summer night is humid but the breeze is cool.

I study the stars. I see the Plough in the west, hanging above the black silhouetted trees. I think of the stars wheeling over the clearing in the woods close to my home.

How many nights did I spend there?

I find Cassiopeia over toward Southwold. The lighthouse flashes beneath her. I follow a line between the two and find the North Star, just as Dad showed me how. And there's a bright star burning low over the woods, its bright bursting fingers touched with red and not twinkling.

Jupiter! Jupiter's rising.

I see Gemini and Leo, Capricorn and Libra. I think of Jack and May. Standing in the garden with them and pointing out the Plough and the North Star just as Dad had done with me. I think of Isla. I think of Isla and Jack and May.

On Jack's seventh birthday we stood in the garden away from the house, looking at the summer stars. Isla had filled the garden with a hundred tealights: tiny candles burning in jars and bottles. They made it feel as if stars completely surrounded us and reminded me of the garden where Isla and I first met. The lights in the house were off. It was humid. The air smelled of harvest dust. We had fir and apple and plum trees at that end of the garden and they were black against the stars and the blue-black-purple night sky.

May stayed close to me, squeezing my hand every time the breeze stroked the trees. Jack had a little torch that he'd got for his birthday and was busy sweeping the hedges back and forth. Crickets filled the air with their chorus that always made me think of Johnny Weissmuller Tarzan films.

Somewhere far off a vixen called. May squeezed my hand even tighter and Jack's torch beam flew across the garden in the direction of the cry. We'd come out to send up a birthday wish, a sky lantern. I'd been working in the study and missed some of the evening while friends and family sat and talked and the children played upstairs, their tiny feet making big noises above. Hiding, screaming, giggling and running downstairs in tears for emergency doctoring, hugs and reprimands. But they had all gone and it was wish time. Isla had sent Jack into the study to get me. It was a three-line whip: no excuses.

We all stood together watching the stars as Isla and I pointed out Leo and Gemini, Jack and May's birth signs. May wanted to know why she didn't have a twin if she was a Gemini. She asked if we could get her one. Jack was appalled by this deep ignorance of the world and told her off. Out of the blue I truly wished we could get her one and I think Isla did too.

Isla and I worked together. The children stood between us while we pointed out more and more stars over their heads. After Gemini, we found the Plough and Cassiopeia and the North Star. Jack's torch became a pointer and I could tell he liked being owner and provider of such a useful device. Then there were planets: Mars was bright and close at the time and Saturn was rising in the east. The little torch beam flashed around the sky and May's grip on my hand relaxed, her beautiful little face looking up in wonder as I dropped in snippets from the Ancient Greek stories that I remembered from Dad. Isla smiled at me over their heads. Her eyes were happy and shone in the darkness. I touched her hand on Jack's back. She took mine, holding it almost as tightly as May had when the fox barked.

'Is it time for the wish?' Jack shouted, looking around. Isla's hand left his back.

Isla looked at me and I nodded. 'Yes!' she said excitedly.

'Yes!' Jack and May shouted with far, far greater excitement.

The paper lantern measured about a metre across. Isla had insisted that it had a bamboo rather than wire hoop. Apparently, the wire hoops ended up getting baled into animal straw and causing all sorts of harm and Isla couldn't bear the thought of animals suffering, even if they were so stupid they didn't know not to eat wire. We stood around the lantern, Isla with May, me with Jack, holding the bovine-friendly double-price bamboo hoop. The two children bounced and shook with excitement, making the entire assembly jiggle constantly.

'Right, hold it steady!' I said, crouching and sparking my brass Zippo that had been specially brought out of retirement and refuelled for the occasion. A flame jumped up and illuminated the white tissue paper with a yellow glow. May let out a little scream.

'Steady!' Isla said. 'Everyone stand back a little.' The lantern was now held at arm's length.

Isla held the tissue paper up above the hoop and I kept the Zippo flame against the fuel bung. The flame found purchase and grew slowly. The brass lighter was getting hot. I held it there as long as I could, the flame taking and moving slowly, slowly. My hand burned suddenly. I flicked the lid shut with a reassuring 'ting' and dropped it into my pocket. The lantern was filled with bright yellow light now. The bung suddenly took properly. The tissue paper filled out and made a straight-edged cylinder.

'Daddy!' Jack shouted simply. May screamed again. She looked around the rim at me and I could see the yellow light twinkling in her eyes. Isla let go of the top. We all held the hoop. It began to tug. It wanted to fly!

'I can feel it!' Jack shouted.

'It's going!' May sang.

'Ready!' Isla called. The lantern was pulling hard. 'Ready! Think of your wish!' Jack screwed up his eyes, his mouth silently forming words. 'Three . . . two . . .'

'One!' we all shouted together.

The lantern climbed away from us and the garden and the little lights in bottles and jars. Up into the stars. It swung to and fro when it cleared the trees and found the breeze before drifting away inland to the west, gliding gracefully and silently, higher and higher. We all watched. We all made our wishes.

'Bye-bye!' May called after it. 'Is it taking our wishes to the fairies?' she asked.

'Yes,' Isla and I said together.

We watched until the lantern became a tiny flickering light among the stars and finally disappeared. It was lovely.

That night, once the children were sleeping with contentedly, Isla and I went back out into the garden and drank wine until the candles started to burn out. I didn't think about work. Then we went to bed and made love for hours. It was warm, delicious, passionate, loving sex, even better than when we were young.

I turn my back to the sea and look west. Leo is above the trees. So bright, the stars are so sharp. My house is there, in the west. I think of that night, of the garden, of home. I think of the roads, the way home.

Six miles.

I think of Isla. Is she there, asleep in her bed, in our bed? Is she sleeping just six miles away? Jack and May. Are they sleeping with her? Did they ever go home? Are they there?

What did I do? Will I ever know?

I look round. There is no one on the silver-grey beach. I am alone. I hear crickets in the marshes. I hear a splash of something small diving into the brackish pools hidden among the reeds.

I think of Isla and Jack and May. I hope they are in the house. I hope they are there, safe and sleeping peacefully. I look down.

What did I do?

I look up.

Six miles!

I look around again. Nothing. Only the crickets, the wind and the moon on the horizon. Henry and Joyce are still promises. But the buses are far away.

Six impossible miles?

I want to see Isla. I want to see my children. I stop. I am still. I look hard at the stars of Leo, the black fringe of the woods swaying beneath. It's time to know, know for sure.

It's time.

I think of Henry. I think of my car. I think of that last drive. I think of Henry looking sad and of Joyce turning away from me. I must know.

But can I? I look down from Leo, straight inland. Can I cross those miles and find them? Will they be there and will I be able to close the gap? I think of those three distant figures on the beach, of running and running and screaming at them but never being heard. Could I ever close that gap? I have to try. It's time. It has to be time. I think of the six miles. I *feel* the distance. It is suddenly vast. But I must try.

I must try.

I think of Joyce and Henry. I know what they would say. I want to wait. I love them. But I must try now.

I must try.

I must know.

I look to the path that leaves the beach and cuts across the marshes. I look at the old post marking it out. I think of the six miles and I wonder if they are impossible. I think of walking away from the promise and the love of Henry and Joyce. I think of Isla. And I think of Jack. And I think of May.

I smile.

Fuck it.

I walk. I walk from the sand and crunch across the shingle. I reach the old bleached wooden post, silver in the moonlight and casting a shadow due west into the mouth of the path. I think of Dad and I think of his stories of Black Shucks. I walk past the post. The path drops down among the tall swaying reeds. The wind stirs them and whispers, but the air is warmer and more humid here. I walk on, the boards of the walkway flexing under me.

40

Isla looked up. Her eyes caught the light from the streetlamps behind me. She studied me. She didn't move, she didn't blink; her face was calm and just a little serious. She was beautiful. I didn't move either. I wanted her. I wanted her body and her soul. I wanted her in my bed and in my life. But standing there, even with my normal confidence topped up with whisky, I felt that she was far out of reach.

She twisted that fucking watch around so that it was in the proper place to read the time and stood up. I took one step closer, raising my hands like I was corralling a nervous animal, just like my Dad had done when the grumpy pony in the back field used to break through into our garden. That pony was a bastard, my dad said so.

'Don't go anywhere,' I said quietly.

Isla smiled apologetically. 'I'm so sorry, Magnus. . . about earlier and, well . . .' She paused. She moved her feet, shifting her stance.

'It's okay,' I said softly. 'Just don't run away . . . not just yet.'

'I didn't run. I . . .' Isla looked at me. I lowered my hands. 'I did, didn't I?'

I nodded. I smiled at her. How could I not? A car pulled up on the street, its lights passing us. I looked around and when I turned back Isla was still looking at me; she hadn't moved. There we stood. A voice raised in quick thanks came from the street and then a door clumped shut. The car pulled away. Footsteps a couple of doors up and the jingle of keys followed. A door opened. We didn't move, we didn't speak and we didn't notice the silence until the door slammed shut and the background hum of Brighton came back to us. Finally, Isla looked down, her hand moving to her watch, turning it round her wrist slowly.

'I've had people run out on me before . . . but never when I was being so charming,' I said, quoting Harrison Ford from *Blade Runner*. Quoting *Blade Runner* was a bad habit I was trying to break at the time, but it was proving difficult on account of the regularity with which Vince, Tom and I watched the film when we were drunk.

Isla laughed quickly. Then she stiffened and looked at me. 'I really made a mess of tonight. The whole thing was a stupid idea. I wanted to tell you that meeting you in Camden was, well . . .' She breathed. 'I wanted to tell you that it was . . . that you're lovely and that's why I left in such a hurry when we got to the station. I wanted you to know that I'm married and that's why—'

'There was no need.'

Isla shifted her stance again and looked up. I took a step toward her. She stiffened. I was sure she *was* going to run away again. I could see it in her eyes and knew that she really was far out of reach; I knew there was nothing I could say. Even the whisky didn't help; it seemed to clear away and leave me sober and bare. I felt the strangest sense of panic right down in my stomach. I'd never noticed the luck I'd had all my life until that moment when I felt it run out. I brought my hands to my face, trying to massage away the ache that the whisky had left.

'The whole thing was really stupid,' Isla continued, apologetically still. 'I really—'

'No, it wasn't,' I said firmly and honestly, looking from between my hands. Isla studied me but didn't reply. There was silence again and for the first time it was uncomfortable; we both felt it.

'What was that you were singing?' she asked suddenly.

I dismissed it. 'Oh, just a song my dad used to sing.'

'I liked it. It was happy. You sounded happy.'

I nodded. We both looked down.

'Why did you leave tonight? I mean, why *did* you run away?' I asked directly. 'Tell me, before you go again,' I added. I stepped aside so that she could pass me and leave.

'Oh, it's a long story. Like I said, I made a real mess of tonight and I'm sorry—'

'Who did the watch belong to?' I took a half step back towards her.

Isla's hand stopped moving and gripping it tightly. 'It was Dad's . . . It was my dad's.' Tears filled her eyes. She wiped her face angrily and then pushed past me. 'Goodnight, Magnus.' I didn't want her to cry and I didn't want her to be angry. I wanted to hold her and make everything okay. I wanted to help her. I put my hands on her shoulders to stop her before I realised I'd done it.

'Don't!' she snapped, pushing my hands away. I stepped back, my hands saying 'sorry, I surrender'. My heart missed a beat. I thought she was going to hit me. 'Goodbye, Magnus,' she said quickly and stepped out on to the street ready to disappear again.

'So he's dead, then?'

Isla stopped and turned back. She looked surprised and still angry, but her eyes answered my question and explained everything – her watch, her Electra-complex choice of husband, the strange sense of distance, everything.

'My dad died of cancer eighteen months ago,' I said without meaning to. It came out like a confession. I don't know why. Isla's eyes widened; the anger left her face. A cat ran from the railings beside her and darted across the road. A taxi with its white painted bonnet had to screech to a halt, its headlights dipping low and then bouncing back. Isla didn't notice as she took a step back toward me. I didn't care if she was married, I didn't care if she could never be mine; right then I just wanted her to know that she wasn't alone in her sadness. I just wanted to comfort her. 'Tonight, when the thunder started, I thought of him because he loved storms. Yesterday I thought of him when I bought a hot sausage roll from the bakers in the Lanes because he liked brown sauce with them, so that's what I had, even though I prefer mustard.' Isla brought her hands together, prayer-like. 'And the day before that because I walked behind someone who looked like him.' And that's how it came out, I think I would have gone on and on if Isla hadn't stepped close and put her hand on my arm.

'Magnus,' she whispered, looking up. Her eyes were wet and searching mine.

'It's okay,' I said. She closed her eyes. She moved against me, putting her arms around me, her head against me. I put my arms around her and held her tightly. We had the same scars and they had suddenly changed everything.

41

I climb the old wooden steps up from the marshes to the wood. The trees are a black wall below the stars. The path forks here, skirting around them to the south and going straight through westward. In life, I was always nervous walking into woodland at night. But here I welcome the trees, the closeness. I walk on. I think of Isla. I think of the first time I held her. I think of her perfume, the subtle shift from night air to flowers that it brought. I remember the feeling of her against me, the dampness of her tears on my chest, the press of her body.

I have to know. I have to look for her one last time.

I think of those six once easy miles, those six impossible miles winding and bending directly to her. I think of the paths and the roads and the fields and the tracks and the land between these woods and my house.

Oh God, I hope she's there.

I quicken my pace. I enter the clearing where Joyce found me this morning. Where Joyce comes to find me. Where Joyce has found me before. She is a promise here. I feel her. I love Joyce. I walk beneath the oak, its branches sweeping and broad. I look up. The leaves are black against the sky. The stars blink through them. They wink and fade, wink and fade.

I leave the clearing. The path is wider here, twin tracks with grass between them. You could bring a Land Rover down here. But I walk. I think of my house ahead. My thoughts race. I think of hills, of the Brecon Beacons. I think of the beach behind me and the smell of the sea. I think of the places I visit. But I must not fade, I must stay present.

I must stay here, I must stay!

I flinch and look around. I didn't mean to talk aloud. The wind stirs the black trees. Patches of silver moonlight flood between the trunks, dappled greys and silvers stretching away. I smile and think of Jack. He feels like a promise to me. The hills feel like a promise too.

I walk on. I'll be through the woods soon. Then it will be out across the heathlands and on toward Westleton. My feet are silent on the woodland path. The air among the trees is thick and smells of the pines as they breathe.

An owl calls! A *toowit!* I stop. I listen for the *toowoo*. Nothing. Even the breeze has eased and the trees are still and silent.

It calls again! Another *toowit!*

I am perfectly still. I want there to be a reply. Is the owl a spirit like me? He must be. Please answer him.

Please.

Nothing. I wait. I am still. He calls a third time. Where is his mate? Is she living? Is she far away in this small belt of woodland? Is she beyond hearing?

I think of Isla and our home. I think of Jack and May. I would weep if I lingered. I walk on. The owl is not answered.

I must see them. I must know.

Isla, I must know.

*

Isla's arms left me and she stepped back. Her make-up, not that I'd noticed she was wearing any, had run; black lines marked her tears. She dabbed at them with a fingertip and sighed. 'I must look like a witch,' she said.

'Yes, you do.'

Isla laughed quickly and looked down.

'But don't worry, I must have got something in my eye too,' I added.

'In your eye,' Isla repeated, looking back up.

'Yeah,' I coughed. The stranger that I knew I couldn't keep had gone. 'Come up,' I said, nodding to my door.

'It's late. It's—'

I winced inwardly at my choice of words. 'Don't worry . . . I mean, I'll make us a cup of tea . . . You can sort your face out—'

'Thanks!' Isla laughed.

'You know what I mean. I even have biscuits.' Then I thought about Vince. 'Actually, no – I don't have biscuits.'

'There's nothing worse than wild claims about biscuits.'

'I know . . . but come up . . . just for a bit. I promise you can keep your dress on.'

'Well, since you're obviously a gentleman . . . I could use a cup of tea—'

'Good—'

'With you.'

I looked at her for a moment. She was beautiful. 'Come on,' I said, holding out my hand. She took it without hesitation. I opened the door and led her past the mountain bikes and the junk mail. The hallway was lit only by the yellow of the sodium lamps from the street coming through the patterned glass. I could hear a TV from the ground-floor flat, muffled speech too faint to understand. The stairs reached away into blackness. Isla squeezed my hand. I slapped the white button switch at the foot of the stairs and the light from the naked bulb above filled the space with brighter yellow and the button started to tick loudly.

'Thirty seconds,' I explained.

I led her up the stairs, our hands still joined, the boards creaking under our feet. On the first-floor landing the same TV programme was coming from flat two and the bright blue-white light from their set was flickering under the door. I thought about Dad and what I'd just said to Isla. About her tears and what she must be thinking. The world of Friday-night television beyond the door of flat two seemed far away from us.

Isla's voice brought me back from my thoughts. 'I can't believe you used that quote,' she said as we started up the second flight of stairs.

'Hey?' I looked over my shoulder to her.

She sniffed and smiled bravely. It was a strong, defiant smile: her smile, a smile I would come to love. 'From *Blade Runner*,' she prompted, but I still didn't follow. 'What you said about running out on you was from the film *Blade Runner*.'

'Oh!' I realised aloud. 'Yeah . . . How did you know that?' I asked, stopping midway between floors.

'Well, I've seen the film.'

'Have you?'

'Yes, of course I have! Everyone has.'

'Right.'

Isla nodded for me to lead on. We started up the last few steps. 'You didn't think you'd get away with it, did you?'

'It wasn't something I really thought about. Just sort of came out,' I explained. We reached my door. Liza in flat five opposite mine had been cooking one of her lentil curries again and the entire landing smelled of coriander and onions.

'Something smells good,' Isla said.

'You think?'

'Yes.'

I unlocked the door and gestured for her to enter. She walked past. Small and lovely.

'Do you like our owl?' I said staying with *Bladerunner* and following her in.

'Is it artificial?' Isla replied, grinning briefly in the dim light of my hallway before her face looked sad again and I knew the light-hearted distraction had come to its end.

42

I reach the far side of the woods. The moon is rising over the trees, bright and full. It's like a false day under its light, a day without colour. There's an old gate across the track here. Its silvered timbers seem ancient.

There's that owl again!

Its call is far off now, way back toward the sea. I listen. Still it goes unanswered. I think of Isla. I think of calling to her and Jack and May on the beach that day.

If it *was* them.

Could it have been them?

And if it was, what does it mean?

Is it neither here nor there?

Is it here *or* there?

The moon has filtered the stars but those that remain are keen. They make me think of frosty winter nights but it's a summer sky. The Plough hangs ahead in the west. It's marking my way.

I remember this gate. I remember it in life and death. But in death I have never passed through it. I have never gone beyond this point. All of what I'm about to do is new.

If I have the strength.

I put my hand on the gate. The wood has a weathered softness to it. I remember the huge wooden tongs that Mum used to haul clothes from washer to spinner in her twin-tub washing machine when I was little. They tasted of soap when I touched them with my tongue.

I look ahead. There's a little lane beyond the gate. It runs west and then turns south to Westleton. I picture my journey clearly, stretching away beneath the Plough: the lane joining the road that runs up to Blythburgh and down through Westleton on its way to strange old Thorpeness, the walk through Westleton itself – the village green with the little barn that has always survived there and the garage on the corner that Jack loved because they fix tractors and Land Rovers – then out again, back on the winding lane, inland to my house, to knowing. To finally knowing.

One way or the other.

The journey, the few short miles, seems like a vast desert to cross, an ocean to overcome, a great mountain to climb. I grip the gate. My eyes focus on the little lane. The tarmac is buckled into ruts and grass has broken through between them. I jump and swing my legs over the gate easily. I think of Isla. I whisper her name: Isla.

*

I led Isla through to the main room of my flat. I liked the feel of her hand in mine, slight and warm. The only light was from the streetlamps below in the square and the fairy lights around my vinyl shrine, winking like coloured stars and edging everything in a twilight of yellows, blues and reds. The smell of smoke and mint had faded away behind the incense I burned when I was alone at night and exploring melodies to match lyrics Kelly and I had written in the brightness of day. The breeze reaching in through the open balcony door still brought a whisper of jasmine from that Thai restaurant in Hove, but, despite the storm, it blew warm and the air that met us was humid and sticky.

'Wow,' Isla said, her voice low.

'Sorry,' I answered, reluctantly letting go of her hand and quickly gathering up the scattered sheets of music and scribbled lyrics covering the floor and sofa. Once clear, the old brown leather looked suddenly lustrous under the tiny fairy lights. I looked back at Isla, my arms full of paper. Standing there in the middle of my lounge, her feet together, her hands clasped at her naval, there was a polite formality about her. She looked disciplined somehow, disciplined and sad. And she looked brave. I think that was the first time she actually brought Audrey Hepburn to mind; perhaps because I'd watched *Love in the Afternoon* with Kelly the previous Monday morning as a guilty treat to get the creative juices flowing. It hadn't worked, our creativity remained becalmed and firmly in the doldrums that were channelling from me.

I remember the whole idea of a polite guest waiting for an invitation to sit striking me as bizarre. Until then I'd only ever had friends eating my biscuits and the idea of guests was odd and terribly grown-up. My parents had had *guests*. I got the feeling that Isla's world and mine, Isla's Brighton and mine, were very different. Finding out how different, how different the same city could feel and appear and *be* to two people as they walked the same streets and breathed the same air, was to be a shock to me. Until Isla I'd had no idea how many different lives could colour the same place. And I'd had no idea that two people could look out across the same vista and see something completely different.

'Make yourself at home,' I said, gesturing to the sofa.

Isla smiled and gave the slightest of nods. She sat down in the corner of the sofa closest to the balcony, the leather creaking. She sat politely with her hands in her lap, her right hand gripping that big old watch. She looked very small. And she still looked brave and she still looked sad. I cast around for somewhere to put my armful of papers, but there were no available surfaces so finally, in an act of desperation, I put them on the piano keyboard – it complained with a fouling of notes that formed a clear *no!*

'I'll get the light—'

'There's no need,' Isla cut in. 'It's nice. I can see out of the balcony like this . . . You're very lucky.'

'Lucky?'

'Yes.' Isla looked around the room and then at me, her eyes warm and bright in the half-light. 'This is such a wonderful place.'

'Oh . . .' I laughed quickly. 'It's a mess and—'

'No, it's just right . . . '. She turned away to face the balcony. I knew she wasn't smiling any more. I wanted to comfort her. I wanted to make things better for her. I wanted to hold her. But I didn't. She was far away again.

'Right. I think I promised you a cup of tea, didn't I?'

'Yes, but you also made a wild promise about biscuits which turned out to be a huge lie. So, I'm not building my hopes up too much.'

'Oh, tea is different. I even have milk.'

'Wow, now I *am* impressed.' She began looking around the room again, her eyes still bright. She studied everything. She was so beautiful that night. It didn't seem right to speak, but the silence definitely needed to be filled with music. So I put the kettle on and then went over to the shrine. I took a minute, looking over the shelves, my eyes adjusting to the light, but I already knew what I was going to choose. There really was no choice at all; it just seemed as if there was.

I dropped the stylus on to Tom Waits' *Closing Time*, a low soft thud was followed by an even softer crackle, like rain pricking against an umbrella. Isla turned to look at me directly. Then Tom's voice singing 'Ol' 55' settled ever so gently over the room. The kettle started to boil. Isla watched me make tea and I watched her watching me. She felt closer.

43

I walk confidently. The distance ahead of me stretches away toward Isla. It feels impossibly far, yet she feels near. I'm determined. I have to know, I have to know the truth.

I will get there!

I look around. I've got to stop calling out aloud! The tall trees dotted along the edge of the road throw down patches of shade in the moonlight. Their shadows are black islands on a silver sea. Broad fields sweep away from me. Sandy acres with heaped rows of legumes. A giant agricultural hose reel and sprinkler catch the moonlight far off. The distant hedgerows are matt grey cut-outs, part hidden by rising mist.

Or is it dust?

I walk through a tree shadow, black and featureless. I step out into the moonlight again. I cast a long shadow that kinks over the low hedge and reaches out across the field.

I feel eyes on me.

There it is, that sense of being watched again. It's like an old wound. I think of the voice that day on the beach. I think of the movement behind me when I walked to the monument.

What is out there?

What is coming for me?

I think of the voice. It came to me after I tried to reach the living on the beach that day. *Enough. Enough.* Raking, foul, threatening. *Enough* . . . I stop walking. A coldness runs through me.

Is that what's out there?

Are Joyce and Henry wrong? Does something guard the living? I look around. I look back to the woods. I think it's there, back there. I finger my wedding ring.

Not this time.

I scan the darkness, the silver shadows and the black trees. Nothing. But I know it's there.

Not this time!

I will go on. I will reach my house. I will know!

I turn my back on whatever is out there, whatever hunts me. I stride forward. I feel those eyes on my back. I steady my focus on the broken old tarmac. I want to sing, sing a compelling song to myself, something to march to. But I cannot sing, not here. I try to think of better times, of better places. I remember walking at night and feeling safe and secure. Feeling happy and safe and secure.

I remember!

My pace is steady now. I walk on. I remember! I was a child. I was with Dad.

It was in the middle of a very long summer. I must have been eight or nine; I'm not sure which exactly. Tom's family had gone away for a fortnight; they'd gone to Butlin's at Skegness. Whilst I'd heard tales of the monorail train that took happy campers all around the site I wasn't jealous because we had our beach hut, but I was sometimes bored on the days Dad was working and we didn't go. It was teatime on one such day. I was in the garden by the apple trees, digging trenches and fortifications for my 1:32 scale World War Two soldiers.

'Magnus!' Dad called from the house. It made me stop and sit up with a start. Not because I hadn't realised he'd come home from work, but because he rarely called me. He would usually come and find me and talk in his gentle slow voice. He called my name again, his voice big and cheerful. I abandoned my reconstruction of Pegasus Bridge and ran up the garden. Our garden was long and narrow and I sprinted along beside the washing line that ran from the house to our little orchard. Inside I found Mum and Dad sitting at the kitchen table. Mum looked excited and just a little proud as she looked from me to Dad and back again. Dad looked up and smiled, cracks and laughter lines reaching out across his big face.

'Sit down, Magnus,' he said. Mum continued to glow with excitement. I sat down between the two of them. 'I've been thinking about my army days,' Dad explained simply.

'I've been playing army. The British paratroops are beating the Germans easy—'

'Good!' Dad grinned. He glanced at Mum. 'Now I've decided that it's time I got my old army kit out, me tarp' and me mess tins an' stuff, and went on an adventure.' I remember my heart stopped. This was major league stuff. I hardly dared to hope, but hope I did. And then it came: 'And I wondered if you wanted to come along, Boh?' My hopes were answered!

'Yeah!' I shouted. Mum laughed.

'Right, that's decided, then. Luckily Mum's already packed your stuff in me bag.'

That was it. Dad had often talked about how when he was a boy he would wander off for days with nothing but a blanket and a bit of canvas to hang over a tree branch as a tent. They were stories of wonder to me, windows on to an exciting world that I longed to see for myself. And that evening we set off to do just that! The plan was to walk until dark, camp and then continue on to reach the beach hut some time the next morning, where Mum and Julie would be waiting with the car.

We walked out of Framlingham, heading east toward the coast. We followed the back lane and reached open country after passing the big house that Dad always called Mud Hall. There was a bright moon but the hedges and the trees cast dark shadows. Usually I would have been afraid, but I was with my dad and nothing could touch me.

It was the best night. We walked and we talked, my dad and me. Dad had a beautiful way of talking, the gentle singsong of old Suffolk. It was quiet, simple and direct. He was either for something or against it. Being against it didn't mean he was at odds with it; it just meant it wasn't for him. And if he was *for* something he'd *go in for it*. There wasn't much time lost to the subtleties of degrees of interest.

I don't go in much for football.

I'm against motorways.

I'm for cricket, although I don't go in for it as much as when I was young.

That old boy used to go in for darts – he loved it!

I go in for sailing.

And if anything was well engineered or if an animal was well kept or a job well done it was simply either beautiful or wonderful.

By the time I got there they'd dug out a beautiful hole.

I go in for sailing. I've got a beautiful little boat with a wonderful red sail.

It's a way of speaking that's gone now. And that's such a shame. Vince and Tom and I used to use the odd phrase as a sort of bond of kinship between us. Like referring to each other as *Boh* – pronounced as in the end of the word 'neighbour', of which it is a truncation – when we were clowning or as thick as thieves.

Do you want a whisky, Boh?

Did you see the arse on that, Boh?

We would also say *Coh* – pronounced to rhyme with *Boh* – to mean 'wow!' or 'oh my God!' A nineteenth-century OMG.

The world is being invaded by aliens!

Coh! Is it, Boh?

We talked about the beautiful and wonderful things Dad had seen that day. We talked about Tom and Butlin's. We talked about the Second World War. We talked about Mum and Julie. We talked about swimming. We talked about getting a dog. We talked about not getting a dog. We talked about Morecambe and Wise. We talked about Mike Yarwood. We talked about Jimmy Savile, about Jim'll Fix It – yeah, that's right, we did, yeah. We talked about the stars and how to find your way by them. We talked about unions. We talked about westerns, about Clint Eastwood, John Wayne and Lee Van Cleef. We talked about rabbits and Dad explained his theory that rabbits give up and die easily because in the wild they don't have much to live for on account of everything above ground trying to eat them and even when down in their holes them being bloody horrible to each other. That got us on to talking about *Watership Down* which we'd all been to see at the cinema that summer. That means I was nine and not eight. Dad admitted that it was one of his favourite films. We talked about *The Professionals* and *Blake's Seven*. And we talked about when Dad was a boy. I remember talking about that after we set up camp by a stream that cut through a meadow close to the village of Kelsale.

Dad had draped his tarpaulin over a low willow branch and we'd had the bread, cheese, crisps and chocolate Mum had packed up for us.

The cheese-on-cheese taste of Wotsits lingered even after I had run my finger round my gums to collect the leftover paste. We were settled by a little fire of twigs and sticks that had burned down to embers, me laying on my nylon sleeping bag and Dad sitting cross-legged. My sleeping bag smelled of our loft and wood smoke. The stream murmured quietly by us and there was the occasional splash of something slipping into the water. At one point, there was a mad flurry of splashing and a strange cry that I fancied was an otter tackling some floating waterfowl. I'm sure there were no otters in that little brook and even if there were I doubt they would have been fussed about water birds, but that's what I guessed at the time. From somewhere over on the other bank we could hear cows moving in the darkness. Dad slowly fed the little fire with stick after stick, each bursting into yellow flames and burning bright for a minute or so before joining the embers. The bright flames made the night as dark as pitch beyond our little camp and strange patterns flickered across the tarpaulin. But all of these things didn't matter. I was with my dad who used to be in the army and used to be a boxer, and there was nothing out there that he couldn't beat up.

Dad was happy. He was content. I remember him saying that life was too hectic and that it used to be simpler when he was a boy. He had a far-off look as he recalled days gone by. I didn't understand, because I was with my dad, having an adventure, and it was brilliant. What could be simpler than that? I guess we were just looking at things differently. That night I fell asleep warm and contented, listening to the sound of Dad softly singing his happy song.

44

Tom Waits' voice continued to gently fill my flat. We'd had 'Midnight Lullaby' and – ironically, appropriately, inevitably, coincidentally, fatefully and absolutely – 'I Hope That I Don't Fall in Love with You' and we'd just started on the timeless, melancholy 'Martha'. I walked around the breakfast bar holding two mugs of tea. One – mine – had a Spitfire banking across a deep blue sky that reminded me of home and the other – Isla's – had a Lancaster bomber. I'd kicked my boots off and I could feel the ridges in the weave of my rug as I crossed over to her.

'This is beautiful,' Isla said, her voice still low.

You're beautiful, I thought.

She still looked small in the corner of the sofa. Her eyes stayed on mine as she spoke and then moved to the shrine, the fairy lights reflecting in them. All the time the music had been playing she had done this: looking at me and then looking away quickly. I would smile but her focus would dart away.

'This is one of those albums that gives more every time you listen to it.'

'Who is it?' Isla asked. This time she didn't turn away, perhaps because I was right there with our mugs of tea.

'Tom Waits,' I said, my voice as much of a question as an answer. Did she really not know who it was? Isla nodded thoughtfully, her hand finding her watch. Still she didn't look away, her eyes staying on mine. They were sad but bright. I don't know why but I thought about Dad and *Watership Down* for a moment. Instinctively I moved cautiously, as if gaining the trust of that same nervous animal from downstairs that might take flight at any moment. Rather than join her on the sofa I stayed where I was. I sank slowly down so that I was sitting cross-legged on the rug. A car horn sounded angrily once and then again from somewhere close by, perhaps down in the Square or across on the esplanade. Isla didn't seem to notice it, her eyes staying on me. I reached forward in slowly and put her Lancaster bomber mug down on the bare boards between the rug and the seat. It was a big heavy mug that clumped on to the wood. I settled back and cupped my own drink in my hands.

'There you go . . . ,' I said cautiously.

Isla's eyes moved to the mug and then back to mine: the spell held. 'Thank you,' she whispered, although I don't think she appreciated the fact that she'd been given the Lancaster.

'You're welcome.' I was whispering too now. 'Sorry about the biscuits.' I smiled.

Isla didn't smile back. Her expression was absolutely neutral. Her eyes traced over my face. She brought her hand up to her chest and began to twist and turn that old watch with the other. She looked up over my head for a moment and I thought the spell had broken. She felt far, far away. I didn't speak.

'Did you get on with your dad?' she asked suddenly, her eyes returning to mine.

'Yes,' I said, stating a simple truth.

Isla nodded slowly. Her eyes shone with tears. I wanted to hold her but I was frozen. 'Are you like him?' she asked.

'No,' I said quickly. 'Yes . . . well . . .' It was a strangely difficult question. 'No. He was better than me,' I said. And in that moment, I knew it. 'He was—'

'I don't believe that,' Isla cut me off, her voice resolute.

'But it's the truth. He was just—'

'I didn't know about you,' Isla continued, ignoring what I was saying. In fact, it was as if she was talking to herself. She looked down and shook her head slowly, her hair falling forwards and swaying gently. 'Martha' faded to a soft crackling shish-whosh, that inter-track vinyl call that always reminded me of far-off waves on shingle. 'How could I have?' Isla asked, looking back at me.

'I, er . . .'

'I never dreamed that you were here,' Isla explained, looking around the room. 'I didn't know you were in the world.' She closed her eyes.

'How could I have known?' She finished so faintly I could hardly make out the words.

I wanted to reach out. I wanted to hold her. But the tiny distance between us felt endless and unbridgeable.

*

I reach the road running down from Blythburgh, the first turn in my journey back to Isla, the first turn amid those few short, but endless miles.

Isla.

The cardinal summer stars still wink through the moonlight. I think of Blythburgh and Dad's stories of Black Shucks. I think of holding Dad's hand as we walked through that night so long ago. I remember thinking about Black Shucks but knowing I was safe with my dad. I remember squeezing his hand and smiling up at him, happy and safe. I remember telling the same stories to Jack last summer and I remember holding his hand while we went exploring with his new torch in the close summer darkness. I remember him smiling up at me and squeezing my hand. I remember May's tiny hand squeezing mine when the fox barked that same night. I remember the magic in her eyes, reflecting back the light of the lantern as she watched it climb into the sky. I think of May and Jack and Isla. Our garden. Our home.

I turn toward Westleton. The road sweeps downhill into the village. I walk on. The moon and those eyes are on my back. I know it. I'm in the centre of the road. My feet fall on the dashed white lines picked out by the moonlight. Crickets chorus in the grass banks either side of me. With the moon behind me my shadow snakes like a thin raggedy spectre.

Birds fly up from behind me!

I hear them take to the wing. I spin around. I glimpse them against the silky night sky. They fly away from back down the little lane, back from where I just came.

It's close now. I know it.

I turn and stride forward. My pace is quick. This night it must change.

This night it *will* change!

This night I will know. I will know once and forever. There can be no turning back. There can be no hiding.

No more secrets, no more denial!

*

Isla opened her eyes and I found my desire reflected back. She didn't look sad anymore and for the first time I realised she was actually younger than me. The distance between us fell away. I slammed my Supermarine Spitfire Mk IV mug down with a decisive thud that sent tea sloshing over the rug. We both stood up. Isla stepped into my arms. Her body was slight and perfect through the soft fabric of her dress and I was immediately ready and aching for her. Our arms moved around each other with a natural ease to make a single whole. As a Hero, I'd known a lot of girls. After every gig there were those who wanted to be able to say they'd fucked a Hero and I'd obliged my share. In bed, I was a filthy-confident but considerate lover and a confirmed pleasure junkie; thrilling a woman, seeing the pleasure in her eyes, was my very best drug of choice. But, pulling Isla to me and kissing her, I knew this was different. I knew this was not to be just some wild fuck; I knew we were to be lovers, Isla and me, and for all my experience and all my confidence my whole body trembled with hers as my hands reached under her dress and traced over her smooth bare skin. Isla broke our kiss and slowly raised her arms, her eyes staying on mine. I lifted her dress over her head and threw it to the side. There she was: her beautiful body. She moved back against me, sliding her knee between my legs. I kissed her mouth and then her neck. She moved her head and sighed low and soft as I kissed downward to her breasts. She ran her hands through my hair. She was perfect. Then we broke and her hands went to my belt. She undid the clasp and worked my buttons. She kissed me on the mouth after each downward glance. She tugged at my jeans, pulling them part down and then her hand found me and she stopped. She looked down and then back up at me. For a moment, for a single beautiful moment of intention, longing and anticipation, we stared into each other's eyes. Then I was pulling off my t-shirt, she tearing at my shorts. Naked, we fell against the sofa. She arched her back and called my name as I entered her that first time. I took her long and hard, driving her down into the sofa. She raked at my back and pulled me into her. When she came she shook and I held her firm, fighting to keep her trembling body from pushing me out. Again she spoke my name. This time it was a velvet whisper, her breath mingling with mine. When her pleasure had subsided, I stood and pulled her to her feet. Our breath was racing and we were both shining with sweat on that humid night.

Old Tom Waits had moved on to 'Closing Time'. I led Isla through to my bedroom. There she was under me, over me, beside me, in front of me and on me as I filled her, tasted her, thrilled her and changed her. We rose and fell through wildly demanding fucking that yielded to passionate, giving, tender lovemaking. Over and over we went, giving, sharing, taking everything from each other, our souls bare and entwined. She shook and sighed and gasped through pleasures that made her eyes tell of far-off places. And I was many things: I was a rutting buck stamping a claim on a stolen prize, I was an experienced wizard skilfully wielding my wand, I was a wily bluesman having my fun, but most of all I was a young man falling in love for the first time. Finally, when we came together in that wrecked nest of sweat-soaked sheets, I rising high with shoulder muscles taut and Isla with legs around me and nails drawing me into her, I knew this was like nothing either of us had known before.

45

Westleton's long narrow green is next to me and the first houses are on either side. I feel eyes on my back.

I *know* I am not alone.

I *know* I am being followed.

But I will go on. I will reach my house.

Isla.

I walk with determined strides. The crickets fall silent. The night is suddenly still. The trees that grow around the green are tall and black. Heavy with leaf they cast inky shadows. This silence, it's like the village is frozen in time. I think of Joyce and Henry talking about time. I love Joyce and I love Henry but they are different. Time still ticks for me, even here. I'm sure of it.

A dog barks!

It's far off across the other side of the village. That proves that time is not still. The village is just sleeping. I continue on. I walk, still in the centre of the road. I feel the living. They are far away but they are close. Closer than they have been for such a long time.

Am I approaching the living? Is this journey taking me to them? Can it? Can I walk to the living? Is that possible? I think of ghosts. I think of all Dad's ghost stories.

A bell tolls!

I stop. I still feel eyes on my back. I *am* being watched. The bell chimes again. It's coming from the church up ahead. Its stone tower rises silver-grey against the night. The chimes continue, light and short. It's the clock. I count. Another dog barks, this time from behind me. I look round. What is out there? What follows me? I continue to count the chimes.

Ten.

I scan the road behind me, the hill stretching back off into the night.

Eleven.

I can see nothing. The stars. The stars have gone. Perhaps the moon is too bright now.

Twelve. Midnight!

I remember Isla took me to see *Henry IV* in Brighton when a small travelling company put on two performances at the Pavilion Theatre.

We have heard the chimes at midnight.

Perhaps I am truly a ghost, a spirit straight out of Dad's stories, walking through the villages. The dog somewhere behind barks again. Another answers it from just ahead. I look around at the windows of the still houses. I feel the living. I do not want to haunt them. I do not want to frighten the children. I move from the centre of the road into the shadows. I carry on, stealing through the night now.

46

Our euphoria, Isla's and mine, subsided through giggling and kissing to holding each other with a tenderness I'd never known before, the sweat drying on our backs and the breeze reaching in through the windows finally bringing a chill to our comfortable nakedness. We smoked cigarettes and talked in whispered voices about nothing and everything, Isla's voice coming like a promise, like spring sunshine that filled me with anticipation. Watching her in the sodium-yellow half-darkness, the line of her fey curves and the warmth of her eyes and lips as she spoke and smiled, there were many moments in which I lost myself. Those drifting moments coalesced into a contented sleepiness.

Lying face to face across a single pillow, I watched Isla's eyes grow heavy, blinking. Then a change came over her, her eyes staying closed for a momentary brush with sleep before opening wide. Her focus moved away from me, far away, her eyes looking down the length of her beautiful body. When she looked back sadness had returned to them. The peace that had enveloped us like the Tide had left her. I moved, pushing the pillow higher with my shoulder, and went to speak. Isla reached over and kissed me first on my lips and then on my forehead, each slow and lingering. She said she had to go. It was the middle of the night and I asked her to stay. She said she couldn't and I knew she meant it. She sat up, looking away from me. I took her hand. She squeezed my fingers and, turning to face me again for a moment, whispered simply that she was sorry. I sat up and pressed her hand to my mouth. I told her not to be sorry. She smiled at me. I said I would walk her home or at least see her to a taxi. Again, she said no and again I knew she meant it.

She dressed in silence. When she looked over I knew she didn't want to leave, but there was that mix of sadness and bravery again, a resolute strength in her.

I wrapped a sheet around myself and went to the door with her. When I reached for the lock she covered my hand with hers and stopped me. She kissed my cheek gently and then lingered as if to whisper something, but she said nothing. She smelled of her perfume and sex and her breathing was soft against my ear. Then she kissed me on the mouth, urgent and passionate. When she moved back her eyes stayed on mine for a long moment. Finally, stepping aside, I opened the door. She walked out into the hall in silence. There she paused and turned back. For the first time I found just a flickering moment of indecision in her face. I thought for just a second that she might stay. But then she was walking away across the landing, head down and hands in front of her, one clasping that watch, with fast little steps like someone hurrying through rain. I watched her disappear down the stairs. She didn't look back; I knew she couldn't. I listened to her footfalls on the steps until I heard the front door open and close. Two great pins fell on to my map in that moment:

I had never been in love before that night.
I had never felt jealousy before that night.

I didn't know whether to cry or sing with joy. The bluesman's lot, I guess. In the end, I started Tom Waits again and took my whisky and cigarettes back to bed with me.

47

The morning after came bright and fresh through my window. I woke blinking into warm sunlight. I was lying naked on my bed and the gathered-up sheets still smelled of sex and Isla. It took me a moment to orientate myself. I turned on to my side, away from the streaming daylight. I found myself face to face with the Stevie Wonder ashtray Vince had given me for my birthday. Old Stevie could barely be seen under the heaped cigarette stubs and ash. I frowned and picked it up as carefully as possible. Leaning over the edge of the bed, I found my whisky bottle empty on the floor and put the ashtray down next to it. I managed to spill a significant amount of the payload, revealing Stevie's sunglasses and some of his smile. I rolled back and stared at the ceiling. When I swallowed, my throat was dry and rasping. I coughed and my chest burned.

I thought of Isla.

Then I noticed the chorus of Brighton coming in with the sunlight: traffic, the rising murmur of so many voices, gulls and a police siren across town. It had been there all along, of course, but I hadn't noticed it. Then more sounds came as I thought about the night before. Music, or at least its filtered bass, was coming through the floor and the bed from Mr Inuit's (Vince's name for the strange man in flat three who looked like Genghis Khan). And there was the rhythmic, crackling shsh-click of my turntable which must have run off the end of Tom Waits hours earlier.

I closed my eyes and thought of Isla. I thought of her there in my bed with me. I thought of our lovemaking, of what we had shared and what we had given. I didn't think of her leaving. I didn't think of her husband or her home or her life in the other Brighton that was filled with the same sounds as the one beyond my window.

Over the years, Isla tried many times to explain how our minds worked and how we thought about some things, noticed some things and skipped over others. About the difference between what reaches our eyes and ears and what reaches our thoughts. About how often decisions and options are illusions or at least made at some basic level within us before our thinking minds pick over them. About how the same place or thing can be so different to two people and how we do not see things in plain sight. About *a priori* evaluations, the filtering of the myriad *facts* that bombard us, subconscious qualitative selection before subjective and objective reasoning. About how Brighton could be two very different places for us. She tried to sum it up with a story about a beer can, a motorcycle in need of a shim and two dear friends that she'd taken from Robert Pirsig. But I never really got her, never really understood until now. But in our relationship Isla was the philosopher and I the artist, and to paraphrase the great Tom Waits: *it was momma and not poppa who was the brains.*

I smiled. By rights and in the name of any sort of justice on earth I should have had a pint's worth of whisky hangover, but I didn't! I realised my head was clear! I opened my eyes and sat up. I ran my hand over my face, my stubble scratching. I looked at the open window and smiled into the sunlight. I got to my feet and stood by the sill, naked and happy, looking out on to the Square and life below. I hauled the sash pane up as far as it would go and leaned out. The air came sea salt touched by diesel. I stretched out into the warm morning. Down in the Square gardens below, a couple walked hand in hand. Again, I thought of Isla. I thought of putting down a blanket and having a picnic with her there in the gardens. It was a plan that would have required me to buy my first picnic blanket. Watching the couple walk, I realised they were older than I'd first thought. Yet they moved against each other, walking lightly and laughing together.

Lovers in the morning, I thought to myself.

Then I was off, a song forming line by line, sentiment by sentiment. Love. Summer. Isla. At last the creative breeze had come again, ready to push us out of those doldrums. It had been so long since a song had come without being raked for. I showered, sentiments and words forming into lines while I washed, the water coming like cold needles against my flesh before finally warming and filling the cubicle with steam. Returning to my bedroom, I went to the dowdy chest of drawers that had come with the flat and which I'd later customised with a glow-in-the-dark sticker set of stars and flying saucers from the newsagent in Churchill Square, and pulled out clean shorts and socks; well, it was already panning out to be a special sort of a day after all. I heaved up my jeans and walked through to the living room, pulling a t-shirt over my wet hair. I picked the phone up off the floor, guiding the cord clear of the standard lamp, and dialled, Bakelite receiver firmly wedged between my ear and shoulder. I knew the number backwards and dialled automatically, my mind still on my emerging song and Isla. Four rings purred at me before the call was answered.

'Two, seven, one, eight, nine, eight,' came Kelly's voice, business-like and ever-so-slightly old-fashioned.

'Kelly!' I shouted with a start, her voice waking me from my thoughts.

'Mags? What are you doing up? What's happened? You all right?'

'I'm fine, Kells, fine!'

'You sure?' Kelly sounded confused.

'Yeah, yeah. I want to work, Kells.'

'Work? You want to work now?'

'Yeah!'

'But we're only over to Portsmouth tonight. We don't need to go until about six—'

'No, yeah, no – I know. I mean, I want to write.'

'Really?' Now Kelly sounded surprised *and* confused.

'Yeah, really. Now come over. Bring the Jazzmaster.'

'You're not pissing with me, are you, Magnus Lancaster?'

'No! Now get over here and wear something nice because I might even take you out to lunch, if you play your cards right.'

'I'm on my way!'

I heard Kelly's phone clatter on to the hook and the line became a near-silence, perforated only by the impossibly distant clicks of circuits way off in the ether of the telephone never-world.

Shuffling, evolving, pairing and linking lyrics first in my head and then out loud, I put Tom Waits away and then spun up a John Lee Hooker CD. The player was set on random and when 'Whiskey and Wimmen' came at me I stopped and grinned. Digging around my kitchen, I couldn't help but nod to John Lee. I opened a new tin of Illy and packed my coffee pot full for a strong brew, which I left bubbling on a low heat while I ran round to the café that used to be at the end of Sillwood Street for takeout doughnuts and bagels. Kelly and I always did our best work on full stomachs. By the time I pulled my door shut John Lee had moved on to 'Maudie'.

Stepping out into the sunlight that morning felt good. Despite the background hum of life in Brighton, there wasn't a soul around on my side of the Square so I jogged up the road thinking of Isla.

48

By late afternoon Kelly and I were well fed and deep into what was already a bloom of new material. We were on a high, we were feeling pretty damn good, pretty damn triumphant. The doughnuts had done their job and we'd lost ourselves to the magic that grew between us when things clicked and we found Vince's (and Jack Kerouac's) *It*. We'd worked on, oblivious to the time, my threat of lunch failing to mature. The only interruption had come in the form of a phone call, a phone call from Isla. She couldn't speak, but just wanted to say hello – just *had* to say hello. She sounded like a schoolgirl and that made me feel like a schoolboy. She said she couldn't stop thinking about me.

Was I going to be home on Sunday?

Yes.

She'd call round late afternoon. Bye!

Well, that just sent me up another gear. I was back at the piano testing tunes and stopping to scribble lyrics before Kelly could ask the *who* or *what* that were all over her face.

And there we were – I at the piano, Kelly standing over me, Jazzmaster in hand, matching chords to my playing, her bare feet tapping; she always seemed to tap with both feet, rising and falling like an understated Irish jig. Our pace was swift, stopping briefly to talk over or edit our jotted lyrics and test-sing a few words, with Kelly joining in or interrupting me excitedly to suggest the next tweak, bouncing notes and riffs and words off each other and driving the work to places neither of us could ever take it on our own. It was good. We were good. Then the intercom buzzer sounded.

'I'll get it,' I said, stepping away from the piano. Kelly nodded without looking up. She was crossing through some words on her pad and writing alternatives in her quick, excited scrawl.

'Heh-low!' I called into the grill.

'Bishop to king seven. Checkmate, I think,' came Vince's voice, crackling, tinny and far away. More *Blade Runner*, I'm afraid.

'Got a brainstorm, hey, Sebastian? Milk and cookies kept you awake, ha? Let's discuss this. You'd better come up,' I replied, running tightly to the script.

I opened the door to the landing and, taking the downstairs key and oversized tennis ball fob from the coat hooks, walked back to the lounge and the sound of Kelly strumming a variation on our second song of the day. Without breaking my stride, I executed a near perfect, if a little theatrical, overarm cricket bowl and sent the key sailing through the open balcony door to the street below.

'The guys are here.'

Kelly looked up from her guitar and nodded. I returned to my seat at the piano and retrieved the cigarette I'd left on top in the ashtray, now more a long finger of ash than anything else.

I heard Tom laughing first, then their voices and finally the sound of their feet tramping up the last few steps. Kelly leaned her guitar carefully against the piano.

'Hey!' Vince called, emerging from the hallway with arms outstretched for a hug. He was, of course, wearing his black suit, this time with a collarless white shirt. His dreadlocks had the voluminous puffiness that they always took on after they'd been wet. 'Hey!' he called again when he saw Kelly. Tom followed, smiling. Tom, even measured by his own standards, was having a particularly sharp day, with a tightly buttoned tailored blue jacket that had a whole Napoleonic thing going on.

Vince got his hug from Kelly, squeezing and lifting her to her tiptoes. Tom, on the other hand, gave her a kiss on both cheeks with an urbaneness to complement his jacket. Then he looked at me. Then he looked at the piano. With a tsk-tsk he waved me off the seat. I got up and let him sit. Wasting no time, he cracked his fingers and tapped a few exploratory notes.

I was aware that Vince was unusually quiet. Looking over, I found him leaning on the breakfast bar, smiling knowingly at me, those eyes a twinkling but sharp inquisition.

'Well?' he said simply.

'Well what?'

'Well . . .' Tom put in, playing an expectant little jingle to serve as drum roll. 'How did it go last night?'

'Oh . . . yeah . . .'

Kelly looked between the three of us with an expression that said my lifted mood was starting to make sense to her

'Did you fuck her, Boh?' Vince grinned.

I looked at him, I looked at Tom, I looked at Kelly. All faces suddenly keen, all eyes on mine, searching for tells of an answer. In my thoughts, I cast Vince's *Did you fuck her, Boh?* against what Isla and I had shared: the passion and the tender intimacy, the joyful pleasure and the loving caresses, the beautiful joining of our bodies and souls.

'Yeah!' I shouted, looking at the ceiling and stretching out my arms like a third-rate impression of Christ the Redeemer. Well, I was young and chuffed. Vince bundled into me first, with Tom's weight slamming in a moment later.

'Jesus Christ,' Kelly sighed.

'Yes! That's my Maggie!' Vince sang, doing his best to get me in a headlock.

All I could think about was Isla. Even in that dreadlock tangled scrum, all I could think about was Isla, the night before, lying together. Holding each other right there in my still unmade bed.

*

I reach the far side of Westleton. I look back at the sleeping houses. I feel the living among them. So far away, yet nearer and nearer this night. I think of my home. Close now. Just a mile or two more. I think of my bed. I think of lying there on warm summer nights in the stillness that comes before dawn. Listening, listening but hearing only Isla's peaceful breathing and nothing of the rest of the world. Listening for dawn and listening into the house for Jack and May. Nothing stirring. Feeling as if I was the only soul awake across all England, across all of the fields and all of the villages and all of the towns and all of the woods and all of the heaths and all of the beaches that stretched endlessly away from my window. The window hidden in darkness and waiting to be revealed by the first blues of day. That limbo place that was mine alone each night toward the end and that now I think was perhaps preparation for this place. Except then there was nothing stalking me beyond the window, nothing watching me from among those fields, or woods, or heaths or beaches. Or was there?

I wonder if Isla and Jack and May are sleeping? Sleeping just over there. Just over there, ahead of me. I walk on. My steps are steady and even.

Isla, I'm coming.

There's a hint of light in the east. I look for movement, my eyes scanning the shadows. Nothing.

But I know. I know I am not alone. There is something there.

I know it.

I focus on the road ahead.

I walk on. My pace is good and steady. I look west, into the darker west. The moon is higher now. I look down. My shadow is a pool of darkness around me. The raggedy spectre has gone. Ahead the stars have moved, the Plough has wheeled south. I study them and think of Dad. I follow their patterns. I find Leo and think of Jack. I trace down toward the horizon in search of Gemini. But it is blank. I search the low sky above the fields. There must be a cloudbank there. Up ahead, toward my journey's end. The stars there are hidden. Pale grey shapes curve along the horizon and hide them. One, two, three great domes. They're familiar. My eyes trace their edges, stars above, nothing below. They are like hills.

Yes! That's it!

They look like the Brecon Beacons. I miss the hills, the beacons. I think of Tom and me toiling on their slopes and standing on their peaks, our customary handshake, and Vince far below in the town, drinking and wondering why we did it.

*

184

'So this . . .' Vince paused from making the tea and frowned his enquiry at me.

'Isla,' I prompted. I loved her name and I loved using it, saying it, speaking it to my friends.

'Yeah, Isla,' Vince nodded. He moved from the left to the right-hand cupboard above the breakfast bar, rising high on his toes to peer inside.

'There's no biscuits,' I said and this time it was the truth.

Vince acknowledged that he believed me with a slow disappointed nod. Then, he gave one of his philosophical frowns along with the quick squeeze of his Elvis lip-stud that in combination meant he was trying to remember what he'd been saying. 'Yeah,' he continued. 'So this . . .'

'Isla.'

'Yeah . . .'

'I like it!' Kelly shouted at Tom. He was running over a suggested tweak to her tune, the piano singing beautifully.

'Yeah,' Vince said for the third time. 'Is she coming tonight?'

'No.' For the first time since waking I thought about Isla's husband, this fucking Duncan cunt, out there in that other Brighton. There it was, harsh, stark and ugly: jealousy, nudging and feeling its way into my life. 'She can't tonight,' I explained simply.

'That's a shame,' Vince replied lightly. He studied the mug tree and carefully selected four, setting them out in a line by the kettle: Spitfire, Lancaster, Hurricane and Messerschmitt 109. I watched him drop a teabag into each one and then move along the line with the milk, working with great care and precision.

'Coffee for me,' came Kelly's voice over the piano.

'Yeah.' Vince laughed quietly to himself, assuming as always that Kelly was joking on the basis that clearly no one drank coffee in the afternoon: coffee in the morning, tea in the afternoon, booze after six. Watching him, I thought about Isla, about her leaving. I found myself wondering what her home was like.

'Tea's up!' Vince's voice brought me back from Isla's house. The piano fell instantly silent and Kelly and Tom walked over. 'Picked this one out for you specially, Tom-Tom,' Vince grinned, his lips curling around the hand-rolled cigarette he'd just relit. He pushed one of the mugs forward.

'I'm not having the fucking one-o-nine again,' Tom replied matter-of-factly.

'Is that the one with the yellow propeller?' Kelly checked.

'Yeah,' Vince confirmed.

'Oh, I'll have it, then,' she said happily. Tom and Vince laughed. 'No biscuits?' she asked.

'No, Maggie-May's let us down again on that one,' Vince replied damningly.

'Shame. I'm starving.'

'Yeah, me too,' Tom agreed, lifting the Hurricane from the worktop and taking a sip.

'Oh, yeah! I forgot to tell you!' Vince suddenly remembered. All eyes went to him. 'This morning for breakfast I did a Findus crispy pancake toasted sandwich!'

Kelly frowned; I think I did too.

'What?' Tom asked on behalf of us all.

Vince put the Lancaster down to free his hands. 'A crispy pancake toasted sandwich,' he said again, this time with a mime of holding a large sandwich.

'What, a Findus crispy pancake *inside* a toasted sandwich?' Tom checked.

'Yeah!' Vince nodded keenly.

'You lie!' I dismissed.

'Vince never lies,' Tom reasoned. Vince nodded with eyebrows raised in agreement. And Tom was right: Vince never, ever lied.

'What was it like?' Kelly asked, taking a sip from the Messerschmitt. 'Ugh, Vince, I said coffee.'

Vince grinned around his cigarette again and gave a short laugh. 'It was brilliant,' he said.

Kelly nodded thoughtfully.

'Why don't you give her a ring about tonight? I mean, it's only Portsmouth; she could easily come in the van. I don't mind sitting in the back if it's only Portsmouth,' Vince offered.

'No,' I said quietly, looking down at the Spitfire and the steam lifting from it.

'Why not?'

'Well, I'm not sure when it's safe to call for a start,' I explained, looking up.

'Hey?' Vince checked. Tom looked down. Kelly looked up.

'Well, you know, if her husband's there or if he answers and . . .' I knew what was coming and sure enough it came.

'Husband?' Vince repeated, his voice flat.

'Yeah . . .'

'She's married? This, Isla bird, is married?' Vince continued.

'Yeah,' I confirmed. I hated saying it. I hated it being true. I put the Spitfire back on the worktop and lit a cigarette.

Kelly looked at me with concern, her big keen eyes suddenly motherly. Tom, who already new about Isla being married, didn't look up.

'We are talking about the bird from Camden, the photographer? The fit one?' Vince double-checked. I nodded. 'She's married?'

'Yes!' I snapped. 'Yes, she's fucking married!'

There was a pause. Then Kelly touched me gently on the arm.

'Well, that's no good, is it?' Vince said, his voice steady, calm and - just to match Kelly's expression - fatherly. Suddenly he looked very much the preacher-man from those Clint Eastwood westerns. 'Not for her *or* you. It's not right,' he concluded simply. I said nothing by way of an ironically filial response.

'It's early days yet,' Tom countered, finally looking up.

'That's what worries me,' Vince replied. He looked at each of us. Kelly frowned her appeal to go easy. Tom looked concerned. I looked down. Vince sighed reluctantly. 'It's wrong,' he said apologetically. 'It's just wrong.'

49

In the end, the rain followed us back from the Downs that last time I visited Vince in Brighton. We were sitting at the little table in his glorious kitchen. We'd been there for a while. It was late afternoon and the rain clouds had taken away the last of the sunshine, the warm colours fading from those few patches of white wall that weren't covered in photographs. The light that remained wasn't gloomy but spoke simply of evening. We'd finished our tea, or rather Vince had; I'd left mine and it had gone cold. We'd talked about this and that, mostly this and that concerning Tom. Vince had phoned Catherine the day before and she'd said the doctors had let Tom come home, which she was thrilled about. The surgery hadn't been *one hundred per cent effective*, whatever that meant, but the doctors were already talking about other avenues to explore, so she and Tom were *keeping positive*. Vince said she sounded hopeful, in good spirits even. It sounded desperate to me and I'm sure it sounded desperate to Vince too. Although when I'd said so he had looked down and smoked his cigarette. We'd ended up sitting in silence.

The room was warm and smoky and with the fading light I'd felt sleepy. I'd found myself listening to the rain spouting and gurgling from the guttering beyond the window and watching it run in rivulets down the glass, pooling on the tatty white gloss woodwork. At home, I would never have stopped and simply listened to the rain, but in Vince's world there was always time for such things: for cloud watching, for rain listening, for talking about days gone by, for sitting quietly. Having not slept properly for days, I found the rain hypnotic and I even stopped looking at my watch. It made me think of Dad. He loved nothing better than sitting by the fire and listening to the rain and the wind outside and my thoughts took me off with him for a while.

Suddenly my thoughts about Dad, the stuff happening with Tom and being surrounded by so many photographs of the past all came together and made me sit up and say what I said next.

'When was the last time you spoke to your dad?' I asked.

'Hmm?' Vince replied, returning from his own quiet thoughts and looking at me across the oversized ashtray.

'Your dad – when was the last time you spoke?'

Vince sat forward, resting his elbows on the table. Even in that light his eyes were still unavoidable. I looked back and waited for him to answer. From nowhere I'd somehow gone from sleepy to angry. This wasn't unusual by then, but never with Vince. I was suddenly filled with a melancholy sense of the briefness of life, of the years that had flashed by since many of the photographs around us had been taken. Of youth gone. Of moments lost. Of people lost. I wished I could talk to my dad. That was a frequent wish in those last months.

I liked Vince's dad. Everyone did. He was a proud man and could come across as a little stiff and old-fashioned, even stern perhaps, but equally he was always patient and understanding: all the traits of his professional life. Sadly, though, he and Vince just couldn't seem to find peace with one another. Ever since we were children they had clashed. Vince's mum said it was because they were so alike and she was right. They still lived in Framingham and I'd bump into them every once in a while, when I was back seeing Mum. They always seemed genuinely pleased to see me, and they adored Jack and May. Vince's dad would make a point of shaking my hand and he'd be keen to talk about me rather than himself, as was his way. He would talk with interest about anything I had to say, but he would never ask after Vince. Of course, if Vince's mum was there she'd mention him and then his Dad would fall silent, disengaging from the conversation and appearing suddenly distant, but his eyes would be focused on me – intense, keen, blue inquisitor's eyes just like his son's that always betrayed the eagerness for news that he was too proud to show. Consequently, you just didn't talk to Vince about his dad. Perhaps that's why Vince took so long to reply. He looked down and put his head in his hands. He messed up his already messy hair. Finally, he looked back up.

'A long time.'

'You should talk to him, you know.'

Vince studied me. 'I wish I could,' he said quietly.

'But you can, Vince, you can. And you won't be able to for ever—'

'I can't, Mags . . . We just – you know how it is . . . and then Mum gets upset and . . .' Vince frowned, searching for words that for once didn't come to him. Shaking his head slowly, he slid another cigarette from the packet on the table. It was my turn to put my head in my hands. I tried to massage the tiredness from my temples.

'Vince, I'm sorry, mate . . . I shouldn't have—'

'It's all right, Mags,' Vince said graciously. He studied me again for a moment and then continued with all solemnity gone from his voice. 'After all, you can't help being a cunt, can ya, Boh?' he reasoned with a wink and grinned around his cigarette. But the grin faded quickly. 'And perhaps you're right,' he finished slowly.

That's where I left Vince, sitting at his kitchen table surrounded by his plants, his pictures and his memories. I suspect I left us both thinking about our fathers; I know I certainly was. It was dark out on the street. The light from the streetlamps caught the rain and the road shone an inky black beneath them. I pulled my coat close around me and ran over to the car, my shoes splashing through the swollen gutters and my feet instantly wet and cold. The car smelled of Vince's cigarette smoke but I didn't mind; in fact I quite liked it. I struggled to get my long coat off whilst sitting in the driver's seat. With some squirming and pulling I managed to get free of it and threw it on the back seat.

I drove down to the seafront and along the esplanade past Bedford Square. I thought of Isla, of when we were young. When we had our love affair. It occurred to me – I think for the first time properly – that Dad had never met Isla. It seemed incredibly strange to me that these two parts of my life had never touched. After Bedford Square came Preston Street and I wondered if Papa's was still there. I thought of our wedding day. Then came the Grand Hotel with its very own lay-by, that little bite of tarmac that had planted something disgusting in me so many years ago on the day two Brightons collided. I looked at the cat in the centre of my steering wheel and realised that, despite all the years, that part of me had never moved on. Finally, I drove up by the Pavilion and the Level, remembering one drunken night when Tom, Vince and I rode a luggage trolley from the station across it as if it was the fiery chariot of the gods. From there I headed out of town, up Ditchling Road, not because it was the quickest route but because it was the road Isla and I always drove up to the big Asda by the A27.

I don't know whether it was because Tom was so ill, or whether it was being back in Brighton surrounded by all those memories, or just seeing Vince and stepping into the enchanted peace of his simple life – probably a mix of them all – but by the time I reached the A23 and turned north toward home I wanted to talk to my dad more than ever. I remember clearly looking in the rear-view mirror and seeing the black line of the Downs against the sky behind me. That was the moment that I finally spoke to him. God knows I'd wanted to; I'd wanted his help, his guidance. I'd wanted him to hear my confessional. Especially at the end, especially in that last year or so. But through all the years I would never let myself believe he could hear me, believe that he was there.

'Well, Dad, that's my last time in Brighton,' I said aloud. I said it because in the last few months I think I knew the end was close. No. I didn't think it. Deep down I *knew* it. I didn't admit it to myself, but I knew. I don't know how, but I did. I think everyone does. I felt as if something was out there, something was coming for me. I felt as if a storm was gathering somewhere out of sight and that something hidden in its shadow was stalking me. Something terrible and dark and bitter. And on that day, I felt for the first time that Dad was close enough to hear me.

The words just wouldn't stop as I drove. I told him how I missed him and how I wished he and I could go for another walk: camp in the meadows and then go to the beach and our hut and his boat, his beautiful little boat with a wonderful red sail. To the beach hut that I knew wasn't there anymore. Then I told him about Isla and Jack and

May, about my family, about the three people in the centre of my world whom he'd never met. I told him that Isla was beautiful. I told him about how brave Jack had been when we left him at school for the first morning, his little determined face when he smiled at Isla and me as we walked to the door. I told him that when Jack had bad dreams he cried for his mum and when May had nightmares she cried for me. I told him how much I loved that. I told him that May liked horses and watched *Black Beauty* over and over and over. I told him that Jack loved *Star Wars*. I told him that Jack loved to ride in the car with me when the roof was down. I told him how his face would light up if I invited him to come for a drive. I told him how May squeezed my hand if I felt upset before I even knew that I did. I told him how Isla did the same. I told him how Jack looked as if he'd burst with pride when I praised him. I told him how when May cuddled up to Isla on the sofa they would both fall asleep and I told him how beautiful and peaceful they looked. I told him how Isla always knew the right thing to say when Jack and May were worried or hurt or upset. I told him how May's voice chimed like singing when she was talking to her toys and imaginary horse. I told him how Jack loved to run. I told him how people smiled at me when I held May's hand in Waitrose. I told him how Jack would cry if May hurt herself and how May would cry if Jack was sad. I told him how Isla smiled at me when Jack and May walked ahead of us hand in hand.

I talked all the way until the Dartford Crossing. Then it happened. Just as surely as if Dad had come back and said it directly, I was reminded of an important lesson he taught me: that lying by omission is still lying. I was edging forward in a queue for the auto-tolls. I looked to my left and saw the side of a tall white van. I looked forward and saw that the silver BMW that had been at the booth when I joined the queue was finally pulling away. I glanced at the dashboard clock: 7.20 p.m. I glanced at my watch: 7.20 p.m. I looked right. There was a family just like mine. Mother, father and two small children: a boy and a girl about the same age as Jack and May. They were in a Discovery. It could have been *our* Discovery. The little girl was crying. The little boy was staring forward at his father, eyes locked on his back. The woman was looking down at her lap. Her eyes were closed. The man kept angrily gesturing along the line of vehicles they'd joined. He'd gesture forward, throw up his arms in despair, look up at the ceiling, bang the steering wheel. When the queue moved their car lurched forward. It was like looking at an ugly mirror. I hadn't told Dad the whole truth about my life.

Once I was clear I pulled over on the hard shoulder just after the tunnel and I wept. I hadn't cried for years and years. The traffic roared past and the car rocked when lorries raced by on the near lane.

50

Dawn came brightly across the meadow to our little camp – Dad's and mine – among the willows. I woke to birdsong. The air was cool and brought the fresh, verdant smell of a new summer day with it. Under the lee of the tarpaulin all was shades of blue. Dad was already dressed, sitting silently on his sleeping bag, looking out across the stream. Hearing me stir, he looked around and smiled, the map of laughter and seasons under the fierce East Anglian sun cracking over his face.

'Morning, Boh,' he said quietly.

'Hello, Dad,' I smiled, sitting up. The air was chill against my bare shoulders. Dad passed me my t-shirt, my favourite blue Adidas with white stripes that looked like an Ipswich Town football shirt and which Mum had to wrestle away from me to wash. I pulled it on and, still in my sleeping bag, shuffled over to him. He was looking out to the east. Strips of morning cloud blazed like mountains of orange and gold along the horizon and told of the rising sun just beyond. A low mist was hanging over the meadow and a lone oak standing far off in the middle was a sketchy silhouette. A distant voice called from farther off still, from the edge of the village itself. Beneath the tree cows stirred, their great bulks suddenly discernible as they moved silently toward the call.

Dad lit the little fire again, building it just high enough to boil the tin kettle he'd brought along and filled from the stream. We had a breakfast of hot chocolate with lumps of sweetener that crunched when I chewed on them and angel cake squashed almost flat and sticking to the cling film it had been wrapped in, but tasting deliciously like vanilla ice cream. The sun reached over the trees along the far edge of the meadow and burned away the mist while we ate. Shortly after 6.30 we were off again, my Dad and me, just walking along the road together, talking this and that on our way to the sea: to Mum and Julie, to our beach hut, to a long happy summer day and a beautiful little boat with a wonderful red sail.

To quote the great Lou Reed, *it was a perfect day*. And it was a perfect day *because* I spent it with my dad. I sometimes worry that with Dad and me both gone those moments have gone too. With no one left to remember them, did they ever really happen? In every quiet corner of the world, every silent, peaceful place, how many stories have been forgotten, how many forgotten lives have touched them? I always thought that perhaps Dad and I would walk in his Meadow he talked about from the Norse stories and that we'd explore the forests and the hills and the mountains beyond the river and talk of such times, but he's not here and so this can't be his Meadow. Can it?

But then I guess it must have happened because it led to so much, so much of me. It led to family camping holidays starting the next year, then to family hill walking holidays, first in the Lake District and later the Brecon Beacons and the Black Mountains that we all fell in love with. We went there every year until college and then I went with Vince and Tom. And it led to high mountains, mountains around the world, first with Isla in the Pyrenees and later the foothills of the Himalayas, then finally solo visits to the Alps when Jack was still tiny, to the moment I told Vince about that last time in Brighton, that pin in my map when I stood on the summit of Mont Blanc.

51

The gig at Portsmouth went fantastically. The Heroes rocked! We had *It* and the unlikely mix of students from the poly' and navy ratings ate it up. It was the sixth time we'd played that venue, a big club near the docks, and we'd developed something of a following that demanded no less than three encores. We'd been hitting a bottle of Wild Turkey that Vince had rustled up when we left Brighton and with the vibe in that room we were on fire. While we played, while I sang and flirted with so many faces, so many eyes wanting to catch mine, I found myself scanning for Isla. I looked over the faces, over the hands that reached up toward me, through the smoke and swaying bodies, and searched for her in every eddy, every glimpse into the sea of people. I knew she wouldn't be there, of course, but I couldn't help but hope; hope that I'd see the camera, the photographer, Isla. And anyway, in the words of the King, by then she was simply *always on my mind*.

A group called the *Excellents* were on after us. They were amazing. There must have been twenty of them! I'd never seen anything like it. They had four singers, all guys, who sang northern soul in perfect harmonies, three backing singers, complete with beehives, swaying behind them, with nothing short of an orchestra in support. They had a full brass section: trumpets, a trombone, alto and bass saxophones, a mix of horns and even a tuba! We stayed backstage listening for a while, still riding the high that that Portsmouth crowd had given us. Tom – Mr Cool – tapped his foot, Kelly and I danced around arm in arm as if it was Dexy's Midnight Runners on the stage and Vince took some pictures. The little flash on his camera caught the eye of one of the backing singers who turned around and swung her hips through a little shimmy just for Vince. It was one of those perfect shots: she looked beautiful and joyful in a way that can only ever come from being on stage in front of an audience like that. In fact, I remember picking her out on Vince's wall that last time I went to Brighton.

Vince had enlisted the help of a group of WRENs on a weekend pass from *HMS Temeraire* and the van was loaded quickly to the sounds of the Excellents filtering out of the back of the club. At some point, he disappeared along with one of their number for twenty minutes, only to return, contrary to our collective guess as to why he had gone, with a feast of Chinese food, bag after bag, tub after tub, enough to feed fifty, let alone the twelve of us. In hindsight, I shouldn't have been so surprised. When a gig went that well and we ended up buzzing with that much excitement, Vince always got hungry before he got horny.

The evening was warm and you wouldn't have known summer was supposed to be at an end. I'd changed out of my black suit, back into my black jeans and t-shirt, and was sitting on the bonnet of the van, leaning back against the windscreen, sharing a tub of spare ribs with Kelly. Kelly was talking about a gig she'd just booked, a posh wedding thing in one of the big Brighton hotels. She said it was paying twice the fee we'd just earned. I was sucking the sticky hoisin sauce from my fingers, which, mixed with the Wild Turkey, tasted like aniseed gobstoppers. Vince, now apparently sated, drummed on the bonnet by our feet and announced there was a party, his eyes twinkling with the energy we were all still feeling. Kelly knew the drill: she smiled and, taking a last rib from the tub, slid down to the ground beside the wing mirror.

'Come on, Maggie! It's time to rock!' Vince grinned. The WREN that he'd wrapped himself around nodded and grinned too.

'What about you, Kelly?'

'Nope, I'm heading back to Brighton . . . leave you boys to have your fun,' Kelly replied through a mouthful of pork.

'How are you getting back?' I asked hesitantly, thinking for the first time of ducking out of a party and heading back to Brighton. Heading back to Isla. It still hadn't fully dawned on me that Isla was far away in a completely different Brighton to the one I was thinking about going back to.

'Train. In fact there's one at seven minutes to ten which I think I can just manage if I get going now.'

'A train?' Vince frowned.

'How the hell do you know the times?' I cut in. It made no sense to me at all: how could she possibly have known?

'I checked times earlier,' Kelly answered in her way of correcting one's ignorance. 'It's called planning ahead,' she added with a nod to prompt my understanding, to dislodge my penny and help it drop.

'A train . . .' Vince said again, slowly this time.

'Yes, Vince,' Kelly laughed. 'You know, long things, locomotive at each end, go from station to station—'

'Full of people who smell of wee,' Vince extrapolated.

'No, that's buses—'

Kelly was interrupted by a cry of amazement from three of Vince's WREN escort. Tom was handing a watch and a purse back to one of them who was asking how he did it. Tom shrugged and as always simply explained that it was magic.

'I don't believe in magic,' she said.

'No?' Tom mused, taking out a pack of cards from his jacket pocket.

Kelly shook her head slowly, smiling at Tom with those motherly eyes.

'Come on, Tom-Tom!' Vince shouted, spinning around, using his new companion as a sort of axle. 'Put your cards away. There's a party to get to, Boh.'

I watched Kelly retrieve her Jazzmaster from the van. I looked from her to Vince who took a slug of Wild Turkey before kissing his new friend. She was quite small and reached up to return the kiss that grew from an exploratory peck to a full and passionate embrace. I imagined sitting on the train with Kelly for a moment, returning to Brighton. I wished Isla was waiting for me in my flat, but I knew she wasn't. But what if she phoned in the morning? What if she couldn't keep away and turned up on my doorstep at breakfast?

'Kelly,' I said.

'Mmm?' she replied, closing the van door.

'Maggie,' Vince said, holding out the whisky bottle then returning to his girl.

'I . . .' I stopped and looked between them just as Tom came up with his group of street magic, blues fans who thought he was the coolest thing in the great coastal city of Portsmouth that night. Something that was almost certainly true.

'What?' Kelly prompted. 'I've got to run, Mags – train to catch.'

I looked between them again. I thought of Brighton, of Isla. I thought of her not being there. I thought, hope against hope, of her being there. Jesus, she really was *always on my mind*, baby. I was no good at decisions then. Even when I knew they had to be made. I was happier just going with the flow. Vince pressed the bottle into my hand. The girl with him reached up and whispered in his ear. Vince laughed loudly and waved a tsk-tsk reprimand with his finger.

'Mags?' Kelly said again.

Fuck it, I thought. 'Take care, Kelly. Is it Saturday today?'

'Yes!' Kelly laughed.

'Let's work on Monday . . . didn't get it all out today . . . lots more to come.'

Kelly nodded approvingly and headed out on to the street.

'See ya, Kells!' Vince called after her.

It turned out that the 9.53 train from Portsmouth Harbour to Brighton that night was delayed due to an incident on the line. Kelly ended up sitting on the platform for an hour. It was an important hour. She met Lucy. Lucy was lovely. She was like Tom, but in female form. Lucy inspired the song 'Lucy Too Damn Cool', which led to the only record the Heroes ever made, a limited run of three thousand singles put out through Dillan Rock Records, a small independent label based in Hastings. Lucy was to turn Kelly's world upside down.

52

I turned off the M25 on to the A12, heading north and leaving Brighton in the south, heading to Suffolk and home, heading to Isla and Jack and May. The rain stayed in the south and I found myself driving under bright stars. I travelled a lot for work and the A12 was like an old friend, a ninety-mile driveway from the world to my house. The traffic dropped away with the rain, leaving me cruising down long empty stretches. Occasionally red lights would appear ahead and I'd absent-mindedly drift to the outside lane with a quarter-mile to spare, passing them a minute later and watching the brighter headlights dwindle away to nothing behind me. Dad was behind me too. I said nothing more to him, although deep down I knew he was close and that there was something else out there with him. My tears had also gone, but unlike the rain and the traffic I hadn't left them somewhere on the M25; they'd just hardened into a decision that I'd made and unmade so many times its costs, its emotions, were as familiar to me by then as the A12 with its service stations, exits to Chelmsford, Hatfield Peverel, Margaretting and Colchester, its turns and inclines, its three-lane stretches and the patches of concrete surface that made the tyre note change like blues to jazz.

As I drove, flicking through radio stations and finding nothing I could bear to be part of, the decision framed itself with the determination that always sat at the beginning of the A12. I had to stop. I had to get off the ride. I knew Isla and I had drifted far apart. She was like a distant shore that I found myself admiring but unable to reach. I knew the drift had been because I was never there, because I was working, always working. Working to make and build and support the lifestyle we had. The lifestyle that looked very different to how it felt: a beautiful place to look into, a cold place to look out of. I switched on the radio again and clicked through them the stations and again could find nothing that settled with me. Again, I switched the radio off. Again, I drove in silence.

I would leave my job, the decision went. I would leave my job and be at home before Jack and May went to sleep. I would read to them every night and make love to Isla. I would be a good husband. I would be a good father. I would be a good person and my children would get to know me, the *real* me. Whoever that was.

My familiar old decision once again followed the familiar old pattern of the A12, fluxing into the age-old sense of sinking the closer I drew to home and the further away I got from the strange thinking of the hinterland that surrounded it. As always, my resolve began to falter as I examined the implications of what just a few short miles previously I had determined to do in the name of love and family and salvation. As the A12 wound onward and each stray vehicle was passed and fell behind, I started to get scared.

I turned on the radio. There were now fewer stations; the number dropped off quickly beyond London, dwindling to only a handful in rural Suffolk. I clicked through them quickly. I turned the radio off. I thought about selling the house. I thought about moving to a smaller house, perhaps just like the one we had left three years earlier, soon after May was born. It was nice. It had four bedrooms; it had a large living room and a lovely garden which the old couple who'd reluctantly sold to us – I think because Isla charmed them – had spent a lifetime happily developing. Nice, but not as impressive as the new house. Not nearly as impressive. I thought about telling Julie and Mum. I thought about telling people, or rather I thought about not being able to see the surprise in their faces when I said we were in the Old Vicarage. I thought about next summer when Jack wanted to ride with the roof down, about explaining to him that we didn't have that sort of car any more. I imagined he'd care. I imagined the people I'd bumped into would care. I imagined having to remind Isla to watch the weekly food bill. I thought about Tom and Catherine, how they lived. I thought about people at work talking about the price of petrol, food and electricity. I imagined worrying about such things. I thought about what it would be like to emigrate to the brave new world of a different

Suffolk. These were thoughts that gnawed at me. Thoughts that laid me naked, thoughts that pissed on so much of what was left of me. Thoughts that stirred the dark ugly thing that had slithered pitilessly between the two Brightons when they collided on that day so long ago, stepping from that little cut of tarmac outside the Grand Hotel and forcing itself on me. It left me so hungry – what a disgusting thing. I hated remembering that day.

I switched on the radio again, changing station the moment sound reached me. The wrong music. Never the right music, never music I could access. I switched the radio off. My mind disobeyed its orders and went without warning to that day when the two Brightons collided and the night I ran through the rain. The night I was crazy. The night Tom saved me as he always did. I gripped the wheel hard. My thoughts returned to the road. I switched the radio on and clicked through the stations. I switched it off again.

53

Shortly after Kelly finally boarded her train at Portsmouth Station, saying goodbye – or rather *adieu* – to Lucy and knowing her life would never be the same again, I came to a strange decision. We – Tom, Vince and I – were at a party in a huge student place over in Southsea. Tom and I were sitting on the first-floor landing. There was a stereo doing its best somewhere on the ground floor but it was mostly bass that reached us, leaving the rest of Nirvana behind. There was a tall sash window that opened out to the fire escape and we were perched on its sill with the night air coming in. Everywhere smelled of cigarettes and ganja. Tom was happy-drunk. He'd got it just right. I still had a little way to go. Tom was still lit up from earlier and he was talking about the crowd and telling me how much he loved Portsmouth. I was agreeing and saying how fantastic Kelly had been when it came to lining up the gigs recently; what with Camden and all, I was saying, my mind wandering to Isla.

'Yeah . . .' Tom nodded enthusiastically. 'I love Kelly too—'

'Oh my boys, my boys,' came Vince's voice, impersonating Richard Griffiths in *Withnail and I.*

I looked around. Vince was emerging from one of the bedsit doors at the end of the corridor. He was barefoot and still faithfully holding the now empty bottle of Wild Turkey in his hand, struggling to pull up the fly of his suit trousers with the other.

'Monty! You terrible cunt!' I shouted. The film quote thing really was getting out of control. Tom started giggling whilst trying to light a cigarette.

'We've run out of booze,' Vince announced, grinning his way down the corridor. A beautiful woman who was older than us, not the WREN he'd been draped over earlier, with blonde hair neatly pulled back in a ponytail, emerged from the same door and followed him. 'And what are we going to do about it?' he continued.

Tom held up the bottle of wine he'd been drawing from and offered it to Vince, who came to a leaning stop against the wall in front of us.

'Excellent, Tom-Tom, excellent,' he grinned. His companion joined him and they sat down on the floor, all but blocking off the corridor. The music changed, but I had no idea to what from the dull thumping that reached us.

'This is Claire,' Vince announced rather formally. Claire smiled and said hello with what I placed as a Yorkshire accent. She was comfortable in her skin and bright. I liked her. 'Three of her friends live here too. I can make introductions . . .'

'Yeah?' Tom checked, frowning slightly in an attempt to present a sober façade. Vince nodded slowly. Claire lit a cigarette and offered the packet around; we all took one, even Tom who had one in his mouth already. Tom pretended to return the packet only to present an empty hand, then *by magic* found the box behind her shoulder with his other hand. Even when he was drunk it was seamless. How *did* he do that?

Then the decision came, before I even realised I'd been mulling it over, let alone taken it. Acting upon it, I stood up.

'Actually, guys, I'm going to leave you to it,' I announced.

'Hey?' Vince checked. Tom smiled at me and raised a farewell hand. 'Where you going?'

'Home.'

'What, now?' Vince looked confused, his eyes moving rapidly as he tried to remember some forgotten reason for us all leaving.

'Yep . . . I wanna get back—'

'Ahh . . .' Vince nodded sagely. 'The boy's in love,' he added, glancing at Claire.

'Yeah, yeah . . . Fuck off, Monty,' I laughed.

Vince laughed, but those eyes of his were serious. 'Don't, Mags. Hang around . . .'

'No, I'm going,' I said, feeling very certain. I stepped over his legs and stood at the top of the stairs. There were people, couples mostly, sitting on almost every step; it seemed Tom and I hadn't been as alone as we'd thought.

'It's no good,' Vince said simply, his voice a cautious neutral. I looked down at him. 'It will get all shitty, and you'll get hurt, Boh.'

'Thank you, Reverend Vince,' I said. 'But I'll be fine.'

Vince studied me for a moment then winked. 'Laters,' he smiled. Give Vince his due: he always knew when he was wasting his time.

Ten minutes later I found myself on a busy road that I think led back toward the venue we'd played. I walked along it and managed to flag down a cab almost straight away. The guy, a rotund, balding old Mediterranean-looking man with thick black eyebrows and grey stubble – Greek, I guessed wildly – dropped the passenger window and raised those eyebrows by way of asking *where to?* I pulled all my paper money out of my back pocket. I had eighty pounds in folded tens.

'Will this get me back to Brighton?' I asked simply. He frowned and scrutinised my outstretched hand.

'Yes,' he replied finally, with a reluctant nod to the back door.

It was to be a long drive to Brighton. Thankfully he let me smoke. Driving through the Portsmouth streets, he seemed to relax and cheer up. He glanced at me in his mirror and asked if I'd had a good night.

'Yeah . . .' I nodded before turning to the window and watching the suburbs slip by. I never really was one for chatting to cabbies.

'Night out?' he asked.

'Working,' I replied simply without looking away from the window.

'Yeah? What you do?' he pushed. I couldn't quite get his accent; Turkish, I thought, revising my guess. He sounded like the Sevim family who ran the Spar on Queen Street. It was their grandfather who came to England, and his sons, born in London, always had a roll to the words that they got from him.

'Musician.'

'Yeah? What, Indie? Grungy?' he asked. This made me smile and I looked back from the window and the edge of Portsmouth. 'Or proper music?' he added, smiling at me in the mirror. This was a good comment. This changed the situation. I stretched my arms out along the back shelf and settled back in to the seat.

'I'm a bluesman.'

'Me too!' he grinned enthusiastically.

'Yeah?' I was dubious on that one.

'You like Floyd Dixon?'

I was amazed: he *was* a bluesman. 'Yeah,' I said and I did.

He fumbled through some tapes and put one into the stereo. We left Portsmouth to 'Mean and Jealous Man', me tapping the seat with the flat of my hand. By the time we got to 'Hey Bartender' my driver – I never knew his name – started to sing the odd line.

'Hmm?' he urged, glancing at me in the mirror. I ignored it and carried on tapping away. 'Come on,' he threw in, his reflection grinning from the mirror.

Before I knew it, I'd started to sing along. Well, I loved Floyd and an audience of one is still an audience.

'Hey!' he laughed, sounding for a brief moment just like the Fonz. He started tapping the beat on the steering wheel, nodding his head and continued singing the odd word here and there.

We cruised back to Brighton, singing all the way from 'Hey Bartender' to 'Blues for Cuba' and everything in between. Then there were tape changes and we left the true blues piste. We had James Brown, we had Elvis, we even got a little Jerry Lee Lewis! The long journey back to Brighton was quick and way too short. My being there in that cab, with the prince that is Floyd Dixon coming from speakers and my balding driver singing – surprisingly well – and nodding his head so much I'm amazed we stayed on the road, seems odd now, but at the time it seemed like the most natural thing in the world. I was happy and I was heading back toward Isla.

54

I drove down the little lane to my house slowly, more slowly than usual.
The radio was off and the car was silent. I'd only been to Brighton but
I felt as if I'd been gone for a long time. I don't know if it was thinking
about Dad, the memories Brighton had stirred or the raking over of the
truth about my life, but I felt as if a page had been turned. I felt as if the
malaise of hive-like activity had had a pin dropped in it – one of my
markers. My plan of changing job, of changing lifestyle, of trading cash
for time, wealth for family, had as always been rationalised, sanitised
and diluted along those final miles, leaving the wider world behind and
returning to the everyday as the practical, the habitual and the real
reasserted themselves. But this time was different – just. This time my
plan hadn't faded to nothing as the walls of the rut I had created for
myself rose around me. This time a small residual core that felt like iron
remained in my stomach. Things had to change. I would talk to Isla.
We *had* to work out how to change things. Before it was too late, before
she was lost to me.

*

I stand at the junction with the lane to my house. By the old plastic salt
bin bedded into the bank and the wooden footpath marker that has
never stood straight and points out across a silent field. I look along the
lane, toward Isla and Jack and May. I hope. I look east. I know
something is coming for me there.

Must stay calm.

It is dawn in the east. Dawn proper now. Cool blues reach across
the sky. Joyce and Henry will be returning there soon. I feel their
absence. I wish they were with me.

I love Joyce. I love Henry. They are both so beautiful.

Soon the sun will show itself. Soon the Tide will pour across the
land and reach me. Perhaps I will feel them then. A promise of them
maybe. Although I know they do not come here. I think only I have

come here, this night for the first time. I'm glad I decided to do this. I have to know. It was the right choice. I look behind me again. My eyes search for movement. Come what may, it was the right choice.

I have to know the truth.

All the stars have gone now, even in the west. Blues are everywhere. Those clouds are still in the west. I study them. It's strange. They really do look like the Brecon Beacons, Cribyn, Pen y Fan and Corn Du. I think of Tom. Dear Tom.

I walk on. My eyes search around the distant hedgerows and treelines that separate the fields and draw the pattern of the land that I grew up on.

I hear gulls!

I can't see them. But I hear them in the east. I look behind me. I see nothing, but I know I am not alone. I know eyes are on me. I look east again for the sun and the Tide and the warmth they will bring, the warmth I need. I walk on.

When I reach my house—

I look behind me again. My focus jumps from shade to shade, from tree to bank to hedge.

If I reach my house I will be safe. I will be home and I will be safe. And I will know. I will finally know the truth.

I think of Isla and Jack and May.

I have to know. I must know.

Almost home now.

Almost home.

55

I stopped on the gravel in front of the house. Well, the pea shingle that we'd replaced the older gravel with. It was dark. The only light came warmly through the wine-red curtains that kept the sitting room snug behind the French doors. Other than that, the house was dark. I knew the children would be in their beds and Isla would be warm on a sofa reading a book or news online; I knew the television would have been switched off when the children went upstairs. I also knew she would be listening for my car. She liked to know where we all were, and when we were all in the house she was at her happiest.

I got out of the car. Instinctively, I pushed the door closed gently, minimising the interruption to the quiet evening with just a padded *clump*. The outside light came to life, shooing away the stars above me with its yellow-white haze. My plan, what was left of it, survived even the final walk from the car, even the turning of the door handle.

The hall was warm and still. Low light filtered down the stairs from the children's nightlight on the landing, just enough to keep the monsters safely locked in the shadows. The doors to the Livingroom were pulled to, but not closed, fissures of yellow light reaching out around them. There was the smell of baking, a savoury smell that left me guessing what Isla and the children had had for dinner. I stopped for a moment and listened to the house's breathing. I looked at the picture of waves crashing over the seawall at Walberswick. I felt the iron residue of the plan in my stomach. I nodded to myself. It was time to talk. It really was time for things to change.

'Hey you,' Isla , looking up from a handful of printed A4 sheets, a paper on child poverty in West Africa that a friend had emailed her to review. She was in the corner of the sofa closest to the fireplace with her knees up under her. She'd pushed her hair behind her ear, a sign that she had been concentrating intently. Her eyes were as warm as the fireside.

'Hey,' I said, walking over. I went to kiss her forehead but she reached up and kissed me on the mouth. She smelled of springtime; I don't know how she managed to but she smelled of April afternoons.

'How was, Vincent?' she asked, putting the flap of A4 down.

'Good,' I said simply, dropping down on to the sofa opposite her. 'He's going to go into the yurt-building business.'

Isla laughed. 'Is he?'

'Yeah.' The iron core of my plan swam in my stomach. 'I . . . I was . . .'

'Are you okay, Darling?' Isla asked, her eyes flitting across my face, reading me as she always did. She unfolded her legs and went to stand. Then it happened. Her phone beeped and gave a buzz-buzz. It was tucked down the side of the sofa. She retrieved it and pushed it under the papers, its illuminated screen going dull again just as she did so. She dismissed it with a tut and came and sat next to me. 'What is it?' she said, her hand on my thigh. 'Has something happened?' she pushed, her eyes still searching mine, her voice calm and soothing.

'No . . . no, nothing's happened,' I explained, looking down at her hand. 'It's just . . .' I paused and looked up. She looked worried; she squeezed my leg lightly and smiled just a little. 'It's nothing to worry about,' I said quickly. 'It's just I had a chance to think on the drive back . . .'

'And that's not something I need to worry about?' Isla laughed. 'You never—'

'About us,' I said quietly. Isla stopped smiling. 'About us and the stuff we've talked about before, about work and you and the children and . . .' I looked down. I put my hand on hers.

'Go on,' she whispered, gently.

'Well, we talk about changing things . . . about just a few more years and all of this,' I looked up and around the room. 'All of this and . . . and more will be really solid and—'

'We don't need more,' Isla cut in, her voice still a whisper but urgent now. 'We don't need *this*.' She joined me in looking around the room.

'Going back would be . . . hard.'

'Why?'

'It would. You need . . . I . . .' I broke off. I thought about the day when the two Brightons collided.

'No,' Isla urged simply.

'It would . . .' I stopped because I wanted to say okay then. I wanted to say what I'd thought back at the beginning of the A12. I wanted to say okay then, we'll sell up, we'll take it as it comes and be happy, take it as a family and be happy as a family. But this wasn't the beginning of the A12; this was off the map at the far end of it. This was the real world.

'Magnus,' Isla urged again, squeezing my hands and moving against me.

'What I'm saying is that I don't know how to do it, but I want things to change. I want us to talk about it, but we can't just run back, we can't . . .' I said clumsily. I took a breath and tried again. 'I know you're unhappy,' I said and surprised myself. It was true, I knew it; I'd known it for a long time but even in my darkest thoughts I'd never admitted it to myself.

'Don't say that—'

'It's true,' I insisted, because it was. 'I hate it,' I went on. 'I want you to be happy and . . . and sometimes I feel like a stranger here and I don't want that. I hate that too.'

'You're not a stranger! We love you,' Isla insisted. Her hand went to my face and turned head to look at her. 'Jack loves you, he adores you, and May . . . May loves you . . . You know the puppet theatre we bought her for Christmas? Well, when the princess is rescued by the knight in armour, it's you – that's *Daddy knight*,' she whispered simply and determinedly. 'Do you hear me?' Isla went on, shaking my hands. She was suddenly angry and there were tears in her eyes. Somehow, they made her look strong because they didn't budge her or deflect her resolve. It was a glimpse of the Isla I felt lost from, the wonderful woman who had hidden herself behind a peacekeeper façade while I lost my way. I studied her. I wanted her to be right. I wanted it all not to be too late. I wanted my Isla, the Isla in front of me. In that moment she felt closer than she had been for such a long time and I wanted to believe that she wasn't lost to me, that she hadn't drifted far away forever, that some new tide had brought her close enough to reach out and bring her back to me. My heart raced. I took hold of her hand, lifted it from my face and kissed it.

Suddenly there was a crash from above us. We both looked at the ceiling.

'Mummy!' Came Jack's little voice through the house. It wasn't the first time May had fallen out of her bed. Then May screamed. 'Mummy!' Jack cried again. Isla jumped up and ran out to the hall. I stood up.

'It's okay, Darling. May's just toppled out of bed,' I heard Isla comforting Jack, her feet falling fast on the stairs. I heard May crying in the background, steady and upset, not pained or frightened. I sat back down, leaning into the sofa and looking up at the ceiling and May's bedroom above. My heart was still racing. I wanted Isla back, my Isla. Then it happened again: Isla's phone chimed and gave another sharp buzz-buzz from under the papers where she had left it.

*

Birds fly up from behind me in alarm! I turn and look. There are dozens, startled into the air from the trees I just walked past. I watch them wing away to the south.

Must stay calm.

I scan the road. Nothing.

I run! I'm running now. Along the lane. I wish the sun would come. I wish the Tide would come!

Almost there. I won't let it stop me. Whatever's coming for me, I won't let it stop me. I have to know.

I have to know!

My head is down and I'm running like when I was a boy, my arms pumping in the corner of my vision, my feet light on the ground.

56

I looked at the papers, the blue-white light of the phone's display just visible through them for a moment before it blinked off. Sitting there I realised how often Isla's phone sounded. It had started around the time she made the collage of photographs, when she commandeered the conservatory over Easter.

I stood up and looked down at the papers on the other sofa.

I realised too that Isla never left her phone anywhere. It was always with her. I knew I was going to look. I didn't want to. It was shit of me. It was shit of me to wonder and shit of me to act on it. But I had to know. I had to know. Even as I moved the papers and picked it up I was trying not to look.

Four threes, the factory code, unlocked the phone.

MESSAGES.>

Don't be sad. You're not alone. I'm always here.

Thank you. I miss you.

I miss you too.

Thank you for yesterday. I don't know what I'd do without you.

Don't be silly. You don't need to thank me. Love Duncan

There were dozens, all sent to and from one name. The name that was the very worst name, the very last name I wanted to find, the name that had haunted me since the day the two Brightons collided as surely as I haunt the world around me now.

> *Duncan.*

> *Love Duncan.*

> *Love, that fucking Duncan cunt.*

It wasn't the name, wasn't the messages, wasn't the words that made me realise just how far Isla had drifted away from me. It was the fact that I put the phone back and knew I wouldn't say anything. Where once there would have been anger, like the blind youthful rage that night when Tom saved me after the two Brightons collided, I knew there would be silent sadness. I blamed myself. I blamed myself because it was my fault, mine and not Isla's.

We didn't finish our conversation because I hid myself away in my study, surrounded by my work. That night I lay next to Isla and wanted to hold her. I wanted to hold her and tell her that I was sorry. I wanted to hold her and tell her that it was okay and that I loved her. I wanted to tell her it would break my heart if she left. But I couldn't. I couldn't touch her. I reached out but I couldn't. She felt so far away. Instead I lay there in the darkness. I fully expected to count the long minutes into the long hours of night, but I fell asleep almost at once. That night Dad came to me in a dream about the beach hut: I was a child sitting on the step, watching him paint his boat, his beautiful little boat with a wonderful red sail. It was a perfect summer day and I sat and watched all night. He didn't look up. It was as if he didn't want to make a thing of it all, didn't want to scare me away, but I knew he was smiling as he worked. He sang his happy song, the words lost by the time the edges of them reached me but the melody familiar. He felt close, very close, just as he had in the car earlier, and it was such a comfort having my dad there that night, right when I needed him most. Did I say that my dad used to be in the army and he used to be a boxer and he could beat up anyone?

57

I woke to the sound of the door buzzer far away. Sleep faded slowly into wakefulness, information coalescing into a gradual awareness of my surroundings like the lazy bubbles in Vince's Elvis lava lamp. For a moment, I thought that it was the taxi driver saying I'd left my wallet on the back seat. Which was especially strange because I'd never owned a wallet at that point in my life. But the bright sunlight streaming in from the open window registered and the fact it was morning became a support column in my emerging world view.

Buzzzz-buzz . . . buzz.

This time it was closer. I rolled on to my back. I was on top of the covers in just my boxer shorts. The light was harsh and bright. I squinted and rolled away on to my other side. I listened for the buzz again and it came short and sharp.

Buzz-buzz.

I swung myself into a sitting position and coughed hard, expelling last night's cigarettes and making room for more. I walked through to the hall but the buzzer stayed silent. I leaned on the wall, looking at the tin box with its grill and two buttons, my arm over it as if I was taking my first piss of the day. Silence. This wasn't unusual; sometimes people buzzed all the numbers to get anyone to open the downstairs door, usually because of forgotten keys or reading of meters or whatever. I walked back to my bedroom but then it came, sliding under the door. A manila A4 envelope pushed almost, but not quite, silently on to the tiles. It was addressed simply with my name: Magnus.

Opening the door in my boxer shorts was never a problem in those days. I stepped over the envelope and opened the door part-way, leaning round to find my postman or rather postwoman. Isla was at the top of the stairs.

'Hey,' I said, just, my voice a grating rasp. 'Hey,' I repeated more clearly.

Isla smiled and stepped back from the stairs. 'I didn't think you were in. You didn't answer.'

'Oh, I was . . . composing, you know . . . Headphones on.'

'You were asleep, weren't you?' Isla guessed, eyes narrowing in accusation, smile broadening. She was wearing a little summer skirt, a white top and a khaki jacket that was halfway military and sort of went with that watch of hers. She looked fantastic, *fan-fucking-tastic*, I thought at the time, and I wanted her.

'Me? Nah.' A moment passed. A good moment.

'Well,' Isla said finally, 'I just wanted you to have . . .' She glanced down at the floor where the envelope was half visible.

'Why don't you come in?' I asked, opening the door fully.

'Composing?' Isla asked sceptically, looking slowly up and down my body.

'I do my best work in just my pants.'

'Do you?'

Isla kissed me. She stepped inside, over the envelope, and I closed the door behind her. I kissed her properly. She put her arms around me. We didn't speak. I pulled her into the bedroom and we fucked each other stupid. We were aching for each other and it was even better than the night before. I think it was just before noon when she arrived and it was just after three when we ended up in the kitchen raiding the sum total of my food supplies: orange juice and Monster Munch. I was naked. Isla had pulled a sheet around herself and wore it like a toga, somehow with style. Even then we ended up pressed into the corner kissing between giggles and mouthfuls of food. When we were done the kissing changed. Isla stopped giggling first and kissed me warmly, lovingly. This time it was she who led me into the bedroom. She pulled the sheet over us and kissed me again and again, gentle, light caressing touches of her lips. I stroked her body, my hands gliding over her smooth skin. Then she turned over and spooned against me, pulling my arm around her and kissing my hand. It was perfect. Finally, I entered her again and the gentle kissing continued as, with our immediate needs and passions sated, we made love and gave more and more of ourselves.

We had such a wonderful day together. In the early evening we talked about dinner, dinner at Papa's, which had already somehow become *our* place. We lit candles that flickered in the breeze from the balcony and turned on the fairy lights around my shrine. Isla was full of questions. She wanted to know all about my music. She had never been particularly into music. At the time, I thought she was keen to change that; it didn't occur to me that it was me she wanted to know and that she understood music was at my heart. I answered in the best way I knew: I played the best of the best, the canon of those who had gone before the Heroes, from Floyd Dixon and my tale of the taxi driver from the night before to the Paul Butterfield Blues Band, Rory Gallagher, Peggy Scott-Adams, Johnny Winter and the arrival of the rock 'n' roll edge through the Fabulous Thunderbirds and, of course, Stevie Ray Vaughan. Isla studied me as I spoke, watching my face while I smiled with the music. Her brown eyes were bright and happy.

At about seven I went for pizza and wine – we'd abandoned the idea of going out by then - and Isla took a bath. I left the flat with an image of her squeezing water from the sponge over her shoulders, her hair up on top of her head with a single curl reaching down, her head tilted away, eyes closed and relaxed, a look of deep satisfaction that was a shadow of when we had made love. By the time I got back the image had bloomed in my mind and I had to have her again before we ate. The pizza was cold but splendid. I'd never really bothered with wine before, but I had picked up a French pinot noir as instructed by Isla and I liked it.

By about ten thirty I was contentedly fed, sexed and watered. We lay together along the length of the sofa. Isla was wearing my bathrobe. I'd forgotten I had a bathrobe, despite the fact it had been hanging in clear view on the bathroom door for months. Another one of those things that are there but not seen, invisible in clear sight. The candles still flickered and we'd settled back to Tom Waits on vinyl. Isla smelled of bubble bath. I could hear a television somewhere, I guessed from the flat on the same level two buildings along. Sunday night was always movie night for them and the traffic had died down from a murmur to individual cars mostly along the esplanade. I felt happy. Isla was stoking my arm and it was as if the sofa was growing in size and I was sinking toward a peaceful place of sleep.

'Magnus,' Isla said softly.

'Hmm,' I replied, rising out of the sleepy depths, the sofa returning to normal size. I remember noticing the cold of the breeze on my arm where Isla was running her hand.

'I have to go,' she whispered.

'No,' I whispered back, kissing her on the nape of her neck. 'You're not allowed to go—'

'I have to, Darling.' *Darling*. She called me darling and I loved it.

'No . . . stay. Let's go to bed right now.'

'I can't,' Isla said quietly. She didn't say no, she didn't say she didn't want to, she didn't express an opinion; instead she stated a fact. She couldn't. It was something from the other Brighton, her Brighton, the one that filled the same space as my Brighton. The Brighton with fucking Duncan festering in the middle of it.

At the door, we made plans to meet midweek. They didn't last and we ended up seeing each other the following evening. We kissed each other. We held each other. We kissed again. Then Isla picked up the manila envelope that had triggered our wonderful day and that I had stepped over on my way in and out, again a thing invisible in clear sight - my mind had been elsewhere. She handed it to me.

'Shit, yeah . . . I forgot,' I said, picking at the gummed-down fold.

'Wait till I've gone,' Isla replied, staying my hand with hers.

'Okay,' I nodded. 'What is it?'

'My blues . . . my music.' She kissed me one last time before walking out on to the landing.

I watched her walk over to the stairs just as she had before. With a final smile, she hurried away and the pattern was set. The pattern of our love affair, because that's what we had then, Isla and me: a true love affair to match her Audrey Hepburn movie-star looks. We stole every moment we could together, we made love, we partied. We ate at Papa's where Luca understood and, like everyone else, fell in love with Isla too. We walked on the beach together. Isla came to *Heroes*' gigs and she became part of my life and my little group of friends. Only Vince had his reservations although he, like Luca, like everyone, couldn't help falling in love with her. It was wonderful, so wonderful. But like all love affairs it had its rules. There must be rules so that they can be broken and everything can, in the end, come tumbling to the ground. Rules that are never agreed, never drawn up, never spoken, but instead form of their own accord in those first few wonderful days. The rules were Isla never stayed the night. The rules were I never asked her to stay the night. The rules were I never thought about where she went at the end of our evenings, never thought about fucking, cunting, bastard, shitting Duncan. I stayed cool with all these through the gift of denial. And then there was the final rule, the rule that we never spoke the words that were in our hearts: we never said that we loved each other. That was perhaps the most important of all the rules because if we had admitted that, acknowledged what was clear and obvious for all to see, then all of the other rules would have broken and the train would have run off the rails, the temple would have cracked and splintered and the wolves would have run in and pissed on the statues. Thus went the rules for the game we played. Always she would leave and head off into the other Brighton that was, of course, just like my Brighton, right outside my door, but which, of course, I chose never to notice, safe in the knowledge that the two Brightons would never, could never, collide.

That night after Isla left I went to open the envelope but stopped myself. It felt important and I decided I had to make a ceremony of it. So, I went to the shrine in search of ceremonial music. It had to be right. After about half an hour of searching, taking out LPs, studying jackets, remembering occasions and nights when they had filled my space, I finally found the correct, the absolutely correct, one: Willie Dixon's *Ginger Ale Afternoon*. I filled my glass with the last of the French wine and sat down with the envelope on my lap just as 'Wigglin' Worm' was making me want to sing. The sofa was still warm from where we had lain. I switched on the standard lamp that had come from the second-hand shop along Lewis Road and journeyed with me ever since student days. I tore away the flap. Inside were twelve black-and-white photographs. All the same size, all, I was sure, freshly printed with a precise three-millimetre border.

The first was a picture of a man sitting at a little garden table under what looked like an apple tree. He was a handsome man in his fifties and the picture somehow conveyed his presence; it was an excellent photograph. I knew at once it had to be Isla's father because his eyes were her eyes, keen, intelligent, knowing, and I realised that was where that uncanny sense of presence came from. I lay it down on the sofa next to me and moved on. Next came Brighton, a summer evening. It was taken somewhere high; my guess was a rooftop on Ditchling Rise somewhere. It too was a fantastic photograph. It took in roofs and houses, the level, the line of Grand Parade, the Pavilion and finally the lights of the Palace Pier. It seemed to come alive the more I studied it, with people on the streets, and on balconies, some a blur, some sharp. It was Brighton, my Brighton, and it was a work of art that gave and gave. Next was a group photograph, on the face of it clearly arranged – perhaps ten families, about forty men, women and children in all. It looked to be a village in Africa somewhere. But it was as if someone else had taken the formal picture, arranged the group, and the one I was looking at had captured them off guard, perhaps just before or just after the 'official' shot; their faces were casual, alive and filled with joy. It was fantastic and I found myself studying each face, wondering about the people and the setting. The next was a camp of some sort. There were tents including a large Red Cross marquee in the foreground. There were crowds of people. They looked confused. In fact initially I thought the picture itself was confused until I saw a Médecins Sans Frontières doctor crouching near the edge of the shot. He was looking into his hands, his face just showing. He was weeping. It sent a cold rush up my spine. It was a haunting picture. There followed more pictures from similar camps, some as haunting, some so hopeful. There was one of a woman being handed a baby by a nurse and both their faces were pictures of pure joy. All of them used people to send a message, to tell a story. No wonder American magazines had snapped them up.

Then came a different picture. It was in Africa still, but on open ground. Dusty, dry, scrubby ground. There were soldiers with rifles; they were corralling people and the people looked afraid. In the centre of the shot was a man looking straight at the camera. He was holding a pistol above his head in one hand and pointing at the camera with the other. He was obviously shouting. His eyes scared me. He was simply a killer. I realised that Isla had taken the shot, had lifted her camera when most would have run. I realised I truly had never met anyone like Isla.

The last picture was of me on stage in Camden. I was pointing at the camera and staring down the length of my arm right into the lens. The microphone was raised high and behind me in my other hand, my body twisting, and the lines of my black suit were blurred with the motion of keeping up with me. Kelly and Tom in my flanks and Vince behind us were also a blur caught up with the lights and the smoke. But my eyes were in perfect sharp focus. The image captured me giving *It* to the crowd, captured the Heroes and how it felt to be a Hero – the rush, the energy, all of it. But that wasn't what the picture was about, because right in the middle of all that it captured a very private moment between Isla and me. The moment my world flipped and she had *It*, the very largest of all the pins in my map, the pinch in my hourglass. Across the bottom corner she had simply written: *Phwoar x.*

Wow. What a time we had, Isla and me, when we were young. What a beautiful, wonderful time.

58

I reach my house!

My house.

The sun finally races warm over the trees behind me. My shadow stretches out, picking its way over the gravel drive, like water exploring and flooding over shingle at the reach of the tide. I stop running. I'm on the road where the driveway, my driveway, splays out to meet the tarmac. I look back along the lane. I expect to see it, see something.

Is this the world of the living? Can I take the next steps? Will it stop me?

I see nothing.

No, wait!

The Tide bursts bright and brilliant into the lane! It's rushing toward me, filling everywhere with dancing light. It cascades against the banks, a wash of light, light within light. I think of the reflected sun sparkling on a calm summer sea, winking with tiny reminders of summer days, long summer days with Dad and brief, fleeting summer days with Jack and May.

It's beautiful, so beautiful. Wonderful.

The Tide touches me. It gathers me up. I am light. I think of the woods, their shade and their comfort and their mystery, and I think of the beach. I *go* to the beach, the shingle underfoot and the sandy patches baked by the sun. I feel the spray of crashing waves blown by winter gales. I think of the towns and streets and squares where I have searched for Isla and Jack and May, the hint of them on the Tide. I think of all the places I visit. I *am* all the places, some close and some far all at once. I feel the Tide flow through me and around me, warm like the sunlight that bathes it. It brings a promise of Henry. Joyce also, but fainter, a far, far fainter promise. I think of Dad and Mum and Julie and Isla and Jack and May and Tom and Vince.

I was loved.

I *am* loved.

I feel it.

I sense love behind me too, from back there. But I can't trust it. Evil comes with many faces.

I turn toward my driveway, my house, my home, my Isla, my Jack, my May. My family.

Must be quick now.

Have I made it? Have I broken through? Can I really take these last few steps?

I swallow. I must move. I must know. Nothing must stop me. I step on to the drive. I walk slowly, cautiously. My feet make no sound on the gravel.

Am I a ghost? A ghost among the living?

I look up, my eyes following the sweep of the drive to my house. Will they be there? This is it. I will finally know. Finally know where they are.

If they—

I shake. I am shaking. Is this physical? I feel my legs weakening. I walk on, slowly. I make myself move on.

59

The next morning, I woke before Isla. I woke into a feeling of restful peace. I hadn't slept that contentedly for months and having Dad so close made me feel safe in the way I had when I was a child. In that waking moment, I was bolstered with the sense of security that had gone with me all my life, unnoticed until Dad's death when I suddenly felt vulnerable. Thank God, Tom had been there to prop me up for those first few months. Dear Tom.

Then the night before returned to me. I listened to the birdsong from beyond the window. The room was cold and I guessed there had been a late spring frost through the night. The light from the window was white and stark. I listened into the house for Jack and May. But I heard nothing except for the bass thrum of the oil boiler firing way off in the scullery. I thought of the messages:

MESSAGES.> DUNCAN

They settled uneasily in my stomach and I knew I wouldn't be able to hide them. Not that morning. I turned my head to look at Isla, the pillow cool against my face and smelling freshly washed, soap powder and some faux-mix of meadows. She was facing away and her breathing was steady and slow. I knew I needed time, time to prepare myself, gather myself, before I could hide the messages from my eyes. I knew for at least that day I had to be away from her if I wanted to avoid confrontation, avoid having to talk about them. I never could hide anything from Isla. I slid out from under the eiderdown, moving slowly and cautiously so as not to wake her. The room was cold and gooseflesh rose over me. I gathered up my suit and shirt in silence and slipped out on to the landing, taking care to work the latch without a sound. I dressed quickly in the family bathroom and padded down the stairs in my socks like a cat burglar in the old films I used to watch with Isla when we were first married.

I was right: there had been a late frost, the last of the spring. Ten minutes after waking I drove away from the house as the early morning sun reached over the fields and started to take the frost from the verges and banks.

*

The house is bathed in sunlight. The lawns and banks and trees are filled with the eagerness of early summer. I look up. The sky is like a blue ocean from the stories Dad told Julie and me. Fine, high white clouds hang lazily across it like wave crest. There is no breeze. The clouds are motionless. Nothing moves. There is no birdsong. All is still. The house is still. Nothing stirs there. All is at perfect peace. I glance behind, back at the lane. Nothing shows itself. I stop where the drive fans in front of the house. There are no cars here. I close my eyes and feel the Tide. It brings courage. It brings hope. I want to smile but I cannot. I feel for Isla.

Can I feel her? Can I feel the children? Is that them or do I imagine it?

I open my eyes. My legs are shaking. I am shaking. I must know, I must know what happened that morning. I have to know. I have to know the truth. At last the truth.

60

His mind returns from the office, from jogging up the stairs and the salutations of colleagues. His thoughts focus on the here and now:

The car.

The road.

The bend.

The time.

The road is low between tall banks now, dappled light streams across the bonnet and over his sunglasses. The bend rushes at him, immediate and imminent. His eyes flick to the dashboard. The mathematics runs and then sinks away somewhere in his mind as the need to act, the need to be present for a precise moment arrives.

He smiles.

His hand flashes in a controlled snap. His feet move in perfect synergy. The car roars under the new gear. He feels the speed drop away through his seat and his neck and his stomach. The bonnet bows down in abeyance. His grip tightens on the wheel, the tiny moments blink down, his arm muscles tense. His grip on the gearstick flexes. The white lines in the road draw close and touch now, a single strip of warning. His hand flashes again. The engine roars louder, the transmission whines, the car angles forward. The speed is stepped down again. He feels heavy against the wheel, his arm tight.

The moment comes. His eyes are locked on the curve now, clawing each blurred leaf and flash of motion into view. He turns the wheel hard and the car lurches in response. His weight shifts, wanting him across the car now. His muscles hold him. He grips the wheel, the gearstick. The tyres call out from the tarmac. His foot is poised over the accelerator, linked directly to his eyes for the instinctive action at the apex of the bend, no need for higher thought. His eyes fix on the racing, blurring feathered blade of the bend; his foot hangs in anticipation.

61

I walk across the drive toward the front door. Still my feet make no sound on the gravel that isn't gravel but pea shingle. This is hard. Each step is a fight. I wrestle with the effort to move forward. I want to cry out. I look at the doors, gloss blue with brass fittings, just as I left them. I lower my head and force another step. My mind reels with the effort. I grit my teeth. I remember climbing high mountains. I remember being miles above the African plain, labouring on Kilimanjaro. I remember the great sloping cathedrals of snow that I fought my way up on Mont Blanc that day when I peaked, that day when I hammered that great pin into my map. I remember my mind forcing me on whilst my body screamed *no*. I remember the burning of fighting through such thin air. I force another step. I guess at how many more until I can reach out and touch the door. I have never failed to find strength before. I have never missed a summit and I will make this last one!

Isla!

I cry out with the effort. So real now, so physical. I move forward. I push and I push. I look up. The great bank of cloud in the west that looks like the Beacons towers behind the house. The sun is on my back. My shadow is reaching toward the house, marking my course. I imagine the heat of the day around me but do not feel it. Another step. Another.

A wind blows down from the clouds that look like hills. I feel it. It pushes against me. I cry out again and push forward. The effort intensifies. My body wants to fail.

Come on!

I push. I take another step. Still the gravel is unmarked.

Where am I?

What is this place?

Another step. The light around me rolls away. It is suddenly dark now. Another step. And another. I lock my teeth. I look up to the house. No lights are burning there for me. I push on. Another step. And another. Close now, almost there.

The wind builds, howls around the house. I think it is calling something. I think its howl is about me. I think I hear my name in it.

I turn my head and look behind. I see nothing, but I hear the wind calling. I put my head down and force the final steps. My mind punishing my body, my will set against my pain.

I will not stop!

I must know. I must know whether they are here or there. I must reach them.

*

Over the following days I did everything I could to avoid Isla, to avoid talking with her. I worked very long hours even for me. I was out of the house from dawn until bedtime. On the Wednesday, I had to make a sales bid in Newcastle and I was grateful for the overnight stay. It was a strange trip because when I was waiting to go in, I sat looking out to a stunning view of the Tyne. It made me think about Dad, triggered a memory of watching a TV programme about the Tyne bridge with him. It was when I was little, but sitting there it felt like we'd watched it just the day before. I'd asking where the Tyne was. He showed me on a road atlas and said it wasn't really very far up the coast. I remember him laughing when I looked surprised and saying he'd sail me up there in his boat one day for a look. His beautiful little boat with a wonderful red sail. He felt close. He never left me in those last few months.

Despite my evasiveness and night away, Isla tried to talk to me about my plan, about what I'd started to say that night I got back from Brighton. She tried several times. I returned to my default position of everything being better in a couple of years' time. She seemed disappointed. I let her go to bed before me, working late into the night in the study, then slipped in next to her once she was asleep. One night she stirred and touched me, her hand resting on my thigh. I pretended to be asleep.

All I wanted to do was hide the fact that I knew about her messages, about fucking Duncan. I wanted to buy time so that I could work out how to bring her back to me. I was convinced I just needed time. But as the days and weeks passed it didn't work out like that. It didn't work out like that at all. I found myself having to fight the urge to steal secret looks at her phone. I found my thoughts filled with the words I'd read. I found myself absent-mindedly thinking of the moment when those two very different Brightons collided all those years ago. The night Tom saved me. Just like that moment, the messages I'd read festered inside me. I couldn't sleep and Isla drifted further and further away. I pushed her further and further away when I needed her most.

My only comfort came during the few hours of stolen sleep that I did manage. Then I would dream of Dad and the beach hut often. His happy song became a soothing lullaby and I knew he was close. I knew he was coming. He was sailing closer as Isla was being blown far away.

*

The wind stops. Light returns, yellow then brighter, golden now. There is silence. I look up. The door is ahead of me, the big brass handle right there. I take a final step. My hand closes around it. It is cold to the touch.

Isla.

I shake again. My hand is shaking. My mouth is dry. I listen but hear nothing. The world around me, be it the living world or somewhere else, is absolutely still and absolutely silent. I feel as if the sands running through my hourglass, passing through the eye that is that night in Camden, that moment in the photograph Isla gave to me when we were lovers, have stopped. I feel that time has stalled and ended.

I turn the handle. The door glides open. I step inside. The hall is warm and still like the outside world. My eyes follow the sweep of the stairs. Are they sleeping up there? Have I broken through? The Tide ebbs around me. I notice the picture of waves crashing against the seawall at Walberswick. I smile at it and remember a good, good day.

Can I reach them? Are they here? I must know.

I walk across the hall and stand at the foot of the stairs. I listen into the house. I listen into the Tide. I feel them, I'm sure I do. And I feel love. My mouth is so dry. I have come so far. I have fought to be here. I grip the banister. I must reach them. Whether I am a ghost or not, whether this is their world or not, I have to reach them.

Isla.

My voice is rasping and barely there.

Isla!

Clearer now. I listen into the house. I listen into the Tide. Silence.

I shout now, loud and urgent.

Isla! Isla!

62

The sea was rough the day the two Brighton collided. The waves were grey plough shears with white crests, booming against the stony beach. The gulls that lived in the old bones of the West Pier were restless and banked around and around, flying over the esplanade and the white buildings before heading back over the churning sea. It was fabulous. It was the first big sea of autumn. The sound of the stones clattering back under the waves between each boom reminded me of Suffolk and home. I was sitting on the seawall eating chips from the little place in the arches below. I'd loaded them with salt and vinegar and the taste made me think of home too. I had no idea that the world around me was resolving itself for the placement of one of the tallest pins in my map. Some pins shine like beacons and sing of hope and joy; others are malignant and seed a growth as destructive as the malfunctioning cells that trigger the cancer which took my Dad. This pin was one of those.

'Hi, Mags. Sorry I'm late,' came Kelly's voice from behind me.

'All right, Kells,' I replied looking up, grinning with a mouthful of potato and grease. "S all right, I got some chips while I was waiting,' I explained, offering up the bag.

'Where's the ketchup?' Kelly asked, helping herself to one of the crispier, darker ones.

'If you do the salt and vinegar properly you don't need sauce,' I explained, quoting Dad verbatim.

'Wow . . . I see what you mean,' Kelly nodded.

The traffic must have been flowing in perfect harmony, perfect alignment with our light conversation, because everything came together without any warning, any sense of importance or foreboding. The two Brightons simply drifting silently but surely together.

'Thanks for coming today, Mags,' Kelly said from squarely in my Brighton, our Brighton, as we finished the chips together. I screwed up the paper.

'No problem, Kells.'

'It's just that this might be the start of a regular gig. We could get on the recommended list for weddings and you can charm the arse off a donkey.'

I laughed, but it was true. She was right. Those were truly this dog's days and I knew it. 'Right, let's do it, then,' I said, standing up and brushing down my black t-shirt.

Together we turned and looked across the road to the Grand Hotel, its balconies and ornate white stonework, its Georgian glory, its proud entrance busy with the arrival of fine guests for some evening do and its very own little cut of tarmac, complete with waiting concierge in a Quality Street uniform.

'Recommended list for weddings, hey?'

Then it came. The other Brighton.

A Mercedes-Benz turned out of the traffic in front of us, Kelly and me, whilst we were waiting to cross the road. It was a big E-Class saloon, silver and new. The concierge stepped forward. The car stopped in front of him. The driver got out: a tall man with neat, short grey hair. He looked like an ancient old man in his fifties to me. He was wearing a dinner suit and bow tie and he looked comfortable in them. He raised a hand to a couple who were walking up the steps to the grand entrance. He spoke over the car roof to the concierge, his words lost in the traffic. The concierge nodded and waved up a lackey whom I hadn't noticed before. The new chap, in a lesser uniform that was more Odeon Cinema from when I was a kid than Quality Street, took the keys from the old man. Then the traffic cleared and Kelly started across the road. I was about to follow when the concierge opened the passenger door and a woman stepped out. She was wearing a red and gold evening dress. I only had a view of her back but it was enough. I froze. It was Isla. And the old cunt was that fucking Duncan cunt.

Kelly reached the other side of the road and looked around for me. I wanted instinctively to hide but I stayed fixed to the spot. Fucking Duncan walked around the car and offered Isla his arm. His face was bright and confident and, although I didn't admit it then, full of love. Together, arm-in-arm, promenading like Mum and Dad, like Isla and me that first evening when we went to Papa's, they walked. There was the Brighton of *I can't stay*, there was the Brighton she returned to when she left mine, there was the Brighton I didn't think about, the Brighton I had chosen not to see. I felt a jealousy like nothing I had known, I felt hate and I felt a love for Isla that I couldn't hold back, and it hurt. God, it hurt. As they walked up the steps, Mr and Mrs Fucking Duncan, and the Mercedes moved off, I watched and it burned. I looked down at my clothes. I looked up at the car. I had never known anyone who had a Mercedes, not even Vince's family with their big house. To me at that time they were things of the rich, things from another world, another Brighton.

How could I compete with that? How could I ever give Isla that?

I turned and walked away. Kelly ran after me, calling my name. I don't think Isla heard. I don't think she ever knew.

She looked beautiful in that dress.

The Heroes never did get the gig at the Grand. When Kelly caught me up she shouted my name and spun me round by the shoulder. Her voice had sounded confused and annoyed. But the moment she saw my face all that changed. She understood without any explanation being needed.

We were still on the seafront, right at the end of West Street. The meeting, the Grand, wasn't mentioned. Instead we went straight to the pub. Not just any pub, not just the nearest pub, we walked over to the Dorset in the Lanes, on the corner of North Road and Gardner Street. The Dorset was a proper boozer in those days and we went there when proper drinking was required. We used it more like a clinic than a pub. Kelly and I got heavy drunk. I was straight on the whisky; Kelly followed soon after. The last of the evening sun was fading outside and it was smoky and dim inside. I remember talking about Isla, about Isla and fucking rich Duncan, while Kelly talked about Lucy, of future 'Lucy Too Damn Cool' fame. They had already spoken on the phone several times and I think she already knew her existing relationship was going to have to end; she knew she'd met the one for her. It was something she had never expected and she was in a mess. It was an evening of two concurrent drunk conversations across the same small table with cracked varnish and the word *PAWG* scratched into it, both of us speaking and neither of us listening. Ironic that I was talking about two different worlds, two Brightons going on in the same place.

Finally, we drifted out into North Street. The chill of the autumn night coming unexpected after the cosy warmth of the Dorset. We went our separate ways. I was shockingly drunk. My memory after that is patchy. I remember trying to buy whisky from the convenience store further down North Street but they refused to serve me. I remember struggling with the push–pull zen of their door and swearing. I remember walking through town. I remember people looking – some laughing, some angry, some afraid. I remember someone pushing me away when I walked into them and me being saved from falling by a telephone kiosk that I backed into.

Then I had a bottle of whisky in my hand. I don't know where I bought it - I have a feeling I stole it. I was shivering. I only remember the taste of it in my numb mouth and a sense of fear as I pulled at it and wanted not to and couldn't stop myself. Then there was Tom's door. I'd drank myself to an ugly place. An angry place. I kicked at his door and my fists were on it. Then there was Tom. I shouted about fucking Duncan, about his disgusting old hands on Isla: vile and repulsive and wrong. I was going to go down to the Grand and fucking kill him. I was going to do this because he was a cunt. Tom's face was bobbing and weaving in front of mine. His hands turning me back by the shoulders to face him again, again. His eyes searching mine, questioning, reading, caring. He spoke my name many times, sometimes an appeal, sometimes a question, sometimes an order sharp enough to cut through the whisky. Then he was helping me walk. Shepherding me, guiding me. Just Tom. The angry faces and the laughing faces and the scared faces of the crowds faded away into the night.

I don't remember arriving back at Bedford Square; only the high-pitched whine of a whisky hangover I woke to early the next morning. There was a glass of water and aspirins by the bed. I took them gratefully. Then I realised Tom was asleep in the corner of the room on the old brown armchair I'd bought at the Fiveways shop on Ditchling Road and carried back with Vince and used as a clothes horse ever since. There were towels and a bowl, my washing-up bowl, beside him. There he had waited like a healer keeping a vigil over a patient, waiting for the fever to break, waiting to nurse me back to health. But that day I had no need of his counselling or his healing. He'd already saved me from the night before and the clinic had worked. The clinic and the whisky medicine had done their job. The other Brighton was already back in its box and my brief view of Mr and Mrs Fucking Duncan with it. Locked away with through my power of denial. Our young love affair continued. Jesus, what a wonderful time we had.

Of course, I'd only put it away not cured myself, the clinic, the Dorset, the whisky, only masked the symptoms; the disease endured and grew inside me, festering unnoticed.

63

Isla! I shout again.

No answer comes. Perhaps my voice cannot reach them. Perhaps I cannot be heard.

No. I must reach them.

I look over at the door to my study. I look away quickly. I climb the stairs. I listen into the house. I listen and listen.

Nothing.

Even the steps do not creak. I *must* be a ghost here. I have no body here, no weight. This must be the world of the living. Are they here?

I reach the landing, the step where Jack would sit and listen to the adult world below. The morning light reaches in through the stained-glass window beside me. A static collage of colour. All is so still. My bedroom door is ajar. I cross the bare boards and the rug. I place my hand on the white glossed wood. My mouth feels dry again. I shake again. Suddenly physical, suddenly connected to the wood. I look along the corridor to the children's rooms. Their doors are ajar too.

Isla.

My voice is nothing more than a whisper. No reply comes. I look at the children's doors again. I must know. I push gently. The door swings open. I look into the room. The bed is empty. The room smells of fresh laundry, the washing soap we used. The bed has not been slept in. The clock by the bed is blank. I try the switch by the door. The light does not come on. There is no power. Why?

Isla!

My shout fills the room. I step back into the corridor.

Isla!

Jack!

May!

I run to Jack's door. I throw it open. Empty. The bed hasn't been touched.

Isla!

May's room is the same. Where are they? What does it mean?

I run down the stairs. Still my feet make no sound.

Isla!

I run to the living room. Empty. The fireplace is swept clean and cold. I try the light switch here. Dead, no power. Nothing is working. I run to the kitchen. No one.

Isla!

I run back into the hall. The front door is wide open. I'm sure I closed it.

Isla.

The photographs! The collage! I stop and look back at the kitchen door. I run back in to check. The collage of photographs that Isla made last Easter is gone. The wall is bare. I feel coldness in my spine. I stare at the blank wall. What does it mean? I back away, out into the hall again. I go to shout again but stop myself. I sink down on to the stairs. I sit. I look around myself. I put my head in my hands and listen to the silence. They are not here. Does this mean . . . If they are not here then they must be . . . I must have . . .

No I can't bear that.

I feel as if I am sinking. I want to weep, weep like I did on the motorway that day, but only the living can weep. I look out of the door and down the driveway now bathed in summer sun and feel so far away from its warmth.

Wait, something moves! There! Down the driveway. I stare and watch a figure emerge.

This has to be it. It has come for me. It is time.

I know I shouldn't have come here. I knew I'd be followed. I've been followed since I found myself in this half-place, this hinterland. But I am not afraid now. I deserve this for what I did. I'm ready.

I watch it move up the drive. It leaves the shadows cast from the fir trees and comes into the sunlight. Its shape seems to change and flow in the heat of the new day, mingling, flowing, splitting and then coalescing. I didn't expect it to be a man.

How could I have done that to them?

This must be my reckoning for what I did. It has come.

I stand up.

A shadow falls across the open door. I look down. I cannot look at it. I feel its presence. I think of Isla, I think of Jack, I think of May. I think of that morning.

Any moment now.

I want to feel my heart racing. I want to feel fear in my stomach. I want to tremble. I want my breath to come short and fast. But I am dead. I am cold and empty and all I can do is keep my eyes closed and wait for its touch.

Any moment now.

My name is spoken! It comes to me in a familiar voice. The voice? Is this the voice from the beach that day?

My name is spoken again.

I know this voice!

I open my eyes and stare into what has come for me.

Henry!

It's Henry!

Henry stands at the door. His round, jolly body, alive with the Tide, fills it. He smiles at me.

He says my name again, his voice calm and gentle, his arms reaching out toward me, extending his greeting across the hall. I love Henry.

Henry . . . How did you?

He says that he followed me, that he wanted to stop me. He says I shouldn't do this to myself. He looks around the hall, eyes roaming high and low, his hands annotating his words. He steps closer. He looks at me directly. The Tide is in his eyes. His warm face is filled with concern. He reminds me of how Dad would look at me when I was afraid at night and he reminds me of how I felt when Jack came to me when he was afraid at night.

But I had to know, Henry. I had to.

He nods slowly. He understands.

He touches me, his hand on my shoulder. I feel the Tide. I feel Joyce closer now, a clear promise aglow in the flow from Henry.

Isla!

I feel Isla too. Not a promise, not like Joyce, but I feel her, I'm sure of it. I look into Henry's eyes. They are peaceful pools in the Tide. Jack and May too. I feel them. I feel the joy they ran and played within.

Henry. I don't understand.

Henry's eyes search mine.

Henry, I have to know. Help me. Help me, please.

I put my hand on his arm.

Help me.

Henry says that I don't need help. He says I already have all of the answers I'm looking for.

I don't. How can I?

Henry's eyes search mine again. He steps back. The Tide is all around him, bathing his curving, shining form.

He says that first I have to be honest, that truth has to start with me. He says *I* must give the truth if I want to find the truth. His hands cup together while he speaks, as if he's holding something precious.

But I am truthful!

Henry stares at me. There is sadness in his eyes. He pinches the bridge of his nose. His eyes close slowly.

He says my name. He says I must be honest. I must hide nothing, especially from myself. He opens his eyes again. They are fixed on me. He says I must tell the truth, I must face the truth. His eyes search mine in haste, jumping from focus to focus, demanding and urgent.

But I do! I'm not hiding. I'm not hiding anything. I tell the truth!

64

The apex of the bend blooms from the feathered, sliding, green horizon of hedge and bank and tree. His foot moves a breath, dipping with the slack given by tendons in a moment between waiting and action. His eyes are needles on the emerging edge of view. His automated response to the familiar, the oft travelled, the known, the trusted, builds through his muscles. His fingers tighten on the gearstick; his arm rises like a lever on a trap. He grips the steering wheel with the cat in the centre, knuckles whitening.

The car flashes forward, tyres gnawing at the road, a great and terrible and deadly mass of steel hurtling forward. The hedges shake with its passing. Animals bolt from the fierce boom of engine and tyres, cutting wakes through the barley in the fields beyond. A family of startled fieldfares takes to the wing.

The sound of the racing air streaming over the car reaches him as a muffled roar in the insulated world of the engineered, the styled and the expensive.

The moment resolves itself. Only power and more speed and a steady hand to deliver them with precision can see the car round. Only then, in the moment of judgement, can he control the out of control, force order and direction on the racing mass of steel and glass and leather that wants to fly straight, wants to burst through the bank and hedge and trees into the barley beyond.

His foot flashes down on the clutch. His hand snaps the stick through its gates. His foot jumps to the accelerator. His hand turns the wheel with certainty. His foot is down on the pedal in the same instant.

The car roars and lurches. The tyres shout. The mass is hauled round the bend on the edge of flight, on the edge of rolling and tumbling, on the edge of chaos. A smile begins to reach across his face. The flashing light from the tree canopy above blurs over the lenses of his sunglasses. He feels the forces he controls pitching through him, his muscles responding, his head heavy against his neck.

Then it happens. A new moment. A moment when everything changes. A moment when one single new variable is added to the precision of the known. An unknown, an unfamiliar, a new, an unpredicted, an unaccounted for. Chaos in the controlled.

SCANIA.

Both hands are on the wheel. His muscles lock. His heart wants to explode. He turns the wheel over and over. The car – the mass, the steel, the glass – begins to lift and tip. Everything is chaos apart from the one new single constant: SCANIA.

His eyes fall on the empty car around him. The slide becomes a spin and brings him closest to the lorry. He closes his eyes.

65

Henry's eyes drift from mine, refocusing on empty space somewhere between us. They dart left and right, tiny hints of motion that speak of thinking, reading what has just passed. They close. He turns his face to the ceiling. He shakes his head slowly. He holds his hands up as if he's testing for rain.

He speaks. I do not understand the words. I do not recognise the language although I feel I have heard it before. I feel as if I spoke it once, in a dream perhaps. His words roll and ebb. They are like the sound of the Tide if it were not silent. Like the edge of a distant song, part heard, part felt, where the words blur and just the melody and sentiment reaches you. Like Dad's song in my dreams. It is strange. It is beautiful.

I know what he's saying. I don't need to speak the language to understand his meaning. I don't need to hear the words to know someone is singing the blues: *For God's sake* has a universal ring in any language, in any number of tongues.

I look at Henry. I watch him. The house is utterly silent except for his strange words. He stops. Now the silence is absolute. He looks back at me. His eyes are bright with the Tide.

He says my name. His voice is gentle but strong. His hands come together slowly. He presses his mouth to them as if in prayer. His eyes do not leave me.

Must stay calm.

He says my name again.

I know what he wants. I know what he is going to ask of me.

He says please. His fingers fanning out, sending his request to the four corners of the room.

Must stay calm

He says please again.

I step backwards. My ankle meets the bottom step. I think of Isla and Jack and May. I can't stop shaking. I drop on to the stairs. I'm sitting. I can't stop looking at Henry.

No!

Henry asks what I have hidden.

Henry, I . . . nothing.

Enough.

Henry's voice fills the house! I stare at him. Enough, enough. The word, the voice.

Henry?

Henry nods slowly. His eyes are filled with love.

You?

Henry nods slowly. He crouches before me, his great rounded body moving effortlessly. I feel the Tide flowing from him. I'm still shaking.

He says enough of this. He says no more. He says please.

I look at him. I can't, Henry, I—

He says I must be honest. He says that he loves me. It's true. I know he does. I love Henry. He's beautiful.

He says my name again, softly. Again, he asks me for the truth.

66

'Daddy, there's a lady coming to our school today,' his daughter begins with excitement. 'She's going to show us all about pianos and—'

The door slams. His daughter's voice is lost. He stops and turns back. His hand moves toward the door. He frowns. His hand stops short, fingers folding in. He turns to walk to his car. The door opens. He turns back.

'Wait,' his wife says. 'You're dropping us off . . . for school. Remember, the Discovery's being serviced—'

'There's no . . . I'm late!' he insists, holding up his arm and watch like a shield.

'We have to get to school!' she snaps finally.

His jaw muscles flex. She looks down and then back up at him, her eyes resolute. The decision is resolved in the silence.

'Two minutes!' He holds two fingers up like a stressed Churchill.

She disappears into the house, her voice calling out to his son and his daughter. He marches across the gravel drive, his shadow long in the bright early-morning July sun.

He waits in the car. He looks back at the front doors reflected in the rear-view mirror. They are still ajar. His focus moves to the stranger staring back at him. He looks down at his lap. He runs his hand over his face and blinks sleep away. His head aches with a dull persistence.

He looks up at the oval clock set into the dashboard.

He ignores the clock and looks at his watch.

He frowns.

He puts the key in the ignition and looks down at the steering wheel with the cat on the boss and starts the engine. He holds down a switch and looks up. Servo motors whine behind him and the windows drop a half-inch. The roof above him lifts and begins to retract. He continues to look. The canvas folds and draws clear, the cream lining replaced with bright early-morning summer sky. A single feathered contrail spreads out across an otherwise faultless blue dome. The air has a chill to it and is heavy with the smell of the conifers along the driveway. The servos stop and the car chimes.

He looks up at the oval clock.

He ignores the clock and looks at his watch.

He looks back at the house. He sighs. He grips the wheel tightly.

He looks at the oval clock

He ignores the clock and looks at his watch.

He looks back at the house, catching another glimpse of the stranger in the mirror.

He flexes his fingers on the wheel, squeezing the thick leather.

He looks at the oval clock

He ignores the clock and looks at his watch.

He feels the slipping seconds eating at him. The journey to the school and then work plays out in his thoughts. Mathematics resolves itself.

His son and his daughter rush from the doors. The car engine revs into life. His son's face is fixed and serious as he runs across the drive. His daughter trails behind, pulling her pink rucksack with a cartoon girl on it behind her. It bounces down against the gravel, half carried, half dragged. His wife steps out behind them. She locks the door. She looks beautiful. She hurries across the gravel, stooping to pick up a pink and red pony key ring that has fallen from his daughter's bag.

67

I'm on my knees. I'm shaking. I slump to the ground. Henry moves to support me. He crouches beside me.

Henry. Henry, what I have I done?

Henry says that it is okay.

They're dead. I killed them. My beautiful children! Isla! I killed them! I killed them, Henry!

Henry pulls me up. He is in front of me. He moves his hands to my shoulders. We are kneeling and facing each other.

He says no.

I don't understand. They must be dead. That's why I could never find them when I searched for them among the living. That's why they're not here.

They're dead, Henry.

I look around me. I listen into the silence. That's why they're not here. That's why the house is empty.

Henry closes his eyes. He sighs. He shakes his head slowly and whispers in that strange flow of language. I'm not shaking any more. This is the end of my road and I don't know what I can do now. There is nothing I can do.

They're dead, Henry. I killed them. My voice is a whisper.

Henry opens his eyes, bright and keen and knowing. He says they're not dead.

Then, where are they? My voice is a shout. I didn't know it would be.

Henry says this isn't the world of the living. He says that I cannot walk back to the living.

I stare at Henry. He's right. I see it in his eyes. He guides me to my feet. We stand facing each other.

He asks if I want to see them. He gestures around the room.

Yes!

Isla, Jack, May, their faces fill my thoughts. I love them. They're beautiful.

TRANSITION

Henry says to take his hand.

I take it. Isla and Jack and May. He turns to the open doorway. He turns back, his face warm and filled with an innocent excitement, just like at the monument when he came for me. It reminds me of when I was little, playing at the beach hut. It reminds me of Jack and May when they acted out stories with their toys, their minds far away and their eyes seeing every detail of imagined worlds. He looks at the open door. He runs at it. I run with him. He calls out to me. He asks if I am ready.

I nod because I am.

He glows in the Tide and the sun, shining with a warm golden lustre. He jumps at the threshold. I leap with him.

The land drops away from us, the driveway, the house, the lane. I see it all in a perfect hemisphere below me, so sharp, impossibly wide-angled and bordered with those clouds that look like hills to the west and the sea to the east, the sea and those clouds that look like land. We're in the Tide!

Oh my God!

We are birds on the wing, Henry and me. This is just as it was when he came for me at the monument. I remember now.

I remember!

We spiral up and up. The air streams firm and cold under me and soft above me. I understand it. Following him is instinct. Moving is instinct. With a reach and a lean and a will, I move as I choose. The Tide is everywhere! Henry looks at me. We stop climbing. The air under us is suddenly warm and perfect like a welcome bath. We glide without moving. Henry looks down. I look too. The world is an impossible dome below us, every detail sharp and absolute.

The sun is everywhere!

The Tide is everywhere!

Henry furls his wings and pivots forward. He drops, spiralling down through the sun and the Tide as if diving through golden waters. I follow. My wish interpreted in the fold of my wings, my downward glide automatic and easy.

Oh my God!

We glide down above the spinning dome of the world. The splitting air warm beneath and cool over me. The landscape rushes at me, the detail divides and blooms, sharper and sharper, greater and greater patterns of land and trees and fields and sky.

And roads! And movement!

Movement jumps out and shines like a beacon. The white of a van moving along the road sings out, irresistible, bright, fleeting, fascinating.

I see my house!

There below Henry. We sweep down and down and down toward it.

We land with effortless grace on a tree at the edge of the driveway, flight and motion to perching and stillness in a single calm instant.

The living world!

The living world explodes at me! The air is alive with smells. Trees and grasses and flowers and earth and dust coming at me and filling the air. Some sweet, some subtle, some ripe, a great collage of flowing scent. The air feels heavy with it and I feel it move over me. And it is moist! I feel the water from the breath of the living around me and in it is the taste of the trees and of the dust rising from the gravel drive. It is spring here. It's so alive.

And the sounds!

The world is alive with sound coming to me from all directions and distances, filled with song, the buzz of life and the whir of humanity. Birdsong is everywhere, coming from far and near and all steps between to paint a picture of a great wide world: a backdrop canvas of mixed song in all directions as my head darts side-to-side. Now individual songs come from points around, near and nearer, whines and pips, fluted calls, joyful, rolling melodies, language to me here. Insects ply the moving, smelling, heavy and moist air, rising and falling in the warm flows above the gravel below me. Some of the songs that reach me tell of them. It is fascinating, beautiful, enthralling, overwhelming.

Henry turns his head and looks at me. I feel the Tide and joy from him. He is beautiful here as he is there. I love Henry. I turn my head, in tiny, sharp steps, focusing, seeing, smelling, feeling, hearing. I want to join the many voices, the many songs. I want to sing.

I want to sing!

Henry jumps to a further branch. I look. His eyes are on the drive. Motion jumps out from gaps between leaves. My heart races. Something is coming. I hear it. A motor, its changing guttural notes. Tyres on the gravel. A humming of mechanical power. I move my head, rapid tiny steps and shifts building a picture from the new angles and the glimpses they give. A car, a blue car, its colour solid against the changing variegated canvas of spring that fills the world around me. The birdsong shifts and flows around it, the points of calls and pips against the canvas of background song accommodate the intrusion but do not fly from it.

I want to sing.

The car moves into view. It seems slow. I move more quickly. The sun catches its body and blazes like electricity in its lustrous blue panels. The buzz of the machine and the dry taste of diesel fumes reach me. They build from faint to distinct. The sun gleams from the windscreen. I blink into it. The brightness moves up to the roof with the final slow creeping of the vehicle.

It stops.

It is fascinating. My head still moves rapidly. Tiny movements bring ever more detail. Silver chrome, form, folds, edges.

The back doors open!

Jack! Jack!

Jack steps from the car. He pulls a bag with him. He is splendid! He is beautiful!

Jack!

His blonde hair is tidy now and shines bright in the sun. He is older – a year, perhaps two. His eyes are bright and sharp and intelligent and there is joy and the Tide in them. He is perfect.

Jack!

He looks at me! He smiles!

I want to sing.

He walks toward the house and—

May!

May steps from the car. Her hair longer now, bobbing like Isla's when we were young. May is older too – seven perhaps? She takes my breath away. My head is still. She is the loveliest thing I have ever looked on. She is beautiful.

You're beautiful! May! My beautiful little girl!

She looks! She looks right at me. The Tide shines in the great depths of her warm eyes.

She looks to Jack and chases after him.

They laugh!

They are so full of life. So alive. So beautiful! I want to sing. I want my joy to fill the air!

Henry hops closer. His eyes blink at me and burn with bright excitement.

The front doors open, both of them.

There, there she is!

Isla steps from the passenger door. She is wearing a shift dress, shades of white. Her hair is in a bob. She is beautiful. I cannot breathe or move or make a sound. She is beautiful. A silver pencil line snakes along her arm, a faint scar across her brown skin. She steps away from the car. She moves with a gentle limp that most would miss. She looks strong. Stronger than ever. I want to sing.

An old man steps from the driver's door. He waits there. He smiles at Isla. He is tall and his hair is white and his face is kind and the Tide flows from him. He looks at Isla with love.

I know him.

Isla walks around slowly. He keeps a hand on the open door. He is very old. Isla puts her hand to his shoulder and kisses the side of his face. She speaks words but they are lost to me. The Tide flows between them. I am glad. Seeing love surround her fills me with joy.

It's Duncan. Not the Duncan of my darkest fears, the rival, the competitor, the danger. The real Duncan, old now, the Duncan who, like all of us, loves Isla.

Thank God she is not alone.

I remember words read. Word of friendship, words of support. Not words of lust or desire. Words of love. The same words but so different now.

MESSAGES.> DUNCAN

> **Don't be sad. You're not alone. I'm always here.**

> **Thank you. I miss you.**

> **I miss you too.**

> **Thank you for yesterday. I don't know what I'd do without you.**

> **Don't be silly. You don't need to thank me. Love Duncan**

Jack and May wait at the front doors, under the shade of the porch. They chatter and laugh. Isla walks toward them, strong and brave and graceful and beautiful. Duncan is back in the car. The engine starts, the sound reaching me in so many layers, a roar over patterns of tapping, rasping, sliding and thudding.

They are so alive!

I want to sing.

The car moves off. Isla stops and turns. She is so close now. She raises a hand. I watch her, every line, every breath. Her hand drops.

May calls out. Isla smiles, her face breaking into laughter as she turns to respond. So much love and so much life!

I sing!

The song burst from me and fills the air. It is Dad's happy song, his song of joy. It comes as harmonies and springtime calls that add to the great flow of song all around, the final immediate voice against the landscape of sound that surrounds us.

I sing!

I sing of Isla and Jack and May. I sing of us and of the times we had. Those precious years that I would have had a thousand of. I sing of my beautiful lover and I sing of little princesses and brave knight sons. I sing of making love, I sing of bedtime stories, I sing of Christmas and of returning home. I sing of summer and winters warm together, I sing of hope, I sing of grandchildren, I sing of all the times we had. I sing of family and I sing of love.

Isla stops and looks at me. Her eyes fixed on me. I sing at her. I sing for her.

She smiles! She smiles at me. The Tide flows in a great bridge between us. Her eyes shine with tears. I sing of my love. I sing of my beautiful and only love. I sing of the children we have made and the joy they add to the world. I sing of our family and the love that still flows between us.

My children are my gift to the world and it is so much the richer for them!

Isla raises her hands and presses them against her mouth. She closes her eyes slowly. She is still.

May calls to her again. Jack laughs.

Isla opens her eyes.

I finish my song.

We stare at each other. I love Isla. She is beautiful. A moment passes.

She turns and walks over to the children, my beautiful children. Isla opens the door. They step inside, their voices and laughter drifting away into the house.

I turn to Henry. My joy is reflected back in his eyes.

He jumps to the wing and banks high up above the drive. I follow.

PART THREE

THE LIGHT

68

Isla stopped at the door and kissed me. I pulled her close, my hands sliding under the jacket she'd just put on, feeling the warmth of her body through the top that had been on my bedroom floor for much of the evening. Her arms slid around me and we came together with her head against my neck. She smelled of the shampoo she kept in my bathroom, she smelled uniquely of Isla, she smelled of our lovemaking, she smelled of love. She kissed my neck and we held each other.

It was March. It had been the first real day of spring with a warm breeze coming off the sea. It was the first time we'd been able to see each other for a week and we'd celebrated with dinner at Papa's. We'd walked back through an unexpectedly cold evening along a deserted esplanade. We talked and listened to the sea clawing at the stones like some unseen animal digging in the darkness, our breath lingering white. A couple, of similar age to us, walked by, hand-in-hand. We didn't hold hands out on the street in case we were seen. In case Isla was seen. But when they passed I felt her hand on mine and we locked arms, close against the cold. Isla smiled up at me, her eyes bright and reflecting the yellow lamps along the prom. They were filled with excitement. It had after all been a week, a very long week. We hurried back to Bedford Square in a huddle together, in a part-jog, part-shuffle, racing-crab kind of way. I chased Isla up the stairs, pinching at her bum, our feet loud on the steps. At my door I fumbled for my key. Her hands teasing at my groin, while she kissed my neck, laughing with mischief. Well, it had been a week, a very long week.

I kicked the door shut and we fell into the bedroom, kissing and pulling at our clothes. Penetration was immediate and urgent. We fucked hard. Then there was giggling, then there were cigarettes, then there was holding each other, then there was kissing, then there was lovemaking.

Later, after midnight, once the duvet was over us and I was slowly sinking into the still and peaceful waters of the pool of warm contented sleep I found myself floating on, Isla kissed me again. This was a different kiss. This was the slow, lingering kiss on the side of my face that was an apology. The kiss that said *I'm sorry, but I have to go.* It was the kiss that triggered a much-rehearsed sequence, the set piece of our evening that always capped off the spontaneity, the fun, the joy. It was a shit but important part of our time together. It was one I had thought about a great deal. It was one, through denial as much as anything, I had made my peace with because I knew Isla couldn't give me more and if that was the best deal on the table I was taking it. Of course, I wanted her to stay; I wanted her never to leave. I wanted that with all of my heart and I knew she wanted it too. But I knew that it was more complicated than that; I knew the other Brighton that Isla went to had duty and promises that I didn't understand but respected because they were important to her. So, I had resolved myself never to make it more difficult for her than it had to be. I was determined that every evening should end well and that she should leave with me smiling at her. So I sat up and I did just that: I smiled. I kissed her. I got up and began to dress; being first to do so had become part of my ritual to take responsibility for that point in our evenings away from Isla.

Isla stepped away from me and put her hand on the latch. Her eyes searched mine and she smiled. I smiled back. She opened the door.

'Come back, very, very soon,' I said, leaning against the wall.

Isla nodded slowly. She stretched forward and gave me a gentle kiss on the side of my face. Then with a last brief smile, her eyes fixing on mine for just a moment, she turned and walked out on to the landing. I moved to the door and leaned against the frame. I watched her disappear down the stairs into the dim yellow half-light. I listened to her feet fall quick and sharp on the steps below. I listened to the front door open, the brass letter flap clanging. I listened to the door close with a bump and then a more determined thud to overcome the stick of the swollen woodwork. The letterbox clattered again. I kept smiling.

I closed the door and walked through to the living room. It smelled of incense and mint. The door to the balcony was a pallid block of yellow in the sodium light of Brighton and the fairy lights of the shrine twinkled. I walked over to the piano, sat and lifted the cover. I switched on the lamp; the keyboard looked like a smoker's teeth under the dim bulb. I started to play pairs of notes and combinations of pairs. Gently so as not to disturb my neighbours. This had become part of my ritual too. When Isla left I played the blues and sometimes I wrote some of my very best material. The rumble of a late train came to me from across the town, dull and mechanical. It somehow suited the tune. I continued to play experimentally. I whispered lyrics as they came to me. I was building a song about Isla, a song about lovers.

Then it came to me: a moment of absolute clarity, an epiphany that could only have come when I was making the blues. Suddenly, I understood what it was to truly love someone, to truly love Isla. And in that moment, I knew that I had to leave Isla's life. I stopped playing, my fingers resting on the old keys so smooth and warm that it was as if they were just my fingers. The late train rumbled in the distance with a random chime of metal sliding on metal joining its song. It was the very worst thing for me, the very, very last thing I wanted to do. That's why I knew it was true. I thought of Vince. And I thought of Tom, his words of comfort coming back to me from the night the two Brightons collided. *It's okay*, he had said. *It will be all right*, he had said. *It will work out*, he had said.

'You bastard, Vince,' I said, because he'd been right all along. He hadn't wanted to be, I knew that, but nonetheless he was right on the money. Tom had been wrong; he'd wanted to be right, but he was wrong. The world would have been a much better place if it had been up to Tom, but unfortunately it wasn't.

I lit a cigarette and inhaled deeply, holding the smoke until it burned. I thought of Isla, of her eyes when they searched mine before she left. She was looking for an answer that could never be found. She was trapped. Our love affair was wonderful. It was beautiful. But we were diseased by it, just as Vince had known we'd be. For me the disease was jealously, growing, dividing, multiplying and festering inside me; for Isla, it was guilt. But where I had denial, Isla had pain. Where I in my own way had made my peace with having Isla in my life in the only way that I could, Isla was paying for every moment of joy, our joy, *my* joy, in full. Her guilt was growing unchecked from roots deep in her good catholic upbringing. I could see it in her. It showed in her eyes when she left me at the end of the evening, when she left my bed and went back to Duncan. She was trapped by promises she'd made when she had needed something secure in her life, promises to reassure a nervous Duncan who'd always known that in the end she'd find someone younger, someone like me. It was as if a light was slowly going out inside her, dimming each time we parted.

I turned the lamp off and sat in the half-light of filtered sodium yellow and fairy lights. How could I leave her? How could I give her up?

Thank God fate decided to step in and mug me before I had to do it.

69

Our feet are on the drive again. We are men again. Henry holds my arm, steadying me. I step away. His eyes still blaze with excitement.

They're alive! They're alive, Henry!

Henry grins broadly, his eyes twinkling with the Tide. He nods. He laughs. He nods again.

It is a beautiful summer morning. Those clouds that look like hills are still there in the west. They catch the sunlight, shifting lazily. The sun is warm and the Tide flows with it. I can still feel them in it. Isla, Jack and May. I feel their love washing over me. It is everywhere.

I feel them! I feel them, Henry.

I look to the faultless blue sky above us.

I can feel them! I cry out. I cannot help it. I want the sky, the world, everything and everyone to know.

Did you see them, Henry?

Henry nods again. He grabs me and hugs me, his great curving body warm against me. I feel his joy in the Tide.

He releases me and we look into the sun and the Tide together. Isla is all around us. Her love. And Jack and May. Their love, their excitement, their promise, their potential. It's all there. In the light and the Tide. Flowing from them. I think I understand now.

The Tide comes from the living?

Henry says it comes from people wherever they are.

It carries their love?

Henry puts his hands on my shoulders. His round face is beaming at me. His eyes look through me to far away. He says . . . He says it *is* their love. He says. He . . . He says it is everyone who has ever loved. It's true. I know it's true. I have always known it. I nod. I grin like a child. I grin like Jack and May grinned at me when we played together. I grin like I grinned at Mum and Dad when we played together.

Henry's eyes come back from that far place and focus on me. They are filled with love, they are filled with kindness, they are filled with joy. He says that is why I was never alone here. He raises his hands and gestures all around us. He says . . . He says that is why *no one* is ever alone.

I turn slowly, looking at the world around me. My house, the driveway, the trees, so green and vibrant, soughing in the gentle breeze. The clouds on the western horizon that make the shapes of the Brecon Beacons shimmer invitingly. I hear the sound of the sea, closer I'm sure than it should be. I smell salt. A gull soars up from over the trees to the east. I have no fear. None at all. The thought of the sea makes me happy. I think of Dad and the beach hut. I think of chasing Julie across the sand and shingle when we were little. I think of Jack and May chasing each other over the same sand and shingle, their laughter, their energy. This place is perfect and beautiful. The Tide flows around us and touches everything with love and beauty. Henry stands beside me. He is looking at the sun. I love Henry. I feel Joyce.

Joyce!

She is a promise with the sea. I think of her and running toward Henry just . . . Was it just yesterday? I remember waiting for her by the path from the marshes and going down to the sea. I remember so many times. I remember them all now, time after time after time after time. Her patience, her calming strength, her love. I love Joyce.

Let's find Joyce!

Henry looks back at me.

I want Joyce to know! I want to tell her about them, about Isla and Jack and May.

Henry nods his agreement. We walk down the driveway away from the house. We leave no mark on the gravel.

70

I knew something wasn't right the moment I pulled up on the drive. It was not long before I was killed – the second Sunday of that May in fact. I finished work early and arrived home bang on six o'clock. Even for a weekend this was an hour or more earlier than usual. It was a perfect evening. It had been a very hot fine day after a week of rain. The garden, the trees, the hedges, the fields were all rich greens and splashes of late spring colour. The sun was a lazy yellow over the row of poplars to the south-west of the garden. Driving back, a thin mist had started to rise in the fields, the land sighing after the heat of the day. There was birdsong when I stepped out of the car, including the distant doleful call of a curlew from over the way toward the brook that crossed the road beyond the church.

Jack and May didn't come to the door or emerge from around the house. This was strange. We had a trampoline and swings and a slide in the back garden and warm evenings like this ended with them having to be ordered in at dusk. I pushed the door closed and listened. Still only the birdsong, joined by the scratchy note of a small bike or moped engine far off. The scent of the honeysuckle that grew by the study window reached me in its fullness and made my nose itch. I looked at the house. No lights were on. Standing there, I wondered if Isla had left me, if she had taken the children. I closed my eyes.

MESSAGES.> DUNCAN

I took a breath. I turned and looked over to the stable we used as a garage. The Discovery was there. I let go of the breath. Isla was in. But where were the children? Why was the house so quiet? I looked up at our bedroom window. The sash was open just a little and the muslin curtain, touched yellow by the late sun, showed in the gap.

I listened. Nothing. Even the curlew down by the stream had fallen silent. I glanced back at the car. I thought about leaving and coming back later, coming back at my usual time. I dismissed the thought and walked over the gravel that was actually pea shingle. The moment I walked into the shadow of the house the evening was cooler and I felt the breeze through my cotton shirt. I tried the door, half expecting it to be locked. It opened smoothly. I stepped inside. Silence met me. I glanced at the stairs. Then, looking away toward the lounge, I called out the children's names.

'Hello! Jack, May . . . Daddy's home.'

*

I'm talking about Jack and May. I can't help it! They are amazing. Seeing them again! Oh my God! I walk with Henry, side by side. We are on the lane that leads back toward the coast. Toward Joyce. The sun is high now and the Tide has settled deep around us, holding the sunlight and bathing the world with love. Henry's been smiling like Jack and May when, well, all time! All the time! Always so full of life and joy and love! They were loved. God, I loved them. God, I love them!

I love them, Henry!

Henry laughs and nods. I think he thinks I'm crazy!

I'm not crazy, Henry! Did you see them? Did you!

Henry nods again I feel the Tide and I feel Joyce there, the promise of her.

They're beautiful, Henry.

They're beautiful! My children are perfect and so full of life! I shout the words.

Henry says yes. His big kind face is full of my love for them. I feel the Tide and I remember him.

I remember!

I saw him in life! I remember! I remember him in the chair by my bed when I was ill in hospital and my drink tasted of plastic and Dad told me about the Meadow, about the hills and mountains and forests beyond the great river-flood that we would explore together, and said that if I went first he would come and find me. Henry was there next to me. He leaned over and put his arms around Dad and me.

I remember!

I remember Dad's words and Henry's silence. I think of Joyce. I think of Dad sobbing silently and me pretending to be asleep. Then there is Joyce, the same feeling as Dad when Henry was helping us. Just the same, and I know she is searching. I think of the little girl I felt running on the beach with Joyce and me and I know, I know she is searching; just as Dad would have done if I'd gone first. I know it. She has always been searching.

She's searching, Henry.

*

No reply came from Jack or May or Isla. I looked around the hallway. I learned over and looked into the kitchen. Nothing. The house was silent and still. I frowned. I put my hand on the banister and looked up the stairs, something in me didn't want to go up but I started to climb the steps, calling for Jack and May again.

'Magnus,' came Isla's voice from the sitting room door. It was calm and low. I let go of the banister. I looked at her. She was standing in the doorway. Her hands clasped at her waist. Even in the low light I could see she was wearing her dad's big old broken watch. My heart sank into my stomach.

'Hey,' I said. Isla took a step toward the stairs. 'Where are the little people?'

'They're at Sally's,' Isla replied calmly. Sally was a friend of Isla's who lived five minutes away and whose son Noah, Jack described as his *primo amigo*. She may as well have said they had gone to the moon; it made no sense at all.

MESSAGES.> DUNCAN

My heart raced. 'Oh?' I said, coming back down the few steps and putting my leather satchel down.

Isla stepped up and took my hands. Her grip was gentle. She looked sad. Then she spoke, but the words weren't the ones I expected.

'Cathy called . . .'

'Catherine?'

'Yes . . .' Isla nodded. 'It's Tom—'

'Tom? What about Tom? What's happened?'

'They've moved him from the hospital—'

'Well, that's good.' Isla squeezed my hands and tugged to stop me.

'They've moved him to St Judith's . . . the hospice.' Isla paused, her eyes patiently searching mine. I looked down. I wasn't ready for this at all. I hadn't even been thinking about Tom really. I'd decided he'd get better and it had been put to the side. I'd been working a lot.

'Fuck,' I said finally. 'I thought he was getting better . . . I thought Catherine had said—'

'I think things have moved quickly,' Isla explained.

'I . . .' I stopped. I didn't know what to say. Isla put her arms round me. I hugged her back. She smelled of Isla. I kissed the top of her head. She squeezed me then looked up into my face. She looked strong. My legs felt shaky. We both sat on the stairs.

'Fuck . . .' I said again, looking down at our clasped hands and Isla's dad's big old broken watch.

'We should go and see him,' Isla said. 'Tonight. Now,' she added and kissed me.

She was right, so I nodded.

'I'll drive us. Sally's good to have Jack and May for the night.'

I looked her in the eye.

'It's fine. Jack thinks it's brilliant and May adores Sally.'

'You should have called me—'

'Cathy didn't call until four and it took an hour to get the children sorted,' Isla explained. 'And I wanted to tell you here. I didn't want you to take the call when you were with people at work—'

'I was on my own . . . but thanks. I . . .'

Isla squeezed my hands again. 'Are you okay?'

I looked down at the hall rug and considered the question. 'Yes,' I said, because I was. I was because Isla was with me. 'We should tell, Vince,' I suddenly thought.

'Cathy already has—'

'God . . . Catherine . . . poor Catherine. How is she?'

'She's . . .' Isla paused. 'She's okay,' she said thoughtfully. 'Yeah,' she said, I think to herself as much as me. 'She's okay.'

I showered and changed. I'd taken longer to shower than usual, standing with eyes closed and face raised to the warm water washing over me. I tried to think about Tom and I did, but also, I thought about Isla and I was relieved that she hadn't cleared the house to talk to me about Duncan.

Twenty minutes later we were driving along quiet lanes, surrounded by fields flooded with evening mist beneath a slowly setting May sun. Isla drove and I sat in silence, watching the fields and hedges and trees and paths and lanes that Vince and Tom and I had always known, slip by. She reached over and put her hand on mine. We drove in silence; there was no need to speak. I was not alone. Isla was with me.

71

The night fate mugged me and stopped me giving Isla up came the week after my late-night epiphany. It was also the night that Tom met Catherine at the Catfish Club.

There was a sizeable queue impatiently shuffling along the pavement by the time Isla and I arrived. Mostly students with a scattering of older rock 'n' rollers and Brighton thirty-somethings. The wind was coming cold and damp off the sea and the mood of the queue was subdued. Not me; I was happy. I knew what I had to do and I knew it would have to be soon. But delay, the putting-off of things, was a brother skill to denial in me. And until the moment came I was determined to enjoy every second with Isla, and besides I'd had a whisky or two and that always made tomorrow feel a lot further away. She was simply a picture. She had her hair in a black beret and her red raincoat stopped above her knees at the same delicious place as the black dress she wore under it. Officially she was working, of course, so she had her leather camera bag over her shoulder. The Heroes were up so I was wearing my black suit. Isla loved it when I wore my suit. We walked up beside the queue. Apple Geoff – so named because he was a puritanical body builder who only ever drank fresh apple juice whilst on duty – was working the door. We squeezed past the front of the queue without too many of the usual protests or threats.

'All right, Mags!' Apple Geoff said, a broad smile breaking out across his sunbed-tanned face. He shook my hand, always a surprisingly gentle grip. Isla got a gracious nod.

'Geoff,' I nodded. 'Are my amigos in yet?'

'Yep, got here, I'd say, approximately thirty minutes ago,' Apple Geoff replied efficiently, stepping by us and resuming his standard *at ease* position at the head of the queue. I always suspected that Apple Geoff secretly longed for a career in the military.

'Cool. I'll see you later on, then.'

We made our way through the lobby, which smelled of faux-roses from the carpet spray they always used. The girl at the cloakroom hatch watched me. I winked at her. She looked away, busying herself with arranging the small book of tickets on the counter. Isla pinched my arse through my suit trousers and barged me toward the stairs.

The basement room – with its stage and dance floor surrounded by a sea of tables, themselves corralled by booths of old velvet benches and mahogany panelling with broken vanish and forty years' worth of drunken graffiti – was a smoky, humid den of bodies and rhythm. We walked in just as a woman I hadn't seen before, who I later found out was called Alice O, had taken the stage. She was unaccompanied and sang to a backing track she'd slipped Southampton Barry, the DJ. She started singing Dusty Springfield's 'Beautiful Soul'. She'd upped the tempo and spun it her way and it worked. Her voice was amazing: huge but gentle. It filled the room. Isla and I both stopped and watched. The sea of sweaty folks on the dance floor began to move. She looked fabulous. She was big and beautiful – you'd have to say fat, with folds of flesh rolling under and around her purple dress, but she carried it with such health, such vitality, she seemed to glow with life. Very much like Henry, now I come to think about it. Isla smiled at me and finally took my hand. I squeezed it.

A loud howl of a whistle managed to cut through the singing. I knew it was Vince even before I looked round and saw him standing in our usual booth. Alice O looked over and Vince clapped high above his head, moving with her rhythm by way of a come-on. She sang toward him, directing some of the lyrics his way. Still moving to her voice, Vince took his camera out of his jacket pocket and clicked off a single shot. We wove through the tables to join the others.

'Hey, Mags,' Kelly said. 'Hello,' she added to Isla, standing up and hugging her warmly. Isla and Kelly were becoming friends and I liked that a lot. Tom was sitting at the end of the booth, talking to a slim and beautiful girl with long, blonde hair and the kind of big, happy eyes that he was a sucker for. Tom was wearing his hero suit and was doing his street magic thing. She was obviously hooked. Tom made a show of drawing back his jacket sleeve and looking at the time. The blonde girl looked with amazement at *her* watch on *his* wrist. She looked at her own arm in disbelief. They laughed together.

'Hey, Tom!'

'Hi, Mags,' Tom replied, looking up. 'And I'!' he added standing up to reach over and kiss Isla. 'You okay?' he asked as always.

'Never better, so long as you keep away from my watch,' Isla chided. The blonde girl smiled at this.

'Oh, yes . . . this is Catherine,' Tom announced proudly. 'Down all the way from Norwich for the weekend.'

Isla and I said hello and sat down. Tom and Catherine melted off into their own conversation at the end of the table before anything else was said, Tom producing a pack of playing cards from his pocket, shuffling them expertly.

'Come and sit yourself down,' Kelly said to Isla, patting the tired, threadbare velvet of the bench next to her. 'Have a chat with me about getting some promotional photos, while Mags gets a round in,' she smiled. Isla sat, swinging her bag under the table.

'Maggie, Maggie. . . Maggie!' Vince shouted. He climbed over the back of the booth and put his arm around my neck, pulling me close. 'Time for a boogie . . . time to go down there and throw a few shapes for that great big saucy bird!' he added, releasing me and nodding to Alice O who was swaying in a sort of figure of eight behind the microphone stand.

'Hi, Vince,' Isla cut in, looking over her shoulder at us.

'Hey, Isla. How are you?' Vince replied, letting go of me.

'I'm good,' Isla smiled.

'Cool.' With that Vince was off. Isla watched him go. Kelly looked at Isla and then to me.

72

A gull soars up ahead, flashing white in the high sun. We are definitely closer to the sea than I thought. In fact, I can smell the salt in the air. I love the sea. I may have a swim!

I think of swimming when I was a boy with Dad and Julie and Mum at the beach and when I was older it was always Tom and me; Vince would sit on the shingle and watch and smoke cigarettes.

You knew Tom? You saw him, didn't you, you met him here?

Henry stops walking. He stands with his back to the west and the clouds that still look like the Brecon Beacons, all hazy under the high sun and the breathing land.

Henry nods happily. He says he did . . . He says so did I.

I never—

Henry says he was there but I couldn't see him.

I think of dreaming of Tom, of Tom's voice on the hills, in the mist on the Beacons.

Henry nods slowly.

Where is he now?

Henry says he has gone on. He says he was only here for a short while. He says that he was ready. He had found peace before he came. I nod. I understand.

I like that Tom was here. I feel him! I look into the Tide shifting bright with the sun and the promise of Joyce. Yes. Yes, just a hint of him, but I can feel him. I breathe. The air is cool and sweet. We walk on.

*

The promise of Joyce grows ahead of us with every step. I think of Jack and May so alive, so free, so full of joy and hope and love. I think of Isla so beautiful, brave and strong, and I am proud. I think of Dad. I am humming his happy song. I stop. I look around. I feel someone back there. I'm sure of it. But I have no fear. There is too much love all around me, ebbing in the Tide, for there to be any fear. Henry stops too. I turn to look at him.

I think someone's back there.

Henry nods.

Do they need our help? Shall we wait for them?

Henry moves beside me so that his back is turned to where I'm looking. I can't see anybody, but I'm sure I can feel someone.

Henry whispers to me. He says he is not the only one who followed me. He says not to look too hard for they are still afraid. He clasps his hands over his heart.

I look at him quickly. Afraid? We must help them.

Henry puts his hand on my shoulder and gently turns me back to the road ahead. I feel the Tide and for a moment I am in the woods again. I am in the clearing where the weather came when I was hiding, all seasons warm and cold and light and dull and stormy and calm. The little girl in the yellow coat is watching me from off among the trees.

I am back with Henry. We walk on.

She wasn't one of the living.

Henry smiles and shakes his head slowly.

We must help her.

Henry says we will.

I know he's right. The Tide shifts gently around us in the warmth of the sun and I feel Joyce. I love Joyce. And I feel Isla and Jack and May, far off, but there. I feel their love and I know Henry is right. I love Henry. And I know we will help the girl in the yellow coat.

73

Isla looked at Kelly and me. 'I don't understand what I've done to offend Vince,' she said honestly.

Kelly and I looked at each other and the back to Isla.

'You haven't offended him . . .' Kelly began, pausing to glance at me again.

'No. No, you haven't at all,' I agreed.

Isla looked from me to Kelly and then back. 'It's fine. I just wondered if there was anything I could do . . . you know, to make peace . . .' She paused and started again. 'He's your friend. I'd like us to get on.'

'It's nothing you've done,' I continued. 'He's just—'

'It's because you're married,' Kelly said flatly.

Isla exhaled sharply and her eyebrows knitted into a question for a moment. 'Really?' she checked.

I nodded.

Kelly nodded.

Isla pressed both her hands to her mouth and looked down. 'He doesn't strike me as the sort to worry about that,' she said finally, looking over to the dance floor where Vince was already making his moves in front of Alice O who was still singing 'Beautiful Soul'.

'He's got quite an old-fashioned view of marriage,' Kelly explained. 'Amongst other subjects.'

'Old-fashioned view of marriage!' Isla laughed and looked happier. 'Now I know you're teasing me—'

'No, it's true,' I confirmed, leaning against the back of the booth between Isla and Kelly. 'Had a very strict Christian upbringing, old Vince did.'

'Christian? Vince?' Isla shook her head. 'No . . . come on . . . '

'He's a believer, baby,' Kelly cut in.

'Vince? Vince?'

'Yep, and you sound just like his dad . . . ,' I added

'I do?'

'Yeah. He doesn't believe it either,' I explained. Isla leaned back and frowned at me, her eyes searching mine for signs of mischief. 'Honestly!' I insisted. 'You should see them together, stubborn old gits, the both of them. His dad says Vince should learn constraint . . . give up his sinful ways. . .'

'Right . . .' Isla said slowly, glancing over at the now gyrating Vince and then to Kelly who nodded an affirmative.

'But Vince says it's not about rules; it's about being decent to people, enjoying life as much as possible without fucking people over.'

'He says that life is God's gift and the sin is not to enjoy it,' Kelly quoted. 'He may not look it,' she added with affection as she watched him dance, now close up to a petite, grungy-looking student girl with a vest top and bright red skirt, 'but Vincey there, he's a very moral man . . . in his own special way,' she concluded with a thoughtful frown.

'You see, he likes you, he likes you a lot . . .   and he doesn't want to see either of us get hurt.' I said the words before I knew they were coming. Isla looked at me and in that moment we both knew that it was true. Isla looked down.

'We'll both have a gin and tonic,' Kelly announced. Isla looked up, brave and beautiful and strong.

While I was waiting at the bar to be served, Beautiful Lloyd came up to me. Beautiful Lloyd was a painfully skinny old man who lived rough in and around Brighton. He had crazy long white hair and scratchy white whiskers that were neither quite a beard nor stubble. He had watery blue eyes and his leathery skin was scarred and stretched and pocked like you wouldn't believe. He was a gaunt, ugly, broken old man whose age was guessed at anywhere between sixty and eighty. He was a gaunt, ugly, broken old man whom we all loved dearly. Nobody knew anything about him really, apart from the fact that Beautiful Lloyd played the trumpet like no other.

'Hallo, Mags.'

'Beautiful! How the hell are you? Let me get you drink, Boh.'

'Oh, thank you, that's kind of you.'

'Whisky?'

'Yes.'

'Whisky it is.' I ordered the drinks including a four-shot whisky for Beautiful Lloyd.

'They say you're up next, Mags. You and the Heroes, that is,' he said in his slow careful way.

'Do they? Yeah, sounds about right. Are you going to join us?'

'Well, yes. That is what I'd like to do if that would be all right with you.'

'Absolutely! We love it when you play with us, Beautiful,' I said, because it was true.

'Good. Well, I shall wait for you to take the stage, then.'

I handed him his tall whisky. 'Why don't you come and support us regular, Beautiful? We'd pay you properly and throw in drinks. It would be fantastic.' It wasn't the first time I'd made this offer, but every time I was hopeful he'd agree. His watery eyes focused on mine and for a moment and I knew he was thinking about it; for a moment, I knew he wanted to say yes, but then a shadow passed over them and he looked down.

'No . . . I'd just fuck it all up, Mags. Wouldn't be fair by you—'

'But—'

It was no good; he'd already turned and started to walk away.

I came back from the bar when Alice O was finishing 'Some of Your Lovin', her second Dusty Springfield cover, again upped in pace and spun her way. It was good. She was good. The crowd were moving slow and sensual. All except, Vince that is, who hadn't really dropped tempo. I put the drinks down and slid in next to Isla. Isla squeezed my leg under the table.

'We're next,' Kelly said, nodding to the stage.

'Sounds like a plan, Kells. Oh, I just saw Beautiful at the bar and he's going to join us!'

'Fantastic!'

'Beautiful?' Isla asked.

'Yeah, he's—'

I was interrupted by cheers and applause as 'Some of Your Lovin'' ended. Before I had a chance to continue, the backing tracked moved on to her third and final Dusty cover. The room went crazy and the dance floor swelled as 'Son of a Preacher Man' came loud and cool. Vince, looking like that desert-crazy preacher from Clint westerns in his black Hero's suit with no shirt and bare feet was in his element, gyrating right in front of Alice whose voice was everywhere. She had it. She really had it. I looked at Kelly and she laughed. Tom looked up from Catherine, smiled and shook his head.

'You must have set this up!' Isla shouted over the beautiful singing.

I laughed and kissed her.

74

St Judith's hospice was a few miles outside Norwich and only about five minutes from the A47, but when we pulled up in the car park, with its screen of trees and low lights lining the paths through the landscaped grounds around the quiet single-storey buildings, it might just as well have been a hundred miles from anywhere. There was a scattering of cars and Isla swung into a block of spaces in one corner. The light had almost gone but the sky in the west above the building itself was still dark blues and deep reds. We sat for a moment in silence, looking out toward the hospice and the sunset beyond it. Finally, Isla reached over, the leather of her seat squeaking, and kissed me on the side of my face, her lips the gentlest touch against my skin. I turned and she smiled at me.

'Right then,' I said. Isla nodded and we opened our doors.

The evening was cool and the smell of cut grass hung everywhere. It was almost silent, just a very faint rumble of traffic or perhaps a plane in the far distance. Isla locked the car, locks clunking and it beeping and flashing the indicators. The beeps seemed rudely loud. Isla slipped her arm through mine and we walked to the entrance.

Inside, the quiet continued and the air smelled of flowers, heavy scented and sticky. The woman in reception was lovely. She was, I guessed, in her sixties, plump and kind-faced. She smiled at Isla and me. I said we'd come to see Tom and, after taking the time to say that he was settling in well, she gave us directions; he was actually in a separate four-bedroom unit across a small courtyard from reception.

'He's a very popular young man, your . . . er . . .'

'Friend,' I answered.

'Yes, your friend . . . he's a very popular man,' the woman repeated. 'He's with his wife – oh, she's lovely, isn't she? – and another friend and, I believe, his parents and the chaplain . . .'

'Right . . . okay,' I replied.

'Yes and we don't like too many people in the room at once . . . It's important that Tom can rest and isn't too . . . well . . .'

'Sure' I said.

'Yes, so if you could perhaps wait until the chaplain and his parents are out . . .'

'Of course,' Isla smiled.

The unit across the courtyard was laid out like a bungalow with a comfortable waiting room in the middle. Isla and I walked in hand in hand and I remember we were talking about stainless-steel cooking pots for some reason. I remember the whole place, us being there, feeling unreal, dream-like. The waiting area had two pairs of sofas facing each other and a side table with tea and coffee things. Like the main building it smelled heavily of flowers. We stopped just inside and the doors swung shut behind us with a swishing over the mat. Vince was there, standing with his back to us, looking out of the window on the opposite side of the room.

'Vince,' I said.

Vince looked up with a start and turned around. 'Maggie,' he croaked. He looked bad. He looked pale and he'd clearly been crying. As soon as Isla saw him she began to well up too. She put her arms around him, kissed and hugged him tightly.

'Isla . . . He's . . .' Vince's words tailed off. I watched for a moment and then put my arms around both of them.

Finally, Vince straightened up and stepped back. 'You've been in, then?' I checked.

Vince nodded slowly and leaned back against the window ledge. Isla put her bag on the ground and perched on the other end of the casement. 'How is he? And Cathy . . . how are they?' she asked.

'He's—' Vince breathed deeply and rubbed his face. 'He's . . . They're . . .' He raised his hand as if to call a stop and sucked in his lips.

I looked at Isla. She held out her hand and I took it.

Vince turned away and faced the window again. He spread his hands out across the sill and leaned forward with head down. 'He's so thin,' he whispered. Then he was silent.

I looked at Isla again and we squeezed each other's hands.

75

Since we had Beautiful Lloyd with us we decided to make the most of it that night in the Catfish and cover all the tracks that demanded brass.

By the time we'd set up, the room was already humming with expectation; the folks of the Catfish loved their Heroes. We stood in a huddle in front of Vince and the drum kit, with Vince leaning over to join the conspiratorial whispering that was there for theatre as much as utility. Beautiful Lloyd stood slightly to the side of us, his head down while his fingers felt their way over his trumpet. We didn't direct the discussion toward him because we knew he wouldn't answer. I limbered up, rolling my shoulders and swinging my arms to make sure my suit was ready to give enough to deliver a good show. I liked to start with a special move or two to really grab them. The murmur of voices responded with an increase in pitch; they knew we were about to go. There was a wolf whistle from way back in the room and when I looked over my shoulder it was followed by a woman's voice giving a *whooaaa*.

'So what are we going in with?' Vince hissed over the drums.

'Gotta be something with a horn, Boh,' Tom replied, adjusting the strap of his bass guitar and running a hand along the beam.

I nodded, still shaking my arms and limbering my shoulders. I'd had exactly the perfect amount of whisky and I was buzzing, buzzing, buzzing. I wanted to own that room; I wanted to give them their show and be in the centre of it. We all looked at Kelly. She took a moment. Another excited wave passed through the chatter behind us. The volume actually dropped, the excitement peaking. Kelly nodded.

'"Mini-Skirt Minnie",' she announced decisively. Vince nodded approvingly and leaned back into his seat. Kelly and Tom placed their fingers on their strings and moved to hide me from the crowd.

'"Mini-Skirt Minnie", Beautiful,' I said to Beautiful Lloyd. He nodded slowly. The crowd cheered. The lights dropped, we were in darkness; Southampton Barry ran the switches and he knew our start-up. The crowd cheered again and whistled and whooped. I loved the Catfish; it was the best of friendly gigs.

Kelly gave the count: 'One . . . two . . . three . . .'

Vince struck out the four-beat lead-in: one, two, three, four. Kelly and Tom backed away from me toward the crowd. Kelly laid down the nine-beat riff on four: once, her Jazzmaster showing its pedigree and commanding the room; twice, the crowd taking a breath; three times. Tom caught it and strummed down the four-step bass. I was crouching with my back to the crowd, looking over my shoulder for my key, trembling with a whisky-and-electric buzz that rushed from my spine and made my flesh tingle. The spotlight on the rig above the bar swung across the crowd. Kelly and Tom turned and parted for it and I jumped high. I spun round into it, my suit lifting and flapping with me. I landed perfectly.

'Mini-skirt Minnie! Oh my Lord! The baddest girl around!' My voice boomed from the sound system and the room answered! Kelly and Tom lifted it further, playing in my flank, three more bars. Then Beautiful Lloyd lifted his trumpet and he blew and he blew and he blew that room away! He'd said many times that the rhythm drew lights around him and he played best when he traced the patterns with the trumpet and that's just what he did. People would often wonder why that ugly, broken old man was called Beautiful Lloyd, but when they heard him play that fucking trumpet they never needed to ask again.

I moved and sang at the front of the stage. Bodies swinging, movements punctuated by Beautiful's trumpet. So many eyes. Isla moved to the front and took her pictures; I pointed toward the lens and forgot the room for a moment, singing just to her.

God, I loved the Catfish. I loved that room and we had it that night. I had it, I had that whole room in my hand. All the spotlights were on us, on me! And I loved it.

76

We're walking in the woods now. The sun is coming through the leaves, winking brightly. It's cool in here. The woodland floor is lush and rich. I smell the rich black earth beneath the green carpet. I hear the brook that runs down into the marshes, chattering to itself down the slope from us where the oaks and chestnuts give way to willows and poplars. Henry is humming Dad's happy song with me. He seems to know it perfectly. A breeze, gentle and warm, comes up along the path from behind us. The leaves answer it. They flutter busily, the dappled sunlight suddenly a kaleidoscope, the winking sun punctuating the changing pattern.

I feel her still.

I look around and see the little girl in the yellow coat way back along the path. She is at the edge of the path, part hidden by the trees. She stops. She peers out from behind the leaves and shadows. She does not run. She does not hide. I raise my hand and smile. She is lovely. I think of May. She steps back further into the shadows but I see her smile! A shy, beautiful little smile. Henry starts to walk on again. I understand and follow in silence.

Ahead the sunlight is dazzling, right where the woods end and the path drops down through the marshes. I think of the beach hut in my dreams, the light piercing through the threadbare curtains. It's wonderful. Someone is there, waiting on the stile above the old steps. It's Joyce. I love Joyce.

It's Joyce!

Henry nods. He spreads his arms wide and smiles into the light.

She is a silhouette against the bright, wonderful sunlight filling the path ahead. I can't take my eyes off her! I think of Isla and Jack and May! Alive! The sunlight is streaming down through the canopy and filling the path and falls warm on my face. I think of Jack and May running into the house. I think of Isla so strong.

I run! I run toward Joyce. I want her to know about Jack and May and Isla. I want her to know the truth, the truth that they are so alive and so beautiful.

Joyce! Joyce!

Henry runs with me. The woodland earth is soft under my feet. Henry runs with grace, his great rolling body swift and silent and golden in the slanting sunlight. He laughs aloud. He laughs with my excitement, I know it! He feels it. He feels it with me and it becomes joy! We feel Joyce. She is smiling at us. She feels it too, she if full of joy and excitement.

*

I was absolutely spun-up by the time we left the Catfish, soaring on a high that only performing to a room like that could give. The night was cold by the time we left, turning the sweat I'd built up down in the basement into an icy breath on me the moment I stepped out. Isla was being drawn along by my excitement and we raced hand-in-hand down the steps to the street. All we wanted to do was get back to my flat and fuck. There was obviously something in the air that night because Tom and Catherine had left just as hurriedly ahead of us with, we guessed, an identical plan. Later we thought Tom had died, because they didn't leave his flat or answer his door for four full days. A truly perfect match made in heaven.

Completely Oblivious to the brutal danger that was ahead, to the razor-sharp pin that was about to stab into my map and change our lives for ever, we walked hurriedly along the esplanade. Crossing the road, the Palace Pier greeted us with lonely pulsing lights and the smell of frying doughnuts as we raced passed; me pulling Isla by the hand, her having to trot every few paces to keep up, both of us giggling.

*

We reach Joyce. Henry laughs. I laugh. It is the same laugh. Joyce laughs with us.

Joyce!

The marshes beyond us sway in the breeze and the blue sky reaching over them to the beach and the sea is endless and wonderful. I take her hands. I squeeze them gently. I feel the Tide flowing through us, running warm like the sunlight. Isla and Jack and May fill my thoughts. So alive, so beautiful! Joyce's eyes widen. Delight fills her face.

They're alive!

Joyce laughs aloud with me. I jump up and down. She jumps with me.

I saw them, Joyce! Jack and May. Little May. Oh God, you should see her!

She pulls me to her and we hold each other. Henry puts his arms around us and the Tide flows.

I watch Jack and May and Isla walk from Duncan's car over and over in my thoughts. So alive, so beautiful, so full of hope and love and promise. And I think of Tom and Henry thinks of him too. I can feel it. When he arrived here he saw only the peace and beauty that is everywhere around me. I know it. Dear Tom.

77

We heard a door open somewhere down the corridor. Isla and I looked over. We heard footsteps and voices. Vince looked back from the window. He really did look awful; I'd never seen him look so pale and I'd never seen him look worried. Isla took my hand again.

Tom's parents and the chaplain, tall and proud-looking in his traditional black suit and clerical collar, appeared at the entrance to the corridor. I hadn't realised who the chaplain was until then; it turned out it was a move to semi-retirement. I looked at Vince, wondering whether things would be awkward. But that wasn't the case at all. The chaplain excused himself from Tom's parents and walked straight over and put his hand on Vince's shoulder. Vince's searching blue eyes met their mirror and he looked down.

'Come and stay with us tonight. Your mother misses you.' Vince looked back up; there were tears in his eyes. '*I* miss you . . .'

Vince nodded slowly. 'Yeah, I'd like that, Dad,' he replied quietly.

Tom's parents came over and his dad shook my hand. 'Thanks for coming, boy,' was all he said, all he needed to say. Tom's mum hugged me without saying a word. She did the same to Isla.

I paused at the door to Tom's room. My legs were numb; they felt like they weren't mine. I honestly don't know if I could have walked in if Isla hadn't been there holding my hand. She moved closer, folding her arm against mine. She kissed me.

'I love you,' she said. And I knew she did.

I knocked on the door.

'Come in,' came Catherine's voice.

The scene inside the room was nothing like I'd expected.

The room was nice. There was some medical kit, mostly on a wheeled metal stack by the bed, but it was more like a Travelodge-type hotel room. Tom was propped up in bed and Catherine was sitting beside him. They were holding hands and they looked *happy*. There was something proud and something brave about their faces. I was reminded of the Tylers and of the two soldiers who had helped each other across my drive to their cars those months before. Except this time they'd got it right. This time they weren't afraid or looking out for the next danger; now they were invincible and nothing could touch them. The room was quite simply filled with love. Strangest of all was that it made me think of when Jack and May were born, how Isla and I sat together and greeted family and friends, Isla proud of what she had endured and done and I even prouder of her for those same reasons; both of us so proud of our wonderful new baby. It was the last thing I expected to be reminded of, the very last thing. Vince was right: Tom look thin. He looked very bad. His hair had gone and he wore a white linen cravat around his neck, covering I could only guess what; but oddly now I remember just Tom, Tom as he'd always been: cool and kind and happy.

The mood in the room put Isla and me at ease immediately. We sat either side of the bed and the four of us chatted and laughed and reminisced and cried and laughed and talked and recounted and laughed. It was easy, it was wonderful, it was so very Tom.

Catherine's parents had arrived so we got ready to leave and let them have their turn. Isla leaned over and kissed Tom, then hugged Catherine. I put my hand on Tom's shoulder and told him I'd come back and see him later during the week.

'Cheers, Mags,' he said, putting his hand on my arm as I stood up. I kissed Catherine goodbye; she smelled of apples – I have no idea why. Isla and I went to the door.

'Oh, Mags,' Tom said.

'Yeah?' I turned round quickly.

'Don't forget your watch!' Tom was holding up the expensive diving watch I'd had for Christmas. He looked pleased. Catherine laughed and shook her head like a mother proud of an incorrigible child. She kissed him.

'For fuck's sake. . . how?'

The boy was a master!

78

A wave fans out over the hard-packed sand, the foam racing and bubbling toward Joyce and me. We run backwards, pulling each other and laughing. We fall on to the shingle bank. Joyce lies flat, her arms outstretched, her face turned toward the sun, her eyes closed. She sighs happily. She seems young suddenly, younger than I have ever thought.

She says it's lovely here.

She's right. It is.

The sun is lower now, a deeper burnt yellow, and the clouds on the horizon that look like land are touched with orange and gold. Henry runs from a wave now. He is already wet from clowning in the surf earlier. He stumbles and falls on to the shingle beside us. He laughs and it infects us. We all laugh together.

What a day!

Since we walked down through the marshes we have run and chased and laughed like children. Just like Jack and May, just like Julie and me when we were young. Jack and May. I can't stop thinking about them. So beautiful.

So alive!

I've talked about them all afternoon too. I can't help myself! And I feel them, Jack and May and Isla too, in the Tide that's moving with the sun. I feel their love. It is everywhere, in the sky, the air, the sand and the stones under me, the water and the tress and the marshes and the clouds that look like land on the horizon and the clouds that look like hills. Everywhere in the warm sunlight. I never knew that love and paradise were the same but now I realise that they have to be.

79

It turned out there were more than just the two Brightons I knew of. I guess there were many more, including the violent and desperate one that came out of the shadows that night after the Catfish Club. The night that fate quite literally ambushed me and my plan to set Isla free. Isla and I were on the beach side of the esplanade just past West Street. Me riding the Heroes high, singing lines from the covers we'd laid down and Isla still having to break into a jog every few paces. Her tugging at my arm and telling me I was crazy, me hauling her forward, kissing her and then racing on. We were laughing. We had forgotten ourselves. We'd forgotten about people seeing us. It was just Isla and me in a great glorious bubble together.

We didn't notice him walk up the concrete ramp from the beach until he was right by us. We didn't really notice him until he stepped in front of us and blocked our way. I almost walked into him. I was looking back at Isla, singing *come on, come on* to her and when I turned back he was right there.

'Sorry, mate,' I said instinctively. Isla, unready for the stop, barged into the back of me. I laughed. Then I saw his face, part shadowed by his hood but enough to know we were in trouble. That's when I saw the knife. He raised it above his waist just enough to catch the light. He glanced down to make sure I looked.

'D'you think you're something special?' he growled.

I was instantly sober. I was instantly and absolutely present. I stood tall and looked at him, measuring him. In that moment nothing else was moving; it was just me and him and Isla. He was skinny and a little shorter than me. His hoodie was red with white stripes along the arms. He was wearing skinny jeans and trainers. He had a sharp little nose and even in the shadow of his hood his face was pale, sickly white. His eyes were wild.

'Don't fucking look at me,' he shouted. He raised the knife higher.

'Magnus,' Isla said.

I thought of Dad. Dad always said don't fight, but if you do fight, then fight; don't be nice about it: hurt them, batter them, break them.

He twitched. He looked over my shoulder. He shook the knife. His eyes jumped between Isla and me. 'Give me that fucking bag, bitch!' he hissed.

I'd experienced flight-or-fight before and flight had always won, leaving me running before I knew it. This time Isla was behind me. I was between her and him and so there could be no flight. I was clenching my fist before I realised what had been resolved.

'Okay,' Isla said calmly, her aid training in Africa kicking in with professional efficiency. 'It's yours.'

'You're not having that fucking bag,' I said, fixing my eyes on his. What I should have said was *you're not having the bag because I'm going to kill you*, because even if he'd have dropped the knife and apologised I'd have battered him. I wanted to kill him. I wanted to hit him until he stopped moving. I wanted his blood. I wanted to break his skull and snap his bones. I wanted to kick his fucking stupid brains out. Finally, his twitching eyes managed to fix on mine.

'Magnus!' Isla cried.

I stared back at him. His eyes flicked to the road. I hit him. I landed a punch right on his pointed nose. It was, and remains, the best punch I ever landed; Dad would have been proud. Blood exploded from his nose. His head rocked back. He twisted down on to one knee, trying to keep on his feet and turn away.

'Magnus!' Isla screamed. She grabbed at my arm, trying to pull me back. It didn't work. I jumped forward and slammed my fist down on top of his head. With a wet cry from the back of his throat, he went down. I was silent. I swung to kick at him. Isla got hold of my arm this time and managed to break my stride. He scrambled away from me like a crab and managed to get to his feet. I broke away from Isla's grip, jumping after him but he bolted away. I have never seen anyone run like that. I chased for a few strides and then the violence left me and he drew away. My flight-or-fight automation had played out and control had returned. I stopped and watched him go. Then came the euphoria, racing with the adrenaline in my blood. A great wave of excited pleasure. I laughed. I laughed aloud. I turned to Isla, expecting in that strangest of moments to find her laughing too; why wouldn't she be? Who couldn't be right then? She wasn't. She was standing a few yards back, staring at me. Her hands were raised as if she was about to catch a football. She was trembling.

'Isla . . . What's the matter?' I said through laughter. I walked up to her just as the euphoria was subsiding into confusion. There were tears in her eyes.

'You stupid . . .' she whispered. 'You stupid . . .' She moved her hands and I thought she was going to slap me. Instead she took my face in her hands and wept. I felt my heart racing and the fullness of what had just happened hit me. I pulled her to me and held her. I kissed her through her hair.

'Magnus . . . I thought—'

'Sshh, sshh.'

We didn't call the police. We didn't even talk about what had happened for a long, long time. We went straight to my flat, just as we'd intended from the moment we left the Catfish. And we went straight to bed, just as we'd intended when we left the Catfish. But we didn't fuck. We didn't make love. We held each other and we spoke our love. We said the words and broke all of the rules and Isla didn't leave; she chose to stay and for the first time we fell asleep together and woke to our first morning together.

80

That night, after our first visit to see Tom at St Judith's, we drove home through the early summer night in silence. There was nothing we needed to say. I drove and Isla brought her legs up on to the seat and leaned into it like a sleepy child. When I looked over, her eyes were on me and sometimes she would smile and reach over to touch my hand. She felt close. She felt closer than she had for a long time.

It was late when we got home and we went to bed quickly, Isla first while I sorted some things for work the next day in the study. This had become a ritual for us. Finally, I undressed in the half-dark of the moonlight that filled the garret window of our room and slipped into bed beside her. The house was strangely quiet without the children, or rather felt quiet without the promise of hearing them. Isla was asleep and I lay on my back, turning my wedding ring around and around. The coolness of the bedding quickly faded and I lay listening to her breathing. Sleep came with unexpected ease.

That night I dreamed of Dad. I was at the beach hut, sitting on the front step and watching him work on his boat. He was painting this time, painting where he had scraped and prepared last time. I watched him brushing the gloss carefully, fast then slow on the edges to make a crisp line. He sang to himself. He sang his happy song. I couldn't make out the words – his soft voice was lost and came to me as not much more than a hum – but I knew the tune. Just as before he didn't look at me. He didn't want to scare me away. But he knew I was there. I was sure of it.

After a while he finished, putting the brush in the little pot of paint, and backing away from the boat to admire his work. He came right up to me, his back toward me. Then he sat, again without looking round, without looking directly at me. I watched him. Still I could not see his face; still he was looking away, slowly nodding proudly at his little boat. Then the smile lines reached out across the side of his face and he put his arm around me.

I woke with a start. I'd taken in a deep breath and I let it out. My heart was racing. The window was blue with the first light of dawn. Isla was sleeping next to me. I felt her slow, steady breathing through the bed. I was still on my back. I breathed again and waited for my heart to slow. I knew Dad was close that night, so close. I told myself it was because of Tom, but I knew, deep down I knew, that that wasn't the reason.

81

I look at the sky and feel the sun and the Tide all around me. I could sleep, it's so peaceful. I sit up. Henry and Joyce sit up now, joining me on either side. I turn to look inland and there are the clouds that look like hills, except they just look like hills now, no hint of cloud remains, they *are* hills, they *are* the Brecon Beacons, I'm sure of it. I look at Henry and he smiles. I look at the clouds that look like land on the horizon. They are brilliant in the sun. I look for a boat, a little boat. Of course, I do not see one, but I can't stop looking. All day I have caught myself looking.

I look at Joyce. I love Joyce. We have had such a wonderful day here on the beach. She is looking away. She is looking along the shingle bank back toward where the path from the marshes comes in.

Henry!

I see the little girl in the yellow coat sitting there on the shingle bank. She's a way off, but it's definitely her. Joyce is looking at her. I want to help her. I go to stand. Henry puts his hand on my leg. I feel the Tide and a wonderful peacefulness flowing from him. I look at him, at his big kind face. I love Henry. He smiles. He shakes his head slowly. I understand.

Joyce stands slowly. Her blonde hair catches the sun. She straightens down her clothes. She is tall and smart and beautiful. I love Joyce. She helped me and she was my first friend here. I think of when I first held her in Woodbridge and felt the warmth in the Tide flowing between us.

I love you, Joyce.

Her eyes are fixed on the little girl with the yellow coat. She takes a step away from where Henry and I sit. She stops and looks back at us. She smiles. The Tide moves through and around us. I feel such peace and such joy from Henry, touched by excitement. Joyce's face is full of love. I feel it in the Tide. We all do. Joyce turns to look at the little girl again. She is still sitting on the shingle bank, lifting handfuls of the tiny stones and letting them fall back through her fingers. She does not look this way. Joyce walks toward her along the flat hard-packed sand. The little waves play around her bare feet.

82

The next day, our first waking morning together, Isla acted quickly. We sat and ate breakfast together with the balcony doors open and the cool spring air coming in. We had fresh coffee that I'd set bubbling while Isla showered and I went to the baker's on Sillwood Street and bought pastries. As we ate there was something different about Isla: she looked well, better than she had for months. The pain had gone.

She left after breakfast, going straight home to talk to Duncan. I offered to go with her, but of course she said no. I spent the rest of the morning worrying about her. So as a distraction and because I *was* a bluesman after all, I spent the time experimenting with tunes on the piano. I found myself playing with ideas that worked best with a trumpet.

Isla returned in the early afternoon. She had bags with her and I went down and helped move them in while she paid the taxi driver. That was it. That was the moment she crossed over and came to live in my Brighton.

Duncan, always knowing the day would come, was a gentleman and had taken it well. Isla said he actually seemed happy for her.

I understand that now.

For Isla, it was an awakening and rediscovering, and for me it was simply wonderful. Isla bloomed. It was as if she remembered how to be young again. We partied and we travelled and our sun shone and we made hay. I took her to the Brecon Beacons and she loved them. We walked often and the hills became the mountains of the Alps and the Himalayas of northern India. We bought the Triumph. It wasn't Duncan's Mercedes, I knew, but it was glorious with the top down. We went to Suffolk and Isla fell in love with it.

Then, in the following spring, we were married. It was a beautiful day and it was a beautiful day. We married, me in a black suit, of course, and Isla in a simple white dress that confirmed she was the most beautiful, most elegant woman on earth; I'd always thought she looked like Audrey Hepburn but that was the day I realised she was so much more. The service at the registry office in Hove was small and perfect. Kelly and Lucy Too Cool, who were a couple by then, sang for us; Vince brought Alice O who had become a true friend of his. There was Tom and Catherine, of course, Julie and Mum and few scattered dear friends and relatives – my relatives, that is; Isla had no family after her dad. From there we walked to Papa's for the reception – and what a reception! What an evening! We were seated to 'O Sole Mio' and Luca played the most beautiful music all night and when we had the *Gianni Schicci* aria he cried so much that Sabina had to help him up to the flat above the restaurant for a lay down.

After we were married we bought our first flat together, the two-bedroom place in Brunswick Square. We had such wonderful years there. The Heroes were doing well, but to help with getting a mortgage I took my first sales job. It was just part-time, set up by a friend from the Catfish, and much to my amazement I loved it. I could sell to anyone. I had never imagined I'd enjoy a regular job, but I would come home buzzing after a big sale almost as if I'd just been on stage. Basically, it was all down to people, I always loved people, meeting them, getting to know them, hearing their stories, sharing a joke, and sales was all about people. Soon I was making much more money from sales than from the Heroes and things gently moved that way. That's what led to the first big job offer in the line that got me back to Suffolk.

Then came Jack and then came May and we were a beautiful family and we had our days: our Christmases, our birthdays, our first days at school, our snowy days and our lazy summer days by the sea. And I could never have asked for more.

83

Joyce sits down next to the little girl with the yellow coat. Joyce says something but I cannot hear her words. The little girl laughs and nods excitedly. They both lift handfuls of shingle and let the tiny stones pour back to the beach. They laugh together. The little girl is chattering now. I look at Henry. Great tears are rolling down his big face. I love Henry. He looks at me and grins. What a beautiful day.

I look at the clouds on the horizon that look like land. So many shades and colours. They shift and thin. They *are* land.

Henry?

I see forests reaching up to hills and mountains beyond. Right there across the sea. I think of Dad and think I understand.

Henry?

Henry looks at the land across the sea and then to me. The Tide flows between us and all around.

He says they are beautiful.

But how, Henry? How can they be there?

Henry says . . . he says they have been there since I arrived.

But . . .

He says I just couldn't see them.

He's right, I know he is. I have always known he is.

I look over my shoulder at the hills that look like the Brecon Beacons, that *are* the Brecon Beacons. I look back at Henry.

Henry nods. He says that's where Tom found me, but I couldn't see him either. Not then.

I look back at the distant land across the sea, bathed in the early evening sun. I think I see a light. Yes.

There's a light!

There's a light on the far shore. A tiny pinprick against the misty slopes, right where I thought I saw the lights of a ship all that time ago when I stood here with Joyce. It grows brighter. It flickers.

Henry, I think it's a fire.

Henry nods slowly.

I think of Dad. I feel him on the Tide. He is a promise now!

The waves fan out across the sand in front of us. It's perfect. I sit with Henry, watching the waves and the orange sun on the water and the deep blue sky stretching over to the distant shore with the tiny light that isn't a ship.

Something moves!

Henry! Look.

I watch the far shore. Something moves past the tiny light, blocking it for a moment. I stand up. My eyes strain. It catches the sun! A glint, there! And there! There's definitely something moving!

Henry stands too. He is right beside me.

We watch together. I can see it now. It's on the sea. It moves with the sea. We watch in silence now.

It's a boat! Henry, it's a boat!

It's moving over the water, growing. It's coming closer, cutting across southwards. I see flashes of white at its bow! It's really racing! I look south. My eyes follow its course.

I know where it's going!

Henry takes my hand. Joy reaches through him. He looks at me. His eyes are filled with excitement! He looks away, turning his face inland. I follow his eyes.

There behind us, just beyond the shingle, is my car! It sits on a road I do not remember. It sits facing south. I look to the boat. I look south. I look along the line of the road. I look at Henry. He smiles.

My car . . . I—

Henry says it's right where I left it. I just hadn't noticed it there.

He holds out his hand. He opens out his fingers. My key, my key with the cat on it. I look at him and he nods. I take the key.

Henry, I—

Henry puts his great arms around me and pulls me to him. He kisses the top of my head. I think of holding Jack and May and kissing them, I think of Mum and Dad holding me when I was a child and kissing me. I love Henry.

84

He – a different he – walks into his kitchen. A piece of forgotten pasta crunches under his foot. The gentle whir of cooling units reaches in through the window and the sounds of the traffic and the people and the lives of Brighton reach in too. The sun is low over the building beyond the window and slants in lazily, catching motes of dust that spiral and drift around him. Vibrant green plants cascade down from the fridge and shelves and the air is fresh with them.

He sits at a little table. His chair complains across the floor as he draws it forward. He looks at the ashtray in the centre of the table. He closes his eyes and runs his hands over his face. He breathes deeply and looks at the ceiling. A cobweb is reaching from the light fitting and swaying in an unfelt draught. He places his hands flat on the table. All is quiet and all is peaceful. He looks around, studying walls covered with pictures of Heroes. He nods slowly.

He sits forward. He puts his elbows on the table, his black suit sleeves falling back past his wrists. He brings his hands together and raises them to his face in prayer. He closes his eyes. His lips trace and form silent words.

He opens his eyes and takes a breath. He looks again at the pictures on the wall and smiles.

85

I drive fast. The roof is down and the road is straight. The evening sun is on my face and the air blows my hair. The cat in the centre of the steering wheel is golden. I think of Isla and Jack and May. I'm so glad it was Isla I took my journey with; it could never have been anyone else.

And we made Jack and May! I remember Isla on our wedding day. I remember our first home together. My thoughts go to her. We are young lovers. We are young parents. We are proud parents. We are with Jack and May.

We are at home!

Jack is a baby. May is a baby. They are toddlers. They are at school. It is Christmas. It is Jack's birthday. It is May's birthday. They are chasing each other and the house is full of laughter. They are sleeping peacefully and we turn off their light and pull the door to and sneak away to our own bed. I am holding Jack. I am holding May. Isla is holding them too. There is love everywhere.

The car rises and falls with the road that runs along low cliffs now. The sun is low but brilliantly golden and touching everything. I race and race. I look out across the sea. The boat is racing too, drawing close, heading south with me. It's beautiful! It's a beautiful little boat with a wonderful red sail.

I leave the car. I have arrived in the old car park on top of the cliffs. I run under the stunted trees that I loved to climb when I was a boy and which Jack loved just the same. I run to the edge of the cliffs and the concrete steps that go down to the beach huts. The boat is so close now, cutting quickly through the water toward the beach.

I run down the steps. I run along the back of the row of beach huts. They seem as big as when I was a child. The evening sun is winking between them so bright and golden.

I am at our beach hut. By the back door. I reach up and turn the handle. The door opens silently. The curtains are drawn across the front and the golden sunlight is blinking through the weave. I step inside. I hear people outside. I hear singing! I hear Dad's happy song. I draw back the curtains. Golden light streams in.

Oh . . . now, that is beautiful.

Printed in Great Britain
by Amazon

41474426R00175